3 4143 10076 8140

ington Lib

KT-174-061

Wish You Were Here

GRAHAM SWIFT

WISH YOU WERE HERE

WARRINGTON BOROUGH COUNCIL	
34143100768140	
Bertrams	01/08/2011
AF	£18.99
WAR	

PICADOR

First published 2011 by Picador
an imprint of Pan Macmillan, a division of Macmillan Publishers Limited
Pan Macmillan, 20 New Wharf Road, London N1 9RR
Basingstoke and Oxford
Associated companies throughout the world
www.panmacmillan.com

ISBN 978-0-330-53583-0
ISBN 978-0-330-53587-8

Copyright © Graham Swift 2011

The right of Graham Swift to be identified as the
author of this work has been asserted by him in accordance
with the Copyright, Designs and Patents Act 1988.

All rights reserved. No part of this publication may be
reproduced, stored in or introduced into a retrieval system, or
transmitted, in any form, or by any means (electronic, mechanical,
photocopying, recording or otherwise) without the prior written
permission of the publisher. Any person who does any unauthorized
act in relation to this publication may be liable to criminal
prosecution and civil claims for damages.

1 3 5 7 9 8 6 4 2

A CIP catalogue record for this book is available from
the British Library.

Typeset by SetSystems Ltd, Saffron Walden, Essex
Printed in the UK by CPI Mackays, Chatham ME5 8TD

Visit www.picador.com to read more about all our books
and to buy them. You will also find features, author interviews and
news of any author events, and you can sign up for e-newsletters
so that you're always first to hear about our new releases.

For Candice

Are these things done on Albion's shore?

William Blake: 'A Little Boy Lost'

1

THERE IS NO END to madness, Jack thinks, once it takes hold. Hadn't those experts said it could take years before it flared up in human beings? So, it had flared up now in him and Ellie.

Sixty-five head of healthy-seeming cattle that finally succumbed to the rushed-through culling order, leaving a silence and emptiness as hollow as the morning Mum died, and the small angry wisp of a thought floating in it: Well, they'd better be right, those experts, it had better damn well flare up some day or this will have been a whole load of grief for nothing.

So then.

Healthy cattle. Sound of limb and udder and hoof—and mind. 'Not one of them mad as far as I ever saw,' Dad had said, as if it was the start of one of his rare jokes and his face would crack into a smile to prove it. But his face had looked like simply cracking anyway and staying cracked, and the words he might have said, by way of a punchline, never left his lips, though Jack thinks now that he heard them. Or it was his own silent joke to himself. Or it's the joke he's only arrived at now: 'We must be the mad ones.'

And if ever there was a time when Jack's dad might have put his two arms round his two sons, that was it. His arms were certainly long enough, even for his sons' big shoulders—both brothers out of the same large Luxton mould, though with all of eight years between them. Tom would have been fifteen then, but growing fast. And Jack, though it was a fact he sometimes wished to hide, even to reverse, already had a clear inch over his father.

The three of them had stood there, like the only life left, in the yard at Jebb Farm.

But Michael Luxton hadn't put his arms round his two sons. He'd done what he'd begun to do, occasionally, only after his wife's death. He'd looked hard at his feet, at the ground he was standing on, and spat.

And Jack, who long ago took his last look at that yard, looks now from an upstairs window at a grey sea, at a sky full of wind-driven rain, but sees for a moment only smoke and fire.

Sixty-five head of cattle. Or, to reckon it another way (and never mind the promised compensation): ruin. Ruin, at some point in the not-so-distant future, the ruin that had been creeping up on them anyway since Vera Luxton had died.

Cattle going mad all over England. Or being shoved by the hundred into incinerators for the fear and the risk of it. Who would have imagined it? Who would have dreamed it? But cattle aren't people, that's a fact. And when trouble comes your way, at least you might think, though it's small comfort and precious little help: Well, we've had our turn now, our share.

But years later, right here in this seaside cottage, Jack had switched on the TV and said, 'Ellie, come and look at this. Come and look, quick.' It was the big pyre at Roak Moor, back in Devon. Thousands of stacked-up cattle, thousands more lying rotting in fields. The thing was burning day and night. The smoke would surely have been visible, over the far hills, from Jebb. Not to mention the smell being carried on the wind. And someone on the TV—another of those experts—was saying that burning these cattle might still release into the air significant amounts of the undetected agent of BSE. Though it was ten years on, and this time the burnings were for foot-and-mouth. Which people weren't known to get. Yet.

'Well, Jack,' Ellie had said, stroking the back of his neck, 'did we make a good move? Or did we make a good move?'

But he'd needed to resist the strange, opposite feeling: that he should have been there, back at Jebb, in the thick of it; it was his proper place.

BSE, then foot-and-mouth. What would have been the odds? Those TV pictures had looked like scenes from hell. Flames leaping up into the night. Even so, cattle aren't people. Just a few months later Jack had turned on the telly once again and called to Ellie to come and look, as people must have been calling out, all over the world, to whoever was in the next room, 'Drop what you're doing and come and look at this.'

More smoke. Not over familiar, remembered hills, and even on the far side of the world. Though Jack's first thought—or perhaps his second—had been the somehow entirely necessary and appropriate one: Well, we should be all right here. Here at the bottom of the Isle of Wight. And while the TV had seemed to struggle with its own confusion and repeated again and again, as if they might not be true, the same astonishing sequences, he'd stepped outside to look down at the site, as if half expecting everything to have vanished.

Thirty-two white units. All still there. And among them, on the grass, a few idle and perhaps still-ignorant human sprinkles. But inside each caravan was a television, and some of them must be switched on. The word must be spreading. In the Ship, in the Sands Cafe, it must be spreading. It was early September—late season—but the middle of a beautiful, clear, Indian-summer day, the sea a smooth, smiling blue. Until now at least, they would all have been congratulating themselves on having picked a perfect week.

He'd felt a surge of helpless responsibility, of protectiveness. He was in charge. What should he do—go down and calm them? In case they were panicking. Tell them it was all right? Tell them it was all right just to carry on their holidays, that was what they'd come for and had paid for and they shouldn't let this spoil things, they should carry on enjoying themselves.

But his next thought—though perhaps it had really been his first and he'd pushed it aside, and it was less a thought maybe than a cold, clammy premonition—was: What might this mean for Tom?

He looks now at that same view from the bedroom window of Lookout Cottage, though the weather's neither sunny nor calm. Clouds are charging over Holn Head. A November gale is careering up the Channel. The sea, white flecks in its greyness, seems to be travelling in a body from right to left, west to east, as if some retreat is going on. Rain stings the glass in front of him.

Ellie has been gone for over an hour—this weather yet to unleash itself when she left. She could be sitting out the storm somewhere, pulled up in the wind-rocked Cherokee. Reconsidering her options, perhaps. Or she could have done already exactly what she said she'd do, and be returning, having to take it slowly, headlights on in the blinding rain. Or returning—who knows?—behind a police car, with not just its headlights on, but its blue light flashing.

Reconsidering her options? But she made the move and said the words. The situation is plain to him now, and despite the blurring wind and rain, Jack's mind is really quite clear. She had her own set of keys, of course. All she had to do was grab her handbag and walk out the door, but she might have remembered another set of keys that Jack certainly hasn't forgotten. Has it occurred to her, even now? Ellie who was usually the one who thought things through, and him the slowcoach.

'Ellie,' Jack thinks. 'My Ellie.'

He's already taken the shotgun from the cabinet down-stairs—the keys are in the lock—and brought it up here. It's lying, loaded, on the bed behind him, on the white duvet. For good measure he has a box of twenty-five cartridges (some already in his pocket), in case of police cars, in case of mishaps. It's the first time, Jack thinks, that he's ever put a gun on a bed, let alone theirs, and that, by itself, has to mean something. As he peers through the window he can feel the weight of the gun behind him, making a dent in the duvet as if it might be some small, sleeping body.

Well, one way or another, they'd never gone down the road of children. There isn't, now, that complication. He's definitely the last of the Luxtons. There's only one final complication—it involves Ellie—and he's thought that through too, seriously and carefully.

Which is why he's up here, at this rain-lashed window, from where he has the best view of the narrow, twisting road, Beacon Hill, which has no other purpose these days than to lead to this cottage. So he'll be alerted. So he'll be able to see, just a little sooner than from downstairs, the dark-blue roof, above the high bank, then the nose of the Cherokee as it takes the first, tight, ascending bend, past the old chapel. The Cherokee that's done so much hard journeying in these last three days.

The road below him, running with water, seems to slither.

Of course, she might not return at all. Another option, and one she might be seriously contemplating. Though where the hell else does she have to go to?

It's all gone mad, Jack thinks, but part of him has never felt saner. Rain blurs the window, but he looks through it at the rows of buffeted caravans in the middle distance to the right, beyond the spur of land that slopes down beneath him to the low mass of the Head. All empty now, of course, for the winter.

'Well, at least this has happened in the off season.'

Ellie's words, and just for a shameful instant it had been his own secret flicker of a thought as well.

He looks at the caravans and even now feels their tug, like the tug of the wind on their own thin, juddering frames. Thirty-two trembling units. To the left, the locked site office, the laundrette, the empty shop—grille down, window boarded. The gated entrance-way off the Sands End road, the sign above it swinging.

Even now, especially now, he feels the tug. The Lookout Caravan Park, named after this cottage (or two knocked into one), in turn named after its former use. He feels, himself now, like some desperate coastguard. Ellie had said they should change the name from The Sands. He'd said they should keep it, for the good will and the continuity. And so they had, for a year. But Ellie was all for them making their own mark and wiping out what was past. There must be no end of caravan sites called The Sands, she'd said, but The Lookout would stand out.

It could work two ways, he'd said, 'Lookout'—attempting another of those solemn-faced jokes of the kind his father once made.

Ellie had shrugged. So, didn't he like the name of the cottage? It wasn't the name they'd given it, after all. Lookout Cottage (usually known as just 'The Lookout'). They could always change the name of the cottage. Ellie was all for change. She was his wife now. She'd laughed—she'd changed her name to Luxton.

But they hadn't. Perhaps they should have done. And

before the new season began, for the sake of uniformity but also novelty, and because Ellie thought it sounded better than The Sands, the site had become, on the letter-head and the brochure and on the sign over the gate, as well as in plain fact, The Lookout Park.

And it was lookout time now all right.

2

MY ELLIE. She'd changed her name (at long last) to Luxton, just as, once, his mother had done. And 'Luxton', so his mother had always said, was a name to be proud of. It was even a name that had its glory.

Both Jack and Tom had grown up with the story, though, because of the eight years between them, not at the same time. But after Tom was born it acquired the double force of being a story about two brothers. It was Vera who mainly had the job of telling it, shaping it as she thought fit—though there wasn't so much to go on—for the ears of growing boys. Their father may have known more, but the truth was that, though the story had become, quite literally, engraved, no one had ever completely possessed the facts.

There was a medal kept at Jebb Farmhouse, up in what was known as the Big Bedroom: a silver king's head with a red-and-blue ribbon. Once a year, in November, it would be taken out and polished (by Vera, until she died). Jack and Tom had each been given, and again by Vera, their separate, private, initiatory viewings. It was anyway for all to see that among the seven names, under 1914–18, on the memorial cross outside All Saints' church in Marleston village there were two Luxtons: 'F.C. Luxton' and 'G.W. Luxton', and after 'G.W. Luxton' were the letters 'DCM'.

Once, most of a century ago, when wild flowers were blooming and insects buzzing in the tall grass in the meadows along the valley of the River Somme, two Luxton brothers had died on the same July day. In the process, though he would never know it, one of them was to earn a medal for conspicuous gallantry, while the other was merely ripped apart by bullets. Their commanding officer, Captain Hayes, who had witnessed the act of valour himself, had been eager, that night, to write the matter up, with his recommendation, in the hope that something good—if that was a fair way of putting it—might come of the day's unspeakabilities. But though he knew he had two Luxtons under his command, George and Fred, he had never known precisely which was which. In their full kit and helmets they looked like identical twins. They *all* looked, he sometimes thought, like identical twins.

But the two Luxton boys were now equally dead anyway. So he had opted for George (it was the more patriotic name), intending to corroborate the matter the next morning, if he had the chance, before his dispatch was sent. There had been much else to concern him that night. But he never did have the chance, since by seven a.m. (another radiant summer's day, with larks), not long after blowing his whistle yet again, and only obeying a futile order that elsewhere along the line had already been cancelled, Captain Hayes too was dead.

So it was George, not Fred, who got a DCM—which was only one medal down (Vera liked to make this point) from a VC—and neither brother would ever dispute it.

No then-surviving or subsequent member of the Luxton family ever had cause to challenge what was set down in the citation and carved in stone. No one else had contested it, though no one had suggested, either, that Fred was any sort of slouch. They were both heroes who'd volunteered and died for their country. It was the general, unspoken view of the slowly diminishing group who gathered every November round the Marleston war memorial that all those seven names on it were the names of heroes. Many not on it had been heroes too. There was perhaps a certain communal awkwardness about the local family names that were represented (only the Luxtons featured twice), perhaps even a particular awkwardness about George's DCM—as if it had been merely attention-seeking of him to capture single-handedly an enemy machine-gun and hold it under impossible odds (so Captain Hayes had written) till he was cut down by crossfire. On the other hand, it would have been in the shabbiest spirit not to honour a thing for what it was. George Luxton and his DCM were in fact the reason why—even long after another world war—many residents of Marleston village and its vicinity turned up in November with their poppies when otherwise they might not have done. The Luxtons themselves, of course, were always there. George Luxton (which was not to forget Fred) was the village hero and no one (not even Jimmy Merrick of neighbouring Westcott Farm) could deny that he was the Luxtons' claim to fame.

Only Jack knows, now, how Vera told the story. He never confirmed it expressly with Tom. On the other hand, he had no reason to suppose that Tom didn't get exactly the same rendition. His mother had given Jack the plain—proud, illustrious—facts, a man's story coming from a woman's lips. And all the better for it, Jack would later think. His dad would have made a mumbling hash of it. At the same time, like some diligent curator, she'd placed the medal itself before him. Jack couldn't remember how old he'd been, but he'd been too young to recognise that he was going through a rite of passage arranged exclusively for him. It was probably early one November, around the time of Guy Fawkes' Night, when they'd light a bonfire at the top of Barton Field, his dad (it was still just the three of them) having splashed it first with paraffin. So in Jack's mind Remembrance Day was always linked with flames and fireworks.

Whenever it was, his mother hadn't played up the soldier-boy side of things, nor had she played it down. But when she'd finished, or when Jack had thought she'd finished, she'd added something that, much later, he realised was entirely her own. That was the story of George and Fred, his mother had said, that's how it was: George won a medal, but they were both brave men. And if, his mother had gone on, those two boys (she'd made the point that they weren't much more than boys) had made it home together after the war, one with a medal and one not, what would have happened, she felt sure, would have been this. They'd have stopped at the gate up on the Marleston road before walking down the track and

George, who had the medal, would have pulled it from his pocket and would have broken it in two. Then he'd have said, 'Before we go any further, Fred, this is for you.' And given his brother half the medal. 'What's mine is yours,' he'd have said. Then they'd have walked on down the track.

The extraordinary thing was that his mother had told Jack this extra, imaginary bit long before Tom was around—long before, in fact, anyone thought that there would ever be, or *could* be, a Tom. Jack was Vera's one and only son. The extraordinary thing also was that you couldn't break a medal in two. Jack knew this well enough. Jack had held the medal, then, in whatever size hand he'd had at the time. He has also held it, much more recently, in his much bigger hand. And what was true years ago was as true now. You couldn't break it in two. It was made of silver. You couldn't break it in two even if you took a pair of the strongest pliers to it.

But his mother had said that what might be true for a bar of chocolate could also be true for a medal.

The last time Jack stood, wearing a poppy, by that memorial cross in Marleston was in November, 1994, and he has every reason to remember it, setting aside that it was Remembrance Day anyway. His father was there with him—or it was more the other way round—but Tom wasn't there, the first such occasion he'd missed. Tom, who would have been nineteen in just a few weeks' time, wasn't around at all, for the simple but, on such a day, highly complicated reason that he was in the army.

It made the inescapable annual attendance at the

remembrance service awkward, to say the least, but it was far from being the only burden of that sorry day.

Vera wasn't there either. She'd been dead by then for some five years. Her grave was in the churchyard close by, and it had become part of the Luxton Remembrance Day ritual that after the service they'd go and stand by it for a moment, wearing their poppies, as if she too might have been mown down on the Somme. That had been duly done—just Jack and his dad—that day.

Over the others gathered by the memorial there hung, too, an awkwardness or an extra sombreness (though it was a sparkling crisp morning) that owed something to Tom's absence, but just as much to the devastations that had visited the region's farms in recent years—to the war still rumbling on, though the thing had passed its peak, with the cow disease. In many respects, the after-effects were as bad as the outbreak itself. While officials blathered about recovery and 'declining incidence', the human toll was mounting. Perhaps everyone did their best, as every year, to picture for a moment the indescribable battlefields on which those Luxton brothers and others had died, but what came more readily to mind were the cullings and slaughterings of recent times and the grief and hardship they were still causing.

You couldn't really blame Tom Luxton, in fact, for seeking his future in the army.

Jack remembers that Remembrance Day because it was the last one he attended with his father and because his father, on this occasion, didn't offer to buy him, as was the regular ritual too, a pint in the Crown afterwards. It was the only day of the year on which Michael would buy his son a drink, doing so with a rather stagy insistence, as if the long-ago deaths of those two lads somehow rested on his conscience. Or perhaps it was more that on this day, with its hallowed meaning for the Luxton family, he liked to make a show in front of the village.

The whole thing was carefully adhered to. Every Remembrance Sunday Michael would put on his rarely worn suit, which Jack knew had been Michael's father's before him, and Jack, when he was old and privileged enough, would wear the suit his mother had once bundled him off to Burtons in Barnstaple to buy him. On that last Remembrance Day it was no longer a good fit, but it was in good condition. There had been little other use for it.

Michael was an unsentimental dairy farmer, un-comfortable at, but grudgingly empowered by, having a hero in the family. He made a display of both feelings. He'd put on his suit with an air of unwillingness, as if the whole performance only deprived him of time better spent, even on a Sunday morning, on the farm. He'd pin on his poppy. Then he'd take the medal, which Vera would have polished, and slip it almost furtively into his breast pocket. His mother, Jack remembered, always put more spirit into the thing, not only buffing up the medal, but making sure to procure the poppies in advance and inspecting them in their suits as if they might have been soldiers themselves. And she wasn't even a real Luxton.

All this had changed and the annual event had acquired a new meaning and a new component after Vera died. But there'd always been—and after Vera's death it included the teenage Tom—that gesture of the pint.

They were certainly not regulars at the Crown. If they had been, it might have lessened the effect when they walked in every November with their poppies and suits.

Drink, Michael would generally say, was money down the throat. And at least he'd never taken the route, as more than one farmer did, of letting drink itself make you forget that. They drank tea at Jebb, pints of it. They called it 'brew'. Otherwise, except at Christmas, they were mainly dry.

Old man Merrick on the other hand, Jack had long suspected, even before Ellie confirmed it, always had a hip flask on the go. Tucked somewhere about him, under those strange layers he wore. A nip here, a nip there— ever since Ellie's mother, Alice, had disappeared one day, when Ellie was still a teenager, from Westcott Farm. Just enough to keep him bright and looking—as he often did with no great reason to—like some twinkly-eyed, contented elf. Yet on all those occasions when he and Jack would meet 'by accident' in the Westcott boundary field and for a few moments do what might be called 'passing the time of day', leaning their backs against the pick-up— with Luke sometimes perched in it—or against Merrick's beaten-up Land Rover, Merrick had never fished inside his wrappings and said, 'There, boysy, take a slug.' Even when the wind was sharp.

Luke was the softest dog going, but he'd always growl and act fierce when Merrick was around and Jack had never known Jimmy Merrick stretch out a hand to stroke him.

Merrick, with rumpled lapels and a poppy, would regularly turn up on Remembrance Day, mainly for the drinking afterwards and for the rarity—it was worth a humble nod to Luxton glory—of having Michael Luxton buy him a pint. If he looked a strange sight in a suit (but they all did), Jimmy wasn't a stranger to the Crown. Michael's view was that he must have a stash of something under the floorboards at Westcott, a pot of something buried in his yard. It had to do somehow with his wife running off. But this was something Ellie could never verify—and she'd certainly have wanted to know about it.

Drink was money down the gullet anyway, Michael would say. Not that he'd want to judge his neighbour. Maybe it was even the point he was making on that Remembrance Day. It wasn't a point about Tom. Tom's name was simply no longer mentioned. It was just that they were teetering on the edge. More so than Jack guessed. Even the twenty-odd pounds he'd need for the two pints (just the two now) plus the others he'd have to stand (you had to look proud) was more than he could muster. Jack always put a twenty, if he had one, in his own pocket so he was covered too. And he'd had a twenty, somehow, that day.

But his dad hadn't even looked in the direction of the Crown. His face was like a wall, a thicker wall than usual, and, after doing the other thing they always did, going to stand by Vera's grave, they'd just driven silently back to Jebb. 'That's that then,' his dad had said and had hardly needed to say even that.

Jack was the passenger, Michael drove, and there was a point somewhere along the road when Jack realised, if not quite at the time itself, that it was too late. Before that point he still might have said, 'Stop, Dad, there's something we haven't done.' And conceivably his dad was testing him, daring him—wishing him to say it. He might have said it even when they were well clear of Marleston and nearing the Jebb gate, the hedges along the road still glittering with barely melted frost. He might have just grabbed his father's arm as he shifted a gear. What a simple thing.

But they'd passed the point, and Jack couldn't have said exactly where it was. Though, afterwards, he was to think it was the same point where Tom, on foot and heading in the other direction, at three o'clock in the morning, almost a year before, must have known—if he'd had any doubts at all—that now he couldn't, wouldn't go back.

And it was the same point, perhaps, where George might have stopped with Fred.

'Stop, Dad.' But Jack wasn't up to it. Though by then he'd long been the bigger of the two of them. One day, years ago, he'd woken up to discover, disturbingly, that he was taller than his father. Now, in some mysterious way, his dad was even shrinking. But he still wasn't up to it.

And his father, Jack thinks now, might just have said, 'We haven't not done anything. We went and looked at her grave, didn't we? Take your hand off my arm.'

They might simply have had a set-to right there, a blazing set-to, pulled up on the Marleston–Polstowe road, the engine of the Land Rover still running. A set-to in their suits. They might even have got out and taken a swing at each other, the swings at each other they'd been saving up for years. And his dad with a medal for bravery in his pocket.

On those previous occasions in the Crown there'd

usually be someone who'd ask, as if they'd been planted there for the purpose, 'So—do you have it with you, Michael?' And his father, perched on his stool at the bar and looking as if he hadn't heard or might even be quietly annoyed by the question, would sip his beer or blow smoke from his mouth and, only after you thought the matter had passed, dip his hand into his top pocket and take it out again, clenched round something. And only after more time had passed and while he still looked at the air in front of him would he open his hand, just for an instant, above the surface of the bar, and then return the medal to where it had come from. It was a perform-ance his dad was good at and one worth its annual repetition. An unsentimental dairy farmer, but capable (though Jack could never have furnished the joke) of milking a situation.

The lights on in the Crown. He can see it now. A grey November noon. The low beams. Poppies and suits. A faint whiff of old wardrobes and moth balls. The beer seeping down, everything huddled and glinting. Then for a moment that extra glint. The glory of the Luxtons.

'Stop, Dad. I want to buy you a drink.' Such a simple thing, but like moving the hills.

3

WHAT WOULD his mum think? That has always been Jack's inner yardstick, his deepest cry.

Vera Luxton died when Jack was twenty-one and Tom was thirteen, of ovarian cancer. Perhaps his acquaintance with cows and calves made Jack better able than most men of twenty-one to comprehend what this meant, but it was anyway an event that changed everything, like a line in history. The cow disease, which came later, was one thing and it was a killer in every sense, but the rot really set in, Jack would say, when Vera died. Michael had run the farm, but Vera had overseen it, had made it revolve in some way round herself. If they hadn't known and acknowledged it at the time—and that included little Tom—they knew it now.

Behind that wall his dad could present to the world, Jack knew, his father was stumbling. There were some things Jack could see through—or that he simply duplicated. He had a face like a wall too, he was stumbling too. It was his fall-back position, to take what he got and stumble on, to look strong or just dumb on the outside and stumble inside. He was just like his father.

But on the other hand (and his father knew it) he'd always been closer to his mum, a lot closer than little Tom had ever been, coming along those eight years later and to everyone's surprise.

'Would you like a little brother, Jack?'

His mother had looked at him with a strange, stern-but-pleading look, as if she needed (though he was only seven) his serious, manly help.

'Because I have a feeling,' she'd said, 'you may be going to get one.'

It had seemed to him that she was somehow floating away, might even be saying goodbye, and this was some sort of offer of compensation. And how, with that look in her eye, could he have said anything but yes?

It was only later that he drew the conclusion—or formed the theory—that Tom hadn't been meant to happen. It was a risk. His mother had problems in that department. She'd had a bad time with him, he vaguely knew. Though he also understood that she'd thought it was worth it. She had an even worse time, as it turned out, with Tom. Between the two of them, Jack sometimes wondered, might they have given her the cancer?

But he'd been truly intended. While Tom, it seemed, had turned up by surprise and at much hazard to his mother. It made a difference, perhaps. It made him feel that Tom was never a rival—the opposite. Jack had been born at Jebb, in the Big Bedroom, with the assistance of an intrepid midwife. But Tom had been brought home one day from Barnstaple Infirmary, with a Vera who'd looked rather weaker than her baby. It made a difference.

In any case, after Tom was there, Jack's mum had a way, from time to time, of drawing Jack aside into a sort of special, private corner—though it was usually in the kitchen or on warm days in the yard, so in no way hidden. Nonetheless his dad, and Tom when he was older, would respectfully steer clear of it, as if Vera had issued an order. When he was in this special space with his mother, Jack would mysteriously understand—even when he was only nine or ten—that he was having a grown-up conversation, something you were supposed to have in life, a sort of always-to-be-resumed conversation, which went on, in fact, right up until the time his mother fell ill and died. And he'd understand that this conversation had to do with something that seldom otherwise came into his thinking, let alone his talk: his future and its responsibilities. Or, to put it another way, his name.

Since it meant something if you were born, as he was, on a farm: the name. The generations going back and forwards, like the hills, whichever way you looked, around them. And what else had his mother borne him for than to give him and show him his birthright? Something his father, for whatever reason—and though it was *his* name—could never do. There'd never been such a moment.

And then the birthright, deprived of Vera's backing and blighted by cow disease, had begun to look anyway like a poor deal.

That had always seemed to Jack to be the gist of those conversations, whatever their apparent subject: his birthright. That he shouldn't worry about Tom, who would always be the little nipper and latecomer. That he should rise to his place and his task.

When he was older, starting to outgrow both his father and that Burtons suit, she'd make tea for just the two of them. He'd smoke a cigarette. She'd top up his mug, without his asking, when he put it down. He didn't know then how much one day he'd miss, and he wouldn't know how to speak of it when he did, the creases in his mother's wrist as she held the teapot, one hand pressing down the lid, and refilled his mug, just for him.

And it was only later, when she was gone, that it occurred to him that another gist, and perhaps the real gist, of those conversations was precisely that. That she was telling him that she wouldn't always be there. It was what she'd had in her mind perhaps—and he'd been right to have those strange feelings—even when she first told him about Tom. She'd be gone sooner than anyone might think.

She was more of a Luxton, it could be said, than the Luxtons themselves. When she died it was as if the whole pattern was lost. Yet her name had once been Newcombe, and until she was nineteen she'd never even known life on a farm. She was the daughter of a postmaster. One day Michael Luxton had plucked her from the post office in Polstowe and carried her to Jebb Farm and, so it seemed, nothing could have better answered her hopes and her wishes.

Something like that must have happened. Jack had never known, even from his mother's lips, the actual story. His dealings with Ellie Merrick didn't seem a useful guide. But he found it hard, or just vaguely trespassing of him, to imagine that his father, his father of all people, might once have carried his mother, her legs kicking, over the threshold of Jebb Farm and possibly even have carried her, without a pause, straight up to the Big Bed—where two years later he, Jack, would be born and where, twenty-one years after that, Vera Luxton would die.

He'd sometimes daringly think that the business of birthright might work in reverse. That his mother's birthing him, more than her taking his father's name, had made a Luxton out of her. She'd had such a bad time with him, Jack supposed, that it had generally been accepted that she couldn't be a mother again. So everything was pooled in him. Or, looking at it another way, it was his fault. Eight long years had proved it. Then Tom had come along and taken away the blame. Which was another reason why suddenly having a little brother around was never a problem for Jack. Quite the opposite.

Anyway, there were those conversations. And anyway, by the time Vera lay dying in that big bed, she'd become so much a Luxton that despite the determined efforts of the health authorities to move her into hospital, she refused to be taken from Jebb Farm. As if she were putting down her final roots.

He'd always remember—though he's tried to forget them—her last days. How she clung, sometimes literally, to that bed as if she wanted, perhaps, to become it. Or the bed, perhaps, wanted to become her. His father, as if not to intrude on this intimate process, had slept, or rather kept terrified watch, close by in a sort of separate bivouac made out of the old wooden chest pushed up against the room's solitary, battered armchair. The room was like some compartment of disaster.

Well, at least she was spared, Jack can say to himself now, the long road to ruin, and worse. Though it was not so long, really, after her death. How it would have appalled and shamed and simply disappointed her. How she must have flinched, again and again, in that grave of hers in Marleston churchyard. But then if she could have flinched—Jack can sometimes lose his own logic—she wouldn't have been spared.

He can't decide the matter. His mother is dead, yet she has never not been, in theory, at his shoulder. He wants her not to have known and suffered or even witnessed all the things that followed her death. Including all this now. But that would be like wishing her dead. Merely dead.

Only yesterday Jack had been obliged to stand close to his mother's grave. Had she known? How could she have borne it to know, under the circumstances? But if she'd known, then surely she'd have let *him* know, he'd have felt some tug—something even like the tug of those empty caravans—and surely she'd have cried out, somehow, when he'd left in that sudden, uncontrollable haste, 'Jack, don't go. Don't rush off like that.' And surely, if she had, he'd have stayed.

All of them there together, for that short, agonising while, all of them under the same pressing circumstances, but him the only one left above ground.

And all of them there (except him) right now, he thinks, right this minute, under this wind and rain. The wind plucking the browning petals from all those flowers, toppling the stacked-up bunches and wreaths, the rain rinsing the gravestones, new and old, the water seeping down through the soil.

Jack can't decide the matter. Do they feel it, know it all, or are they spared? He could say he's about to find out.

4

WHAT WOULD his mother think (he tries not to think about it) if she could see him now?

But what would she have thought, anyway, to see him no longer at Jebb Farm but here by the sea, tending a herd of caravans? What would she think to see him hitched up—properly and officially married—to Ellie Merrick? But that once-impossible yet inevitable thing—who else was it going to be?—would surely have been only what she'd have wished. If only she'd had the power to knock two stubborn male heads together and make it happen herself.

But it hadn't happened, anyway, in Marleston church. No wedding bells reaching her, six foot below in the Devon earth, making her smile. My son Jack's getting married today. And he hadn't felt her presence—her touch, her whispered approval—in that registry office in Newport.

And now, look, with a gun on their marriage bed.

And what would she have thought to see him and

Ellie taking off every winter, for three weeks or a whole month sometimes, to sun themselves under coconut palms and drink tall drinks with paper parasols stuck in them? Never mind that they were here by the seaside, near a beach, in the first place. But that was what Ellie had thought they should do, they could afford it and they should do it, and why shouldn't *they* have their holidays? And he, with a little coaxing at first, had gone along with it. And not a bad arrangement at all. Certainly according to the caravanners—the 'Lookouters'. We get a week in the Isle of Wight, you get a month in the Caribbean. Not bad, Jack, for an out-of-work farmer.

It was the regular backchat, not ill-meant, but he'd had to find a way of handling it. No one got short-changed, no one got a bad deal at the Lookout. He couldn't arrange the weather (any more than he could at Jebb). You'll get as good a holiday here as you'll get there, he'd say, in a way that, he could tell, they felt he really, mysteriously believed. He'd risen to that task: talking to the caravanners, making them feel at home and befriended. He'd been surprised at his talent for it.

He took his holidays these days in the Caribbean. And what of it? Once he'd been tethered, all year round, to a herd of Friesians.

Though, if the truth be known, after a few days of lying under those palm trees and sipping those drinks and smiling at Ellie and rubbing sunscreen on her, he'd sometimes start to think anxiously about his caravans. Whether they were all right. Whether they were with-standing the winter storms. Whether that security firm—Dawsons—was really any good and whether anyone was actually patrolling the place, while he was lying here where once he could never have dreamed of being. And then he'd think, because it was the thought he was really always having to bat away, like batting away one of those big bastard tropical hornet things that could come at you suddenly out of nowhere: what would his mum think?

Well, Jack, my big old boy, it's a far cry from Brigwell Bay. That's what she'd think. Or from hosing down the milking parlour.

And then he'd think of Tom.

'Farmer Jack'. He never quite knew how the word had got around. Farmer Jack, milking his caravans. Here comes Farmer Jack in one of those shirts he got in Barbados. The ones that make your eyes hurt. What would *they* have thought if they could actually have seen him in the parlour in his faded blue boiler suit and his wellies? Being barked at by his father. What would his mum have thought if she could see him in one of those shirts?

But never mind that. Never mind the Lookout Park, formerly the Sands, or the winter holidays in the Caribbean. What would she have thought to see how it all went at Jebb? To see it now, not a Luxton in sight, its acres all in new hands and the farmhouse no longer a farmhouse. A country home, a 'holiday home' (that was the phrase Ellie herself had once used) for people who already had a home. What would she have thought to see all the things that didn't bear thinking of? (Though had she seen them anyway?) To see Tom, little Tom, but a big boy himself by then, simply slip out one cold December night and disappear?

But Tom's with her right now, Jack thinks, he could

scarcely be closer. He was walking right back to her, that night, without knowing it.

And what would she have thought to see those burning cattle?

All the generations going back and forwards. It had been so for centuries. The first farmhouse on Jebb Hill had been built by a Luxton in 1614. The oak in Barton Field was perhaps old even then. And who would have thought—let alone his own mother—that he, Jack Luxton, would be the first of all the Luxtons (as he was now the last) to cut that long, thick rope on which his own hands had been hardened and sell Jebb Farmhouse and all the land and become, with Ellie, the soft-living proprietor of a caravan site?

He could blame Ellie if he wanted to. He'd been the only man left around the place, and who else made the decisions? But Ellie would surely have known the weak spot in him she was touching (so would his mother) when she came up with her plan. And what other plan, what other solution did he happen to have?

'I've thought it through, Jack, trust me.'

To become the proprietor of the very opposite thing to that deep-rooted farmhouse. Holiday homes, on wheels. Or 'units', as they'd come to refer to them. But they'd been good at it, he and Ellie, they'd made a good go of it—with a lot of help at the start, it's true, from 'Uncle Tony'. And they'd made more out of it than they'd ever have made out of two doomed farms. And, for God's sake, it could even be fun. Fun being what they dealt in. 'Fun, Jacko, don't you think it's time we had some?' And every winter, on top of it all, they flew off to the Caribbean.

But not this winter. Obviously. Or it had seemed

unavoidably obvious to him. But not to Ellie, apparently. And that was the start of all this.

He looks now at the rain-swept caravans. The tug of it, still. Lookout Cottage up here, the caravans down there, no more than little white oblongs at this distance. The joke was that he had a telescope constantly trained, he wasn't just Farmer Jack, he was also sometimes the Commandant. Driving down or strolling down every day to see if all was well. In fine weather, dressed the part: shorts and Caribbean shirt (extra-large) and one of those baseball caps they'd had run up, free for every guest, with LOOKOUT and the lighthouse motif—gold on black—above the peak.

Thirty-two units. All 'top of the range', he could truthfully say, even if the range wasn't quite the topmost one. He could never have said that about the milking machinery at Jebb.

The tug he'd never expected. Empty half the year, but then sometimes, strangely, as now, all the more tugging. Occupied for the other half by this shifting temporary population—migrants, vagrants, escapers in their own country.

It was only ever an encampment down there, that was the feel of it, like the halt of some expeditionary, ragtag army. It might all be gone in the morning—any morning—leaving nothing but the tyre marks in the grass. That was the tug. Not cattle, not even caravans, but people.

5

ELLIE SITS IN the wind-rocked, rain-lashed Cherokee, in the lay-by on the coast road at Holn Cliffs, thinking of her mother.

The car is pointing in the direction of Holn itself and so in what, on any day till now, she might have called the direction of home. And on a clear day it would be perfectly possible to see from where she sits not just the fine sweep of the coastline, but, on the hillside running up from the Head, the distant white speck of Lookout Cottage. It had been built there, after all, with a now-vanished lighthouse above it, because of the prominent position. And on a clear day, a fine summer's day say, it would be equally possible to see from Lookout Cottage the distant glint and twinkle of cars—with perhaps an ice-cream van or two—lined up in the lay-by at Holn Cliffs while their occupants admired the view.

Today there is no view. Even Holn Head is just a vague, jutting mass of darker greyness amid the general greyness, and Ellie can only squintingly imagine that at a certain point, through the murk beyond her windscreen, she can see the pin-prick gleam of the lit-up windows of the cottage.

The wipers are on, though to little effect. Thirty yards along the lay-by, barely visible, is another parked car, a silver hatchback, doing what Ellie is apparently doing, and Ellie feels, along with an instinctive solidarity, a stab of envy. *Only* to be sitting out the storm.

How could Jack have said what he said?

Ellie hasn't seen her mother for over twenty years—and can never see her again—so that to think of her at all is like seeing distant glimmers through a blur. Yet right now, as if time has performed some astounding, marooning loop, thoughts of her mother—and of her father—have never been so real to her.

How could Jack have said it?

Ellie's mother disappeared, one fine late-September day, from Westcott Farm, Devon, abandoning her husband, Jimmy, and her only child, Ellie, when Ellie was barely sixteen, and though she would never see her again, Ellie would come to know—familiarly and gratefully—where her mother had eventually made her home. Ellie's mother once lived in that cottage whose lights Ellie can only imagine she sees, and had she not done so, Ellie and Jack could never have made it their home as well.

Though now Ellie wonders if it is any sort of home at all.

The exact cause of her mother's sudden flight all those years ago Ellie would never know, but it had to do with a figure whom Ellie, back then, would sometimes call, when in intimate conversation with Jack Luxton, her mother's 'mystery man'—using that phrase not so much with scorn but with a teasing fascination, as if she would quite like a mystery man of her own.

Her father must have had some clue who the man was and even communicated indirectly with his runaway wife on the subject, if only to become an officially divorced man and get back the sole title to Westcott Farm. But his lips remained sealed and, anyway, not long before her father's death, Ellie was to discover that her mother had replaced that original mystery man with someone else and had lived with him on the Isle of Wight.

A few miles along the coast road behind her, in a cemetery in Shanklin, Ellie's mother—or her ashes—lies buried, under a memorial slab placed there by her then husband, whom Ellie would one day refer to as 'Uncle Tony'. Ellie has lived now for over ten years in her mother's and Uncle Tony's former home, but has never been to see her mother's nearby resting-place, and until recently this would only have expressed her mixed feelings about her once renegade mum: blame, tempered with unexpected gratitude and—ever since that September day years ago—an odd, grudging admiration. She hadn't quite condemned, but she hadn't quite forgiven either, and she wasn't going to go standing by any graves.

And until recently this would only have expressed Ellie's position generally. The past is the past, and the dead are the dead.

But two mornings ago when Jack had departed, all by himself, on an extraordinary journey whose ultimate destination was a graveside, Ellie had felt rise up within her, like a counterweight, the sudden urge to pay her long-withheld respects. She'd even had the thought: As for Jack and his brother, so for me and my mum. The only trouble was that she didn't have the car, Jack had it, and she'd baulked at the idea of getting the bus. But she has the car now—she has unilaterally commandeered it—and, only within the last desperate hour, Ellie has attempted that aborted journey once again. And failed.

She'd driven blindly hither and thither at first, sometimes literally blindly, given the assaults of the rain, and because much of the time her eyes were swimming with tears. How could Jack have said that? But then how could she have said what *she'd* said, and how could she possibly, actually act upon it? Then the thought of her mother had loomed, even more powerfully, once more. Shanklin. Forget Newport. Forget Newport police station. That had just been a terrible, crazy piece of blather. Shanklin. And now, after all, might really be the time.

Hello Mum, here I am at last, and look what a mess I'm in. Any advice? What now? What next?

And if no answer were forthcoming, then at least she might say: Thank you, Mum, thank you anyway. I'm here at least to say that. Thank you for deserting me and Dad all those years ago. Thank you for leaving me to him, and to the cows. And the cow disease. Thank you for being a cow yourself, but for coming right in the end, even if you never knew it. Thank you for giving me and Jack— remember him, Jack Luxton?—these last ten years. Which now look like they're coming to an end.

And thank you, if it comes to it, for offering me your example.

Rolled up in the back of the car is one of the oversized

umbrellas they'd had made for use around the site and to sell in the shop. Yellow-gold segments alternating with black ones displaying a white lighthouse logo—meant to represent the vanished beacon—and the word LOOKOUT at the rim. The umbrellas matched the T-shirts and the baseball caps and the car stickers—all things that (like the name 'Lookout' itself) had been her ideas.

It would have gone with Jack, she realised, on his journey. She suddenly hoped it hadn't rained on him. What a fool he'd have looked putting it up at a funeral. Let alone at a military parade. But driving madly just minutes ago through the blinding rain, Ellie had seen herself clutching that same wind-tugged Lookout umbrella as she stood by her mother's rain-soaked remains.

Hello Mum. What a day for it, eh?

But what a fool *she'd* look. And what a miserable exercise it would be. Picking her way through some wretched cemetery, through the puddles and mud. In *these* shoes. All to find some little, drenched square of marble, while a seaside brolly tried to yank her into the air. Jesus Christ.

And as for that advice, that example, did she really need to stoop, cocking an ear, by her mother's grave? It was stored up, anyway, in her memory, like an emergency formula for some future—rainy—day. She could hear her mother's forgotten voice. Skedaddle, Ellie. Just skedaddle, like I did. Cut loose. While you've got the car and while you can. With just the clothes you're in and what's in your handbag. Now or never. Cut loose.

Somewhere near Ventnor, with a strange little yelp at herself, she'd turned round and driven back along the coast road, into the teeth of the oncoming gale, only to find herself immobilised now, fifty yards—across a sodden verge, a wind-rippled hedge and a strip of field—from the edge of Holn Cliffs.

Everyone has their limits, Ellie thinks, and her mother must have reached hers, for her to have left a husband and a daughter who'd only just turned sixteen—even with a mystery man on hand. And her own limits must have outstretched her mother's—but then she hadn't had a mystery man, she had Jack—for her to have stuck it out with her dad for another twelve years. To have stuck it out with him, as it happened, to the very end. Even being with him, holding and squeezing his hand, in that hospital in Barnstaple just a few hours before he died. And she'd have been with him at the end, if she'd known and if it hadn't been at two in the morning.

How could Jack have said what he said?

Everyone has their limits, and it seems to Ellie that she might have reached her limits now with Jack—or whoever that man was up there in that invisible cottage. She might be about to turn her back on him, as she'd never, in fact, turned her back on her father. Or, before now, on Jack.

But here she sits, pulled up in this lay-by, not going anywhere, within a mile and (on any normal day) within sight of home. And it wasn't the perilous weather that had made her stop, or even the pursuing ghost of her unvisited mother, but the sudden, clear, looming ghost of herself, driving madly once before, through the still, golden sunshine of a late-September afternoon.

*

Barely sixteen, but she knew how to handle a Land Rover. Even if she wasn't allowed and was even forbidden by law to drive it on the road. Nonetheless, on the third day after her mother's departure and while her father seemed to have taken resolutely to the bottle for the day, Ellie had gone out with the keys to the ancient vehicle in the Westcott yard, got in and driven it, for the first time in her life, right up the Westcott track to the gate and the road, and beyond. With no real intention of returning.

It wasn't a planned escape. She'd taken nothing with her, but it had evolved, in the very fact of motion, in the familiar quirks of the gear stick beside her and the mud-plastered pedals beneath her, into a frantic bid for free-dom. In any case, there was the sudden sheer, wild glee of taking the thing out onto the road and seeing what it could do. Swerving to miss traffic, taking arbitrary turns, and, in the narrow lanes, finding out that she was entirely adept, even aggressive, in dealing with an oncoming vehicle in that one-to-one situation when either they or you have to find the passing-spot. If she could manage this Land Rover in a muddy field, do natty reverse-work in the yard or buck along a rutted track, she could do all this on a solid road now.

The early-autumn sun had filled the air and drenched the berried hedges. The window was down, her hair flew. There was petrol in the tank. Ellie can see, now, her bare teenage knees as she pumped the pedals, her little smoky-blue, thick-corduroy skirt, no more than a band of ribbed fabric—this was 1983.

She began to laugh, to sing—selections from Duran Duran. Was her face also shiny with tears? Had this old

Land Rover ever been given such a ride? As she drove, a sort of plan, a purpose had come to her. Wherever she was going (if she was going anywhere) she couldn't go there alone. Or she couldn't leave her mates behind without letting them at least know she was on the run and offering them the option too. There was room in the back.

She thought of going to get Linda Fairchild and Susie Mitchelmore in Marleston itself, Jackie White in Polstowe and Michelle Hannaford at Leke Hill. Liberating them all. A skidding halt, a loud blast on the horn. Quick! It's me, Ellie! Come on! She thought of going to that bus shelter near Abbot's Green, where much was thought of and discussed and giggled over but not so much done, and scrawling a last, filthy, farewell message on its wall. She thought of scooping up the whole Abbot's Green School bunch and saying, 'Right! Here we go!' The chances of a police car round here were a hundred to one. And, to hell with it, she could even go and pick up Bob Ireton's mopy sister Gillian—Bob who was set on becoming a cop.

All this was like some glorious net—a freeing net— flung out from her racing mind. She'd scoop up anyone who was game for it. Boys too, yes, any boys. But at some point in the great rush of her thoughts—she was actually swooping down Polstowe Hill—she calmed down (relatively) and knew what she had to do.

Could it really be anything else? And it wouldn't be just an act of liberation. It would be a test. A test of herself. Could she? Would she? She stopped and reversed, swiftly, with a pleasing belch of exhaust smoke, at a farm gate. All the farm gates, all the bloody farm gates. Someone blared a horn at her. She blared back. She raced again through Polstowe. People couldn't have helped noticing by now. This was at least the third time. That was Jimmy Merrick's Land Rover, wasn't it? But that wasn't Jimmy, surely, at the wheel.

She sped back towards Marleston. Could she really do it? She certainly saw herself doing it. She sees herself doing it now, as if there's still somehow a need. She sees herself stopping by the Jebb gate and opening it. Sees herself driving through and not bothering to do any closing. My God, this is a first. She sees herself roaring into the Jebb yard and lurching to a halt, hand slammed on the horn. No guessing where Jack might be on the farm at this time of day, but in the scene in her head Jack is somewhere conveniently near the yard. And he's heard this meteor coming down the track.

She sees the family turning out to confront her amazing arrival. Michael. Vera. There's a difficulty there, she knows it—to tear Jack from his mum. And standing beside Vera is little Tom, aged seven. A difficulty there too—and there always will be. There's a difficulty now. But it's only Jack she cares about. My Jack.

And there he is. She looks at him and he looks at her, astonishment denting his not often dentable face. A test for her. A test for him. But she's already passed hers, by being there—it was always like this, her making the first move—and by sticking her head now out of the window and yelling, 'Come on, Jacko! Now or never. Quick! Jump in!'

But she doesn't go through the Jebb gate. She doesn't even stop by it. And Jack will never know that he was once part of that never-enacted scene. She thinks of her dad who, even now, in his sozzled state, is perhaps unaware of her flight. How can she do it? Ensure that in the course of three days the only two women in his life will have deserted him, and stolen his Land Rover. She thinks of her abandoned dad who, when he hears her driving back down the Westcott track, will surely think, in his half-stupor, that it must be his wife coming home. Coming back! Allie and Ellie and Jimmy, all together at Westcott again.

She drives along the Marleston road. There's a straight, clear stretch after the Jebb bend, but she's lost now all the thrill of speed. In any case, she slows for the Westcott gate. She can see the square tower of Marleston church poking up ahead. She gives a strange, pained cry (she gave the same cry again, exactly the same, today) and runs a forearm over her slippery face. She stops, gets out to close the gate dutifully behind her—having left it defiantly open on her way out. She hears its familiar clang.

The twin hedges take her in their grasp, the golden sunshine mocks her. She drives on down, along the dry ruts, to her father who, indeed, since he's been seeking oblivion anyway, will never know, any more than Jack will, what Ellie has done today. The things we never know. She drives back into Westcott Farm, to her mother's absence, to her sleeping father (who when she wakes him with a mug of tea, doesn't want to be woken) and to the mooing, snorting, pissing, shitting fact of cows to be milked.

6

It was deep, steep, difficult but good-looking land, with small patchy fields that funnelled or bulged down to the woods in the valley. They had one field up on the ridge where they grew occasional wheat and autumn feed, otherwise it was down to grass and like almost every farm for miles around: sheep or dairy, and they'd always been dairy—beef calves for sale, and dairy. It was hard work for the softest, mildest thing in the world. It was all about turning the land into good white gallons, as many as possible. And it was all about men being slaves to the female of the species, so Michael Luxton had liked to say, with a sideways crack of his face, when Vera had still been around, especially in her hearing. They were all bloody milksops really.

Each one of those carcasses that were carted off after the cow disease came was a potential hand-out from the Ministry. But that didn't allow for the slowness or down-right shiftiness of the bureaucracy, or for the simple fact that there was nothing much to bridge the gap. Not a single one of their herd had ever been confirmed. The words were 'suspect' and 'contiguous risk'. They just couldn't be moved, that's all, though they had to be fed. Nor, at first, could their milk be moved, though they had to be milked. And then they'd nearly all (except for the new calves) been moved anyway—as carcasses. The farm like a ghost farm, the loss of all that penned-up company strangely bereaving. No milk flow, no cash flow, and precious little in the bank. He and Tom got the impression, from their dad's silences, that the precious little wasn't even theirs. Meanwhile, when were they supposed to start restocking again and know it wouldn't be cost and effort for nothing?

Tom hadn't waited for the final reckoning. Though you couldn't say it was a sudden move either. He waited till his eighteenth birthday—till he'd be his own man. And you couldn't say it was a bad move. He'd seen the way the wind was blowing.

And why hadn't he, Jack, thought of it first? Just to clear off out of it. But it had never occurred to him. And why hadn't he minded when Tom said that it had been occurring to him all right, for more than a year? 'This is just for your ears, Jack.' As if then it became a pact that they'd both entered into, and it was down to Jack, while Tom made the actual move, to cover up for him. And to take it, of course, from Dad afterwards, take all the stick for it, but not say anything for weeks, months, feigning dumb ignorance, buttoning his lip, like some good soldier himself, and only speaking, finally, because he thought his dad must surely have guessed anyway—what else does a boy do?—and because there was no real chance of his father's getting Tom back.

No, he didn't know where Tom was. Which was only

the truth. Because Tom was in the army and who could say where the army was? Catterick? Salisbury Plain?

Good luck, Tom. As if Tom was doing the escaping for both of them.

Why had he never minded, or even thought about it most of the time? That Tom was better, quicker, smarter at pretty well everything. Including, so it seemed, deciding his own future. Eight years and, for a long time, several inches between them. And no competition. He could knock Tom down any time he liked, but he never had. Had never even wanted to.

Even that gun lying there, Tom was better at that. At twelve or thirteen he could swing it round and *make* the rabbit hit the shot. Good with a gun—so a soldier's life for him. But Tom was even better, after Vera died, at taking her place, at being, for them all, a bit of a mum himself. Was that something the army required of a man too?

Jack should have been the one, by rights, to step into her space. Eight years her only boy. And all those mugs of tea. But it was Tom who, at thirteen, was plainly quicker and better in the cooking, washing and looking-after department too. And Jack, at twenty-one, was a big, outdoor man with mud on his boots. If he'd tried to take his mum's place, Dad would have mocked him. So it was Tom who one day put on Vera's still flour-dusted, gravy-spotted apron. He and Dad simply watched him do it. It had been hanging on its hook on the corner of the dresser where no one seemed to want to touch it. But it was Tom who took it down and put it on. Like some silent declaration. It was Tom who piled eggs and bacon and triangles of bread into the pan and filled the kitchen with a smell and a sizzle as if someone might be still there who wasn't.

And not just pile. He could crack those eggs one-handed, just as Mum had. Two neat little half-shells left in his fingers. Jack knew, without trying, he could never have done that. They'd have been eating eggshell for breakfast, spitting out the bits.

Mrs Warburton, Sally Warburton, Mum's old pal, had come in for a while every day to 'tide them over', as she put it, and perhaps to set them all her own example in being a bit of a mum to each other. Maybe Tom got some of it from her. Maybe Tom had puppied up to her while he and Dad did all the heavy work.

And it was a pity, maybe, that Mrs Warburton wasn't just Sally Warburton, or just Sally somebody, and not Mrs Warburton, wife of Ken Warburton who ran the filling station at Leke Hill Cross. Because then she might have become the next Mrs Luxton and they might all have got a permanent second-best mum. But she stopped coming after a while, presumably because she thought they were tided over. And then where was Michael to turn? He was fifty-two. Jack never knew what his mum might have said to his dad, even as she was dying, on this score. If she'd said anything at all. But after a certain passage of time Michael made the desperate move of advertising in the *Courier* for a 'housekeeper', and every-one knows, when a recently widowered farmer does that, what it really means.

No takers. (And how could he have *paid* a house-keeper?)

That's when Jack had felt his father starting to turn old. To shrink. And to turn sour-tempered, something which, for all his slowness to raise a smile, he'd never been. You'd see him kick at something, a feed trough, the corrugated iron round the muckheap, for no reason at all. Swing back his leg and kick. That's when Jack had felt that, though Tom was no longer such a little brother, he had to be a shield for him against his father's weather. He had to stand in between and take it. Why had he never minded?

First Mum, then Tom. In between, most of their livestock carried off for incineration. Then just him and Dad. And Dad looking at him with a look that said: And don't you try it, don't you even think about it. When he wasn't wearing that other look which said: Why don't *you* solve the issue, Jack boy, why don't you do something about it? The issue of there being no Mrs Luxton. Which was a mad look, if ever there was one, a look where Dad had himself tied up into a knot, because unless his son was supposed to go foraging (and how might that occur exactly?) it was like saying that Jack should do the very thing there was no question of his doing. The real knot being the knot that he and Ellie Merrick could never formally tie.

Jimmy Merrick and Michael Luxton should have got married themselves, Jack has sometimes thought, they should have married each other. If such a thing were possible. About as unlike as two men could be and with as little liking for each other as two men could have. But both battling with the same things: both of them wifeless, both working, on different sides of a boundary, the same sweet but tough, now disease-hit land. Both of them going to the dogs and watching each other like hawks to see who'd get eaten up first.

In Jack's memory it was the Luxtons who'd had the upper hand (having anyway the finer-looking farmhouse and the prettier acres) especially after Merrick's wife, Alice, had run off and abandoned him, leaving him with a sixteen-year-old daughter as his only companion and domestic workforce. An event as surprising (though Michael liked to say it was no surprise at all) as the Luxtons suddenly acquiring after eight years a second son, which, though the timing might have been better, only added to the stock at Jebb Farm and so to the abasement of the Merricks.

But then Vera had died, leaving the two men, in that respect, similarly placed. Then Tom had done his own bit of running off. Meanwhile, there was a cow disease. All of which left the two farmers, neither getting any younger, in a state of more or less equal dereliction. If anything, it was Jimmy who now had the edge, since he'd had years to get used to misfortune, while Michael, after a fair time of not doing so badly thank you, had incurred a quick succession of troubles, and anyone could see he was going down fast.

They should have got damn well hitched themselves. Or, as would have been the more customary solution and one which had only been staring them in the face for years, Jack should have married Ellie and linked their situations that way.

But that would have gone against all known history and deprived the two fathers of their fuelling disdain for each other. It would have robbed one of a daughter or one of a son, since where were the happy couple supposed to live? Did Michael seriously think that Ellie was going to hop across the fence and settle in at Jebb, when she was so clearly needed at the side of her dear old dad?

And all of this despite the fact that the son and the daughter had been chummy with each other for as long as they—or anyone else—could remember. And not just chummy. For years now, from even before Alice Merrick's abrupt departure, he and Ellie had been pretty much behaving with each other (if only on certain weekday afternoons) as if they *were* married. Which was not only common knowledge in the region of Marleston, but was actually abetted, even smiled on by the two fathers, even while it retained its clandestine trappings—on the basis, presumably, that there had to be some compensation for the fact that real marriage was impossible. At the same time (and Jack had only slowly come to recognise this) it was a concession that kept them both, the son and the daughter, firmly in their places: on their own farms (except, for Jack, on Tuesday and sometimes Thursday afternoons) and in each case a slave to it.

In the beginning, Jack had simply driven over in the pick-up, with Luke in the back. This would be at times when, according to a cautious-seeming Ellie, old Merrick wouldn't be around. He and Ellie would go up to her bedroom, knowing that they couldn't take too long about it, especially if they wanted, which they always did, to sit and have a cup of tea in the kitchen afterwards—with Luke, who seemed to know when to make himself scarce, stretched out by the stove, eyeing them meaningfully. It wouldn't have seemed right without the cup of tea, and that had always been the pretext, or pretence: Jack had simply popped over on a neighbourly visit (though why the hell should he do that?) and stayed for a neighbourly cup of tea.

But this had gone on for so long, without any discoveries or interruptions, that it was clear there was no real need for haste or secrecy, or to divide their time between bedroom and kitchen. Jack had begun to wonder, in fact, what it might mean if they were to have their cup of tea in bed—if Ellie might suggest it, or if he might. But he'd anyway long forgotten when he'd first twigged that Merrick might be staying away on purpose on these afternoons. Or when the idea of Jimmy's coming back and catching them at it had become just an idea, a game, that added a little spice to proceedings. Nor did he need to have Luke sitting outside, to sound the alert if necessary. He just took Luke for the company. And Luke knew that too.

And then there was no Luke anyway.

But they'd kept up their pattern: first the bedroom, quickish, then the kitchen. Which naturally began to wane in excitement, even sometimes in satisfaction. There was a period during the cattle disease when it acquired a new adventurousness by the banning of even human movement between farms—something that generally shouldn't have troubled the Merricks and Luxtons. Jack had let it pass for a week or two, and then thought, Hang it, and made the traditional journey (would there be government helicopters spying on him?), and found that he was greeted with some of the old fervour from the days when they could at least kid themselves they were doing something forbidden. One good effect of the cow disease.

But mostly Jack had begun to feel that these visits, though he couldn't do without them (what else did he have?), had become just a little humiliating. Maybe Ellie felt the same. Though she'd never said, 'Don't bother, Jack.' (What else did *she* have?) Jack even felt that his inexorable traipsings over to Westcott Farm represented the final triumph, so far as it went and after so many years of its being the other way round, of the Merricks over the Luxtons. It might be his dad who was going down the harder now, but didn't his son's situation only clinch it?

When old Merrick contrived to bump into him, in that supposedly unplanned way, on his returns to Jebb, there'd be an extra gleam, Jack thought, in the old bugger's eye. Or it was an extra nip, perhaps, of whatever it was he took. And the gleam seemed to be saying: Well, boy, your dad might be suffering, and so am I, and those cows might have been up against it too, but who's got the shortest straw, boysyboy, of all?

They wouldn't linger now when they met each other like that. Jimmy would just stop, stick his head through the window of the Land Rover, pucker up his face and say a few words, or just twinkle under the brambly eyebrows, and lurch off.

For some reason, if only because Jimmy was Ellie's father, Jack couldn't help liking the little pixy-faced bastard. And, once upon a time, those interludes when he'd trundle back after seeing Ellie—whether old Merrick appeared over the horizon or not—had simply been some of the better moments of his life.

He still thinks it now. Still sees himself rolling a cigarette, with just one finger crooked round the wheel of the jolting pick-up, as if it would know anyway how to steer him home. Sometimes, even if old Merrick didn't appear, he'd stop, all the same, on the Luxton side of the boundary, just to take in the view. Something he never did otherwise. To breathe the air. He'd get out and stand with his back against the pick-up, one Wellington boot crossed over the other, one elbow cupped in one hand, ciggy on the go. The breeze riffling through the grass. And Luke, still alive then, lolloped by his feet, ears riffled too. And Tom just a nipper. Just a baby really.

A sense, for a moment, of simply commanding everything he saw, of not needing to be anywhere else.

'I wouldn't bother, Jack.' She'd never actually said it. Though she'd sometimes said, at dullish moments, as if to make him feel he had rivals or he was just some stopgap (had been all those years?) that what she was doing was waiting for her 'mystery man' to turn up, her mystery man who'd also in some way be her real man, like the mystery man who'd been real enough once for her mum to be persuaded to run off with him. That wasn't 'Uncle Tony', that was someone before. Even his name seemed a mystery.

Jack never knew if she was just joking or saying it to niggle him, or if what she really meant was that this mystery man ought actually to be him. If he would only *do* something. Whatever that might be. So how about it, Jacko? It was all right somehow when she said it when they were only seventeen, but when she said it again when they were past twenty, when she said it after those cattle had been bolt-gunned down on both their farms, it was different, it was troubling.

At some point he'd started having the thought that what Ellie was really waiting for was for her father to die.

Not that she was actually hoping he would have one of the several forms of fatal accident open to farmers, but it might be her only ticket out. And it might be a long wait. Merrick was as tough as a thistle, all twinkle and wire. And it seemed that people couldn't catch the cow disease, or not in a hurry anyway.

And then again, not having to live with him round the clock, Jack couldn't actually hate Jimmy (but then, did Ellie?), as sometimes he could hate his own father. Jimmy, after all, had let them have all those afternoons. And God knows when Jimmy would have last had intimate female company of his own. But clearly that didn't of itself cause a man to waste away and die. Or God help us all.

But, as it happened, Jimmy did start to waste away. And die. And not so long after Michael died.

7

'WE'D BETTER cancel St Lucia.'

Ellie had looked at him and he'd known he shouldn't have said it, or not then. He should have waited for the right moment. It was a secondary consideration—and it went, surely, without saying.

But he'd blurted it out straight away, like some clumsy gesture of reparation. And Ellie had looked at him and he'd known even then, with the letter back in his hands again after she'd read it, that this thing that had arrived out of the blue would drive a wedge—he could hear the blows of the hammer striking it—between them.

There was a separate mail box at the site and Jack would go down most mornings to check it, except during those mid-winter weeks when they'd be away and would arrange for their post to be held back (and suppose this letter had come then). Not much mail came directly to the cottage.

But that morning, a dank, grey early-November morning nine days ago, a red post-office van had swung up the narrow winding road he looks at now, to bring the private mail, including one very private letter, though the envelope bore the words 'Ministry of Defence'. And it must have been redirected by someone with a long memory since it also bore the original, now lapsed address 'Jebb Farm, Marleston'.

And Jack had known, before he'd opened it.

Once he *had* opened it and truly did know, there was no way he could prove that he'd known beforehand, and it didn't matter. Yet he'd known, even as he held the unopened envelope. His mind was no longer the usual slow mechanism. It was quick as a switch, it had turned electric. His big, heavy body, on the other hand, seemed to be draining through the floor and leaving him power-less. The roof of his mouth went dry. In the same bright flash of knowing, he thought, absurdly, of his long-dead mother, raised in a post office.

Even before he'd opened the envelope he'd called out, 'Ellie! Ell! Where are you? Come here.'

She'd been up here, in this bedroom, changing that duvet cover. By the time she was with him, he still hadn't opened the letter.

And now that it lay opened between them and he'd said what he'd said and Ellie had given him that unco-operative look, he thought, seeing it all again, of the last time a letter, seeming to change everything, had lain between them. A letter to Ellie that time, and she'd been waiting—she'd certainly picked her moment—to show it to him. They'd both been stark naked at the time and he'd wondered where the hell she'd been hiding it.

He saw again Ellie's tits sway as she handed him a letter. The July sky at the window. They were in the Big Bedroom.

Out of the blue? But *this* wasn't out of the blue—

setting aside that it was a gloomy grey morning. This had always been a cloud, a possible cloud, lurking over the horizon.

Yet he'd thought, all the same, of blue summer skies. Skies with smoke, perhaps, rising somewhere in them. He'd thought of barbecues. They were allowed down at the site (though every unit, of course, had its kitchenette), but only by permission and with approved equipment. Sometimes, of an August evening, the whole place smelt of charring burgers.

Blue, burning skies. They'd have to cancel St Lucia.

Though that wasn't till after Christmas. This was still early November. Ellie, he could see from that look—his super-fast brain could see it—was already calculating that this thing (was there some proper word to give it?) would have blown over by then. In a month or so it would be behind them. The air would be clear and blue again, even bluer. That cloud, having arrived and shed its burden, would no longer be there. Ellie was actually thinking, even then, that if this thing had been going to happen, it had been well timed. All the more reason for taking a holiday. A problem behind them.

Whereas he'd thought, how could you take a holiday after this? How could you just fly off into the blue?

So he shouldn't have said it. And perhaps, if he hadn't, Ellie would have been with him, at his side, three days ago. She'd have been with him in the car as he drove all those long, solitary miles. And he wouldn't be sitting at this window, a gun at his back. None of this would be happening.

Had he even had the thought, even then, the letter between them, that this thing that he'd always feared, which was the worst of worst possibilities, was really, perhaps, the thing Ellie might have wished? Her best possibility.

'Well, thank God, Jack, at least this has come in the off season.'

She should never have said *that*. And even from a practical point of view—surely Ellie saw this, she being the one who always saw things so sharply—that gap of almost two months ahead might not be so roomy after all. There was no date given in the letter. That is, the letter itself was dated and there *was* a date, very clearly, uncannily, given in it. Jack had tried to remember what he'd been doing on that date (it was a Saturday), whether at any point he'd felt anything turn over mysteriously inside him. But there was no *future* date. And there was thus a question, which he thought he'd quickly answered, of two flights. There was the flight about which the letter said he'd be kept closely informed. And there was the flight, which wasn't going to happen, to St Lucia.

Though the letter hadn't used the word flight. It had used a word which Jack had never encountered before but which would lie now in his head like some piece of mental territory: repatriation.

Once upon a time, and it would have been the same too for Tom, the notion of being anywhere other than England would have seemed totally crazy to Jack and quite beyond any circumstance that might include him. Though he knew that the world contained people who went, who flew, regularly, to other places. He knew that the world included other places. He'd done some geography at school. He'd once learnt, if he couldn't remember them now, the capitals of Argentina and Peru. But, for all practical purposes, even England had meant only what the eye could see from Jebb Farmhouse—or what lay within a ten-mile journey in the Land Rover or pick-up.

There'd been a few day-trips to Exeter or Barnstaple. Two stays, once, in another *county*: Dorset. Even the Isle of Wight, once, would have seemed like going abroad.

If you'd have said to Jack that one day he'd find himself in St Lucia—and, before that, twice in Antigua and three times in Barbados—he'd have said you were barking. (And, anyway, where *were* those places?) It still seems to him, even now that he's done it several times, like something impossible, a trick, even somehow wrong: that you could get into an aeroplane, then get out again a few hours later and there'd be—this completely different world.

It was Ellie who, a bit to his surprise, had been seriously up for it. Not just what she wanted, but, so she'd said, what they deserved, what they should definitely do. It was their world too. Everyone else did it.

'So how about it, Jacko?' She'd ruffled his hair. 'Live a little.'

If he'd known, on those afternoons when he leant against the pick-up, rolling a cigarette, looking around him. If he'd only had an inkling.

And had Tom had any inkling? Or was it, in his case, even something that had pushed him? Up that track. The world. And he'd seen it, apparently. Lived a little. Basra. Palm trees there too.

Later, Jack would receive a thing called his Service Record.

*

On that grey morning Jack hadn't just seen in his mind's eye blue, hot, summer skies, he'd seen himself floating, flying in them.

It had been during their last time in St Lucia, in one of those periods of sweaty, anxious restlessness that could sometimes come over him. He'd wanted to shake off the mood. He'd wanted to say to himself, 'Hey, lighten up, you're on holiday.' 'Lighten up' was a phrase of Ellie's, often used by her in the days when they'd been about to move to the Isle of Wight, like a motto for their future— 'Lighten up, Jacko'—and now he'd use it, from time to time, like a reminder, on himself.

He'd wanted even to demonstrate to Ellie that he had indeed become a new, lighter, gladder, luckier man, and it was thanks not just to luck but to Ellie's really rather amazing sticking by him. He'd anyway finally done something that Ellie had been urging him to do, daring him to do—as a joke, it seemed, because he was never really going to. On the other hand, she'd placed a bet on it, which she hadn't withdrawn: a bottle of champagne at dinner, which in this place would cost a small fortune. And it was something that could be done at pretty well any time of the day. You spent a lot of time, in fact, watching other people do it.

He'd gone down to the beach and the little spindly jetty, where there were some grinning boys in caps and T-shirts, and a couple of motor boats in their charge— who'd strap you into this harness with a long rope running to the back of one of the boats and, attached to your shoulders, though it had yet to open, a big, curved, striped, oblong parachute. Like a giant version of one of Ellie's plastic hairgrips. And they'd rev the motor and power off, and you couldn't help but be lifted off and up, way up high, above the water.

He'd said, 'Okay, Ell, moment's come. Ready to stump up?' And he'd just walked down there, in his shorts and shades. He'd had the sense not to wear his cap (and it was a Lookout cap too). He'd just walked down, trying to do it at the easiest saunter.

And then, moments later, to his surprise, he really was up there, just dangling—being pulled along, but somehow just floating too—with this great taut tugging thing above him, trying to drag him still higher, and the boat below and in front of him, with its white wake and the boys waving at him, like some little separate toy that had nothing, perhaps, to do with him. And all the people dotted on the beach and under the palms and sun umbrellas and round the blue-lagoon pools looking as if someone had just sprinkled them there. And Ellie somewhere among them, on her lounger, no doubt waving at him too, but it seemed silly, somehow, to try and spot her and wave back.

He hadn't felt frightened and, strangely, he hadn't even felt very excited—or triumphant, given that he'd won the bet now, he'd actually done it. When he walked up later from the beach, Ellie had said, 'My hero.' Had he felt like a hero? No. He'd just hung there, Jack Luxton, like some big baby being dandled, or rather—with that thing above—like some big baby being delivered by a stork. Thinking, if he was thinking anything: I'm Jack Luxton, but I can do this. Sixteen stone and six foot one, size-eleven feet, but light as a feather really, light as air.

As he'd been carried up he could see inland, beyond the resort's perimeter. He could see that the resort, with its bright greens and blues, was like an island on the edge of an island. Somewhere in the distance there were slants of smoke. They were burning crop waste maybe.

And all the time he would have been floating up there and all the time he and Ellie would have been lying there in the hot sun at the Sapphire Bay, thinking of chilled champagne for heroes at dinner, Tom would have been in the hot sun, in Iraq.

She shouldn't have said that thing about the off season. But suppose this had come in August. In full swing. What would they have done? Carried on? Carried on, but hung a flag at half-mast at the site? They didn't have a flag. They didn't have a flagpole. He was sometimes known as the commandant and the site office was sometimes known as the guardhouse, but they didn't have a flagpole. Maybe they should have thought of it, as a feature, along with all the other stuff, a Lookout flag fluttering in the breeze, gold on black, like the baseball caps.

Carried on, but explained? Carried on and faced the questions, sympathy, puzzlement—when it became not just their private news but an item, with names and photos, in the papers? The papers available in the site shop. We never knew Jack had a brother, he never said. A brother in the army. Jesus.

Would it have clouded *their* holiday mood? Could they have fired up those barbecues in quite the same way?

But it had come in November, and by the spring it would all be history. And if the regular Lookouters, meanwhile, had noticed it at all, seen the name in the papers and made the link, then he and Ellie might have dealt with the questions, such as they might be, faced any music, without being still in the immediate shock.

Though, now, Jack thinks, they won't have to face any music at all.

He looks down at the site. It was what they'd done, with a lot of help from 'Uncle' Tony, whom neither of them had met, since he was dead, but who'd lived here once, so it had emerged, with Ellie's mum (her third husband and with this one, it seemed, she'd landed squarely on her feet), and run the Sands, as it was then.

People could help by dying, by dying at the right time. Had that always been Ellie's position? Even with this?

And perhaps those regular Lookouters, scattered now in their homes round the country, wouldn't have noticed. Though they'll notice *now*, Jack thinks, they'll notice *this* story. That other story, it wasn't such a big one, not even necessarily headlines these days, though Luxton wasn't such a common name.

There was a war going on, that was the story. Though who would know, or want to know, down here at Sands End? A war on terror, that was the general story. Jack knew that terror was a thing you felt inside, so what could a war on terror be, in the end, but a war against yourself? Tom would have known terror, perhaps, quite a few times. He'd have known it, very probably, all too recently. It was saying nothing, perhaps, to say that he'd also have been trained to meet it.

Does Jack feel terror right now, with a loaded gun

behind him? Oddly, no. Terror isn't the word for what he feels. Has he ever known terror? Yes.

What they meant, of course, was a war on *terrorism*. But then it became a matter of who and where, of geography. Was it conceivable that terrorists—Islamic extremists—might want to operate out of a holiday facility on the Isle of Wight? Or, on the other hand, want to crash a plane into it? Target a caravan site? He didn't think so.

Yet it was sometimes, nonetheless, a subject among the Lookouters. It was surprising how often, in fact, people who were here to have fun, to get away from it all, to have a *holiday*, could drift, of an August evening, with their sun-reddened faces, into conversations about the dire state of the world and how, one way or another, there was no hope for it. Jack would try, which wasn't so difficult, not to get too involved. It was simply part of his obliging, humouring proprietor's role, to go with the flow. So he'd nod and smile and now and then throw in some meaning-less remark.

But once, down at the Ship—he couldn't remember if it had been the war on terror then or some other global emergency—it had all got too much for him and he'd blurted out suddenly (the Lookouters present would remember it): 'Well, I wouldn't worry, any of you. In a few years' time, if what they say is true, we'll all have gone down anyway with mad-cow disease.'

8

'CARAVANS,' Ellie had said, as if it were a magic word, the secret of the universe she'd been saving up to tell him. And she must have known how it would have touched something in him and made him prick up his ears and listen and not just think it was a damn stupid answer to anything.

'Caravans, Jacko.'

There they were, sitting up in the big bed at Jebb on a July afternoon, and he'd realised later that she must have planned it that way. Not that he'd resisted. And anyway for him the word did have a kind of magic.

Ellie would have remembered—though she hadn't been there—those weeks in Brigwell Bay. One week in July, two years running. She'd have remembered him talking about them afterwards, talking at a gabble, perhaps, that wasn't like Jack's normal way with speech. He was thirteen, fourteen, so was Ellie. Not so long before her mum made her run for it.

Ellie hadn't been there. 'Send me a postcard, Jack.'

And he had. Greetings from Brigwell Bay. 'Miss Eleanor Merrick, Westcott Farm, Marleston . . .' God knows if she'd kept it. Or kept them, since she'd got another one too, the second year.

Maybe they were here right now, those postcards, in the Lookout, in some secret stash of hers. Maybe they were at the back of a drawer, right here in this bedroom. They might have been the first postcards Ellie had ever received. They were certainly the first Jack had ever written. And the first of the two would have been a serious struggle for him, if his mother hadn't helped him and, after a little thought, suggested he write, 'Wish you were here.' And he had. He hadn't known it was the most uninventive of messages. He'd written it. And he'd wished it. He'd even thought sometimes, there at Brigwell Bay with Mum and Tom: suppose it was just him and Ellie, just him and her in the caravan. It was a sort of burning thought. But on the other hand, sometimes he was having such a whale of a time that he forgot altogether about Ellie.

And then again, perhaps those unoriginal words on the back of a postcard might have touched a tender, even burning spot inside Ellie, such that she would have wished to send an answer back (though it was only a week), 'Me too, Jack.' But she hadn't sent an answer or even, later, expressed the wish. And after he'd come back and spouted on about the good time he'd had, she hadn't even given him much of a thank-you for that postcard or seemed to want to pursue the subject. By which Jack understood, at least by the second time around, that she was jealous.

And then her mum had skedaddled.

So Jack had been careful, ever since, out of respect for

Ellie, not to mention those visits to Brigwell Bay or the postcards he'd sent each time. As if, even for him, after a while, those two trips hadn't really meant so much or remained so special in his memory. Whereas the truth was they were fantastic. They were the best times of his life up to that time. Maybe even, he sometimes thought, the best ever.

How could he have said that to Ellie, 'They were the best times of my life,' when she wasn't even there, without inflaming her jealousy? Girls. But how many girls did he know? He only knew Ellie. How could he have said it by the time they were having those private sessions at West-cott Farmhouse, without getting into even hotter trouble. What, not *these* times, Jacko?

Let alone say it when they were sitting up like that, each cradling a mug of tea, stark naked, in the Big Bed-room.

So he'd shut up and pretended it was all forgotten and had never been so important to him. For Ellie's sake. He could be good to Ellie.

But Ellie would have known he was only covering. He had a wall of a face, he was born with it, but Ellie was trained in seeing through it. And she'd have known, that afternoon, what a tender spot she was still touching in him and how it couldn't fail to put a seal on things when she said that word. Caravans. As if it was the password and the key to their future.

And the truth still was: those weeks had been fantastic.

When Jack was thirteen and Tom was not yet six Vera had taken them both for the first of two holidays at

Brigwell Bay, Dorset, not far from Lyme Regis. And what had made them particularly fantastic was that they'd stayed in a caravan.

They'd gone on their mother's instigation and insistence. She must have said to Michael, with perhaps more than her usual firmness with him, that she was going to give those two boys a holiday, a seaside holiday that when they'd grown up they'd always have to remember. They weren't going to go without that. And Michael must have relented—for two years running—though Jack would have counted then, even at thirteen and fourteen, as full-time summer labour on the farm.

So they'd taken what was for them an epic journey, part bus, part train, to the south coast of England and (if only just) across the border into another county. And they'd stayed in a caravan, in a small, three-acre field, with hedges all around it, a little way back from the cliffs and the beach below. There were only six caravans, positioned any old how, and compared to the snazzy, lined-up giants Jack can see in the distance now, they were like rabbit hutches on wheels. But they each had a name, and theirs, both years, had been 'Marilyn'.

Those two stays in a caravan in Brigwell Bay were, by the time Jack sat up in bed with Ellie on that July afternoon, the only two holidays he (or Tom) had ever had, and he still might have said that during each of them he'd never been happier. So much so that during the first one, finding himself suddenly so clearly and unmistakably happy, he'd wondered if he'd ever, really, been happy before.

When he sat down at the tiny pale-yellow Formica-topped table in the caravan and wrote his postcard to

Ellie, it was with a mixture of honesty and guilt. Yes, he really did wish she was there. But if he really wished that, how could he be so happy in the first place? Wishing she was there was like admitting he was happy without her. It was like saying he was writing this postcard because he'd betrayed her.

And in Ellie's case, on that July afternoon, the total number of holidays she'd ever had was nil. And 'holidays' was another word she'd invoke and let ring that afternoon, like the word 'caravans'.

How strange, to have been born into a farmhouse, into a hundred and sixty acres, yet to have felt so happy, perhaps for the first time ever really happy at all, in a tin-can caravan in a little grubby field, with in one corner a standpipe with some rotting sacking around it and a dripping tap.

Yet so it was. Jack knows that, at thirteen, he might very well have taken the view that he was too old for it all, it was kids' stuff, buckets and spades—he should have been above it. But the truth was he knew he was only getting these holidays now because of Tom. And those two years, he later realised, would have been his mother's only realistic window of opportunity. So he owed them to Tom. And the fact that he himself had missed out when he was smaller only meant that during those weeks Jack was, most of the time, perfectly ready to regress. It wasn't, in fact, so difficult. It was as though an unspoken agreement operated between him and Tom that while Tom should try to act as if he were thirteen, Jack should try to act as if he were five or six. Then, between them, they might be like two boys of nine.

Yet in practice it was Tom who led the way in being just a kid—who was better and quicker and more naturally equipped to excel even at that. It was Tom who found the secret route, like a tunnel, through the hedge to the clifftops, and then that other path, not the one everyone used, down through the tumbled, broken bit of cliff to the beach. It was Tom who made better sandcastles.

Why had he never minded? Even then. In the evenings, it was true, back at the caravan, it could all turn round. Something quite new could happen to Jack. It could seem that he might be twice thirteen. It could seem that he and Mum were a couple and this was their little home and, for this one week at least, he might be Tom's dad. That was how it could seem.

And if ever he'd had the chance to learn from his mum how to crack eggs into a pan and how to put together a breakfast, that was it. But he hadn't, and the fact was it was Tom, just a little kid, who picked up before Jack ever did on things that weren't just for little kids. It was Tom who asked him, years later, if he'd ever noticed that each of those caravans had been named after a Hollywood film actress. There was a Betty, a Lauren, a Rita. Jack had spent a week each year, two years running, inside Marilyn Monroe, and never even known it.

Mum must have had that tough conversation with Dad, must have argued and insisted. Those two boys. And Dad must have yielded. Acted the martyr, no doubt, but finally reached in his pocket. 'Your doing, Vee, not mine.'

It was mid-July, after the hay was in, when work on the farm was lightish. On the other hand, it was peak-rate time for renting a caravan.

And the situation for Dad while they were away was that he'd have to 'fend for himself'. Jack could remember his mother using that phrase with a sort of edge to it, as if when they returned they should expect to find Michael looking half-starved and the farm gone to pot—which had mostly come true later when Mum was permanently absent. But this was just a week in July, although the days were long and, to Jack at least, they weren't like ordinary, unnoticed days—they were fantastic. Yet when they returned, both times, Dad had said, in his slow, dry way, 'Back already? Hardly seems you've gone.' Or some such words. Mum had taken a careful look around while Michael had looked patient. Then he'd said, or just meant it with his eyes, 'See, not gone to rack and ruin yet.' And his face had finally cracked with pleasure to have them back again.

So they'd always have it to remember. Well, if that's how she'd put it, Jack had never forgotten.

Ellie had surely picked her moment. The hot afternoon, the cool of the farmhouse, its timbers creaking, breezes wafting about it. And before that, he came to realise, she must have done her homework. Talked to those lawyers, talked to all the right people, checked it through, checked to see if it was real and not some leg-pull. She'd even made a trip out here on the sly, so it emerged, to see for herself, to see the lie of the land. But she'd saved it all up for the right moment. To drop that word first into the air, she'd known how it would chime for him. Then show him the letter.

And all, Jesus Christ, in the very bed where his own mother had breathed her last. And consummated her marriage to Michael Luxton, and even once, in the small hours of a September night, given challenging birth to a son called Jack.

Ellie had whisked him up there pretty smartly, and could he say he'd even feebly resisted? As if there was no time to lose and it couldn't be anywhere else. As if it was her own damn bedroom.

'What's the matter? Afraid your dad'll catch us? Afraid your *mum's* going to see?' She giggled. 'Hey, lighten up, Jack.'

And if the truth be known, the sheer outrageousness of it had got to him, driven him, tipped him over. The sheer fact of it. They could do it, do as they pleased now. They were king and queen now of their (ruined) castles, of their finally united kingdoms, even if Ellie was about to spell out to him what he didn't exactly need telling, that the only way was to sell up and leave, cash in and leave—and now they could. But with an answer all ready, up her sleeve, to the inevitable next question. If you can have an answer up your sleeve when you're wearing nothing.

She'd had that letter with her anyway. Hidden some-where. From 'Uncle' Tony, or rather from Uncle Tony's lawyers.

Ellie's vanished mother Alice had, so it seemed, fallen ill and died before her time—not unlike Jack's mother (though in a nursing home in Shanklin)—without having broken her silence with her estranged daughter, or having revealed that she was now married to a man, Anthony Boyd, many years her senior. But not long afterwards Uncle Tony had fallen ill and died too. And he was the one, it seemed, who'd died with a conscience.

'It gets better, Jacko. Listen. It gets better.'

Was there any argument, once Ellie had produced that letter? For some while Jack had been imagining that the next stage in the decline of Jebb Farm might be when the whole damn farmhouse and all its outbuildings would start to slide physically down the hill, crashing to pieces as they went.

Yet, just for a moment, as they'd sat there with their tea, he'd let himself slide into the opposite picture, and almost believe it. That this was their place now. Here they were at last, where they should be. He'd felt that, even as he'd felt the other thing: that they were like two ransacking burglars who'd burst into a place that wasn't theirs at all.

'Still sleeping in your little cubby-hole, Jack? But you've got the run now. This is the *master* bedroom.'

He'd never used that expression. He vaguely knew it was an expression used by estate agents. It was the Big Bedroom. For years now Dad had slept in this bedroom, in this same big bed, all alone, till one night he couldn't bear to any longer.

And he *had* still been sleeping in his own little cubbyhole. Ellie saw everything.

'Well,' she'd said, a little later, 'at least you can't say we never gave it a whirl.'

She'd sat up with her back against the bedhead, not minding that her tits were on display. He'd pulled himself up against the bedhead too. Like a shameless king and queen, yes, surveying their realm. Through the window before them, across the drop of the land, you could see the far side of the valley, the line of the hills. A blue sky, a puff or two of cloud, the speck of a buzzard wheeling. In between was the green, stirring crown of the oak tree.

'Now,' Ellie had said, 'you stay here and I'll go and make us a pot of tea.'

And she'd gone down, in her bare arse, to the kitchen, Ellie Merrick, in her bare arse in the Jebb kitchen, in Jebb Farmhouse. And he'd thought, it wasn't a bad arse (nor all the rest), if it wasn't the baby arse he'd first clapped hands on fifteen years or more ago. How long had he known Ellie? Long enough to have forgotten how long. Long enough for it to have been at times an on-and-off thing. Long enough to have watched her change and change back again, to come in and out of her best. He must have done the same himself, even if he'd never noticed. Always feeling anyway like the same old lump.

He couldn't say, by any stretch, that he was a connoisseur of women, but he was a connoisseur of Ellie. And, judging by Ellie, it was strange the way time could work on women, and not always against them. There was no saying when suddenly they might hit peak condition.

She'd gone down and come back with a tray with the tea on it. But on the tray too, of course, though he hadn't noticed when she'd put it down on the floor on her side of the bed, must have been that letter, taken from her bag in the kitchen.

'Caravans, Jacko.'

He couldn't help seeing—as she let that word hang for a while and took a long sip of tea—Tom, aged six, hopping ahead of him down that path. Or seeing the wiggly letters by the door, with its two steps up: 'Marilyn'. Or smelling salt between his fingers. Or smelling the smell all over that field, in the morning, of frying bacon. And when just a little later he was looking, himself, at that letter, he couldn't help seeing that little yellow tabletop and that first postcard, with its blue sea and white band of cliffs, that he'd written to Ellie.

So just when he'd been thinking that this was his bed now and Ellie belonged in it, he was suddenly also thinking he was really all hers now, he belonged to her. She knew the places in him, she had him.

He'd said, as if at least he must put up some token opposition, 'But no one takes their holidays in a caravan any more.'

But apparently they did. Or they did at the Lookout, formerly known as the Sands. The caravans weren't like the ones Jack remembered from Brigwell Bay (and how much had that farmer charged for a week?). Nor were the caravanners. They were all sorts. With thirty-two units, when they were all on the go, you got all sorts. There were die-hard old couples who'd been coming for years and weren't so sure about that change of name, but liked the fact that the place had 'stayed in the family' (how sad, about Alice and Tony). They seemed to know more about Ellie's mum than Ellie did—or even wanted to. There were big burly families, all tattoos and noise, who in the course of a week became gentler, sweeter. There were two- or three-unit gangs of young people with windsurfing gear who, when they weren't wearing wetsuits, wore hardly anything most of the time and liked to party all night.

All this had fascinated Jack. It had brought something out in him. You never knew what might be going on in any one of those units at any given time. It was certainly a form of livestock. You never knew what might be arriving next. Caravans. It would make him think, sometimes, of a circus, and it could sometimes be like a circus. Entertaining, raucous, a touch of danger. You had to be a bit of a policeman sometimes. You had to be their smiling host in a joke of a shirt, but there were times when you had to show them who was in charge. Jack had found he was surprisingly good at this. At both things: the smiling and the policing. Perhaps his big, lumbering weight was on his side. Or maybe it was that he'd just sometimes let slip, with his straight, blank, unreadable face, that if there was any *real* trouble, he kept a shotgun handy, up in the cottage, having been a farmer once, and he knew how to use it.

As for the caravanners, the Lookouters, they generally took the view that Ellie and Jack were okay. They ran a good site, they looked after you. It was all right for some, of course—sitting up there all summer long, then winging off to the Caribbean. But, at the same time, there was something a bit misfit and oddball about the two of them. There didn't seem to be any little Luxtons, you couldn't even be sure if they were really married. Something just a bit hillbilly. But that was okay, that was fine. There was something just a bit wacky and hillbilly about taking a holiday in a caravan anyway. And when you were on holiday you wanted colour, you didn't want dull and ordinary. You didn't get it, either, with those shirts of his.

Farmer Jack. It's well over ten years now since they sat up with their tea in that bed at Jebb and Ellie uttered that word. And he'd never said then, if there had to be some token, or more than token, opposition: 'There's Tom, Ellie. There's Tom.'

A steep learning curve (Ellie's expression) at the beginning. But the main thing was, it paid. Thirty-two units. He was still good at sums, in a farmer's way. At Jebb it hadn't been the arithmetic but the numbers themselves that were wrong. Compared to anything they'd known before, they were in thick clover now. What with the capital from the sale of two farms, even at knock-down prices, even with debts to pay off.

Ten years. And something more than a learning curve. A release, a relaxation curve, a lightening up. He saw it in the way she smiled at him and he saw, from her smile, that, even with his great brick of a face, he must be smiling too.

But he can see it, now: the steep drop away from the farmhouse, the full-summer crown of the oak tree. The hills beyond. The exact lines of hedgerows and of tracks running between the gates in them. White dots of sheep, brown and black-and-white dots of cattle. For a moment, though for over ten years now Jack has breathed sea air, which some people find so desirable, he can even smell the land, the breath of the land. The thick, sweaty smell of a hayfield. The dry, baked smell of cooling stubble on an August evening. Smells he never smelt at the time. The smell of cow dung mingling with earth, the cheapest, lowliest of smells, but the best. Who wouldn't wish for that as their birthright and their last living breath?

9

THEY'D GOT the letter nine days ago, though, strictly speaking, there was no 'they' about it, the operative phrase being 'next of kin'. Tom must either have put down his brother's name from the very beginning, or made the substitution when necessary.

On that question Jack could never be sure, seeing as Tom had never answered any of his letters. There'd been precious few of them, it was true, but they'd included the letter that had cost Jack an agony to write, about the death and funeral arrangements of Michael Luxton. It had cost him several long hours and several torn-up sheets of paper, of which there was never a big supply at Jebb, though even as he'd written it he'd wondered how much pain in it there would really be for Tom. Why should Tom care? He'd finished with his father nearly a year before, and it was vice-versa now, their father had finished with everything, all fixed and concluded.

'I hope,' Michael had once said, according to Tom (and why should Tom have made up such words?), 'someone some day will do the same for me.'

So where was the agony in it for Jack, knowing there

might be none in it, really, for Tom? Unless that itself was the agony, that there wasn't any. Over such a thing. Or maybe it was that for Jack writing any letter of a personal nature—any letter at all—was agony. 'Send me a postcard,' Ellie had told him, with a little sad pout, as if he might have been going off to war himself (so you'd think she might have been more pleased when she got one). And he'd agonised, in his way, over that.

Well, he wouldn't be writing any damn last letters right now. One thing off his mind. And Ellie wouldn't be reading any.

But Jack couldn't ever be sure about that question of next of kin, seeing as Tom had never written back, or otherwise got in touch. Seeing as Tom wasn't there when they'd lowered Dad down beside Mum in Marleston churchyard. He'd thought: what was she saying to him, what kind of greeting was he getting? This is a fine way to be coming back to me, Michael.

Jack couldn't be sure if Tom had just decided not to be there and not even say he wouldn't be there (though Jack knew there was a thing called compassionate leave) or if Tom wasn't there because he'd never in the first place received that letter that had cost so much to write. Maybe sending a letter to just a name and a number in the army was like sending a letter to the North Pole.

There was no doubt, in any case, when Jack read that official letter, addressed to him from the MOD, that he *was* Tom's next of kin. There wasn't any other. But he wanted to believe—still wants to believe even now—that Tom would have put down his brother's name as next of kin from the very first point of the army's requiring it. Hadn't it, in a way, been understood between them?

Good luck, Tom.

It was almost his first thought as he'd read that letter, that the next-of-kin thing would have applied. That was why this piece of paper was in his hand. As he'd stared at it and tried to make it not be real, he'd thought: and now there wasn't any next of kin, not for him, not in the true meaning, even though he'd married Ellie. There wasn't any next.

And that was a touchy point.

Or perhaps his very first thought had been that, though this letter came from the army, from the Ministry of Defence, it came, in a sense, from Jebb, bearing that crossed-out address. It was like several letters that had reached them for a while. It was an arrangement you made—or Ellie had made it, and the same for Westcott—with the Post Office. But those letters had petered out years ago, which was just as well, since each time (even if it wasn't someone demanding money) it couldn't help but hurt and accuse him to see those words—'Jebb Farm'—on the envelope.

Now, with this letter, they were like a stab.

Since Tom had never known *that*. Whether or not he'd ever received any of those other letters or cared, if he had, what was in them. Jack had never written with that bit of information. It had been his decision. Since Tom had never appeared at the funeral, or ever replied. Since he didn't even know any more where Tom was.

Or Ellie's decision. Lots of his decisions were really

hers. Maybe most. Though he could have said it, nonetheless, been the first to raise the subject, that afternoon, 'There's Tom, Ell. What about Tom?'

And now it didn't matter anyway. Because there wasn't any Tom. Because that letter that had been a little delayed in reaching him, having been addressed to Jebb Farm, informed him that Corporal Thomas Luxton, along with two others of his unit, had been killed 'on active duty' in Iraq, in the Basra region of operations, on 4th November 2006. It informed him that, failing other attempts to contact him directly, this news was being communicated by letter with the deepest regret, and that every effort would have been made prior to his receipt and acknowledgement of this notification to have kept Corporal Luxton's name from public disclosure. It very respectfully asked that Mr Jack Luxton make himself known as soon as possible—a special direct-line telephone number, as well as other numbers and addresses, was given—so that arrangements could be made for Corporal Luxton's (and his comrades') repatriation, which, for operational reasons, would in any case be pending clearance by the in-situ military authorities.

It was a grey, murky autumn morning, the sort of day on which it can be good to know that a holiday under hot, rustling palms is in the offing. Palm trees, for some reason, had flashed through Jack's mind and had made him blurt out that stupid thing about cancelling the Caribbean.

Perhaps it occurred to him as he stared at that letter that he might already have read, without knowing it, as an item in a newspaper—though he was not a great scourer of newspapers—the anonymous announcement of his own brother's death. Public disclosure. But no, he couldn't remember any moment when his insides had turned mysteriously cold. And though, by now, such items of news weren't so rare, he'd always told himself that Tom might be anywhere.

On the other hand, he might have made enquiries. Not so difficult, not so unreasonable. Being next of kin, for God's sake. And he'd known that some such message as he held now in his hand was not out of the question. Now that it was in his hand it had the eerie, mocking truth of something not entirely unanticipated. His hand shook. As if the anticipation might have forestalled it. As if the anticipation might have caused it.

And the fact is he'd known, before, what was in it. This was the thought that, before all the others, sprang up to overwhelm him. That his heart had started banging, as if it had jumped loose in his chest, even before he'd opened the envelope.

And when he'd passed it to Ellie, he'd known that she, too, knew already what was in it. There's such a thing as body language. And that tone in his voice when he'd called up to her. She looked miffed, all the same, to have been dragged from her task. He'd always had a struggle whenever he tried to get that damn duvet cover on. And when she looked at the letter he'd known at once from her face that she wasn't going to make it any easier for him. It wasn't easy in the first place, but she wasn't going to make it any easier. She wasn't going to make it any easier because one thing he could see in her face was that she thought that this *made* things easier anyway. It drew a neat and simple and permanent line. And the fact is, if he were honest, *he'd* had the same thought too, just the tiniest flash of it. But what for Ellie was a thought that made things easier was for him like a trap snapping on him. The very fact that he could even think it.

People could help by dying. Yes, they could. No, they couldn't. He could see that Ellie's position was going to be that this was his, Jack's, business, he shouldn't dump it on her. Next of kin, and Ellie wasn't. Ellie, when all was said, and despite that marriage ceremony ten years ago in Newport, was a Merrick. He could see that Ellie's position, if he pushed her, was going to be that he had helped Tom make his departure all those years ago, had seen Tom off. And wasn't the last thing he'd wanted, or wanted these days anyway, was for Tom to show his face again?

Jack could see all this even as he felt himself starting to tremble inside. Even as he had the briefest but clearest picture of Tom standing right there, in the doorway of Lookout Cottage, grinning and looking bigger than he used to be. In a soldier's uniform. Anyone at home?

The last thing he'd wanted? No.

This was all his fault, Jack had thought, this letter and all it might mean was his fault. He thought it even as Ellie passed the letter back to him. It even seemed like a letter he hadn't just opened but had been keeping in his pocket for some time and had only just decided to show her. Like that letter she'd shown him, the blue sky at the window, at Jebb. Here, read this.

He thought it even as she moved towards him, because she could see now he was actually trembling. Not just his hand. His shoulders were shaking, his chest was heaving.

Even as Ellie put her arms round him and held him—she smelt of clean cotton—and pressed her mouth to the side of his neck and said, 'It's okay, Jacko, it's okay.' And what did that mean—just that it was okay for a grown man to cry? Even as the hot tears came gushing out of him—they had to—out of Jack Luxton's eyes, that were stony-grey and, most of the time, cool and expressionless like his father's. Well, people weren't fucking cattle.

10

RAIN WEEPS DOWN the window in front of him, but Jack isn't crying now. And he'd put a stop to his tears soon enough on that grey morning. He'd gasped them back into himself and wiped a sleeve across his face even before Ellie could grab a clump of tissues and hold it out for him.

It should have been like this then, he thinks. Then the weather might have made his tears seem less conspicuous or might have done his crying for him. But, outside, the morning had been merely grey and damply still.

He couldn't remember when he'd last cried, not counting when he was a nipper and it was allowable. Or if he'd cried at all since then. But yes he had, of course he had, and he could remember exactly when. Tears on his pillow. But never in front of anyone. Certainly never in front of Ellie. So it had been a shock to her. Perhaps even a disappointment.

Not even when his mum died. He hadn't let his eyes well up in front of Ellie. As if Ellie would have had any softness left for missing mothers. And he'd been twenty-one by then, a man's age. And now, when he was thirty-nine, he'd felt as Ellie put her arms around him just a touch of hardness in them, just the hint of a restraint in their comfort. I'm not your mother, Jack, don't cry like a baby.

True enough. If it was all his fault, how should tears come into it? Tom had gone off to be a soldier—and he wanted to sit here and cry? He'd dried his eyes before Ellie could dry them for him. But he'd known that he hadn't cried enough, not nearly enough. That little bit of crying had only made him aware that there was a whole lot more crying left inside him, a whole tankful. He'd just put the stopper back on his tears. As for Ellie, her eyes hadn't even gone dewy.

And that maybe settled something, finally took away, on that painful day, one foolish niggle. Namely, that he'd always wondered and never could quite put the thought aside, whether Tom and Ellie had ever . . . Whether Ellie and Tom . . . On a Wednesday afternoon, say. Given Tom's general quickness off the mark.

Surely not. Though would he actually have minded—even that? Just once in a while. If Tom, as it turned out, was going to pack himself off anyway. But the question was more whether he'd have minded to know it now. Now that Tom was packed off for ever. No, he wouldn't have minded. He wouldn't have minded it even back then, if he'd known then that one day Tom would be packed off for ever. What's mine is yours, Tom.

Surely not. But when Jack, after Tom left, had gone over to Westcott Farm to spend afternoons with Ellie, Tom's name had rarely come up between them. And Jack, with his sliver of suspicion, had supposed this was because Ellie would have wanted to stay off the subject, while he didn't want to force it either. Finished business anyway.

But even on that July afternoon at Jebb, with that other letter in the Big Bedroom, when the subject of Tom should have come up, when *he* should have brought it up, he'd kept warily silent. It was Ellie who'd brought it up for him. 'I know what you're thinking,' she'd said, holding her mug of tea under her chin. 'But he made his decision, didn't he, and when did you last hear a peep out of him? I don't think you have to tell him anything. Forget him, Jack.' And if she could say that, then perhaps his mind should have been settled all along. At least on that score.

He'd wiped away his tears and Ellie's eyes had stayed dry. Then a silence had stretched between them, a silence in which the look on Ellie's face had seemed to say: Don't make this difficult, Jack. This is tough news, don't make it tougher. And even he could see, even then, that it might have been tougher even than this. Tom might have come back in a wheelchair. He might have come back like a big, helpless baby.

Then Ellie had gone to fill the kettle. Certain moments in life, it seemed, required the filling of a kettle. Kettles got filled every day, without a thought, several times over. Nonetheless, there were certain moments.

He heard the gush of water in the kitchen. It would have been a good inducement and a good moment to shed a few more tears while Ellie wasn't looking. And an opportunity—if that's how it was—for Ellie to do a bit of private gushing herself. But he didn't think so. He only imagined how her hand might be grasping the tap a bit more tightly and for longer than was necessary.

How many kettles had Ellie filled? That had been the first ever kettle she'd filled at Jebb. And she'd done it stark naked. But she'd filled enough kettles for him before that, over the years, at Westcott. And she'd have filled enough, anyway, for old man Merrick. He felt, with a letter lying in front of him that weighed, of itself, next to nothing, the weight and strain in her arms of all those kettles Ellie would have filled for Jimmy Merrick. What had she thought that day when *her* mum had disappeared? And it was a big old farmhouse-kitchen kettle too, it wasn't like the natty plug-in thing they had here at the Lookout.

When she came back with the tea he knew it was up to him (if it was all his fault) to break the silence, to say something appropriate to the occasion. He might have said any number of things, poor as he was with words. He might have just said, in fact, 'Poor Tom. Poor Tom.' But he felt he might already have said that, during his short burst of tears. Though the words, if they were there, had got so mixed up with the tears that he wasn't sure if they'd come out like any sort of words that Ellie would recognise. It was just a general choking.

He might have said, 'I wonder how, exactly.' Or, 'I hope it was quick.' He might have said, looking at Ellie, 'I hope it was damn well quick.' He might have said, 'Why him?' On the other hand, he might have said, 'We always knew it was a possibility, didn't we, Ell, something like this?' And added, 'But we blanked it out, didn't we?'

He'd thought: this is like the cow disease. It was a

strange thought to have, but he'd had it. This was like when the cow disease and its real meaning had hit, and he and Tom had waited for Dad to say something, to gather them round the kitchen table, a proper farmhouse meeting, and give them his word. So what now? So what next?

But Dad had never gathered them round, and his strongest course of action had been to stand in the yard alone and spit.

And the truth was that while that kettle had boiled and even as these useless thoughts had besieged him, a whole series of practical considerations and estimations had also run through Jack's head, which had added up to the unavoidable certainty of a journey. A journey that he— he and Ellie—would have to make. The certainty of one journey. And the impossibility, under the circumstances, of another.

So, of all the things he might have said, he'd said that stupid thing. Though he'd said it, he remembered, as if he was truly sorry and as if he was breaking now, to Ellie, a piece of terrible news.

'I think we'd better cancel St Lucia.'

And Ellie had looked at him as if it might, indeed, have been the worst thing he could possibly have said. And he'd thought again: All those kettles.

11

LATER THAT MORNING Jack had called the special direct-
line number in the letter. How could he not? But he'd
had to brace himself to do it and he'd felt, as he spoke,
like a man calling a police station to turn himself in.

'I am Jack Luxton,' he'd said, like the start of a con-
fession.

And only the next morning, which was also grey, damp
and still, a smart black saloon had driven up the winding road from Holn, which Jack surveys now, and after
making the climb in a slow, unfamiliarised fashion, had
pulled up in the turning-space opposite the cottage. Jack
had watched it, from this very window. On a still day any
car ascending the hill—it was a rare enough event—would
announce its approach, even if you weren't already waiting. Then he'd watched an army officer get out, reaching
as he did so for his peaked cap on the passenger seat and
for a brown leather document wallet beneath it.

Jack had been informed of this visit and the timing
was spot-on, it was eleven-thirty almost exactly. But when

he saw the officer emerge from the car, Jack, who thinks now that Ellie might return in convoy with a squad car, was for a moment in no doubt that the officer had come to arrest him, to take him prisoner or to do whatever army officers were empowered to do. To have him shot, possibly. Yet at the same time, when he'd seen the khaki uniform, he'd had the distinct thought: Tom might have done this. Tom might have driven up one day, out of the blue. He might have turned out, who knows, to have become an officer.

But the officer, whose name was Major Richards—and Jack had spoken to him the preceding day, as requested, on the phone—was in his early fifties and, before he'd put on his cap, Jack could see that his hair was grey and receding and that he looked, in some ways, more like a visiting doctor or some peculiarly burdened schoolmaster than an army officer.

Major Richards had stood for a moment and put his cap on very squarely, pulled his tunic straight and, tucking the wallet under his arm, had coughed into his hand. Then he'd walked the few paces to the front door of Lookout Cottage not quite as if he were marching, but as if ceremony and dignity were not out of place and he knew he might be being watched.

Major Richards had explained, even rather insisted, on the phone that this was how the battalion did things. A personal visit, regardless of how notification had actually been made, to express the battalion's condolences and sympathies—and loss, and gratitude. And to explain related matters. In the circumstances, nothing less was proper, and he was the appointed visiting officer. So Jack had found himself agreeing to an imminent visitation by the army. He hadn't consulted Ellie, but he'd said after putting down the phone, and repeating Major Richards's words almost exactly, that it was how they did things and he'd agreed to it.

So they'd had to tidy up the place—though it was not an inspection—and Ellie had put on something smart and vaguely solemn—she chose her black skirt and pale-grey V-neck with her imitation pearls—to go with Jack's black trousers and white shirt (things he was never normally seen in), and they'd both prepared to pretend that this was how they always loafed around the cottage on a weekday morning. Ellie had looked at him with a strange, appraising tenderness as they'd dressed in this unusual way. It was like the day they got married. And even as Major Richards strode towards the front door, Jack, having descended the stairs, was on the other side of it, waiting in his crisp white shirt and, in spite of himself, not quite resisting the urge—he'd feel it again in the coming days—to stand to attention.

Major Richards had said, 'Mr Luxton?' And had asked very formally if he might come in and, when he did, had removed his cap with a distinct and formal gesture. It had been on his head for just the few steps he'd taken from his car. He'd shaken their hands and at once, while still on his feet, had expressed again, to them both, the battalion's profound regrets and condolences. He'd said that Corporal Luxton was a brave and exemplary soldier who'd done his duty to the utmost, so that the army was proud of him, and that this was a great blow to everyone.

Jack had lost the immediate sensation of being under arrest or that he was about to have some order barked at him, but he'd felt that, though it was he who'd shown in their visitor and introduced him to his wife, it was more as if Major Richards was greeting them and ushering them into his world. Everything was the wrong way round.

Only when Major Richards had sat down, placing his cap very carefully on another seat close by and the leather wallet on his knees and meanwhile accepting cordially Ellie's offer of a cup of tea, did the thing relax, if such a thing can relax. With his cap off, he didn't seem so intimidating.

Looking at them both very attentively, his eyes making regular sweeps between them, Major Richards had reiterated the point about the battalion liking to do things this way. He apologised for the letter's having reached them by its delayed and roundabout route. He apologised (though it wasn't his fault) for the need for the letter at all. In most cases, the news, the sad news itself, would be communicated directly, and very quickly, in person. There were what he called 'army families'. Jack understood that he and Ellie, if they were a family at all, were not an 'army family'. In other cases, Major Richards had explained, it was only wise to avoid what might be a wasted or impractical initial journey. As to his own journey right now (since Ellie had kindly enquired), it had actually been quite short—not that shortness mattered: Wiltshire, not so far from Salisbury, to the Isle of Wight.

And not such an unpleasant one, Major Richards might have added, if the circumstances had been different. He might have said something complimentary about the really remarkably pleasant situation they had here. The fine view, even on a grey day like today. As he'd parked the car he'd noticed the caravans, in their neat rows, down below.

He'd looked at Jack and Ellie attentively, as if silently confirming permission to proceed, then had unzipped his leather wallet. He'd said that Corporal Luxton had been killed, as stated in the letter, on the fourth of November and at approximately three p.m., local time. It was not possible for him to give many details at this point—he was obviously just a home-based officer—but he could confirm that Corporal Luxton would have died instantly, on active, front-line duty, and that his record was such that he would undoubtedly have been promoted soon to sergeant. He'd been trained as a sniper—had himself been a trainer of snipers—but had been killed when the armoured vehicle he was in had triggered an exceptionally lethal roadside bomb. Two other members of his section had been killed and two wounded, one seriously. It was a very grave incident and a very great loss. These were things, nonetheless, that soldiers in Iraq risked every day.

Major Richards had left a little measured pause, though he did not actually say, 'Do you have any questions?' Then, taking out a pen and one of the documents from his wallet, but with an air of being ready to reverse or modify these simple actions if necessary, he'd said that he was sorry to have to ask for such information at such a time, but there were certain matters he needed to confirm.

That Corporal Luxton was never married.

'No,' Jack said, though he wouldn't have known.

Had no children?

'No,' Jack said again, though he might have said, 'Not that I know of.'

Or other dependants?

'No,' Jack said.

Parents?

It seemed to Jack that Major Richards had somehow delayed this question and that he might have done so in some knowing or meaningful way. That it might even be a trick question.

'Dead,' Jack had said. It was surely the correct and the quickest answer, but the word came oddly and echoingly from his lips, as if Vera and Michael might have died, too, in an armoured vehicle in Iraq.

'There are no other relatives,' Major Richards had then asked, 'or persons close to Corporal Luxton whom you feel should be informed—I mean, officially informed, other than by yourself?'

'No,' Jack had said.

'You are, in fact, the only living relative?'

'Yes,' Jack said, huskily, as if this might be another trick question, an even trickier question. He felt quite clearly now that he was under suspicion, if not under interrogation or on trial. So he was surprised when Major Richards suddenly said, using words he'd used before, but looking at him directly, in a different, softer way, 'Let me offer you my personal condolences.' He said it as if he, Major Richards, might have suddenly become a relative of the kind just denied, some sort of temporary father, and might have wished even to reach out and grasp Jack's arm, so conveying that he understood that Jack was of the same stuff as the dead man being referred to, that he, Jack, and Tom were interchangeable. The Luxton brothers.

And Jack would never forget it. As he'd never forget that moment, looking from this window, when after the black saloon had stopped in the turning-space—the same turning-space that is now, beneath him, a lacework of ruffled puddles—he'd had the impossible thought that this figure in a uniform might be Tom.

Jack had felt himself starting to tremble again, under Major Richards's gaze, as he'd done under Ellie's gaze when they'd both first read the letter, and he'd started to want Major Richards to leave.

But Major Richards, now handing Jack a number of papers from his wallet, which were Jack's copies to keep, had begun to explain that 'because of the circumstances on the ground' it was not possible to say as yet exactly when Corporal Luxton would be repatriated, but that it would be soon and that Jack would be kept closely informed. There would be a ceremony, of course, and all due assistance would subsequently be given, following the coroner's release, in whatever funeral arrangements might be decided upon. Meanwhile, Jack shouldn't hesitate to call at any time.

This was adding little to what had been said in the letter, and Jack was able to wonder, as Major Richards spoke, whether the unspecified delay and the word 'circumstances' and that strange phrase 'on the ground' (where else did circumstances happen?) might all be to do with the fact that there was no body really, or not in the usual sense of that word, or that the manner of Corporal Luxton's death, and his comrades', might not have been so instant after all. That the 'incident'—that word had been used at some point—required the army's own careful investigation. No one yet had used the word 'body'.

But mainly Jack was trying to control the trembling of his own body.

Perhaps Major Richards saw this. He saw anyway (and he was not unpractised in this observation) that this visit, though there were other matters still to be dealt with, shouldn't be extended very much further. He'd brought with him, for example, just in case, copies of recent photographs of Corporal Luxton, but he quickly calculated that this wouldn't be the moment to produce them from his wallet. The principal purpose of his visit, that it should simply have been made, was fulfilled. The battalion had been represented in person and in uniform. This, Major Richards knew, was, among his several duties, the most important and most symbolic, and often the most difficult. But Major Richards was only too aware that soldiers had to do far tougher things.

It was now very unlikely that Major Richards, who quite frequently regretted the course of his career and the fact that he was not by now a colonel, would be called upon to do those far tougher things. And, of course, demanding as it was, being the messenger was far easier than being the receiver. He made conscious efforts to remind himself of this.

On a number of occasions now—and recently these occasions had intensified—Major Richards had been required to announce the actual news in person himself. Of a death (not so often, thank goodness), of a wounding

or hospitalisation. Since, with the army's increasing tend-
ency to merge regiments, his duties effectively operated at
brigade level (though he still thought of himself as 'First
Battalion') and since he'd been deemed good at them,
he was not inexperienced. There could be a wife, small
children. Or just parents, brothers, sisters. The average
age of a soldier meant that his family might very often
still all be in one place. This could be both convenient
and not. You might walk in on some cluttered, ordinary
domestic scene. Everyday havoc. They would always look
guilty and apologise for the mess.

He'd taught himself always to look them directly in
the eye. Of course, it helped you, but didn't help them,
that they invariably guessed why you were there, as soon
as they saw you in your cap. They often even said the
words for you: the worst words—which he might be able
to correct. Not killed, no. But if it was the worst, or even
not (not killed, no, just paralysed) then the reaction could
go any way, any old way at all. If, say, it was a young
mother and two toddlers. They could explode straight
away, or later. Sometimes they could tell you, and it was
an order you couldn't disobey, to make a swift exit. You
had to be ready and alert.

It gave Major Richards little satisfaction that he'd
acquired the tactical if hardly military skill of knowing
when to beat a retreat. Having sat in Lookout Cottage
for barely half an hour and having drunk the statutory
(but decent) cup of tea, he sensed the need to exercise
this ability once again.

Major Richards had never been in Iraq or Afghanistan
or indeed in any place where, at the time, actual explo-
sions had occurred and bodies been fragmented. He'd

missed the Falklands, as a junior officer—which, for a while, had rankled. Even his tours in Northern Ireland had been quiet. But he had, in recent months, been an intimate witness to some immediate consequences of what was happening in Iraq and Afghanistan. He had, as it were, been present at several scenes of devastation, enough to know that such scenes were proliferating and increasingly pockmarking the land (though they were as nothing, he understood, to the frequency of such scenes in Iraq or Afghanistan). Enough to give him a curious sense of the country in which he dwelt and to which he owed a soldier's allegiance.

Mostly he did what he did by a process of becoming accustomed to it, if you could ever be, and by the application of instinct. He couldn't say, as a soldier in Iraq might say, that he was trained. Often he felt like a civilian in uniform, a pretend soldier. As to the rights and wrongs, the whys and wherefores, of the operations in the Middle East, he couldn't speak, he couldn't comment, even when (though it was surprisingly rare, one of the less-encountered complications) they demanded that you did.

But this case—Corporal Luxton—was really very simple. Just one living relative, as he'd now confirmed. That had its peculiar sadness and bleakness perhaps, but there would be no further family network (it was a sort of comfort) to trouble, no further connections running like underground wires for further domestic detonations to occur. Just one relative and a wife. And—seeing as they'd had time already to absorb the basic news—there'd been no distressing outbursts. None of the howls or moans or terrifying speechlessness he'd sometimes known.

And, as it happened, he'd never been, in all his life, to the Isle of Wight. When he'd crossed the water, a strange, light-hearted mood had gripped him. Hardly appropriate. But he thought, not for the first time that day, as he strode back to his car, cap on again, shoulders square (he knew from experience that they still might be watching or that, once the door closed behind you and you'd straightened your back, all kinds of collapsing might be going on inside) that, had he not been in uniform, he might have taken the chance for a mooch around. A walk. A breath of sea air. His uniform was the bind. It was so mild and still, the sea, from here, like a sheet of polished steel.

What a marvellous spot. Lookout Cottage.

It would hardly have been right to say, on such a day, that he even felt a little envious. It certainly wasn't typical, not typical at all, of the places he had to visit. Housing estates, military or otherwise. He wondered how someone from a farmhouse in Devon—that was the previous given address (and the man had spoken with a real Devon burr)—came to be living in a cottage in the Isle of Wight and running a caravan site. And what must that be like to do? Not bad at all, maybe. He'd looked again at those white oblongs.

No outbursts, anyway. The wife had looked pretty steady, in fact, even a little hard-eyed. Well, it wasn't her boy, just a brother-in-law. No children, apparently. Just them. An odd couple perhaps, something not quite as one between them in the face of this news. But you saw all sorts of things.

As for him, Jack, the only relative, well yes, that was tough. Your only brother. Your younger brother—Major Richards had reckoned that the gap must be several years.

And he'd noticed before he left (it was even why he'd left) something going on inside Jack Luxton, something deep and contained, that might need its outburst at some time. On the other hand he didn't look like a man given to outbursts, or to much extravagant self-expression at all. He looked pretty hefty and—what was the word?— bovine. He looked—and judging from those photographs still in his wallet his brother had been just the same—like a big strong man.

12

QUICKER AND BETTER at just about everything. He would swing that gun, when it was still too big for him, swing it far too much, Jack would think, and fire as if the shot were like a rope that couldn't help tighten on its target. Rabbit, crow, pigeon. Pigeons were the trickiest. Big, clumsy birds, sitting on the bare branches in Brinkley Wood, sitting ducks you'd think, but they knew when a gun was being pointed. Though not, apparently, when Tom was pointing it. A sniper. Two pigeons dangling by their necks on a string from Tom's belt, wet with Luke's saliva. None for himself. Three misses, in his case, all hitting the space where a pigeon had been. But he hadn't minded. 'That's two between us,' Tom would say, and mean it.

Walking back through the wood on a grey, hard January morning. Time off, after milking, on a Sunday morning. Time off to be just two brothers. Even Dad could recognise and concede it. Like Mum fighting for those two holidays. After a long, unyielding silence: 'Well, off you go, then.' An hour's shooting on a Sunday morning. Dad wouldn't come himself, though he was a decent shot. Perhaps he knew that Tom could already outshoot him. And he'd give the permission as if he, Jack, were just a kid too, needing permission, though he was turning twenty now and the idea, the concession, was that he was supposed to be Tom's teacher. Tom didn't need his father watching over him. Tom was old enough to learn to shoot and Jack was old enough to be his teacher. As if Tom needed any teaching.

Coming back through the wood. The crack of twigs. Luke snuffling through the dead leaves ahead of them. Tom was only twelve, thirteen. Mum was still alive. It wasn't even a thought: that she might not always be. Mum had raised Luke herself, from a pup—the only one they'd kept from big old Bessie's last litter.

Tom didn't have his height yet and Jack would sometimes think that the difference in scale between him and Tom was like the difference in scale between Tom and Luke. But Tom had the two pigeons.

Through the trees and from all sides of the valley would come now and then the small, bouncy 'pop-pop' of other guns. Sunday-morning shooting. The farming fraternity would call it 'going to church'. The wood, on a still, grey morning, with the pillars of trees, was not unlike a church. 'The farming fraternity': that was a phrase Dad would sometimes use, keeping a straight face, though you knew he thought it was a joke of a phrase.

Along the track to the gate, then up the steepening slope of Barton Field, past the big oak, breathing hard, their throats taking in the cold air and sending it out again as steam. Jack had the gun—it was heavy, for a boy, to carry up the hill—but Tom had the pigeons. And then at some point, before the farmhouse came into view above them, beyond the rise and swell of the field, they'd stop to draw breath, and Tom would untie one of the pigeons and give it to him. True to his word. 'Here, Jack.' The dead black eye of the pigeon in Jack's hand would look at him as if to say, 'And I won't say a word either.' Then they'd carry on up the hill, all the valley and the far hills opening up behind them as they climbed, they didn't have to look behind to know it.

Pigeon pie that evening.

Pigeons. Sandcastles. And, it couldn't be denied, girls too. Quicker and better. Too young then, at twelve. Probably. But he was already going to Abbot's Green School, waiting every morning by the Jebb gate for the school bus to swing round the bend and scoop him up. Half a dozen or so already inside, two or three girls among them. Kathy Hawkes from Polstowe.

Once, five or six years before, the same bus with the same driver, Bill Spurell, would have picked up Jack and, a little further down the Marleston road, Ellie Merrick. But with that eight-year gap between them, Tom didn't have any big brother around to cramp his before-and-after-school activities, and even perhaps by the time he was thirteen, by the time Mum had died, he would already have got started. Maybe saying to himself that, given the new situation, given that Mum wasn't around and Dad wouldn't waste a chance to haul him out of the class-room, he'd better make the most of his opportunity. He'd better make hay, while he could, with schoolgirls. What other kind of girl was there going? And maybe girls go for a boy who's just lost his mum, they can't help it. It's a sure-fire recipe, and Tom knew it. Maybe that's why he could crack those eggs so damn neatly.

He got through them anyhow, girls, while he could. It wasn't for Tom like it was for him, Jack, with Ellie: the feeling that this one, the one that seemed to have been put there specially in front of him, was the one he should take, for keeps if he could. And he'd better not move on and see what else might be going, because he might end up having nothing. Her being his age, too, and just across that boundary hedge. Not just an after-school thing. The two of them down in Brinkley Wood sometimes, not shooting pigeons, or going to church exactly.

He'd always thought he should stick with Ellie. Generally speaking, Jack was a sticker, a settler. He didn't have the moving-on instinct, or he never really thought he *could* move on. Whereas Tom, clearly, was a mover-on, in more ways than one. By the time he was eighteen, very clearly. A mover-on and leaver-behind. And no doubt as a soldier he'd have got his quota of passing female company, as soldiers do, no difficulty. And that would have suited him and was just as well, now. No sticking, nothing for keeps. Like pigeons.

Would he have stayed clear of Ellie? She was eight years older and she was his brother's—say no more. But would Ellie have stayed clear of Tom? It might have made a change. He could almost see it from Ellie's point of view.

But he knew, now, that nothing had happened, he was sure now of that. Though it would have been a strange comfort all the same, if Ellie had broken down and confessed: 'Oh, Jack, there's something I've never told you . . .' If he'd been able to put his arms round her and say, 'It doesn't matter.' Or even: 'I always had a feeling.' If it had meant that Ellie could have wept too over his little lost brother, last-but-one of all the Luxtons. And if it had made her say, like she should have done, that yes, of course, she'd come with him, she'd be with him, no question, on that awful bloody journey.

Why the hell hadn't she, anyway?

And, really, he wouldn't have minded, now, if she'd confessed at the time or if Tom had even given it as one of his reasons: 'I'm getting out of your way, Jack, if you know what I mean. No more stepping on your territory. She's all yours now.'

Everything would be all his.

Always the feeling, even when Tom was several jumps ahead, that he was Tom's protector. So if Tom had taken a turn or two with Ellie, it would have been like teaching him how to shoot pigeons.

When Tom was born Jack was eight, and he hadn't expected, any more than anyone else, that he'd ever have a brother. But then there was this tiny, gurgly, spluttery baby, and there was Vera, looking for a while as if she'd been pulled through a baler. And for a short period of his life Jack had felt not so much like a brother, but—long before Tom would show the same aptitude—like a bit of a mother. And a bit of a father. There were times when, since he was only eight, he'd find himself alone with his mother and this new little pink-skinned bundle.

Up in the Big Bedroom, stowed away in a corner, was an old-fashioned wooden cradle—hardly more than two thick chunks of wood joined in a 'V' and fixed to a pair of rockers. Everyone knew it was very old. Like so much else in that room, like the big bed itself and the old wooden chest, it was an heirloom, and there was no saying how many Luxtons had been rocked in it. Those two Luxton lads on the war memorial, surely. And Michael had been rocked in it, which was very hard to imagine. It was very hard to imagine any big-framed Luxtons ever squeezing themselves into a cradle.

But Jack had been cradled in it, and had been told so. When he was still only eight it was not so impossible to conceive of having once been in it. But now there was Tom in it anyway, fitting it perfectly.

And Jack had rocked him. Pretty often. Like a mother. In fact, few things were better and sweeter for Jack when he was eight years old than to be told by his mother that he could rock Tom for a bit, if he wanted to. It wasn't really a matter of permission or even of invitation, but there was a thrill in receiving the prompting, and nothing was better and sweeter, Jack felt, than to be rocking Tom under his mother's gaze, to feel and to hear the tilt and gentle rumble as the cradle, and Tom with it, swayed from side to side.

Jack rocked Tom in his cradle. Also, when he was allowed to, he would pick Tom up and carry him around. He'd even sometimes kiss Tom on his funny little head. He'd grip Tom under his shoulders and—standing himself at his full eight- or nine-year-old height—lift him right up so his legs dangled. At eight or nine, Jack had possessed his window of opportunity for doing such things, before his dad had begun to frown on them.

But he'd never said, later, to Tom, even if Tom perhaps might have imagined it: 'Tom, I rocked you once. In that cradle.' He'd never said, 'I dangled you.' How could he ever say it? And now he never would. And he'd never know if his mother had ever said it for him. Never in Jack's hearing anyway.

How could he have said it, or when? When they were down in the woods, shooting? Or sharing the milking? Or when Tom had come home from school, down the track from the gate, after his hand had been up Kathy Hawkes' skirt? 'Tom, I once—'

Or before Tom climbed, for the last time, up that same track, that December night? Though how could he have said it then, of all times? Though perhaps he had said it—thought it anyhow—into his pillow. As he'd said it to himself, a thousand times, while just watching Tom grow.

Ellie wanted a child, children, he knew that. And he didn't. For his own reasons, but for reasons that Ellie knew perfectly well in her way. He simply hadn't wanted any more of himself, of his own uprooted stock, after Tom had left and then he and Ellie had left too. And Dad had gone anyway. He hadn't wanted any passing on.

'No more Jebb, no more Luxtons, Ell.'

It was how he'd felt. And it was part of an unspoken pact between them, along with the caravans and the cottage and the holidays in the Caribbean. Along with the steep learning curve and the lightening up. He wasn't conceding quite everything.

The subject had certainly hovered between them, that afternoon at Jebb in the Big Bedroom, as the word 'caravans' had hovered, as if that word itself might even have been a code for it. What better place for it to hover than in that big bed? And it had been a real enough prospect then. As real and as natural as that oak tree beyond the window. And Ellie wouldn't have so long, perhaps. Her window of opportunity. Jesus, she might have been planning something right then.

But the subject had only hovered, then flitted away. To be considered later, maybe. One thing at a time. And he had a lot to consider. Everything he was looking at, for a start, everything you could see from that window. And that letter.

Over in the corner, in the shadows, the wooden cradle would still have been there. And Ellie's eyes, that afternoon, had been doing their roaming. She'd never seen the inside of Jebb Farmhouse at such close quarters before. She must have noticed the cradle. And she might have made some joke, as her way of broaching the subject, about him once having been in it, and look at the bloody size of him now. But she hadn't broached the subject. So she must have seen his thinking, his position on it, already in him. Or decided to leave it till later. Enough work for one summer's day.

But she must have noticed that cradle, and maybe her simple thought was: Well, Jack once had *his* damn baby. And that was why she'd said that thing about Tom. 'Forget him, Jack.' Or she might have just thought: Time enough, time enough still. Not yet twenty-eight and in peak condition.

Her eyes had done their roaming anyway. When he and Ellie came, about a year later, to do the selling— separately but together, as it were—before they had all those people round (their eyes roaming too), he'd said, 'And what about all the stuff? I mean the stuff inside, the furniture.' He hadn't meant the stuff at Westcott, that was Ellie's business. So why should he have asked on his own account about Jebb, as if he needed her instruction?

'You sell it too, Jack. *We* sell it too.' She'd even looked a little impatient with him. 'You might be surprised what you get for some of those things. I'd say you've got enough there to fill a whole antiques shop.'

And so, because Ellie had given him the go-ahead and because anyway it was like giving her a sort of sign, he'd sold the cradle. What would they want with a cradle? Though it had cost him a wrench, a hell of a wrench.

But he hadn't sold the shotgun. Or the medal.

13

WHEN ELLIE HAD shut the door behind Major Richards—it was she who'd shown him out, she could see Jack wasn't up to it—she'd felt, for the first time since that letter had arrived, like crying herself. This was different from the letter. It was different when a man in a uniform turned up at your front door. You knew then it wasn't just a piece of paper. And it wouldn't just blow away as pieces of paper could.

Of course she could remember Tom. Little Tom, then big Tom, just as big as his brother. Big enough, certainly, to go off and be a soldier. When Jack had told her—but only after it had happened—that this was what Tom had done and that he, Jack, had known all about it beforehand, she'd breathed, she couldn't help it, a grateful sigh. She'd been surprised, but she'd been glad, though she'd tried not to show it. There wasn't any reason to be cut up about it—if, so it seemed, Jack wasn't. If it was what Tom had wanted and planned and he'd gone and done it, then good luck to him. And if Jack had been in on it and wasn't cut up about it, then so much the better.

It was Michael Luxton who'd been cut up about it,

and had taken it out on Jack. But Jack had just taken that in his turn, so it seemed, as if he were doing it for Tom's sake, not even telling his dad, till he thought it was safe, where Tom had gone. Though he'd told her, one January afternoon at Westcott. 'He's joined the army, Ell. You don't know that I told you this.' As if his dad might have come round and throttled it out of her.

That day, that January afternoon, had in fact been one of the better, brighter days of her life. She'd squeezed and hugged Jack's big, familiar body with a new eagerness (had he noticed?), but also with a delicacy, as if he might have been bruised by real blows from his father. Michael Luxton, it was true, could sometimes scare her. He wasn't scary in any obvious way, but he could sometimes frighten her. If there should be a choice of fathers with whom you'd have to live alone for the foreseeable and barely thinkable future, then she'd choose her own father, small and nimble, not towering and looming. Small and sly and with a regular glint of mischief in his face, which she knew was a mask (even though she could be a sucker for it), a bravado put there mainly by alcohol. Her father owned her, but he didn't scare her. She'd choose him of the two. But then she'd chosen Jack, who could sometimes look the image of his father.

'This is just between you and me, Ell.'

She'd run her palms softly over his big frame as if she'd never done it before. Their situations were the same now, equal. They each had to shoulder their fathers, just their fathers. Tom was gone. A soldier. One of the better days of her life. Though she could feel, beneath the skin, beneath the imaginary bruises from his father, the wound of Tom's departure hidden in Jack's heavy flesh.

It was a grey, bitter January afternoon, the heater ticking in her bedroom—'their bedroom'—and some- where out in the cold of the farm, if he was only consulting his hip flask in the Land Rover, her dad was keeping his distance, as usual, so they could have the house. It was how he kept her there—it was the deal. What a pittance of a deal. And, Jesus, they were both twenty-six.

But Tom was gone, and this was one of the better afternoons. There was more than one kind of soldiering. Not all of it was done by soldiers, or by men. She'd shut her eyes and run her fingers over Jack's shoulders, down his spine, as a blind person might seek to recognise the shape of something. The shape—the ache in her own flesh—of her love for him.

Sometimes Ellie could think she didn't know, she didn't understand at all, this man she'd known, in fact, as long as she could remember. Since long before he was a man or she was a woman. That was how it was. Man and boy, girl and woman. Sometimes the thought of it, as if they'd been born together, could make her smile, sometimes it would crush her. She knew that other women might have thought: What a shame. What a shame for poor Ellie Merrick that it wasn't the other way round, that Jack wasn't Tom. But she'd never, honestly, thought of it like that, and when she imagined those other women, shaking their heads, her blood could gather and she could feel she had claws she might fiercely use in defence of Jack Luxton.

She could feel as she supposed Jack must have felt when he copped it from his dad on account of his little runaway brother.

Ellie didn't know much about the army, but she could see it was a simple, all-in solution for a man of Tom's age, and Tom would hardly have been the first. One moment a cowshed in a gone-to-pot farm, next moment a barracks. The main thing was he'd *got out*. He'd shown it could be done. Tom was not unlike her mother. And Jack might have done the same himself, as much as eight years ago, or more. But then *his* mother would have still been alive, and Tom would have been barely ten.

And, anyway, if Jack had ever gone off to join or do anything, it would have meant deserting *her*, Ellie.

She didn't know Jack? She didn't understand how it truly was with him and her? Oh, but yes she did.

Once upon a time, when Ellie was still a pupil, like Jack, at the tiny primary school in Marleston, jealousy had entered her life in the form of an unexpected new arrival at Jebb Farm. At first she'd supposed that this strange, nagging emotion was because she would have liked the same for herself, a little baby brother or sister. Up until then she and Jack had been equal in not having either.

But no surprise event like the one that had occurred at Jebb Farm was to occur at Westcott Farm and there was certainly fat chance of its ever occurring once, several years later, Ellie's mother had made her sudden exit. By then, so far as new arrivals went, there was a much greater chance that Ellie herself, if she wasn't careful, might get pregnant. But by then, too, Ellie had grown up with her jealousy and knew that it wasn't so much that she wanted any more a little sibling of her own, but that she was jealous of that part of Jack that belonged to his brother.

How it had once pained her, and how she'd had to hide it, when the three of them—Jack, Tom and Vera—had gone away together those two years running. Only a week, but how her jealousy had seethed. But then how her heart had soared (though she'd never said so) when she'd got that postcard from Dorset.

'We are all living in a caravan called Maralin.'

Jealousy wasn't even the word, perhaps, by the time her mother had done her bunk. Ellie had grown up resenting Tom Luxton, resenting him and hiding it. Hiding it to the extent sometimes of even pretending that she too, like his big brother, loved him. Wasn't he just so lovable? They'd played games, once, she and Jack, of pretending they were Tom's mother and father.

Wasn't he just so adorable? All of which acquired its complication when, many years later, Tom was old enough to be interested in girls—and vice versa. Of course she could see that Tom was the kind of boy any girl would fall for. Fall over backwards, like little Kathy Hawkes. Well, good luck to her. And of course she could see that there was even sometimes just a touch of unease, of jealousy coming in the other direction, from Jack.

Well, it levelled the score a little. She didn't exactly tell him not to be so daft. But couldn't he damn well see? Couldn't Jack see? Eight years was eight years. And couldn't anyone see by then, even if Jack couldn't, that —call her stupid, call her not choosy—she was Jack's and Jack's only, plain and simple. It was how it was, it was how she was. Where else did all that resentment come from?

But Jack had simply never seen, never noticed what would have been the biggest reason for his not needing to have any jealousy of his own. That she could have done without little Tom altogether. Tom himself could see it, she knew that. He had sharper eyes than his brother. But he'd just shut up about it.

It was something short of the whole hundred per cent, that part of Jack that she could call her own, and what she did have, she only had properly, after her mother's departure, on a couple of weekday afternoons. And that only as a pay-off from her father. Jack, too, was a slave to his father, and he was his mother's favourite (she knew that and she didn't blame Vera) and there was this big chunk of him anyway that belonged with his brother. How much did that leave for Ellie?

But then Vera had died. Then Tom had gone away. And Jack, on the surface, didn't seem so cut up about it, though Michael was. And, though she took care not to show it, Ellie's hopes had lifted—so far as that was possible when everything was laid low by the effects of mad-cow disease. Because at least now she was shot of Tom.

From then on Ellie had begun to do some extra wishing. What could she do but wish? And when, not so very long after Tom disappeared from the scene, Michael Luxton, in his own way, dropped out of it too, she'd begun to feel that wishing wasn't such a useless thing to fall back on, since it seemed it could have real effect. On the other hand, there were limits, serious limits, to wishing, even secretly. And she'd begun also to be a little afraid of her wishes. 'Shot of', it was only an expression.

But then there'd been that letter, out of the blue, from

the man she chose to call, as if she'd known him all her life, her 'Uncle Tony'. Or rather from his solicitors, Gibbs and Parker, of Newport, Isle of Wight, with their condolences and kindest regards.

In all her secret wishing and hoping, Ellie had never been so foolishly wishful as to rely upon some stroke of sheer magic. True, she'd liked to tease Jack sometimes about her 'mystery man'. But now that a stroke of magic had occurred—and there was, in a sense, a mystery man—she quickly enough converted it into a stroke of justice, even giddy justification. So, she hadn't been wrong, after all, not totally to condemn her mother. Because in the end, and without knowing it, her mother had made amends.

'Caravans, Jacko.'

She'd waved the magic wand of that word over Jack's head and filled in the picture for him of their combined and fully provided-for future. Though she'd had to wait. She'd had to wait for another necessary, preliminary event to occur. Which had occurred, in fact, more quickly than she could ever have imagined, or—hand on heart—wished. Though now that it had happened, she could see that it might seem to have happened because she'd wished it.

But in any case Jack had said, 'Yes. Okay, Ellie.' If he hadn't said it quite as simply and readily as that, and if it had cost her, one way or another, a good deal of patience, trouble and heartache.

Though wasn't that afternoon, that afternoon at Jebb, just the best ever? Wasn't the world, at last, a good place to be in?

There was just one gap in the picture, and that was the gap that corresponded to the part of Jack that still belonged to Tom, even though Tom had been absent now for over eighteen months and hadn't even answered any letters. She'd known not to push it too quickly or firmly. When so much else was going their way, and when, after all, she was still not quite twenty-eight. Though when she did in fact push it—gently, she'd thought—the answer she'd got from Jack, pretty quickly and firmly, was that if he was going to leave Jebb, if he was going to be the last Luxton ever to farm there, then there shouldn't be any more Luxtons at all.

As if she'd pushed him over some edge. Or as if that was his condition.

Well, she'd thought, that was his mood of the moment. It was a big moment—they were going to sell two farms—and a big condition. And he was still, perhaps, in grief for his father. Grief and shock. It was a different sort of grief, Jack's grief for his dad, from hers for her own father. It was a different sort of death. Though wasn't it a well-known remedy for grief: you lose one, you make another? It's how it's been known to happen.

Time was still on her side, she'd thought, so far as that gap in the picture went. Time and a change of scene. But she'd been twenty-seven then, she was pushing forty now. Years had passed. And though Jack had come out of the shell of his past long ago, even become a new kind of man (all that too had seemed the result of her wishing it), she knew that the obstacle was still Tom, who was still in the picture though out of it.

So when that letter had arrived, via Jebb Farmhouse, saying, with deepest regret, that Tom was dead, Ellie had felt her hopes fly up once again. Though she hadn't shown it. It wasn't so difficult to disguise the feelings she'd always disguised. On the other hand, she wasn't going to disguise them now to the extent of shedding false tears. Even when Jack had suddenly broken down in tears in a way she'd never seen before.

Her hopes had soared. She couldn't help it. Tom was truly out of the picture now. Her mind had even foolishly raced ahead—even as Jack, holding that letter, had begun to tremble. She and Jack were in the clear now. Tom would never show up. And, who knows, one immediate, unstoppable effect of all this might be that she would suddenly get her long-thwarted wish. Jack might swing now completely the other way. Who knows, in just a few weeks' time, in St Lucia, at the Sapphire Bay, in their air-conditioned bungalow with the hot night outside, they might get down to serious work on it. If it was a boy, they might call it Tom, if that's what he wanted. She wouldn't mind.

And if it was a girl (she didn't care) they might call it Vera. Or Marilyn.

All this had flashed through her mind as she'd watched Jack Luxton tremble, then begin to shake, then spill over into tears. It wasn't a familiar sight, or a pretty one. She'd put her arms round him and felt his big bones grate inside him.

And then, just as quickly, her thoughts had dropped back, sunk back into her own bones, as she'd understood a bigger truth that would only grow bigger, clearer in the hours, days, that would follow. That though Tom wasn't coming back, yet he *was* coming back. So far as Jack was concerned, he was coming back big-time. He was coming back to bloody haunt them.

She'd seen the bit of Jack that belonged to Tom, even though he was dead, only growing bigger and the bit of Jack that was hers only growing smaller.

And then Jack had said that thing about St Lucia.

In Ellie's life, and she was only thirty-nine, there'd been, up to now, only three significant written communications. One was the letter just received by Jack. The second had been that miraculous letter from Uncle Tony's lawyers. But the first and incomparably the most important at the time had been the postcard that had come once from Jack. She could still see its bluer-than-blue sea and sky and curving beach and crescent of white cliffs, like someone's broad smile. And she could still see the face of her mother, Alice Merrick, as she still was then, who'd handed it to her one morning with a smile.

How her heart had soared. Seethed and soared. Ellie, at that time, had never seen the sea. Now here she was with Jack, living right by it. Sands End, the Sapphire Bay. One sea or another.

So when she'd shut the front door behind Major Richards, she'd felt like crying herself, having her own portion of tears. Not for poor Tom Luxton, but for all the stupid, patient, stubborn lengths a woman will go to for a man. All the things she will do. All her life long. When he wasn't even, perhaps, when you stood back and looked, that much to speak of really, that much to bloody write home about. Other women might say, '*Him?*'

But he'd been all that she had and most of the time, truly, all that she wanted to have. How her fingertips had searched his big body. If only she could have all of him. And she'd thought once that at last she even had that, and had made a whole future for both of them.

'Dear Ellie, Wish you were here.'

14

WHEN HE WATCHED Ellie close the door behind Major
Richards, Jack was still trembling inside. He felt as if he'd
just been told again that Tom was dead, and this time it
was real. The first time had been just a rehearsal, a sort of
fire drill. But he knew he shouldn't cry again, not in front
of Ellie. Once was enough and even then he'd been brief.
It hadn't helped the first time. It didn't help anyway.

So he hadn't, though it had cost him a struggle. He'd
looked at Ellie, who'd remained standing oddly by the
front door, her back to it, as if there was something bad
beyond it, though she'd looked, too, as if she were
struggling with something inside her. It was the real shock
and truth of it all, perhaps, only now getting through.
But he didn't get up to go to her. He knew that something had come between them since that letter. All it took
was a letter. But there was an invisible wall. If he walked
across to her now, he'd hit it.

They'd both listened to the sounds of Major Richards
starting his car, turning it and driving off down the road
to Holn. Ellie had stood there in that strange way by the
door. He'd thought: Is she going to cry now, is she finally

going to cry for Tom, so I don't have to? But she hadn't cried, not then, nor at any point in the days that followed, and when, the next day, Major Richards had called again, Ellie had picked up the phone and more or less handed it straight to Jack as if it were some matter that was none of her business. 'Major Richards,' she'd said as if Jack now had friends in high places.

Major Richards had told Jack he could now confirm that Corporal Luxton's repatriation, along with that of the two soldiers who'd died with him, would take place on the following Thursday. He'd given the name of an airbase that Jack had vaguely heard of, though he wouldn't have been able to place it in Oxfordshire. Major Richards had also explained that because of the unusual delay in arranging repatriation (he didn't explain that this delay was partly down to the delay in contacting Corporal Luxton's next of kin) and because, meanwhile, thorough post-mortem procedures had been completed overseas, the Oxfordshire coroner, having read the MOD report and satisfied himself of the facts, would be prepared to grant an effectively immediate release. That is, an inquest would be formally opened and at once adjourned on arrival of the repatriation flight, while the bodies could proceed directly, for their funerals, to their respective undertakers.

Major Richards pointed out that, in his experience, this was quite exceptional—for the civil authority to accept the military authority's findings—and even suggested, in his tone, that Jack ought, really, to be grateful. Jack, who had his own experience of coroners and inquests, didn't feel it was exceptional. Or, rather, he felt that everything was now exceptional, so exceptionality had become the norm.

Major Richards was spared from explaining, as he normally had to, though often hinting that it wasn't a recommendation, that next of kin had the right to view the body while it rested in the coroner's care. In this instance such a matter would be between Jack and his undertakers. But Major Richards hoped it had never entered Jack's head.

The situation, anyway, was that Jack was now free to make plans for Corporal Luxton's funeral—in which, of course, there would be full cooperation. In case Jack hadn't understood these last remarks, Major Richards spelt it out that Jack would need to decide whether he wanted a private funeral or a funeral with military presence. This could be arranged. That in any case an undertaker's hearse would need to be at the airbase to receive the coffin following the ceremony and that the costs of this transportation, as well as all the costs of Jack's and Mrs Luxton's 'compassionate travel', would be met by the army.

Jack (after a silence) had found himself saying the word Devon. The funeral would be in Devon. He'd even blurted out to Major Richards the name of an undertaker—since, limited as Jack's dealings were in many areas, he'd had dealings in this area, too, before. Babbages in Barnstaple. He'd had to arrange once, with Babbages, his father's funeral. He knew the ropes in this area. On the other hand, the ropes now were rather different. Then again, his father's ropes hadn't been so simple.

Jack had said, 'Marleston. Marleston, north Devon.' Then explained for Major Richards's benefit that the nearest large town was Barnstaple. At the same time Jack had thought: the Isle of Wight to Oxfordshire, then to Marleston and back again. It would mean at least one night away somewhere.

Major Richards had explained that Jack and Mrs Luxton would be sent further, full details of the ceremony. And of course a formal invitation. To Jack, the word 'invitation' didn't seem like a word that went with the army, though in this case it didn't seem like the right word anyway. Major Richards had said that meanwhile he'd continue to 'liaise' (which seemed a real army word) by phone and even, if convenient, by a further visit, and that Jack shouldn't hesitate if there were anything he wished to ask.

Though this last point was one Major Richards had made before, in person and with genuine kindness in his voice, Jack somehow felt that, now, it really meant its opposite: that the decent thing was actually to hesitate completely—not to ask anything at all. It was as if Major Richards had become his commanding officer and had just said that any man was free, of course, to back out if he wished, but the decent thing was not to. It was like a test of soldiership.

It had always been, in any case, Jack's basic position in life to hesitate to ask too many questions. He knew that he would never ask (though he would certainly wonder) exactly how—let alone why—his brother had died (he knew that the army would prefer him not to ask such questions). In the same way that he'd never raised with Ellie the question, the peculiarity of their two fathers dying in such quick succession. Was death so infectious?

*

When he came off the phone, Jack explained to Ellie that they were bringing Tom home. He'd been given a date. There would be a ceremony, at some airbase. And they were free to make immediate arrangements for the funeral.

So far, there hadn't been much discussion between them about this inevitable prospect. It would have to be at Marleston, of course, Jack now said. It was his decision. Though he wondered soon afterwards—and he wonders still now—how different it might have been if he'd said that they should have the thing done locally. For the closeness and the convenience. At least then Ellie might not have wriggled out. Though would she have liked the idea either?

In the twenty-four hours following Major Richards's visit Jack had felt that invisible wall settle only more rigidly between them—the wall, so he might have thought of it, of Ellie's failure to reach out and comfort him. Except it sometimes seemed—it was like an unjust reversal of the situation—that this might stem from some baffling failure on his part to comfort her.

As if he should have said, 'I'm sorry, Ell. I'm truly sorry.' Without knowing what for.

A local funeral. A cremation even. So then they might have scattered the ashes—scattered Tom—over Holn Head. Or into the waves at Sands End. Stood together on the beach. Or in among the caravans. But Jack didn't like the idea of cremation. It called up bad pictures. Being a farmer, he naturally went for burial. And he had the distinct feeling that Tom might have been half-cremated already.

But, anyway, Marleston. Where else? He might have said: where all the rest of them are. All Saints' churchyard.

They would have to go to this—ceremony. Then they'd have to go on to the funeral in Marleston. They'd have to find somewhere to stay. Though, of course, they'd be just a mile or so from Jebb and Westcott, their former places of residence.

It was important to Jack, though it was also natural, that when he explained these things he used the word 'we', just as Major Richards had said 'you and Mrs Luxton'. In the pit of his stomach there was starting to form a tight ball of fear about this journey, this two-stage journey as it now turned out—about all the things, known and unknown, that it would entail. He hadn't yet begun to contemplate every daunting detail. Yet it had to be done. It was, though the word was hardly good enough, a duty. And it wasn't as if he, Jack, was being asked, like his brother, to enter a war zone, and so was entitled to this onset of fear. They'd have to go to a couple of places in England, that's all, one of them very familiar. And Ellie, Jack told himself, would be beside him.

But Ellie, apparently, had other notions. Ellie, when he gave this account of some of the necessary consequences of his brother's death, took rapid and rather violent exception to his use of the word 'we'.

'Who's this "we"?' she suddenly demanded. 'Who's this "we"?' He saw her again, closing the door behind Major Richards, but remaining pressed against it and, so it seemed, trying to resist some further attempt at entry.

'Leave me out of this, Jack. I can't come with you.'

Jack was totally unprepared for this, but there was no mistaking the firmness of her position.

'I just can't. He's not my little brother.'

He understood that she was backing out. It was a

legitimate option, though he hadn't offered it—as if he were Ellie's commanding officer. He hadn't said he was asking for volunteers and that any man or woman was of course free to opt out. His big mistake, maybe. If he'd said, 'You don't have to come if you don't want to, Ell,' then perhaps she would have come. It was how such things worked. But he hadn't said it and she hadn't done the decent thing anyway. She hadn't even backed out decently.

Setting aside the fixed look on her face, Jack couldn't be sure which of her words struck the hardest. That she wasn't going to come? That he could no longer take the word 'we', meaning Ellie and him, for granted? That Tom wasn't her brother? That last statement was of course entirely correct, but Jack felt there was a sense, in this particular case, in which Tom *was* Ellie's brother, in which anyone as close to the matter as Ellie was would have felt, at least for a short while: 'this is my brother.' He felt another tremor of that bewildering need to comfort her.

Since Jack was a man already hit hard, he was, in one sense, numbed and immunised against these further blows Ellie was now delivering. But afterwards he realised that it was the word 'little' that had hurt him the most. Ellie hadn't had to say that. Yet it was the word, it seemed, she'd used with the greatest force. 'Little.'

It wasn't true of course, if it had been once. Tom was no longer little. You could say, maybe, that he was less than little now, since now he was nothing—he might not even be just one piece of nothing. And for some time now he'd been out of Jack's life and Jack had tried, mostly, not to think of him. So in that sense, too, he'd been little, or nothing. But in the normal sense he wasn't little at all, and hadn't been little for years. He hadn't been little on that night he'd left Jebb Farmhouse, though Jack had thought of him then, and sometimes since, as little. The point was that 'little' was his own word, his own special word, it wasn't Ellie's.

On the day following Major Richards's visit they'd seen something in the paper that Major Richards had warned them to expect. The names—so far withheld and for an unusually long time—would now be released, of the three men who'd died in the incident previously reported. Along with the names there would be photographs, as well as some words from relatives and commanding officers. Major Richards had asked Jack if, for the purpose, there were any particular words he wished to say. Then Jack had found Major Richards suggesting—composing—a statement for him. It seemed to Jack that Major Richards had already had the statement ready in his head. It was a bit like writing that postcard to Ellie.

It was at this point that Major Richards might have produced the photos in his brown wallet, but since he saw by now that Jack's whole body was trembling, decided against it and simply said that when the thing appeared in the newspapers they should be prepared for there being pictures.

The photograph of Tom—of Corporal Luxton—showed a man wearing a badged beret, moulded very familiarly to his head, and a camouflage shirt, the sleeves rolled up neatly above his elbows. The arms were thick, so was the face. And the expression was—expressionless. There was no hint of a smile, no hint of anything in particular. You couldn't have said: This man could be my friend or, on the other hand, my enemy. Though you might have said this man would be good to have on your side in a fight. A word you might have used was 'solid'. But the man in the photograph certainly wasn't little.

Jack had looked at the photograph and recognised, of course, the man he was looking at. Yet at the same time it had seemed appropriate for him to ask, deep inside: Do I know this man? Can this man really be my brother? He'd wanted the face to have some indication in it that Tom might have known, when the photo was taken, that one day his brother would look at it.

Among the many strange feelings Jack had felt since that letter had arrived was the feeling that *he* was the little brother now. Big as he was, he'd turned little. And it went now with that little, concentrated ball of fear in his stomach. He felt simply small. So when Ellie had used that word, he'd felt she might as well be using it of him.

Do I know this man? But he'd felt just the same about Ellie, he realised, when she'd demanded to be counted out. Do I know this woman? This unwavering woman. There'd been an odd touch about Ellie, in fact, of the man in the photograph. You wouldn't want to mess with that man. He might even shoot you, no questions asked. Similarly, if Ellie could be so unbudging about a thing like this, then there was no saying what else she might do. Or—he'd think later—might have done already.

The words he'd finally spoken in reply to Ellie hadn't sounded like his own words. He couldn't have imagined himself ever saying them or ever needing to. He'd drawn a big breath first.

'I'm asking you, Ellie, if you'll come with me to my brother's funeral. If you'll be with me when I get his coffin.'

He'd felt when he said these words a bit like he felt when things occasionally got out of hand down at the site and he had to step in—usually with remarkable effectiveness—and deal with it. So why, when he said them, had he also felt small?

'And I'm saying,' Ellie had said, 'that I can't.'

They'd stared at each other for a moment.

'Okay, Ell,' he'd said. 'If that's how you feel. I'll go by myself.'

15

So, THREE DAYS AGO, Jack had driven off alone in the same dark-blue Cherokee that Ellie has driven off in now.

It was not yet six-thirty. Still dark. But he'd been awake since five, staring at the luminous face of his still-primed alarm clock. Fear, among many other fears, of being late had made him decide on a perhaps excessively early start. And he was gripped by a strange mood of secrecy. He'd slipped out quietly, carrying just a small holdall and his black parka jacket (it was the right colour at least—and since when had Jack Luxton had use for a proper overcoat?).

Ellie hadn't come to the door to see him off. She hadn't even stirred or muttered a word as he'd crept from the bedroom, choosing for some reason to tread softly when he might have thumped about assertively. But he hadn't believed she was asleep. When he'd stepped outside—she still hadn't appeared—and crossed to the parked car, he'd wondered if she was nonetheless listening, intently, to his every sound. Or if, in fact (though he hadn't demeaned himself with any pathetic backward glance), she'd even got up to part the curtains and watch him leave. From this same window from which he watches for her now.

He sees himself now, as if he might be Ellie watching his own departure, beginning that journey all over again. He sees himself covering every mile, every strange, bewildering stage of it again, even as he waits now for Ellie's return. He hadn't known then, as he departed, if *he* would return. Or if Ellie would be there if he did. That was how it had seemed.

With him, as was only natural on such a journey, had been his mobile phone. Who knows, he might have needed to call Major Richards, to say he'd broken down. (Or to say he'd been suddenly, unaccountably, taken ill.) Also, of course, he might have needed, or wanted, to communicate with Ellie. Or she with him. But, just before leaving, he'd made sure it was switched off, meaning to keep it so. If she couldn't even say goodbye to him.

It's switched off, emphatically, now.

The air had been fresh and a little damp, with the hint of a quickening dawn breeze. He could barely make out, white as they were, the caravans below, but, beyond the lights of Sands End and Holn, it was just possible to discern the faint sheen of the sea—dotted anyway by the small, almost motionless lights of distant shipping that, now and then, if only because they reminded him of the former purpose of the place where he lived, Jack would find oddly comforting.

He wore a white shirt and his only suit, which, fortunately, was a charcoal grey. Along with the strange sensation of stealth as he'd moved round his own home had gone an equally unaccustomed demand for dignity. He'd dressed carefully. He still hardly ever wore a suit. This was not the same suit his mother had once bought him in Barnstaple, but it reminded him of it and of being viewed by his mother when he'd emerged from the curtained cubicle in Burtons. Her little, approving nod. So what would she think now?

He'd thought, as he dressed, of the empty hearse that must have left Barnstaple by now. Or would it have been driven up, so as to be sure, the night before? Either way, it had better be there.

He put on his black tie, arguing with himself as to whether he should do this now or at a later stage. The knot took two attempts. The small holdall, with a change of clothes in it, was the same one that served as a carry-on bag on their winter holidays. It had been to the Caribbean and back several times.

He'd stood for a while by the front door, wondering whether to call up to Ellie—even to go up to her before he left. But he wasn't going to call up if she wasn't going to call back. And he wasn't going to go up if Ellie wasn't going to say, 'I'll be thinking of you, Jack. And I'll be thinking of Tom.' That would have been enough. But she wasn't going to say it now if she hadn't said it already, he knew that. And if she could say it at all, then she'd be coming with him now. She'd be standing beside him, glancing in the mirror by the front door, dressed and a bit breathy, a touch of scent in the air. Like when they left on their winter breaks.

'All set, Jacko? Tickets? Money? Smile?'

He'd shut the front door quietly behind him—he could have chosen to slam it—as if he might, indeed, have been intending to leave undetected. Like Tom, that night years ago. He couldn't help but remember it. That night *he'd* been lying awake in bed, listening for every small sound. The last sounds of Tom he'd ever heard.

He started the engine, but coasted almost silently, on the brakes, slowly down the twisting hill. With his lights on, the sea had disappeared, but as he pointed east the sky in that direction showed a dim, feathery mix of greys and pinks above a just-emerging horizon. He had to arrive before eleven-thirty and in good time, but, even allowing for the crossing and the traffic there might be on the other side, it hardly seemed necessary to be leaving in darkness. From Portsmouth it was some eighty miles. But (unlike Ellie) he'd never lost the farmer's habit of being up with, or before, the dawn. In the summer he'd sometimes sit outside the cottage with a mug of tea at five in the morning, wondering how long it would be before the first of those caravanners (and every unit might be occupied) would make a move. Lazy buggers. But they were on holiday, they didn't have to hurry, their days were their own. They were having fun—thanks to him and Ellie. There'd be just the mew of gulls and, in the quiet, as if it too had barely woken, the faint, sleepy wash of the sea.

In any case, best to be early. The Isle of Wight to Oxfordshire: it was unknown country to him. Like the Isle of Wight had once been. Never mind the bloody isle of St Lucia. It was all unknown country now.

16

HE TURNED LEFT at Holn, the patch of pinkish sky
directly ahead, then turned left again a few miles later,
towards Newport.

Before leaving the cottage he'd taken another, vacillat-
ing decision, along with the decision to put on his black
tie. Into the holdall, to add to the clothes and sponge bag,
he'd finally slipped a small, black, hinged box. Then as
he'd stood before the mirror for a last check, he'd revised
even that decision. He'd unzipped the bag, taken out the
box and slid what was in it into the breast pocket of his
suit, patting its small weight against him. Then he'd
returned the box to the bag. He couldn't have explained
the logic, if they had any logic, of these actions. His hand
had shaken a little.

When he took off his jacket to lay it in the back
of the car he transferred what was in the breast pocket
to the breast pocket of his shirt, the same white shirt
he'd worn for Major Richards's visit, so that small weight
was now almost against his skin. When he stopped outside Newport to fill up with petrol, and throughout the

two days of travelling ahead of him, Jack was wearing the DCM.

He reached Fishbourne in good time for the seven-thirty ferry. By then it was light and, beyond the inlet where the ferries docked, the sea that from the Lookout had been a mere hinted presence showed choppy and active, the combination of a briskish breeze and the rays of the just-risen sun turning the waves inky black on one side and brilliant on the other. The yachts moored in the inlet swayed and rattled.

Though Jack had lived now for some ten years in a former coastguard's cottage and had looked every day at the sea, to be on it didn't come naturally to him. He could point the caravanners towards several boat-bound activities, but had never developed the yen to have a boat himself, to chug around Holn Head in a dinghy with an outboard motor, maybe lowering a fishing line. The six-mile ferry ride across the Solent had been his first experience of being on a vessel and remained his only one. Similarly, until he'd flown with Ellie to the Caribbean he'd never known what it was like to be in a plane. The two unfamiliar experiences were linked, since in order to drive to Gatwick Airport it had been necessary first to take the ferry, and those winter holidays were virtually the only occasions that demanded making the crossing, so that even that experience had never become casual.

Travelling now to an airbase, Jack could remember that first journey, by way of a ferry, to catch a plane. The whole thing—though it was a holiday and was meant to be fun and people did it, apparently, all the time—had unnerved him with its elemental audacity. Even the previously unpenetrated landscape of Sussex had seemed alien. Even the ferry crossing had made him tense.

The truth was that he was that common enough creature, a landsman, by experience and disposition. His big body told him this. He liked his feet anchored to solid ground. How on earth had he ever let himself be plucked into the air on a parachute pulled by a boat? But the truth also was that Jack had become an islander. The ferry crossing was fearful in itself, but it also went, when travelling in this direction, with a queasy distrust of the looming mainland—that yet contained his roots and his past. He felt both fears now, knowing that when he soon drove off again onto dry land, this would in no way cure his qualms. He touched the medal against his chest, as if for his protection.

The ferry throbbed out into the gleaming water, keeping close for a while to the wooded shore and passing near the other ferry point at Ryde, then heading into the open channel known as Spithead. Other ferries and a few merchant ships moved in various directions, smaller craft scattered among them. There was the feeling of some haphazard relay race. Against the dazzling light to the east appeared the silhouettes of squat island-forts.

The shoreline on the far side remained for a time one indistinct, built-up mass, punctured by the white thorn of the Spinnaker Tower. Then Portsmouth gradually separated itself from Gosport, and Southsea, with its beach front, from Portsmouth. Individual blocks of buildings flashed and glinted.

The ferry swung hard to make its entrance. Beyond the ramparts of the narrow harbour mouth could be seen, as if trapped among streets, the masts of the old ships, the *Warrior* and the *Victory*, and beyond them, at the water's edge, the sharp bows of a berthed naval vessel, its grey hull and turrets bleached almost white, with an apricot blush, by the low sun.

Jack had slipped something else into his pocket before departing: his passport. Major Richards had told him he would need it, for identification, on his arrival at the airbase, along with other documents that would be sent to him. His passport showed a mugshot face not unlike that face with the beret and camouflage shirt in the newspaper photo.

Jack knew well enough that he wouldn't need his passport in order to disembark from an Isle of Wight ferry in Portsmouth, but he felt as if he might. He felt, in fact, as the ferry slid through the jaws of the harbour, like a man who, even with his passport on him, not to mention a distinguished-conduct medal against his breast, would, as he came ashore, immediately be arrested.

17

IT WASN'T THE cow disease that had swung it for Tom. For Tom the trigger had been Luke. In more senses than one.

Michael pulled Tom out of school when he turned sixteen, to be a prisoner with his brother on Jebb Farm. No more making hay with schoolgirls. He might have made his escape—by the same route he eventually took—even then. But he waited till his father wouldn't have the power to haul him back, till he was his own free man. And perhaps, even with Vera gone and life at Jebb like a lost cause, it was still not yet a clear thing. He bided his time. Sixteen to eighteen. In between, there'd been an ongoing cattle disease, but also there'd been Luke.

A sort of sliding scale: that sloping line between them. As Tom got bigger, the way it was between Tom and Luke became like the way it once had been between Jack and Tom. When Tom left school to take up full-time attendance at Jebb Farm, Luke somehow became Tom's dog.

And Jack hadn't minded even that. Luke had been the farm dog, the family dog (and he'd been around almost as long as Tom), but he'd been, especially, Jack's. Sitting there in the back of the pick-up, ears flapping, as they'd bumped over to Ellie's. But then he'd become Tom's. It was Luke's own choice and doing, and who could have said exactly when, or why, the crossover occurred? But it was how it was. Maybe it was that Tom had that bit of a mum about him, so Luke hung around Tom because Luke too missed Vera. Or maybe it was that Luke had worked out, just as Jack had, that Tom, though he was the younger brother, was simply superior at most things, including—and one of Luke's functions was to be a gun dog—being a better shot.

But then Luke had got sick. He wasn't young any more. This was some while after the cow disease first struck, but you might have said that Luke, though he'd taken his time, had only come up with his own disease in sympathy. He got sick anyway, just slow and sluggish sick, not mad sick, but he steadily got worse and, on top of it, he seemed to be going blind. They didn't know what to do except hope the thing would solve itself, or that he wouldn't linger, Luke would just spare himself and die. They were all thinking still, of course, of the last time, not so long ago, when there'd been a death pending in the house.

But it had just dragged itself out. Luke dragged himself out. It got a bit too much to take.

One heavy, sullen August morning Michael drove the pick-up into the yard, fetched a spade from the lean-to and put it in the back, then went into the house, unlocked the gun cabinet between the kitchen and the stairs and carried the shotgun out to the pick-up too. Jack and Tom were both in the yard at the time, but felt from the way their father was looking and moving that they shouldn't speak. Then Michael went into the kitchen where Luke was by now confined to his blanket in a corner—beyond even padding his way to the door—and lifted him up and carried him out and put him in the back of the pick-up along with the spade.

He hadn't said a word, but now he stared at Jack and Tom in a pausing-for-breath way, as if he might have had a statement prepared. But what came out was: 'No, neither of you's coming with me.' Both brothers were looking hard at their father and both had perhaps stepped forward, perhaps more to restrain him than to join him, but this is how Michael chose to interpret the situation. Then something in Tom's eyes, or something in his own thoughts, must have made Michael change his mind, because before he got back behind the wheel he said to Tom, and not to Jack, 'Okay, if you must. Fetch another spade.'

Maybe that was all it was. He was thinking it would be quicker work, and not so much that by then Luke had become Tom's dog. But if so, he might just as well have picked Jack or told them both to go and grab spades.

And then Michael, with Tom and Luke and the shotgun and two spades, had driven off.

Later, though not all at once, Tom told Jack everything—or everything that he wanted to tell him—but the scene itself, from which Jack was excluded, has only ever, like some other scenes from which he was absent yet which were crucial to his life, played itself out in his imagination, seeming each time to be both real and unreal.

But there's no doubt that he heard the shot. His ears had been straining for it. And, later on, he saw the little mound of freshly patted-down earth. Luke had been too weak to raise his head above the side of the pick-up as it drove away, so that he and Jack could take a last look at each other, and Jack realised when it was too late that he hadn't even been allowed the chance to say goodbye to him or give him a final stroke. His father had driven off fast, over-revving the engine, as if there were no time to lose or as if he were afraid of changing his mind.

Then Jack was alone in the deserted yard, with the receding sound of the pick-up jolting its way down the hill. In the muggy air, a hatch of flying ants was buzzing round him. His mother, he knew, would have found where the nest was, then boiled the kettle. But Jack just stood, listening, in the yard.

Tom said they'd driven down Barton Field, his father stamping on the brake, past the big oak, to the low, flat corner by the wood where the ground, even in summer, was nearly always soft. Then they'd stopped and Dad had gone round to gather up Luke, who must by then have formed his own conclusions. Tom didn't say if anything had been spoken on the way down or if, at this point, there'd been any argument. You don't have a tug-of-war with a sick animal. Dad had carried Luke a few yards from the pick-up and put him on the grass. Then he'd gone back for the gun. Tom said he hadn't wanted to touch it himself, he hadn't made any move in that direction.

Dad had the cartridges in his pocket and while he stood and loaded the gun—both barrels, just in case—he told Tom to get the two spades from the back. Jack asked Tom how their father had spoken, and Tom had thought for a bit and said he'd spoken like he was giving orders. This wasn't a nice thing for either of them (or for Luke) and there was no way of speaking about it nicely. All of which Jack could understand. Then Tom had added that his father had spoken like a complete bastard.

Tom said that while Dad loaded the gun Luke had just sat there on the grass where he'd been put. It's true, he couldn't move much now anyway, but he'd just sat there like a good dog sits, front legs out before him, waiting for what's next. Of course, he was perfectly familiar with that gun.

Jack asked Tom (though he already knew the answer) if he thought that Luke knew, all along. Tom said, of course. Of course Luke knew. Luke was half blind and he hadn't made a move, but Tom said he was sure Luke knew, even as they'd bumped down Barton Field. And Jack knew he hadn't needed to ask.

But Jack would never be sure about the next bit in Tom's description. Though why should Tom have made it up? Tom might have just said that Dad had simply walked towards Luke, aimed and fired. But Tom said that, after loading the gun and snapping it shut, Dad had turned in Luke's direction, paused for half a second, then turned again and held out the gun to him. He'd offered it—if offer was the right word—to Tom.

Tom said that he couldn't tell, even after thinking

about it, if his father had only just got the idea then or if he'd had it in his mind all along, and that was why he'd wanted Tom—Tom specifically, for some reason—to be with him. He'd got the idea, perhaps, looking at them both in the yard, and he'd singled out Tom.

Jack had thought (to be charitable) that it was possible Dad had held out the gun to Tom because he'd realised suddenly he couldn't do it himself. But Tom had read Jack's thought and said it wasn't like that at all. There'd been a look in his father's face, a tone in his voice. He'd said, 'Here. You do it.' It wasn't an offer, it was another order. Then Tom said, 'Like an even bigger bastard.'

Tom couldn't do it, anyway. He'd just stood in front of his father and shaken his head. He couldn't put a finger on that gun. And maybe—though Tom didn't say this, it was one of those things Jack's imagination had to supply—Tom was never meant to. It was just a bluff, a game, to make Tom feel like a worm, to make him wish he could disappear into the ground.

Several seconds passed anyway, Tom had said, while Luke sat there, not moving, and his father had still held out the gun.

Then, according to Tom, Dad had said, 'No? Can't do it? But it needs to be done.' And then he'd turned, taken a few quick strides forward and shot Luke between the eyes. One shot was enough.

And up in the yard, in that still air, Jack had heard the shot clearly enough, like something hitting his own skull.

Tom said—it was plainly difficult for him to give these details or even to remember them precisely, and Jack would come to know how he felt—that Luke had never turned away as Dad came towards him with the gun, though at the very last moment he might have lowered his head. He just might. He couldn't be sure either if, just a fraction before he'd fired, Dad had said, 'Goodbye, Luke.' Or if it was a fraction afterwards. Or if he'd just imagined that Dad had said it. (Jack, listening to Tom, thought: Tom said it, Tom said it himself. He said it aloud or just inside, but Tom said it himself.)

But after firing the shot, Tom said, Dad had turned and even as he broke open the gun and fished out the unspent cartridge, said, clearly enough, 'And I hope one day, when it's needed, someone will have the decency to do the same for me.'

Dad had walked back to the pick-up to stow the gun. Then he'd grabbed the spades lying in the grass and held one out for Tom. Tom didn't say if he held it out in the same way as he'd held out the gun, or if he'd said anything along the lines of: 'I hope you can do *this*.' But it seemed that from that point on there hadn't been much conversation except for Dad saying, 'Deeper.' Then again, 'Deeper.'

Tom said it was a good, safe grave, it wouldn't get disturbed by some fox coming out of the wood.

Finally Dad had said, 'Deep enough.' Then he'd gone to pick up Luke, or what was left of him, and, kneeling and stretching, had lowered him in. Dad had done the shooting and Dad had done the burying. But he'd said to Tom, 'Okay, now fill it in.'

Then he'd gone to the bottom gate, into Brinkley Wood, where the little rill ran through the ditch at the edge of the trees, to clean himself up. Tom said there'd been a lot of blood and stuff left on the grass. The crows and buzzards and the weather would have to take care of that. Tom said it looked like where a ewe had dumped an afterbirth.

They'd both patted down the last soil with their spades. If there was a question of a marker—a grave-stone—it was never discussed. There'd be a little grown-over hump, anyway, in the corner of the field. They'd hardly forget the spot.

Then they'd driven back to the house with the gun and the spades, and with the air—Jack could see this as they pulled into the yard—thick between them. He didn't understand the thickness of it till Tom, and it took a little time, had given his full account.

But the air (still busy with flying ants that had escaped that kettle) was thick and heavy anyway, heavy with the sultry August weather, but heavy with the strange, hollow weight of there being three of them now where once there'd been four. Just as once there'd been four of them where once there'd been five.

18

JACK DROVE OFF the ferry into the hurrying morning streets of Portsmouth. No one had detained him or regarded him with special interest, but he whipped his sunglasses from the dashboard not just against the glare of the low sun. His instinct was to hide his face. It was absurd to think of being recognised, but in his white shirt and black tie, even inside the car, he felt painfully conspicuous. He had safely got ashore, but at any point now, he felt, as he strove to navigate the currents of purposing traffic around him, he might be stopped and asked to explain his own particular purpose. And how would he do that?

I am going to meet my brother.

As the ferry docked, the ball of fear had tightened in his stomach. He told himself, for no clear reason, that the innocent have nothing to fear.

He looked frantically for road signs—his instinct also being, on finding himself in the middle of a city, to get out of it fast. Portsmouth was not the biggest of cities, but it was more than big enough for Jack, who in all his years—save in appreciating that most of the Lookouters came from them—had rarely had to deal with cities. The word 'city' itself was foreign to him, as was the word 'citizen', though that second word, he somehow appreciated too, hung, almost like its explanation, over this journey.

When, some eight years ago, in order to take a holiday in the Caribbean, Jack had acquired a passport, he'd understood that he was now a citizen. It said so. Not so long before, the very idea of possessing a passport would have seemed ridiculous. A farm was its own land, even its own law, unto itself. And as for being a 'citizen'—citizens hardly lived on farms. Though, apparently, you didn't need to live in a city to be a citizen. Or even require a passport. A passport merely confirmed something that came with you. Even little babies—even little babies born on farms—were citizens. It was a birthright.

But it had still seemed strange to Jack to discover that he was a citizen and that in order to pass through Gatwick Airport he had to prove it. Gatwick Airport itself had seemed like some weird, forbidding city, though he hadn't felt like a citizen, shuffling through and showing his clean new passport. He'd felt more like a cow at milking time.

Yet he'd thought, very recently, how shaming it would have been if when Major Richards had said he should bring his passport he'd had to say: I don't have one.

He didn't feel like a citizen today. Though today he knew, inescapably, he was one. It felt like some imposition or even incrimination when he knew it should be the opposite: a privilege, a protection, a guarantee. The fact that he was a citizen should be dissolving that primitive ball of fear in his stomach.

If he were stopped, then he had his passport. Not only that: in his jacket pocket he had other papers (not all of which Major Richards had said he need bring with him). He had a letter from a Secretary of State, personally signed. Truly. He had a letter, and an invitation, from a Colonel of the Regiment. Who else in this flood of morning traffic around him was carrying better credentials, was better authorised to be going about their business?

It ought to be the case, Jack told himself, that rather than being stopped, he should be waved through, with saluting respect. Lanes should be cleared for him.

But he had to get out of this city.

He looked at signs: London, Southampton, Winchester. He definitely didn't want London. He briefly passed, on his left, the long, fortress-like walls of the Dockyard. Not just a city, but a navy base. And he was travelling to an airbase.

The funnel of the M275 seemed to find him rather than he it, feeding him onto the westbound M27. The whole length of the M27 skirted a mainly urban sprawl: Southampton was a city too. He needed to be free of this region of thick habitation. On the motorway he put his foot down, but after a few miles took it off again, realising that he had no need, or wish, to hurry and that he risked, indeed, being absurdly early. All the same, the proximity of large populations—all of them citizens— oppressed him. On the fringes of Southampton he joined the M3 and only when, after passing Winchester, he left the motorway and was heading north across the broad downs of Hampshire did he begin to feel calmer, though this was not for long.

Big, sunlit sweeps of land now faced him, but clouds were rapidly gathering. More to the point, this open country, with its unimpeded views of the road ahead, was only drawing him inexorably and all too rapidly closer to his destination. In preparing himself for the other immensities of this journey, he had over-allowed for its simple distance. In both miles and time his journey was already half done.

He bypassed Newbury, then at a service station just short of the M4 intersection he stopped, to empty his bladder and simply kill a little time. It was not yet ten—though the mere reflex of looking at his watch, the noting of passing minutes, made him sweat. The tightness in his stomach reasserted itself and, as if to smother and quell it, he forced himself, in the cafeteria, to consume a large, sticky Danish pastry and drink a cup of coffee.

Around him was the random sample of the nation (another word, like 'citizen', that had come in recent days to nag him) to be found in any service-station cafeteria on a weekday morning. The bland, communal atmosphere both soothed and troubled him. Jack didn't like cities, but this wasn't because he essentially minded people—or people removed from the context of cities. The caravanners had, unexpectedly, taught him that. The caravanners could comfort and beguile him—just as he saw it as his role to keep them contented.

He thought now of the travellers who might stop here in the summer on their way south from cities like Birmingham or Nottingham, bound, perhaps for the first time, for the Lookout Caravan Park. Bound for a little off-shore island that, in their minds at least, was entirely set aside for the purpose of holidays. He felt a sudden tender pang for them.

But this was November. Outside the sky was now mainly grey with a hint of rain. He no longer sensed that he might be liable to sudden arrest and interrogation, but he wondered if, in his black tie, he was being scrutinised by those around him. There would be an obvious conclusion (though it would fall some way short of the actual mark) about his purpose. Who was he? What did he do, with his big frame and big hands? Was it unseemly for a man wearing a black tie to be stuffing his face with a Danish pastry?

He thought again of the hearse and of its separate journey: Devon to Oxfordshire. There were some strange tasks in the world, some strange purposes.

But around him, in fact, was a majority of solitary, preoccupied men (though none in a black tie) doing just as he was doing: pushing something sticky into their mouths and chewing on it needily, but with no particular sign of pleasure. Were they all—though none of them, surely, could be on a journey, a mission like his today—nursing, feeding their own little balls of fear?

This was peacetime in the middle of England. But there was a war on terror.

He took out his mobile phone. It was something else these men were doing. But he merely stared at it and returned it to his pocket. The coffee or regathering fear, or simply the sensible precaution before he set off again, made him head for a second piss. In the hard white light he looked at himself, again, in the mirror. He didn't look, he thought, like he'd looked, only hours ago, at the cottage. He should have got his hair cut, perhaps, specially. It was wispy at the neck and by his ears. He was going to meet the army. He tweaked at his tie, though it was fine already and it hardly mattered while he was driving. His heavy face, gazing straight back at him, seemed not to know him.

Did he look like a citizen, a good citizen, in his white shirt and dark suit? No, he looked like a gangster.

19

WHEN DAD AND TOM had returned from disposing of
Luke, a silence hung over the farmhouse as if some
explosion had occurred much bigger than the small but
significant one Jack had heard volleying up from Barton
Field. Thick hot clouds filled the sky, but it was one of
those times when the thunder doesn't come. Jack didn't
get Tom's full account till the following morning. He felt,
after hearing it, and trying to put himself into Tom's
shoes, that though Tom had been unable to shoot Luke
(and who could blame him?) it was perfectly possible that
Tom might one day raise a gun to his own father. Such a
thing seemed perfectly possible on their forlorn, milksop
dairy farm in the deep, green hills.

Tom was big and tall enough by then, but Jack still
had the feeling, when it came to relations between his
dad and Tom, that Dad should pick on someone his own
size, and that it was up to him, Jack, to intervene accordingly. He wondered what he would have done if he'd been
down there too, a witness, in Barton Field. Would he have
snatched the gun Dad offered to Tom, and shot Luke
himself? And would that have settled the question of how

things stood at Jebb Farm for ever, of who now would rule the roost?

He wondered how it would have been if it had been just Dad and him down there, not Dad and Tom.

It was a long time—not till after Tom had left Jebb—before Jack told Ellie the full story that Tom had told him. He'd just told her at first that Dad had had to shoot Luke. It was tough, but necessary. No more Luke. Even when he'd told her the full story he'd hesitated to repeat those words which he'd remembered as clearly as Tom had seemed to remember them. 'And someone, some day . . .'

When Luke met his sudden end the cow disease and its consequences had been with them for some time. It had peaked, some said, but it still hung in the air like those sultry clouds, and perhaps it was then, on that morning when that shot rang out in Barton Field, that the madness had really set in.

Yet what had saved the immediate mood, restrained and sobered them all and perhaps prevented some further explosion, was the simple fact of Luke's death. His absence. It was only a dog's death and, when all was said, it had been a mercy, but it left a more than dog-sized gap and there was that echo—though none of them dared say it—of the death of Vera.

Trying to put himself in his father's shoes (and he was not so good at putting himself in anyone's shoes), Jack felt that the way his dad had brought about Luke's death must have had to do with the death of his wife. As if the sudden swift killing of an animal that was only getting sicker and sicker might have cured Michael of all the grief, anger and abandonment gnawing away inside him. But it hadn't worked. It hadn't worked for any of them. It just caused more sickness. On top of the cow disease.

When Tom and Dad got back from Barton Field, Luke's old basket, with the rumpled tartan blanket—still bearing Luke's scattered hairs, his smell and the dent of his body—remained in its corner in the kitchen. It remained there, untouched, for days, like a judgement on them all. Michael, who'd been able to blow Luke's brains out, seemed barely able to look at it. No one knew what to do. There was, perhaps, the shared, unspoken thought that Luke should have been buried with his blanket. It would have been the right thing to do. Or at least Luke should have been carried down in comfort to Barton Field in his basket and blanket, instead of being snatched up from them and plonked down in the pick-up like a calf for the abattoir.

But in any case, Jack had thought, Luke would have had a pretty shrewd idea. And with his blanket under him, he'd have had an even shrewder idea. Dad had done the right thing, maybe. There was no nice way of doing some things. There'd been no nice way, when they'd finally got round to it, of carrying out a culling order.

And, anyway, Luke's basket and blanket, still sitting there, were like a buffer, blurring and softening the difference between Luke's presence and his absence. A judgement and a comfort, like Vera's apron.

And it was Tom, again, who finally made the move, with a suddenness, Jack thought, that was just like his father's when he'd bundled Luke out to the pick-up. No one dared stop or challenge Tom on this occasion either.

He was still laundry chief, and, so far as it went, the housekeeper and the mum of the family. And maybe Dad had never been able to abide it.

Tom gathered up Luke's blanket, carried it out into the yard and shook it and slapped it. Then he proceeded to wash it, very thoroughly. There was an old zinc tub that suited the purpose. Hand-washing a dog blanket is quite a big and stinky job, but Tom did it very carefully. The stink was Luke's stink. Only after several washings, rinsings and wringings did he hang the blanket—as he'd hang the bed sheets—on the line in the yard, where it began to dry soon enough in the August warmth. There was no odour of Luke left, just the soapy, airy smell of something that's been well washed.

But Tom hadn't finished. When the blanket was still just-damp, he unpegged it and actually took the iron to it, a wet tea towel spread on top, to smooth out the wrinkles. Then he folded it very neatly into a small oblong and, when it was dry, carried it upstairs on the tray of his arms to the Big Bedroom. It was in the Big Bedroom that Mum had made sure that all sorts of things were kept—like that wooden cradle—though they no longer had any use. And Dad couldn't say, now, 'I don't want that, I don't want that thing up there.' And he didn't. Tom put the blanket on the top shelf of the wardrobe, with other old spare blankets, where he knew Vera would have put it.

Then he carried Luke's basket to the bonfire that regularly smouldered near the muckheap, and set light to it.

Whatever Dad thought about Tom's actions, he certainly never removed the blanket from the bedroom. He would even have had the option, on cold nights, of taking it from the wardrobe and spreading it over him. It was only a blanket, after all. In fact, Jack knows that there was one night, a cold, frosty one, when his father did do just this—the only instance that Jack was aware of. But he's never told anyone.

What would people have thought if he'd tried to point out that he'd never seen it spread on that bed before and that, really, it was a dog's blanket? If he'd come up with the whole dog story? Someone might even have thought he was only pointing it out because he'd put the blanket there himself. So he'd done the right thing at the time—which in most cases, in Jack's experience, was to shut up or say very little.

It should be there right now, Jack thinks, on that bed behind him, under that gun. It would only be appropriate. But it was among all the other stuff (from farm machinery to teaspoons) that Ellie had 'sorted out'—for auction, for sale, for ditching, for sending to charity (charity!), as part of what she called her clean sweep.

'A clean sweep, Jacko, a clean sweep is what we need.'

Well, it hadn't included that gun.

When Tom had finally let Jack in on his plan of making off from Jebb—only a few weeks before it was carried out—he'd said that it was on the day that he'd washed and ironed Luke's blanket that he'd really made up his mind. It was the army for him—if he'd have to be patient for a while yet. The army could take him in. No more

Jebb. By the time he told Jack, he'd long since found out all about it and got the forms that would take effect when he was eighteen. One day, a couple of months after Luke was shot—November and Remembrance Day were coming up—Dad had given him time off and a handful of grudging twenties (it was meant to square things between them perhaps) and told him to go to Barnstaple and get himself a suit. He couldn't turn up in his school blazer any more. But Tom had actually got the bus to Exeter, bought a suit in an Oxfam shop, kept the cash left over, and walked into a recruitment office.

So now he knew what he'd need to do.

Maybe the army likes a man who not only knows how to shoot, but who knows the value of a blanket, who takes good care of a blanket. Blankets go with the army. Whenever Jack remembered Tom ironing that blanket and folding it up so carefully and holding it, as if it might have been Luke himself, across his arms, there was something about it he could never place. But now he can. It was as if he was handling a flag.

20

IT WASN'T LIKE Gatwick Airport. It *was* like Gatwick
Airport. It was even a little like a city—approached
through its own ancillary town.

Lodged in Jack's mind for some days had been the
almost calming notion 'airfield', suggesting something
grassy and forgotten, but this place, he realised at once,
was anything but peripheral. This place in the centre of
England was a hub, and—clearly—seriously and constantly busy. It had, he soon saw, its own terminal, check-
in areas and car-rental facilities and the air had the blast
and tang about it of ceaselessly refuelled, long-range
activity. So that, though he'd never been anywhere like it
before, he was reminded of nothing so much as that first
passage, with Ellie, through Gatwick Airport.

He felt, all over again, as if he might be about to enter
for the first time that ominous opening called 'Departures'
and then (after much nerve-wracking queuing and waiting) find himself strapped in the long, imprisoning tube
of an aircraft, about to be hurled into the sky. Ellie had
gripped his hand with sheer, brimming excitement—it
was a bit like when she'd first yanked him up the stairs

at Westcott Farmhouse—but he'd gripped hers, though trying not to show it, like some great big boy holding on to his mum. He'd been suddenly, acutely aware of the immense desirability of taking a holiday in a caravan.

But the big, obvious difference about this place was that none of its manifest and elaborate purposefulness had to do with the taking of holidays.

He found the Main Gate, then found Control of Entry— this was where he had to show his passport and other documents. He was spoken to at this point, so he thought, with a marked deference and ushered on as if he might have been a VIP. At the same time he had the feeling that his own reason for being here was just one, unusual reason in a general ungentle pressing of reasons. The place hadn't shut down because of why he was here.

Temporary arrowed signs indicated 'Ceremony of Repatriation'. Among other things he'd been sent by Major Richards was a 'Visitor Pack', with a map, directions and a check list. There was also an 'Order of Ceremony' and a 'Provisional List of Those in Attendance'. It had all amounted to too much to carry on his person, and he'd shoved the bulk of it in the side pocket of his holdall, thinking even then that it was not unlike the wad of stuff you take with you, along with your passport, through Departures. But, of course, his business now was the seemingly much simpler (and usually paperwork-free) business for which, in fact, Jack had never entered an air terminal before: the business of Arrivals.

I'm here to meet my brother.

The sudden proximity of it, the realisation that he

would have to do this incontestably personal thing, but in these heartlessly impersonal surroundings, hit him like some actual collision—even as he drove at a careful five miles an hour, peering hard through the windscreen for further signs.

He found what seemed to be the appropriate car park. Despite his fear of being early, it was now nearly a quarter past eleven. The final miles of the journey had been along the slowest roads and he'd cut it, in the end (though he wasn't entirely sorry), a little fine. The car park was almost full and he had to search for a space. People—some in remarkable costumes—were converging from it towards an ordinary glass-doored entrance nearby, but as if they might be approaching a cathedral. This clearly wasn't some small event. But of course it wasn't.

After switching off the engine he lingered in the safety of the car, as though some desperate, final choice still remained open to him. Then he took several deep, involuntary, labouring breaths and with each one said aloud, hoarsely, 'Tom.' Then—he wasn't sure if he said it aloud too, in a different tone, or simply thought the word: 'Ellie. Ellie.'

He eyed himself in the driving mirror, smoothed his hair, fingered his tie for the hundredth time. At Control of Entry he had already put on his jacket. Such documents as he thought he might still need were in its inside pockets. Official invitation. Order of Ceremony. Passport (you never knew). The letter from Babbages. In another pocket was his silenced mobile phone. But he was hardly going to activate it now.

From his shirt pocket he took the medal, warm to his touch, and slipped it into the empty breast pocket of his jacket. He could not have said why. So it would be closer to Tom. Then he got out of the car and locked it.

From then on Jack was like a puppet, a lost man, somehow steering himself or letting himself be steered through what lay before him. He might have used, if it had been one of his words, the word 'autopilot'. He might have had the same sense of not being himself if he had been called to Buckingham Palace to be knighted by the Queen.

Beyond the glass doors (a sign said 'Ceremony Reception') he was met—and ticked off a list—with an intenser version of the courtesy he'd received at Control of Entry, but with also, he couldn't help but detect, a faint, disguised relief.

I am Jack Luxton.

There was now ahead of him, through another wide doorway, a throng—he was somehow sucked into it—that included a great many uniforms, some of them of an astonishingly resplendent and seemingly high-ranking nature. His plain suit felt instantly shabby. There were swords, sashes, gold braid—medals—epaulettes. It was fancy dress. Some of the uniforms were so besmothered and encrusted that Jack wondered if they didn't mark the point where they mysteriously merged with the regalia of dukes and earls. And he'd previously noted, from the List of Those in Attendance, that he would indeed be in the presence of one viscount (whatever a viscount was) and more than one lord. It hadn't given him any sense of privilege. It had scared him.

Among the uniforms were a number of women in

what seemed to Jack extravagant forms of dress and hat, as if this might be a wedding, and wearing also, in some cases, a kind of smile that wasn't a smile at all and reminded him of zip fasteners. There were also at least two men wearing uniform but with long white lacy surplices on top.

Among it all too, though somehow distinct from it, were two clusters of civilians (that word, like 'citizen', now also forced itself upon him) who seemed to Jack not so unlike himself, either in their clothing or in their air of dazed incomprehension. He instantly knew who they were and instinctively felt it would be good, though also difficult, to be close to them. The two clusters were quite large, both consisting of more than one generation, from grandparents down to small children. In one case there was a child so small that it needed to be carried in its mother's arms. The mother looked not only weighed down, but as if she were standing on ground that had given way. All the children looked as if they were there by mistake.

This was all suddenly quite terrible: these people, these floundering women (he vaguely grasped that the ones with the hats and smiles must be there to provide some token balance), these children, among all these uniforms. The two clusters seemed both to cling to them-selves and to cling, separate as they were, to each other, and Jack realised that he was a third cluster. He was *the* third cluster, a cluster of one. He felt both a solidarity and a dreadful, shaming isolation, that his cluster was just him.

But at the same time he'd glimpsed something else distinct from the gathering—standing at a distance from it, yet overshadowing it, overshadowing even these important human clusters. On the far side of the large room was a wall of mainly glass, such as you might find near a boarding gate in any airport building. And through the glass, beyond the jostle of heads and hats, could be seen, out on the tarmac, a single large plane. Around it was none of the usual clutter of baggage carts and service vehicles that surrounds a parked plane at an airport, and it was stationed with its nose pointing outwards so that, even from where he was, Jack could see the dark opening into its belly, beneath the tail, and the ramp leading down.

When he'd first had to picture this event, Jack had vaguely supposed that everyone might watch the plane fly in, then unload. But of course it wouldn't necessarily be like that. The plane had been there perhaps for some time, while preparations were made. It had landed in darkness, possibly. It had slipped over the English coast, perhaps, even as he'd slipped down Beacon Hill.

Jack had known it would be there. But seeing it like this was nonetheless a shock. It was a big plane, for three coffins. It stood there, seemingly unattended, under a dappled, grey-and-white, autumnal sky in Oxfordshire. It must have stood not so long ago on a tarmac in Iraq.

Major Richards was suddenly and mercifully at his side—barely recognised at first, since, though Jack had only ever seen him in uniform, he too now wore a sword and a sash, as if he might recently have undergone (though he hadn't) some promotion. Even as this contact was made—an actual, quick touch on his elbow—Jack realised that Major Richards must have been keeping an eye out for him, not just to make sure he was there, but, as it now seemed, to compensate, so far as was possible, for Jack's being just a cluster of one. He and Major Richards, if only temporarily and for the purposes of negotiating this gathering, would form a cluster of two.

Major Richards already knew that Jack was the last of the Luxtons, the only one left. There was a whole story there perhaps, he'd thought, though it was not his business to enquire. But then, only yesterday, Jack had got in touch by phone to explain that, 'as things had turned out', he'd be coming alone. There was a whole story there too, no doubt, but Major Richards felt it would be even less appropriate to pursue the point. His own wife wasn't here either (though why should she be? She wouldn't want to be). He was only a major, after all.

Major Richards said, 'Journey okay?' As if they might have just met for some sports fixture or were about to compare notes on the traffic on the A34. But Jack didn't mind this at all.

'Yes.'

'Good. Good.'

After this, Jack was not always sure what Major Richards was saying or what he was saying himself (now and then he opened his mouth and words came out), but he understood that Major Richards was doing his duty, a special kind of duty. He was leading him around, introducing him briefly to people, leading him on again so that no single encounter became too much. He was being a cluster with him and getting him through this thing. And

Jack realised that he, too, in spite of himself, was somehow stumblingly doing his duty, which was to be, unavoidably, introduced to people in extraordinary get-ups with extraordinary voices and have his hand shaken as if he himself had done something extraordinary, and have things said to him and over him (while he said, 'Yes,' or, 'Yes, I am,' or, 'Yes, it is') which were no doubt meant to make him feel good.

And Major Richards was definitely being a special cluster with him, because those other clusters surely deserved Major Richards's attention just as much as, if not more than, he did, though perhaps they didn't necessarily want it and anyway they had each other. The point soon came, however, when Major Richards piloted Jack towards them. It was what Jack both wanted and dreaded, since what could he possibly say to these poor stricken people which could be of any use to them? Their grief was multiple, if also shared, and they'd see before them just this big, roughish man. Perhaps they'd think: Poor him, all on his own. But what they would also see, Jack felt certain, since it would surely and damningly be glaring out of him, was that he was here to meet his brother, because he had to, though he hadn't seen his brother for almost thirteen years, hadn't even written to him for twelve, hadn't known where he was, and had even tried not to think about him most of the time.

Despite this feeling of being a blatant culprit, Jack had nonetheless wanted to open up his big arms and embrace as many of these people as he could, as if he might have been some returned, lost member of their family. In his head he'd wanted to say, 'It's okay. I'm just me. It's you lot I feel for.' But what he actually said, over and over again, while shaking more hands and wondering what was showing in his gormless block of a face, was: 'I'm Jack Luxton. Tom Luxton's brother. I'm sorry, I'm very sorry. I'm Jack Luxton. I'm very sorry.'

Then the hum of voices all around suddenly subsided and it became clear that they were now to proceed outside for the ceremony. For this, with the exception of a few uniformed ushers, the parties of relatives were given precedence and it seemed natural to Jack that he should find himself bringing up the rear. Just as it seemed natural—and reassuring—that outside, in the designated area, he should find himself standing at the edge and at the back of the civilian group. People would have to turn round if they wanted to see him.

He also became separated at this point from Major Richards. But not before Major Richards had said to him, confidentially, 'Afterwards there'll be ... more.' Then paused and looked carefully at Jack and said, 'But I'd just slip away, if I were you.' Jack wasn't sure what Major Richards meant by 'more', or if Major Richards knew himself, but he felt that these words were perhaps more than Major Richards might have been required to say or even ought to have said (was he under military orders to say only certain things?). But he also felt he might have opened his arms to embrace Major Richards, too. He wondered if Tom, in his last days, in Iraq, had had such a commanding officer.

What followed seemed, at the time and later in Jack's memory, to go on for an unendurable length, but also not to be nearly long enough, as if this procedure of under an hour was all there might ever be to stand for the whole life of his brother. Inside the building, despite the uniforms, the mood had been unregulated. Outside, everything ceded to military discipline. The air was cool but not cold, a little breezy, the sky overcast with only the weakest suggestion now and then of a break in the clouds. The tarmac was damp and puddled. Earlier in the morning, unlike in the Isle of Wight, there'd been rain. Perhaps it was raining now at the Lookout.

There was that reek of fuel and the sense, after that crowded room, of being on the edge of something huge and remorseless. As if, though this was Oxfordshire, war was being waged only just over the skyline. At ground level, the plane now looked vast, and, with its cavernous rear opening directed at the onlookers (though in the dull light and with the elevation of the fuselage you couldn't quite see inside), it seemed to Jack that it might be there not to unload, but to gather everyone up. The climax of this event might be when they were all—the generals and earls, or whoever they were, the ladies in hats, the white-frocked padres and the black-clad mourning families—scooped up into the big, dark hold and taken off to Iraq.

The high-rank uniforms and their entourage had formed up separately from the relatives' group, by a low platform which Jack guessed would be for saluting. Some of the officers detached themselves for particular duties. Jack lost sight of Major Richards. To the left of the relatives' party, at a little distance, three hearses (this was both a relief to see and utterly distressing) were drawn up in a row facing away from the tarmac, their rear hatches raised in a manner that imitated the solitary aircraft.

His hearse—Tom's hearse—was there. Tom's trans-port was waiting. That 'side of things', Major Richards had already whispered to him, was in place, there was nothing Jack needed to do. All the same, actually to see the hearses was heart-stopping, and Jack felt he should at some point at least make contact with the driver. He should slip him a twenty. Would twenty be enough?

On one of his earlier phone calls, Major Richards had delicately explained that normally on these occasions there would be no flowers. These occasions weren't funerals in themselves and the army didn't deal in flowers. But Jack could see now, placed in readiness beside two of the hearses, a small, defiant offering—a cluster's worth—of flowers. He felt a moment's abject misery and humiliation (and sympathy for his upstaged hearse driver). He'd have had to peer very hard indeed to see the single wreath he'd ordered (though he'd specified large) to await the coffin's eventual arrival in Marleston.

The padres in their fluttering surplices had walked out to the plane. Everyone was straining to see inside it. Though everyone knew. There was now a general barking of orders. Three detachments of six bare-headed soldiers marched out towards the plane, each led by a bare-headed officer. Other officers, with caps on, stood to attention near the ramp leading into the plane and now and then performed strange gestures with their swords. Positioned on the tarmac, in red tunics and white-and-gold helmets, was a small-scale version of a military band.

The first party of bearers moved into the plane. Then a bugle blew as the first coffin, completely wrapped in a

Union Jack, was carried off. Jack felt there was a sort of silent gasp, an invisible but detectable flinching among the relatives' group. He'd been told, and it was in the Order of Ceremony, that Tom's coffin would be the last. He didn't know why, and hadn't asked, and didn't know if it was in any way significant or even constituted an honour, but he felt, now, that the two preceding coffins would prepare him.

The other two soldiers were called Pickering and Fuller. Before this event and throughout its duration it never quite got home to Jack that these men, having been privates, would have been in his brother's charge. He had among the relatives a technical, proxy seniority. But he felt like the lowest of the low.

The bearers stood for a moment at the foot of the ramp, close to the padres, while the officer for the bearer party took his place behind the coffin. Then a single muffled bass drum began to beat the rhythm of the slow march, followed by a muted growling of brass instruments, and the coffin was carried along a carefully planned route so that it passed in front of the heavyweight uniforms on the platform—all standing at a salute—then in front of the civilian party, before delivery to its hearse.

When the drum began, Jack felt it was being struck inside his chest, and though he was required to do nothing more than stand and look, he couldn't prevent his arms going stiff at his sides, the thumbs pointing downwards, he couldn't prevent himself lifting his chin and pulling back his shoulders and coming to an instinctive, irresistible attention. This he did for all three coffins. And the fact was they were all the same. They were, all three, just Union-Jacked boxes borne on six shoulders and looked interchangeable. This was both bewildering and unexpectedly consoling. Each coffin received an equal and undiscriminating fullness of attention, as if there might have been a bit of each man in each box.

But Tom's coffin, Jack realised, had a genuine distinction in being last. There was nothing else now, in reserve, on which the onlookers might unload and exhaust their emotion. It was the final chance for everyone to focus their feelings. It was also, specifically, why Jack was here.

The bugle sounded again, for Tom's coffin. It was a recognisable bugle call, though Jack couldn't think of its name: Reveille. When it sounded, some second person inside him, it seemed, gave a little inner cry. He hoped that none of the group in front would now turn and give him, however well intended, sympathetic looks. None did. They were looking at Tom. They were thinking of Tom for him.

The drum was pounded again. In the minutes that followed, almost every remembered moment he'd spent with Tom seemed to flow through him in a way he couldn't have predicted, willed or even wished. Yet he was also aware of all the time they'd not spent together. He thought of the letters he'd written to Tom, with great difficulty, and the letters he'd never written. And the letters he'd never got back. He thought of the things that had and hadn't passed between them and that, perhaps, didn't matter now. The things that Tom had never known and the things that he, Jack, had never known. He had gone into caravans. Tom had gone into battle.

He thought of the last time he'd stood like this— though it wasn't like this at all—at his own father's funeral, when Tom wasn't there. The whole village saw that Tom wasn't there. But Tom, everyone knew by then, was in the army. He thought of how he would have to stand there again, very soon—he would have to go through it all again. He thought of those Remembrance Days. Marleston churchyard. The grey and yellow lichen on the memorial, the rasp of leaves. He thought of how if he was required, following this ceremony, to make a speech, he would say how Tom, his little brother Tom, had always wanted to be a soldier, ever since he'd learnt about his two great-uncles who'd died in the First World War and how one of them had won the DCM. Or some such crap. He'd say it. Though thank God that he didn't have to make a speech. How could he, Jack, ever make a speech? How could *anyone* ever make a speech? But he'd brought that medal with him. He couldn't say why. He could hold it up, for effect, in his speech. He touched it now in his breast pocket.

He thought of the bar in the Crown. Jimmy Merrick in a suit. He thought, or tried to think, as he'd tried to think many times before now, of Tom's last moments, but he couldn't think of them, couldn't imagine them, his mind flicked away. He thought, as the coffin passed directly in front of him and he wanted to touch it, to be one of the six bare-headed soldiers or somehow all of them: what would his mum think—his and Tom's mum—to see both of them now?

When all three coffins had been transferred to their hearses a tense silence remained. This was, Jack understood, a pre-arranged part of the proceedings (it was like those Remembrance Days), but it was also like a natural, inevitable response. How could this thing simply end? After delivering the coffins, the parties of bearers had formed up, each in two ranks with their officers before them, beyond the hearses, at an angle to them, like some third, flanking group of onlookers. Then a separate detachment of soldiers, with rifles, had formed up in front of the hearses.

By now Jack had noticed that the three drivers of the hearses were not (of course) alone, each had—what would you call them?—a co-driver. It was a mark of respect and standard practice. No man should be asked to drive a corpse across the country alone. Alone, as it were. But Jack had imagined Tom's hearse having a solitary driver because he'd imagined that driver being himself. Each pair of drivers stood now, erect and still, by the rear of each hearse. Had they been instructed to do this? Was it regular undertaker's training?

Major Richards had explained that there would be rifle shots—it was a tradition of the regiment and had been done in the Peninsula (an old foreign war). But, even with their preparatory commands and drill, the shots came like jolts. The relatives again seemed to buckle, as if they were being fired at themselves. The noise of the shots rattled round the sky—even this big wide sky—as if it couldn't find a way out, the echo of the last shots still trying to flee as the next were fired.

Then it was over. The whole thing was, as it were, stood at ease and dismissed. The army had discharged its obligations and returned these three soldiers to their civilian claimants. Repatriation was complete.

Even now, for a moment, the civilian group seemed not to want to move. Then it began an impetuous, almost mutinous surge towards the hearses. Having seen, till this point, only the backs of heads, Jack noticed now several tear-stained, choked and ravaged faces. He saw handker-chiefs. He also noticed several cameras being fumblingly produced and held up. He thought of Major Richards's words. If I were you. But he felt like scum for even imagining he might now simply peel away. He was caught in the general drift. And there were the hearse drivers to acknowledge.

But none of those things, Jack knew, was what impelled him. He wanted to be near the coffin, as near as he could get. He wanted to touch it. The previously solemn and restrained gathering of relatives was now milling round the three hearses like visitors let into some show. The drivers stood back like mere attendants. So too did all the military personnel. It seemed that this was one part of the programme that had not been rigorously planned. The cameras flashed and clicked. The names—names and nicknames—of the other two soldiers were suddenly being called, like strange animal cries. Jack felt he could not open his mouth now to say the word 'Tom'—he had done the right thing, perhaps, to say it in the car in the car park—but he was saying it inside. He felt like scum, nonetheless, because all the attention was on the other two hearses, all the name-calling was directed at them. Because they had those tributes of flowers. Because his drivers, the pair of them, must surely be ashamed to be driving his hearse, to have got this job of the three.

He was Jack Luxton, Corporal Luxton's brother—people knew by now—and he stuck out plainly with his height and his size, but he would surely go down in people's memories, Jack thought later, as the mysterious man who simply came and went all by himself, the mysterious man who'd stood at the back, but had gone up afterwards to the hearse where his brother's coffin lay, to the open rear door, and simply bent and touched the coffin—no, held it, clung to it, for several long, gluing seconds, gripped the two wooden corners nearest to him with his big thick hands as if he might never let go.

Many of those around him saw him do this. Just stand there like that, attached to the coffin. Then when they looked for him again a little later—he'd disappeared.

The two drivers, realising who he must be, had simply stepped aside. The flag had been removed. There was just the bare wood, with a brass plate (and no garlands). This was different from the other two coffins—and everyone would notice and remember this too—and was all, in fact, according to Jack's instructions. Major Richards had explained on the phone that, in this exceptional instance (since the hearses weren't provided by the army), the flags would be either retained or, according to the bereaved's wishes, removed and folded by the bearers and presented to the mourning parties. Major Richards hadn't pushed it either way, but Jack had felt again that it was as if he'd been told he was free to step down, though the done thing was not to move.

But Jack had said—it had just come out, it was one of his occasional, forceful blurtings—that he didn't want the flag. If it was his say-so, then he was saying so. He didn't want it left on the coffin, and he didn't want it himself. He said—and this had just come out too—that he wanted it given to the 'battalion'. He'd used Major Richards's word. He wanted the battalion to have it.

And what would he have done with it? Where would he have put it? They didn't have a flagpole, he thought once again. But, anyway, he didn't want the present of any flag. Major Richards, down the phone, had been silent for a while, then had said (with a detectable but awkward sigh of relief), 'That's—a fine gesture, Mr Luxton. But, if you should change your mind . . .'

He wrenched his hands from the coffin, from its bare wood, then turned to the two drivers. He was surprised by the sudden outward authority and decisiveness he seemed now to have acquired. Had it come from the coffin? He shook the drivers' hands. He said, 'I am Tom Luxton's brother, Jack Luxton. I am very grateful.' It seemed oddly like the reverse of the hand-shaking he'd done a little while ago inside the building. It seemed as if he were some senior, elevated dignitary acknowledging these two black-clad drivers in their great loss. He felt a sudden pity, but also an admiration, even a strange envy for these men who would have to drive his brother's body, sitting with it behind them, for some hundred and fifty miles. He had a sudden sense too of having imposed on them outrageously and of having ducked out of what should have been his own task. Had it been possible— had the coffin fitted—he might have offered to lower the back seats in the Cherokee and take over their job.

But they'd looked at him as if they might have saluted. They said, 'Sir,' and 'Mr Luxton.' He wanted to gather these men, too, into his arms. But, instead, he took his wallet from his back pocket, opened it and felt the edges of the notes inside. He didn't care if this were the right thing or not. And he didn't care that it would be forty now, for the two of them, not twenty. When would this ever happen again? He'd had no idea what his incidental expenses might be for this extraordinary journey, but he'd drawn out a good wad of cash just in case. It was only money that would have been spent in St Lucia.

He handed them each a twenty. They might have made some small, token gesture of protest, but they said, 'Thank you, sir . . . Thank you, sir,' as if he'd pinned a medal on each of them. And he had a medal too.

'Will I—see you tomorrow?' he said.

'All Saints', Marleston. Ten-thirty,' one of them quickly said. 'We'll be two of the bearers.'

He would be a bearer himself, he knew this, along with five undertaker's men (Babbages had arranged it)—not having anyone else he could easily ask or choose. Well, Jack thought now, three of the party had been shown how the thing could be done. Should he make that joke? Would they all expect another twenty tomorrow? That would be a hundred all round, on top of this forty.

'It will be an honour, Mr Luxton,' one of them said. It was what they always said, perhaps, what undertakers were trained to say, but it occurred suddenly to Jack that these men might actually have volunteered for this job. They'd never done anything like it before. Nor had Jack. It seemed that both of them were a little awed by what they'd witnessed. It couldn't surely be that they were in awe of him, Jack, for being the brother of a man who'd died in the service of his country. Couldn't they see he felt like scum?

'I'm Dave,' one of them said. 'Derek,' the other said.

One was thinnish and sandy-haired, one thick-set and

dark. There was no way they could have been taken for brothers. He shook their hands again. They seemed to want it.

'I'm Jack, I'm Jack.' They already knew this, he'd already said it, but he said it again. 'Call me Jack. I'll see you tomorrow, then.'

Then he simply turned away. Walked—sloped, slunk away. He could do nothing else, was good for nothing else. He'd kept in mind where the car was and had spotted already how he could get to it without having to go through any door. He could cut across a stretch of grass, then slip behind the corner of the building from which they'd all recently emerged.

He simply turned and walked away. He didn't care if everyone was watching him. Didn't mind the feeling of needles in his back, the feeling of being a deserter. Didn't mind if there were all sorts of other things he still should have done or was expected to do. He simply walked away.

As Tom once had simply fucking walked away.

He reached the car, ripped off his jacket, flung it, with the medal still in the top pocket, on the back seat, and started the engine. He knew he'd already passed from people's sight after rounding the building. He was back in the inconspicuous, unceremonial world of car parks. He reversed out and drove off along the route by which (it seemed now long ago) he'd driven in. Had barriers come down to prevent his departure, he would have put his foot down and burst through. But he passed Control of Entry without incident (was Exit also controlled?) and reached the main gate, after which he could accelerate and just drive. He drove through the camp-like town with a distinct sense, now, of being an escaper—word would surely be put out about him—then sped into open country. He knew he had to find the M4, then just point west.

He couldn't have given any coherent reason for his fugitive haste, which didn't diminish even when he was free of the town, but a strange, hounding explanation came to him even as he drove. It was the hearse. He had to get away from the hearse. It would be making this same journey too—M4, M5—and though, by definition, a hearse was a slow vehicle, he was afraid of its coming up behind him, of seeing it in his mirror, bearing down on him. This was all crazy and unlikely. It wouldn't even have left yet, and it would surely have to travel, at least at first—and no doubt in company with the others—at a solemn snail's pace. But the thought of its somehow gaining on him, of encountering it at any point on the journey now before him, afflicted him like a nightmare.

Only moments ago he'd actually wanted to be *in* the hearse. That was his rightful place. Having held that coffin and having wanted not to let go, how could he be afraid now of being followed by his own brother? But that was the point. He'd separated himself from his brother (and what was new about that?). He had to be in this damn Cherokee. Therefore he had to avoid the hearse and its pursuing indignation. To put distance in between.

But he'd hardly gone five miles, and he couldn't have said where it was—it was somewhere in the unknown heart of England—before he'd had to pull over into a lay-by while a series of great, wracking shudders made him, stopped as he was, hang on to the steering wheel as if he might wrench it off.

21

But it wouldn't have worked anyway, would it? If
he'd had to get up and make a speech and had said that
Tom had always been stirred by those two Luxton boys of
long ago. Because that would have been like saying that
Tom had really wanted to go off and get himself killed as
well. As he had done. And what kind of war, exactly, had
Tom been going off to fight when he'd slipped out of
Jebb Farm thirteen years ago? What kind of war, exactly,
had he even been fighting now?

At least those two Luxton lads had known the score.
Maybe.

It wouldn't have worked because it wasn't true. But it
wouldn't have worked, anyway, because Jack Luxton
could never have got up to make a speech—before lords,
ladies and colonels—even to save his own damn life.

He looks now through the rain-spattered cottage window
and remembers pulling up in the car, among strange,
bare fields, just to shake and weep. Tom was the traitor,
my lords and ladies, Tom was the deserter, the runaway.

Running away from the war against cow disease and agricultural ruin. And against his own embattled father.

Good luck, Tom.

One morning, at milking (by then they had a sort of herd again and they could sell the milk), Tom had told him the whole story. About his trip to Exeter to buy a suit, more than a year before. About how he had it all planned now, for his eighteenth birthday. His own man. December 16th. Bugger Christmas. And bugger birthdays, if it came to it. What kind of birthday did anyone get, these days, at Jebb Farm?

The cows had twitched and steamed in the stalls. It would have been this time of year—November, not so long after Remembrance Day, when Tom would have worn that suit, only the second time for the purpose.

'This is just for your ears, Jack.'

'And the cows',' Jack might have said if he'd had the quickness of mind.

Though Jack had needed to think quickly, and seriously, enough that morning. And one of his first thoughts was that Tom hadn't had to say a thing. Tom might have just cleared off, according to his plan, leaving him, Jack, as surprised and left in the lurch as their father was going to be. But Tom was telling him now, so Jack had thought, because Tom was a brother. He'd been saving it up and it had been a matter, perhaps, of careful timing, but Jack didn't want to go into that. Tom was telling him now.

And that meant that Tom was really putting before him a whole set of alternative positions. Like the position

179

of saying: You can't do this, Tom, you can't bloody do it. Or the position of simply ratting on him to his father. Or the position of thinking why hadn't he, Jack, done something like this years ago and left Tom to Michael's mercy? Or the future position (the not-so-distant future, it now seemed) of being left, himself, to Michael's mercy and having to pretend he'd never known a damn thing about it.

But none of these theoretical positions had really exercised Jack much at the time, because of the overriding position Tom was putting him in, which was the position of trust. Tom hadn't had to say a word. But what are brothers for?

The steady hiss and clank of the machinery, the familiar parade of swollen udders and the splat of cow shit had seemed, for Jack, to say that though Tom had just announced, in effect, a division, a parting in their lives, nothing was altered, everything would stay the same. Or the same as the cow disease and the price of calves had left it. Or the same for him at least, Jack. Since he wasn't going anywhere.

His own man.

He'd said, not stopping in his work, 'I understand, Tom. I understand what you're telling me.' In the middle of milking you can't pause, sit back and say, 'Let's talk this over properly.' Maybe Tom had reckoned on that.

They'd both had to raise their voices through the sound of the machinery. That noisy old machinery. It was like speaking in whispers while shouting. Then after some moments, when the last udders were being relieved of their burdens, he'd said, 'Okay, Tom. You can rely on me. Your secret's safe with me.'

'And with the cows,' he might have said, if he'd had the wit for it.

Jack could never have got up to make a speech if he'd tried. But Jack had thought he could never write the letters he'd had to write, more or less a year later, to Tom, not even knowing then where they would find him (or, now, if they'd reached him at all). About the death of Michael Luxton. Which had required an inquest. How did you write to your brother about such a thing? But not only that. About the fact that Michael had made a will, as farmers do, and in his will, according to its latest revision, he'd left everything (such as it now was) to his first-born. No mention of his second.

'All yours, Jack.'

Tom had never actually said those words. Or said, in some other form, that it was the deal between them—if he was to go and Jack was to stay. But Tom had never written back to him, or shown up for the funeral, for whatever reasons, perhaps simply practical or perhaps—uncompassionate. There'd been two letters to write to Tom. One about the death and the inquest. One to tell him the verdict (though was there any doubt?) and to tell him, consequently, the details of the funeral. And of the will.

Babbages, Barnstaple. November, 1994. The month, so it seemed, of funerals. And Ellie had been there—had helped him, steered him through it all, been at his side then. But no Tom, for whatever reason, perhaps merely military. And no word from him. And hadn't that settled the matter? Wasn't that even Tom's way of saying it again—what he'd never actually said in the first place? All yours, Jack—and you're welcome to it.

And Ellie had said, said it more than once: 'Forget him.'

Tom was the deserter, the traitor? But if so, Jack was a traitor too, for covering for him. Or Jack was doubly loyal. To Tom, for not betraying him, and to Dad, or to the farm, for staying put himself.

One late December afternoon—it was the eve of Tom's eighteenth birthday—Tom and Jack had spoken to each other, knowing that this was the moment for their saying goodbye. Tom was to slip out at three the next morning (Michael could sometimes stir at four, even in December) and Jack was to pretend that he'd been sleeping, as he usually did till his dad's stirrings roused him, like a log.

They were once again in the milking parlour, making sure they were out of their father's earshot. Jack at this point had asked Tom to write to him and let him know where he was. Tom had said of course he would. And so he had, using the non-interceptible method of sending the letter to Jack care of the tiny and soon to be closed sub-post office in Polstowe (where their mother had once been a girl), and letting him know the postal particulars by which he, Jack, could write to him in future. But that was all Jack ever heard from Tom after he left.

Tom said he would just take the clothes he'd be in—several layers, for the cold—and a backpack with extra stuff. It would soon be the army's job to clothe, feed and house him. He'd hoof it through the night, then get the first bus to Exeter. He'd already, by the time they'd spoken, hidden a pack of sandwiches and a thermos inside the Big Barn at the far side of the yard. It was like the usual rations he might have taken with him to do some job on the far side of the farm. He'd breakfast on the march.

Jack had said that thing about writing, and had remembered that first card to Ellie (seeing again the little fold-down table), but there was another written message that had gone with that moment in the parlour. It was almost Tom's eighteenth birthday. It was true what Tom had said: no one bothered about birthdays these days at Jebb, they hadn't since Vera had died. But Jack had found a moment, all the same, to go into the Warburtons' store at Leke Hill Cross. Would they have any cards, even one for eighteen? Yes, they had. Inside the card it said: 'You're Eighteen! Now the World is Yours!'

Jack had desperately hoped when he'd entered the store that neither Sally nor Ken Warburton would be behind the till, so there'd have to be some conversation about Tom being eighteen now. Though he was prepared to pretend to either of them—since he was prepared to pretend to his father. But he was in luck. The shop and the whole forecourt, it seemed, was being minded by a girl who looked hardly out of school, though Jack vaguely knew her name was Hazel and she must be Tom's age, give or take, and, while he glanced at her black-sweatered breasts (and she looked at him as if he were an old man), wondered if Tom had been there.

Jack had added some words of his own to the card and given it, sealed in its envelope, to Tom that afternoon and said, 'Happy birthday.' Tom had looked at Jack and after a short, questioning pause had said he wouldn't open it yet, since it wasn't yet the day, was it? He'd open it in the morning. And Jack had said, 'Okay.'

Then Tom had said, 'Well, I suppose this is when . . .'

And Jack had said, 'I know.' Then he'd said, 'Good luck, Tom. I'll be thinking of you.' Which was a foolish thing perhaps to have said, because it was exactly what he'd written in the card.

And it was a foolish thing perhaps to have given Tom that card at all. Since it turned out, the next morning, that Dad had actually got Tom a card too. It went against all recent custom but, as Dad himself put it, 'It *was* his bloody eighteenth.' But by this time it was apparent, anyway, that Tom had disappeared. So Michael had been able to make a big demonstration of the card he'd specially bought for Tom: by ripping it up in front of Jack. What's more, it was the *same* card, the same card with a gold, embossed '18' on it and the same message inside, that Jack had bought, and that Dad, too, must have dropped into the store at Leke Hill Cross to buy. Had that girl noticed?

Jack, of course, hadn't said and couldn't say anything about his own card. But this had only meant that his father was able to round on him and demand: and where was *his* card then? If he'd known nothing about all this, where the hell was the card that Jack had got for Tom? And Jack could only answer that, well, he'd forgotten it was Tom's birthday.

*

Tom, holding the unopened envelope in the milking parlour, had said, 'I'll be okay. I'll be thinking of you too.' And he'd looked at Jack with a look, Jack thought, that wasn't just a brother's look but perhaps a sort of son-and-father look too. Then he'd said, 'Thanks, Jack. Thanks for everything. I won't forget you.' And Jack had never ceased to wonder about that remark.

Then they'd hugged. Jack couldn't remember who'd put their arms out first and perhaps it didn't matter. The last time they'd hugged each other was when Vera had just died.

'Three o'clock,' Tom had said.

'Three o'clock,' Jack had said.

Jack hadn't had to repeat it, like some pre-agreed appointment, but he knew why he was doing so, though he didn't actually say the words: 'I'll be awake, Tom.'

And so he was. He'd stayed awake pretty well all through the night—which was rare for him—just to be sure. He was awake at three o'clock to hear Tom's stealthy departing movements, while he himself remained motionless and as if asleep.

He heard Tom creep along the passage and down the stairs. Tom would know, even in the dark, where to put his feet, which steps would creak and which wouldn't. Those steps were part of him. Jack heard the sounds in the kitchen and then the sounds—this was tricky for Tom because the hinges were far from noiseless—of the door into the yard being opened and closed again. It was all done as quickly and as quietly as possible. If Tom had been a soldier, specially trained for such a night-time opera-tion, you could say he'd done it well.

Jack thought he heard a few faint scuffs of footsteps as Tom crossed the yard and again as he slipped in and out of the barn. But it wasn't a case of hearing, so much as of imagining and seeing in his head. It wasn't difficult to do. For Jack in his head, as for Tom on his feet, the walk up the track would be like going to get the school bus when it was still dark in winter. How many times had both of them done that—always separately, because of those years between them? In the dark, but knowing every step and, because you knew every step, not using a torch, though you had one with you. The small bravery of not using it, not needing or using any light—till the blazing headlights of the school bus, rounding the bend, caught you, like the eyes of some snorting monster, and you'd be gathered up.

Tom would be thinking perhaps of all that now. Jack couldn't hear or see Tom's footsteps, but he could picture them, count them, every one, as if they were his own. He could see as if he were holding, even if it wasn't needed, a torch for Tom, every thick, ropey rut, hard with frost, and the splays of ice in between. The high, hedged banks on either side, stars peeping through the thorns. The bend where, on the way down, you'd catch your first glimpse of the farmhouse, just its roof and chimney. Or where, on the way up, you'd pause to look back. Would Tom look back? But everything would be in darkness. Or if a moon was up, there'd be the glimmer, maybe, of the roof slates under which he, Jack, was lying.

One hundred, two hundred paces. Three hundred ascending, lung-rasping paces—to freedom. If that's what it was. Was the army freedom? Tom must think it was. It wasn't Jebb Farm. Three hundred paces, his heart thumping, breath smoking. Then the gate.

Good luck, Tom. He'd said it into his pillow as he counted him up the track and pictured him swinging quickly over the gate—there'd be no opening it. Dropping his pack over first. Then the road towards Marleston. If there was a moon, it would light up the pot-holed surface. In twenty minutes or so he'd pass the churchyard and the war memorial, and his mother's grave. Would he pause?

Good luck, Tom. Since when had he, Jack, a grown man, ever whispered into his pillow? Or ever felt his pillow damp beneath his cheek?

Good luck, Tom.

He'd said it inside himself the next day, as if for his own preservation, when Dad had gone ballistic, after ripping up that card. And he'd said it many times, over and over, in the weeks, months and even years to come, as if to make something true that wasn't. Till something he'd really known all along had sunk in on him. That Tom had simply gone, gone his own way. He would never hear Tom's voice or see his face again.

22

MAJOR RICHARDS watched Jack walk away across the grass and disappear behind the corner of the building, and blamed himself. 'I'd slip away if I were you . . .' But that hadn't meant the man should simply turn tail and make a beeline. 'Slip away' implied some tact.

Major Richards felt vaguely disappointed. Nonetheless, as he watched Jack walk away, he found himself oddly willing him on. He was walking in an intent, obstinate way, like some big child clinging to the absurd hope that he might be invisible. As a soldier might walk, Major Richards thought—though he'd never been in a position to see such a thing—from a battle.

And there was no question of stopping him. You allowed in a civilian under the sway of great distress what you would never allow in a soldier facing possible imminent death. What you would never have allowed in any of these lads lying here in their shiny black hearses.

When Jack reached the safety of the building, Major Richards felt a small flutter of relief, even of something like envy.

*

Derek Page and Dave Springer, the undertaker's men from Babbages, also watched Jack turn and walk off across the grass, like a man, it seemed to them, who'd just remembered some other appointment. Then they looked at each other. Well, that was a bit sudden. But it was the privilege of the bereaved to act how they liked (Derek and Dave had seen some examples). They could laugh their heads off if they liked and be excused for it. And he'd done the decent thing, made contact, when that wasn't in the rule book either, and they'd pocketed twenty each.

And he'd certainly made contact with that coffin.

The look they gave each other registered many things, but it included certain physical assessments. Had they been totally free to speak, one of them might have said to the other, 'Big bugger, wasn't he?' They were, themselves, of similar, slightly below-average height. Not that this affected their current task, but so far as tomorrow went, it could only mean, if the other bearers included Andy Phillips and Jason Young, also from Babbages, that they'd be at the back with the thing sloping down in their direction. They'd be taking most of the weight. What they didn't know yet was that the few yards they'd have to tread from the church porch to the grave were also on a downward slope, which would correct, even slightly reverse the imbalance. And it would be a short journey anyway, nothing like these soldier boys had just had to do—down the ramp of that plane and then across a hundred yards or more of tarmac.

A hard act to follow. They'd already had the thought.

But having now met Jack Luxton—the older brother —they both gave renewed consideration to what those six soldiers had carried and now lay in their own charge. In this case, of course, you couldn't exactly be sure if Jack Luxton's bulk was any sort of guide. You didn't know quite what was in there. They hadn't had to deal—a mercy maybe—with the body. It might be light as a child's. They'd find out, perhaps, when they started the hearse. A sensitive foot on the accelerator, when you had to go slow, would tell you pretty quickly if any extra gas was needed to cope with the load.

But the thing weighed upon them anyway, quite apart from these gaugings of physical weight. It weighed upon them in a way that their work seldom did, since they were used to it by now. But they'd never done anything like this. 'Big bugger', had they spoken it, wouldn't have excluded the sentiment 'poor bugger'. In fact, the first phrase could almost have stood for the second, and 'poor bugger', had it been used of Jack, would have equally stood for the occupant of their hearse. Poor buggers both.

Derek and Dave were twenty-nine and thirty respectively. Neither had a brother. Dave had a younger sister. Derek was an only child. Each was married. Derek had two kids, Dave just the one. All the children were still so small—still learning to walk in one case—that it wasn't yet an issue how they would be told what their daddies did for a living. They'd both drifted into the trade for the same simple reason: it was available work, which not everyone wanted, and they'd both thought of it as a stop-gap. Now they'd both become stuck, at assistant level, in a business that they knew very often ran in families, and both wondered exactly what the future held. They'd worked together often now. They were mates. It was not beyond them to think, in this case: suppose it was your brother. Nor beyond them to think that *they* might have been out there, in Iraq. There was no call-up, of course, and they'd opted years ago for this other, though now it seemed not entirely unconnected, form of employment. Corporal Luxton had been not quite thirty-one.

Being undertaker's men, they were not unfamiliar with ceremony, but they'd never been at anything like this before, and the chances that they might ever again were thin. You couldn't deny it was a privilege and an honour, it was certainly something special—to pick up the body of a soldier who'd actually died, in action, for his country. But both Dave's and Derek's thoughts when they went in this direction tended to get a little lost. He'd been carried off that plane, anyway, here in Oxfordshire, wrapped in a bloody great Union Jack. Which had then been whisked smartly off the coffin by those same six soldiers who'd done the bearing, like some precious tablecloth that had to be put away in a drawer. Which had presumably been at the request of the bereaved—that man who'd just stomped off. So they might have been a little miffed. The two of them had just been denied the opportunity of driving a coffin, draped in a Union Jack, halfway across England. Which would certainly have turned heads. More than a hearse usually does.

And, when you thought about it, to anyone turning their head, it could only have meant one thing.

But now that they'd met Jack and seen him clutch the coffin like that and then each shaken his big hand, they weren't so sure if they felt cheated or in fact glad at not having the flag. They weren't sure either, from what they'd occasionally seen on the ten-o'clock news, if even words like 'in action' were quite the right words to be thinking of.

They had to be thinking of making their departure, anyway. A sudden chill breeze swirled through the crowd round the hearses, fluttering skirts, lifting ties from jackets, making hands go to hats. The weather was changing. They had to show respect, of course, to these other two lots. The original plan, so they'd understood, was for a slow initial procession, the three hearses one behind the other, through the main gate and through the town. They'd been looking forward to that. But how would that look now: two coffins with flags and one without? And, again, there was no book of rules. They had to take some initiative—a little like Jack.

But too quick an exit wouldn't do either. It wasn't so often you got to be in the presence of three deceaseds, and neither Derek nor Dave was sure of the strange, clinging mood around them. Their hearse, with its un-adorned coffin—and now without its principal attending mourner—made them feel like poor relations at a wed-ding. On the other hand, they drew a vague sense of precedence from the fact that their coffin was a corporal's, as against two privates'. They had the rank. And from the evident fact that even the army, in full parade splendour, seemed to have handed over command now to a few men in plain black. The decision was theirs and they felt strangely stirred by the possibility of unilateral action.

They looked at each other, then at their watches, like skippers judging the tide. It had already been agreed that Derek would do the first shift of driving. As, with appropriate, unhurried dignity, they got into their seats and started the engine, they were briefly the centre of a re-solemnised attention, everyone automatically standing upright and still. And no doubt of puzzlement too, but they couldn't help that. They were in charge of Tom Luxton.

They moved off and crept back along their route of entry. It was not as anticipated. All the same, people going about other random business stopped and stood, a little nonplussed, as they passed, those in uniform saluting promptly enough, despite the absence of the flag. It was like being temporary, absconding royalty. They reached the main gate, then continued to creep—a touch more right foot perhaps—through the strange semi-military town, where again, on either side of them, there was some half-surprised but guessing observance, even scattered saluting. As if their one vehicle were a whole procession.

Only with the town behind them did they begin to pick up speed. Nothing crazy, of course. In their calculations as to when to leave, they'd given due attention to Jack's prior departure. Abrupt as it had been, it was in a way a good thing—signalling that they too, if they wished and dared, were free to go. But they had to give him a head start. It was unlikely—it would be like the tortoise catching the hare—that they'd catch him up. But they didn't want to find themselves (though they had no idea what car he was driving) coming up behind him. He would be making essentially the same journey and there was only one real route. Get past Swindon, then M4, M5.

Why they felt there shouldn't be this mutual sighting they couldn't have explained, but they felt it. Why shouldn't two brothers, in these circumstances, have kept as close to each other as possible? If you could put it like that. If Jack Luxton had insisted on driving in convoy with them (in front or behind), they'd have had to respect it. Though it would have been awkward.

As it was, they knew they had to press on, being as discreet and minimal as possible about their swap-overs and comfort breaks. You couldn't drive a hearse for a hundred and fifty miles just any old how. Though neither of them had in fact driven a hearse nearly this far before.

As they gained the open road, an unaccustomed taciturnity clung to them, which didn't just have to do with what was behind their backs. They were used to that and used, whenever there was a chance and no one was looking—as now on a country road—to breaking the rules of decorum. To having a chat about this or that.

But this was different. A hard act to follow. As broad, rolling vistas opened up before them, as they crossed from Oxfordshire into Wiltshire, clouds breaking over the hills to let through beams of sunshine, they both withdrew into themselves, became thoughtful, even grave.

The truth was they'd both been affected by what they'd seen. It was not possible to disregard, as they normally could, what they had in the back. It had come out of that plane, it had been flown all the way from Iraq. It? Now it was nudging, as it were, at their shoulders. They didn't have the Union Jack and that meant that anyone seeing them would have the usual thoughts that people have when they see a hearse with a coffin inside. They wouldn't imagine or guess. So only *they* would know, just the two of them, exactly what they were carrying halfway across the land.

The thought was a sobering one, as was the actual length of the journey in prospect—in such special company.

Though they would never talk about it and though they eventually broke this meditative hush, both Derek and Dave would feel that in this journey they formed a definite bond with their cargo. It didn't happen on the usual short trips, quite the opposite. But this was like having a third person along for the ride, there were definitely three of them. The conversation, or concatenation of unspoken thoughts, was somehow three-way.

It was—well, memorable. But more than that. The word was really (though neither of them said it) haunting. When they finally reached their destination, Marleston church, back in Devon, where the coffin would rest overnight, they felt relieved, but also vaguely sorry, even deprived.

By then the sky had cleared and the November afternoon had turned still and chilly. The air in the churchyard smelt smoky and raw. They'd phoned ahead and the rector, Brookes, and some local men were on hand to help with the final carrying into the church. In the fading light it felt like an act of stealth.

They were certainly exhausted. They'd need a drink or two, in the Spread Eagle, once they'd garaged the empty hearse in Barnstaple. Tired as they were, they didn't wish this long mission to be over. They weren't at all resentful that they'd have to go back to the church in the morning, to make contact again with Jack Luxton (who hadn't been sighted en route, so far as they could tell) and to finish the job.

The sky to the west, as they drove the last few miles to Barnstaple, had reddened while the hills had darkened. They'd seen a lot of hills today, a lot of land. Even that seemed haunting now, or haunted. This was Corporal Luxton's land, his country, as much as theirs. He'd been returned to it—with a little help from them. One of those ready phrases that had sprung into their heads earlier now seemed as shadowy as the nightfall. Corporal Luxton, who'd ridden with them, must have been a pretty good soldier, especially if he was as big as his brother. But to say, as is said of soldiers, that he'd died for his country— no, that wouldn't be exactly true, would it?

23

CORPORAL LUXTON, Tom Luxton, then a lance-corporal and between tours, had seen those shots of burning cattle, huge roaring piles, on the TV in a West London pub—tanking up before a night of it—but had simply sniffed, swallowed more beer and said nothing to his mates. Roak Moor, Devon. Foot-and-mouth this time. Well, there were worse sights in the world (Hounslow Barracks, for example). And now he could feel sure—as if he hadn't known all along—that he'd made the right decision.

But he kept the TV picture of those burning cattle in his head as if it was a real and actual memory, and it was a useful memory to have, somehow, whenever he saw a belch of black smoke, after the explosion, rise up above the flat rooftops, over the palm trees—which was getting to be most days now, sometimes you'd see two, three or more palls of dark smoke. It was a good guide and reference point to have, whenever you had to think of or sometimes look at what those clouds of smoke meant. Burning cattle, slaughtered cattle. Like the ones he'd seen carried off from Jebb Farm because they might be mad.

Not were, but might be. They might have been going to catch or spread the madness.

It was a good guide. Tom could remember another news clip, on the telly at Jebb, when the mad-cow thing was just starting, but in some other part of the country and they hadn't the slightest idea it was actually going to hit *them*.

It was a clip of a cow, in a pen somewhere, that had got the disease. It was falling down and getting up, then falling down again, its legs skidding sideways. It didn't know what it was doing, it was going round in circles. It wasn't a good picture for him and Jack and Dad to be looking at, even if it was only a picture on the telly, and they were all thinking it couldn't possibly come their way.

And it was pretty much the same when Willis got shot, their first serious casualty. Everyone was dreading carnage, major detonations, someone with a nasty parcel under their shirt. But it was a single bullet, a sniper. No one even seemed to have heard the shot. They just saw Willis acting funny, not being Willis any more, moving around like a big, jerky puppet with some of its strings missing, no one understanding why. A bullet that just nicked his spine, but it was enough. Enough to stop Willis being Willis any more, for the rest of his life maybe. The first of theirs to be shipped home.

And because he was Corporal Luxton now and had to make sure they got that picture out of their heads pretty fast, he'd had to act for them like someone who'd seen this sort of thing before, maybe a dozen times, and knew how to hack it. And the only thing that had helped was that cow on the telly—the memory of sitting round at Jebb and thinking: surely not.

It had flashed through his brain, while God knows what was flashing through Ricky Willis's brain. That and the fact that he himself was a sniper. Or had been. More of a regular corporal these days, only a part-time sniper. If you were going to shoot a man, then do it cleanly, so he'd never even know about it. It made him angry, that poor bit of snipering. From then on (it was already there, but Willis helped to sharpen it) there was a general feeling that if it was going to be your turn and if it wasn't going to be something nice, like just a foot or an elbow, then let it be something you'd never know about, not some crap like Willis got.

He'd had the thought, later, that the army ought to have its own equivalent of a squad of MAFF slaughtermen to come as quickly as possible and finish off cases like Willis. It would be a mercy, it would save a lot of trouble. It would only be doing what any soldier might sign up for. If you'd do it for an animal.

He'd got the picture of Willis out of his head by remembering that cow. Strange, that it was just a cow on the telly. But then *they*, B Company, were just pictures on the telly for most people back home, though they didn't get the pictures like they got of Willis. And that picture on the telly at Jebb wasn't funny. There were real cows across the yard. It wasn't just a picture, even if they didn't know the thing was coming smack in their direction. You might have said they'd been served notice.

Or he had. Though he hadn't yet made up his mind. He'd make up his mind down in Barton Field. What you'd do for an animal. The cow disease, when it came, was like some not quite final warning. A disease had already been eating away at Michael Luxton and was starting to eat away at him, Tom, too. He'd got it from his dad. Jack was made of tougher stuff, maybe, better stuff than he was. A good brother, a better brother. And a better father, sometimes, than his father.

But after that morning with Dad and Luke in Barton Field he wasn't going to stick around any longer than he needed, with bad thoughts in his head that he might just one day put into action. Let the cow disease seem like his reason. What should he have said? Why don't we both do it, Jack, you and me together, why don't we both just hop it? But he'd looked hard into Jack's eyes and seen, first, that what he did actually say would be safe with Jack, safe as blank ammunition, and, second, that Jack had never even dreamed of it himself.

Well then, Jack could keep it. Keep what he was leaving. Let that be the deal. He'd never break it or ask for his share back. If that took away the weight of guilt that settled inside him as soon as Jack said, there in the parlour, 'You can rely on me, Tom.' If it made Jack the good brother and him the bad one, so be it. If it made Jack the fool and him the smart one, so be it. He'd slipped out of the farmhouse, like a fox from a henhouse, at three a.m. on his eighteenth birthday. His mum had told him once that he'd been born at three a.m., but that had nothing to do with it, it was just a coincidence. And Jack had told him that 'born' wasn't quite the word for it anyway. Jack had said, 'That's when you finally came out.'

He had a backpack and he was wearing all those layers—less to carry—against the cold. He had rations (he'd better get used to that word) hidden in the Big Barn. And he had Jack's birthday card, which weighed next to nothing but was like an extra load of blame to carry with him. A big gold '18' and a big 'Good Luck, Tom' inside. He'd kept it for a long while, hidden in his locker. Signing up on your birthday wasn't exactly like a birthday. If he'd wanted punishment, to go with his guilt, then he'd get it in the army.

But he certainly no longer had the card by the time he was sitting in that pub, watching those cows burning on the telly. Though maybe the 'Good Luck' still applied, now as then. It had stopped him, so far, from being like Willis.

Apart from the card, only three other written messages had ever come his way from Jack. Which wasn't a complaint, since he, Tom, had never written back—or only the once, and briefly. He'd very quickly found out that he just wanted to be out of communication in this world he'd chosen, this world of strangely unresented punishment, his whereabouts unknown.

Now the World is Yours.

The first letter from Jack had been after two weeks or so, and was just a line hoping he was okay and saying that everything at Jebb was fine—which was surely Jack being a well-meaning liar. And then, since he hadn't replied to that, there was a long, long gap. It looked like that was that. They'd really said goodbye to each other and known it, that December afternoon in the milking parlour. Meanwhile, he'd been moved around a bit anyway.

Then those two letters had come, soon after each other, the first looking like Jack might have spent a whole week writing it and torn up several versions along the way. But the main item was perfectly clear. That Jack was all by himself now, not counting Ellie (assuming Ellie was still a feature, and how might she not be?). The old man had cleared off too, so it seemed, in a manner of speaking. And then the second letter had come soon afterwards, about the funeral, since that had to be delayed. And that had included that other item of news: that Michael had left the whole farm—though Jack had seemed to want to emphasise that there was a whole heap of debt to go with it—to Jack and Jack only. Well that was no surprise. That had even been the deal.

And he hadn't replied to either letter. He hadn't got on the phone to Jebb Farm. He hadn't done a single thing about either letter, though he'd stared at them both long and hard enough. Those letters reached him, as it happened, in Germany. Before Bosnia. It would have been difficult, but, with that delay for the funeral, not impossible. And there was such a thing as compassionate leave. And he'd felt compassion, definitely. For his brother.

But he hadn't done a thing. He hadn't applied to the CO. He imagined the CO's face. My old man has shot himself.

He hadn't lifted a finger. It was a bastard thing to do to Jack, but then, maybe, it had been a bastard thing he'd done in the first place, that night in December.

All yours, Jack. Now it really was, and Ellie's too, if Jack had any sense. And good luck to them. But it wasn't his ticket or what he was made for, he knew that too now.

He was a private in B Company, earmarked for the sniper section, currently stationed in Germany, occasionally on active duty with a Helga from Hanover, when he might have been the owner of fifty per cent of Jebb Farm, of a hundred and sixty acres of England. So be it. He couldn't go back on the deal, and he couldn't go back anyway to the place itself, compassionately or otherwise.

Couldn't have gone back to that churchyard to stand by the grave, even for his brother's sake, and look down and think: it was a fine line, it was a fine bloody line. And Jack maybe thinking it too. And maybe if he didn't show up and didn't even send a message it would be like a clear enough last signal. All yours, Jack. Forget about me.

He'd stared at each letter in turn. So his father had done what no one else, now, would have to have the decency to do for him. He'd done the decent thing himself. He'd stared at both letters together. Reading them was a little like reading Jack's face, but he'd never have to do that any more. He put the letters away, and he never did speak to the CO. Later, he found an opportunity privately to burn them. The barrack room had an old-style stove with a lid. Simple. A small fire, compared with piles of cattle going up in flames. And a small matter, he'd come to think, compared with some of the things that come a soldier's way. Bosnia. He'd watched those cattle burning on the telly six years later, in the spring of 2001. And it wasn't so long afterwards that a couple of planes had flown into a couple of big towers—another TV picture to remember—giving a whole new meaning to the act of suicide and having a range of consequences, including ones for British soldiers, which would make a spot of cow disease seem piddling.

And all he'd wanted was the get-out, the complete alternative package. No finer reasons. He'd never once said to anyone that he'd had a great-uncle who'd got the DCM. (Posthumous.) When he'd walked, that icy night, with his backpack, past the war memorial, he'd never turned his head. He hadn't felt brave, or even that he was doing something that really took so much initiative.

He'd started life as a soldier by running away. Which was a common enough story. It was what half of B Company had done in their different ways. What were the alternatives? They'd handed over the problem to the army. Take me in, please, sort me out please, the whole package. With some of them you could see, clearly enough, that if it hadn't been that, it might have been prison eventually, one way or another. You could picture their faces sometimes (and now he was a corporal, he'd sometimes tell them) behind bars.

And that might have been his case too, and it might not have been petty crime either. But that was all taken care of now. He stared at those letters.

But he'd still think about cattle. They haunted him and helped him, gave him a sort of measure. If he wanted, now, to get bad stuff out of his head, bad human pictures, it helped to replace them with cattle. He could still remember the wet jostle of the milking parlour, the smell of iodine and udder. He could still remember that daily treadmill of extracting milk from cows, and the thought that would sometimes come to him while doing it, that it was only the same essential process (so hardly a man's job) by which human babies were nursed and eased into the world, by which he himself had once been nursed and eased—late and (apparently) tough arrival though he was. And it was a wonder how the grown-up world still needed, by the churn-load, by the tanker-load, this white, soft, pappy baby-juice.

He'd had that thought, especially, after Vera died, and wondered if Jack, in the next stall, was having it too. Their mum had died, but these damn cows still had to calve and be milked. But, at that time, the milking parlour was the best place to be.

What kind of thoughts were they for a future soldier? What kind of training was milking? But it was a cattle-existence often enough, a cowshed existence. They were mostly hard-nut townie boys and liked to think of him as a softie country boy, a bumpkin. But there were those who were hard outside and all mush inside, you could do without them. And there were those who might look soft on the outside (though not so much of that these days) but were hard underneath, and he knew now he was the second kind. Now and then they'd get a glimpse of it, too, and knew they shouldn't argue—one reason he'd made corporal, and would make sergeant pretty soon.

By the time they were out here, most of them had that hard and soft stuff sorted out. They knew they didn't have their mums around any more. They'd better be their own mums to themselves, and that wasn't a joke. He could do that too. Set them an example. Sew on a button for them just like his own mum had done. Bite off the cotton. 'There you are, Pickering. Now say thank you.' Another reason he'd make sergeant. But he could also shoot people dead cleanly. Not like that useless cunt who'd shot Willis.

Another big advantage of being the country boy. Crows, pigeons, bunny rabbits. He'd been put on the sniper's course and passed, flying colours. He had a skill to bring to the army.

Though no one had noticed that what he'd brought

with him too was his anger. Sniping was supposed to be icy-cool, precise and careful, it was the opposite of blazing away. Yet it was anger that had driven him, that cold night, up that frozen track. Two years' worth of simmering anger and of keeping a lid on it. He might have just done a bunk after he left school. He might have just legged it—and nearly had—that night after Luke got buried. Would Dad really have got him back? This is my boy and he belongs on my farm, he doesn't belong in the army. Or would he have spat and said, 'Good riddance'? Either way, he wanted it to be certain and clear. So he'd arrived on the army's doorstep with at least two years' worth of anger.

And was that, too, so unusual? The army welcomed anger. Was happy to channel and redirect it, even, maybe, cure it. If you were lucky and patient, it might even find you a real enemy to take it out on. And Tom didn't mind who that was. A war on terror? That sounded like an open day for enemies, that sounded like a perfect opportunity for firing off lots of cool, disciplined, single rounds of anger. The first time he'd fired for real and seen his man drop, he'd felt anger fly out of him, he'd felt a great whoosh of sanity and calmness. Now he'd done it. He'd even thought he might never need to do it again, but of course it was required of him, it was what he was there for. As for the man he'd popped, he didn't think about him. And *he'd* never known about it. It was clean killing. Not every soldier could do it, or wanted to.

But he was a corporal now and less of a sniper. He'd been credited with that other skill the army needed: leadership. And he liked it. Sniping was a solo business and he was a sniper these days only by occasional solo detachment. Otherwise, he had eight men to look after—seven, after Willis. When he'd been made corporal he'd felt for the first time like a big brother. Now he had some little brothers. And he no longer felt angry. He'd sniped it away, maybe.

Eight—seven—men. All townies, and him the only bumpkin, the one in charge. It was the accent of course that did it, the broad buttery burr he couldn't get rid of, any more than he could get rid of the memory of milking. But no milksops among them now, especially after Willis. They were okay and would be okay, if he had anything to do with it. Some of them even found his voice soothing now, when he wasn't barking at them. It wasn't the obvious voice of a corporal, it was the voice of a cowman. It made them think of green English fields, perhaps, out here in the dust and crap. Well, they'd better forget all that. He could tell them about green English fields,

More the leader, less the sniper, but he still had the same, secret equal-vote of a wish they all had: that if his moment had to come (and if they had to do without him) it would just be clean and he wouldn't know about it. Death by sniper would do, and in his case might even be called fair. But not, please, like Willis. Wheelchair Willis.

So when the IED—and it must have been a whopping IED—blew up under them, the whole section riding home, dog-tired, to beddy-byes, he thought it was unfair, but there was nothing he could do about it. He could see that Pickering and Fuller were out of it and he didn't know who else might be okay or not, behind. He couldn't move to look. It was all madness, but he was clear and calm and strangely comforted, not by his own burry voice, which didn't seem to be working, but by the fact that he couldn't hear anything. There must be a lot of racket, screaming, yelling, gunfire even, but he couldn't hear any of it and he had no sense, either, of how much time was passing, if time was passing at all. He could smell fuel. He knew he was trapped under mangled metal, by his legs, but he couldn't feel or move his legs, couldn't move anything, even a hand, even, it seemed, his lips. Well, it would be all down to Lance-Corporal Meeks now, Dodger Meeks, if Meeks was still up and dodging.

Was this terror? The thing they were fighting? He saw the ball of flame bloom out, and he knew he wasn't going to die by nice clean sniper fire, but was going to be burnt to death, but there was nothing he could do about it, and it seemed he had plenty of time to think about other things and the peace and quiet to do it in. He could think about not being in a blown-up armoured vehicle in Iraq, but being in the back of the school bus with Kathy Hawkes. He could move his hand then, all right, every fingertip. And he could think about being in a caravan, a caravan with just Jack and Mum. He could even think about Marilyn Monroe. He knew now that he should have written to Jack, at least answered one of those letters that he'd dropped in a stove in Germany. He could see the red, round opening of that stove. He'd write now, if he had a piece of paper and a pen and could move his hand. He'd explain that when Dad had thrust the gun at him he hadn't taken it, for the simple reason that he'd known he'd have used it on Dad first, then on Luke. Or on Luke first, then on Dad. A tricky question, but same difference. There were two barrels. And he'd known, from the look in his eyes, that Dad was half expecting it, even wanting it, and that's why he'd said that thing about decency. He'd known, anyway, when Dad had turned away with the gun, that he, Tom Luxton, had the killer instinct in him. And he'd have to put a lid on it.

So I joined the army, Jack. Now here I am in sunny Basra. Wish you were here. No, not really. Remember me to Ellie.

But he wasn't here either. He was there. He was back there in Barton Field. There was the big oak, its leaves brushing a big blue sky. But there was no Dad, no Luke, no gun. And no Jack. But he was lying in Barton Field more or less where Luke had been shot and had known all along it was coming. It was summer, it was warm and the grass was full of buzzing insects. And then he could hear something else, getting closer. He hadn't heard that sound for a long time now, but he knew straight away what it was, and if he could lift his head he might just be able to see them. It was the unmistakable, steady 'tchch ... tchch ... tchch' of browsing cattle, the slow, soft rip-rip of cows' mouths tearing up grass. It was the most soothing sound in the world and it was utterly indifferent.

24

ELLIE SITS BY Holn Cliffs, looking at the vanished postcard view. The occasional white, whizzing missile of a wind-hurled seagull is almost the only sign that there's anything out there.

Their seaside life, vanished too now, toppled over a cliff. Their Isle of Wight life. She'd come here once, all alone, to see for herself, when it was still her secret, her gift in store, like some unborn child. Twenty-seven years old. Fine spring weather. The view had been glorious then. Her dad was in a hospital bed, knowing no more about this excursion of hers than he'd known about that spin she'd taken when she was sixteen. And thank God it wasn't the same Land Rover. She'd taken the ferry to Fishbourne, gone up on the sun deck, as if she were on a pleasure cruise.

Their Isle of Wight life. The beauty of it: a whole separate land, with only a short sea to cross, but happily cut off from the land of their past. Not exactly their 'isle of joy'. It wasn't Tahiti. Look at it now. Or St Lucia (that would come later). But nonetheless it was a fact, and it had become their purpose, that they were in the business of pleasure. And it had become *theirs*, not just 'The Lookout', but 'Ellie's and Jack's'. Once it had been Alice's and Tony's—Allie-and-Tony's. Now it was Ellie-and-Jack's.

She'd stood beside him, in a straw-coloured dress, in that registry office in Newport and not minded at all that she was changing her name. It seemed a good name. Luckston. Later, outside their front door—it was a mild October afternoon and the caravans below even looked like something spread out for a wedding—she'd said, 'Well, come on, you won't get another chance.' And he'd done it as if he'd been planning it all along. My God, he'd scooped her up as if she'd been as light as straw herself.

He'd come out of his mourning for Jebb, and not so slowly, and actually started to look happy. Farmer Jack. She'd even thought she might settle for there not being any other kind of birth, for the sake of this remarkable rebirth in him. And hadn't she caused it to happen? And, anyway, was it so out of the question that there still might be both kinds of birth?

So was it any wonder that she'd been both flattened and glad—glad—when that letter came?

'Leave me out of this, Jack.'

She should have gone with him, back into the wretched past. For a moment she sees before her not the November rain of the Isle of Wight but the soft flaps and veils of midsummer rain over the Devon hills as she drove into Barnstaple the morning after her father had died. She'd called Jack from a pay-phone in the hospital to give

him the news without any tearfulness and with hardly a
tremble in her voice. She'd wanted to convey to him that
she was being practical and steady—and he was still in the
grip of his own father's death. It was over, it had been
expected (and, yes, all those years, since she was sixteen,
were over too). In a little while they might start to think
of their own lives.

'No, it's okay, I don't need you with me.'

And he'd done two lots of milking.

And he'd needed her with him two days ago.

She should have gone too, been at his side, even wept
a little. She was weeping now. But she just couldn't do it.
Stand on some grim piece of tarmac, while it all came
back, in a flag-wrapped parcel, by way of Iraq, their old,
left-behind life. Then stand, again, in that churchyard.
By Tom's grave. By her father's.

She just couldn't do it—any more, apparently, than
she could go and stand by her mother's. She just couldn't
do it, even if Jack had to. She could see there was no way
round it for him.

She'd listened to him leave, two mornings ago. It
seems already like two weeks. Heard him moving downstairs in the kitchen, heard the front door, his feet on the
road outside. The car starting. She'd actually thought:
Poor man, poor man, to have to be going on such a
journey. None of his noises had sounded angry, there was
no slamming. It was almost as if he'd been trying not to
wake her.

How could she have let him do it without even seeing
him off, without standing in the doorway, without so
much as a kiss or a hug or even an 'I'll be thinking of
you'? My poor Jack, my poor one-and-only Luxton left.

But how could she have said or done any of those things when, in the first place, she might simply have gone with him?

It was still dark. She hadn't moved. She'd even pulled the duvet tighter up round her. There was a brief brightness at the curtains as he put on his headlights before slipping down the hill. Even as he'd left she'd wondered: would he come back? Was this the sort of journey and the sort of starting out on it from which he might never come back?

The fear had taken hold of her that he might not come back. How absurd. When she might have gone with him. She'd left all those messages on his mobile, none of which had been answered. Well, she'd asked for it. I'm thinking of you. I love you. Forgive me.

Strangely, in all the time he was gone, she'd hardly thought of Tom, returning, in his own way—being returned—to where he'd come from. Or put herself in the terrible position of some mother or wife receiving back, but not receiving back, a soldier-husband, a soldier-son. She'd thought of her own mother, of going to be with her, and failed to do even that. Failed twice now. All she'd wanted was for Jack to come back.

Well, he had come back. And he hadn't. And now it seemed she might sit here in this lay-by for ever.

25

JACK SWUNG THE Cherokee back onto the road and sped off as if from some delay not of his own making. He'd wasted valuable time getting choked up. Part of him recognised that it was the whole point of this journey, to get choked up. It was its essence. But some other part of him was now trying to outdrive this immobilising stuff inside him. He looked in the mirror, half expecting to see the black hearse on his tail.

The road was clear, in both directions. The November day was brightening again, the grey clouds breaking, so that a whole hillside would suddenly light up while everything else seemed to darken.

He crossed the infant River Thames, back into Wiltshire, but the countryside, the passing signs to innocent-sounding villages, now vaguely oppressed him, unlike when he'd left the motorway to drive north in the morning. He was relieved when he joined the M4 and was sucked into its tunnelled anonymity. He saw himself as a mere moving speck on a map—the blue line of the M4 draped like a cable across the land. The road was everything and, despite the names that loomed at junctions, might have been anywhere. Chippenham? Malmesbury? Where the hell were they?

But for the first time he became conscious of the empty seat beside him, of the pointedness of its emptiness. What was Ellie doing now? The Isle of Wight seemed already far away, as far away, almost, as Iraq. He couldn't imagine what Ellie was doing now. He couldn't imagine that she was sitting now at the Lookout, trying to imagine what he was doing. Wishing that, after all, she was sitting next to him.

Was she packing her bags?

It seemed to him that there was now a difference, a gap, between Ellie and him as plain as that strip of choppy sea he'd crossed this morning. For her, Tom's death meant quite simply that Tom was gone now for good and was never coming back. He could see that this was a perfectly sound position. But for him it meant just as simply—though it was a position much harder to argue for—that Tom *had* come back. He understood it truly now. He'd come back as surely as if that letter announcing his death had really been Tom himself knocking on the door. Can I come in? It was as if Tom, whom he'd lived without for thirteen years, could no longer, now he was dead, be lived without. He'd been trying to drive away from this nonsensical, pursuing fact, and yet it was true.

There was even a simple test. He asked himself a question that, lurking inside him though it may have been, he hadn't dared confront till now. Perhaps it had only become a question since he'd made his bolt for it, after the ceremony, back there. Who would he rather have right now—right now between junctions 17 and 18—in that empty seat beside him? Ellie? Tom?

It wasn't an easy question or even a fair one. For a moment he failed to answer it. But then, for a clear second or two, and by way of an answer, Tom was there. He had a corporal, in battle gear, sitting beside him while he drove, under a brightening sky, down the M4. This was the first time this had happened on his journey, and it wouldn't be the last. Jack wasn't frightened or even surprised. He was even relieved. He didn't need now to worry about the hearse, about outstripping it, because Tom was with him anyway.

It's because he's really come back, he thought. It's because I touched the coffin and held it. Like a kind of contamination, but a good one.

Then he thought: Am I going mad?

Last night (was it only last night and not last week?), when Jack had asked Ellie one last time—he wasn't going to insist or demand—if she'd come with him, she'd shaken her head and taken a deep, exasperated breath, as if she might have been going to say, 'It's him or me, Jack.' He was sure she was going to say it, that was the look in her eyes, but she hadn't said it.

And he should never have said that thing, at the start, about St Lucia. Then Ellie would be with him now. He'd seen the same look come into her eyes then—as if, strangely, now Tom was dead, she could no longer rely on his absence. And hadn't he just proved her right? The simple word was ghost.

'So what are you going to do, Jacko? Mope around here all winter?'

The word was 'mourn', he'd thought. Mourn, not mope. But he couldn't say it—'Mourn, not mope, Ellie.' The word had stuck in his throat. Like St Lucia hadn't.

And if Ellie were with him now, sitting right beside him, would that mean Tom wouldn't be, couldn't be? That there couldn't be any ghosts? Now all the other ghosts, it suddenly seemed to him, were waiting for him too—sensing his approach, beyond the end of this blue, snaking motorway. Including Jimmy Merrick, with an extra, needly twinkle in his eye. 'What—no Ellie with you, boy?'

Was he going mad?

Bristol, like some phantom presence—a thickening of traffic and junctions—passed somewhere on his left. He filtered off the M4 onto the M5, confused by the lanes. Bristol, Avonmouth, Portishead. The sea could not be far away. A different sea from the one he'd seen and crossed this morning. The Bristol Channel. The map of England wheeled in his head. Portsmouth, Southampton, Bristol. He was on an island. And he was in Somerset now, a sign told him. The West Country. Clevedon, Weston-super-Mare. He'd never been to Weston-super-Mare, but the name smacked of caravans.

Beyond Taunton—most of his motorway driving was behind him now—he pulled into a service station, needing to piss and eat. It was more that he was empty than hungry. He needed to fill himself as he might have needed to fill the car. He needed to drain himself, though he felt already drained. In the Gents he could have sworn that, again, for just a moment, he'd seen Tom, three urinals along. Desert camouflage, slung rifle. Had he simply imagined it this time?

He walked back out towards the cafeteria, past a row of busy, brightly coloured miniature cars on stands, each occupied by an eager child who could only just have been released from a real car. He was still feeling, himself, though he was on his feet, the sway and thrum of being on the road. The cafeteria was a near-replica of the one he'd sat in, near Newbury, this morning, but now he wondered how many of those around him—or how many of those who would pass through here today—would have some link, no matter how remote (a cousin, a brother-in-law) with someone in Iraq. There ought to be a badge, perhaps, a means of recognition. No there shouldn't. If there was a war on terror, that would be a stupid idea. Could bombs go off in motorway service stations?

That place in Oxfordshire, he thought, had been like a great big bloody service station—for the services.

It was not quite three o'clock, but the day was waning. The light outside seemed fragile and taut, already preparing to depart. He'd made good time and there was now no particular need to rush, but he had an odd fear of having to drive in the dark. Though he wasn't afraid of seeing Tom again. It had happened twice now, so the possibility was strong. He was no longer afraid of the hearse—which, even while he sat here, might whizz sneakily past. Perhaps, in some quite feasible and arguable way, Tom was no longer in the hearse. He stared at the empty chair beside him, which stayed empty.

It was clearly something Tom had control over, not him.

He pushed aside his plate, got up and walked back to where he'd parked. It was distinctly cold now. The sky was virtually clear and the edges of things had sharpened. His thin shadow, like a pointer on a dial, went before him across the car park. He still wore the black tie, not even loosened. His suit, which he'd have to wear tomorrow, would now be hopelessly creased. He laid the jacket again on the back seat. The medal went back into his shirt pocket.

Only a few minutes and a few miles further on, he crossed into Devon. 'Welcome to Devon.' Did he feel he'd come home? Did he feel he'd crossed a special line? Within half an hour, on the outskirts of Exeter, he turned off the end of the motorway onto the westbound A30. The possibility had certainly occurred to him of exiting at an earlier point and taking a route along slower country roads that would eventually have led him into landscapes that he knew. But he instinctively wanted to stave off till tomorrow—and even then, perhaps, to keep it as brief as possible—encountering any views that were familiar. This wasn't memory lane. The dual carriageway of the A30, as well as being fast, had the numbing virtue of being like any busy trunk road anywhere.

But even as he sped along it, he began to see, on his right, a certain kind of bulging hill, a certain kind of hunched, bunched geography that he intimately recognised, and ploughed and scooped out of it, here and there, were areas of bare earth with a familiar ruddy hue. In the late-afternoon light it even seemed to glow. These sights brought an unexpected tightness to his throat. 'Earth with dried blood in it,' Michael Luxton had once moodily said.

The sky was darkening, with a reddish tinge to match

the scours among the hills. He switched on his side lights. On the left, Dartmoor loomed. Its distant, cloud-hung outline had once been the regular sight at Jebb. So, he couldn't deny it, he was back now. On the other hand, he had never *been* to Dartmoor, and he was about as close to it now as he'd ever been. Though it had been constantly there once, on the horizon, it might as well have been the Isle of Wight. And he'd understood that it was a tourist place, where holidaymakers went in the summer. Also a place, he'd understood, where there were signs saying, 'Army: Keep Out'.

Before day had quite given up to night, he turned off the A30 and descended into the nestling town of Okehampton. He was now in a place he knew, though not well. Even Okehampton—like Barnstaple or Exeter—had been a rare excursion. He had dim memories of being taken there to see his mother's Aunt Maggie. A bus ride, shops, a cream tea in a cafe with rickety chairs. But hotels didn't feature in his memories. There'd been no reason for them to. In all his life—and despite being himself in the business of providing accommodation—Jack had only ever stayed in three different hotels, and all of them had been in the Caribbean. Now he was to stay in a hotel less than twenty miles from where he was born.

He'd chosen the Globe Inn from a website, back at the Lookout. Since Ellie wasn't coming, he wasn't inter- ested in anywhere smart, just a place for the night. He'd almost self-denyingly gone down-market. Should he sleep in luxury while his brother slept in a coffin? He'd chosen Okehampton because it was about the right distance from Marleston. It might have been Barnstaple, which was nearer, but he'd plumped for Okehampton. He was definitely not going to stay anywhere in the direct vicinity, certainly not in the Crown (if they had such a thing as a room). Technically, there would still be people around who, in the circumstances, might have put him up. But that thought—he was Jack Luxton who'd cleared off over ten years ago—horrified him.

He knew now in any case, as he entered Okehampton, that he might as well have made no booking and taken pot luck. Okehampton in mid-November was not exactly in demand. The streets were scarcely busy, despite some glittery gestures in shop windows to a Christmas still weeks away. And when he found the Globe Inn, parked in its yard of a car park, and entered through its rattling front door, he was glad, at least in one sense, that Ellie wasn't with him. Her tastes and requirements had been raised considerably in recent years. So had his, it was true, to keep up with hers. But now his had rapidly dropped away, though with no real sense of indignity, as if he felt that he deserved something only just above the lowest.

This was Tom's homecoming and he'd gone for cheapness. But it wasn't Tom who'd be staying here.

The Globe was little more than a pub, but its lack of any style was vaguely comforting and as he entered, there, briefly, was Tom again, behind the cubicle-like reception desk. As if his brother was there to welcome him (though with a chin-strapped helmet on). He was standing with his hands resting on the wooden counter. Then he was gone.

Jack pressed the bell on the counter—though without supposing this would resummon his brother—and a woman waddled into view and smiled. This also comforted Jack and made him put aside his feeling of foolishness at having booked in advance.

He gave his name and heard it being drawled back to him. 'Lu-uxton'. He had a momentary terror of being found out. She'd surely have read the name in the local paper, where it must have been a story. But the voice (which had something in common with his own) had no particular meaning in it. She took a key from the rack behind her and smiled again. 'Breakfast in the back bar— that way—seven to half-past nine.' He wondered if he were the only guest.

The room was better than he'd expected, much better than the mere cell he felt was his due. There was a large window, beneath it a radiator that was barely warm. He found a plug-in heater that made ticking noises, and drew the curtains. Then he lay sprawled for several moments on his back on the bed, closing his eyes. The bed seemed to tremble and rock under him as if he were still travelling. He saw the plane parked out on the tarmac.

He got up again quickly, as if to rest was fatal. His watch showed it had just gone five. In his bag he had a change of clothes, for this one evening, so that he could preserve his suit, with a fresh white shirt for the morning. The medal had been in his top pocket when he entered the hotel. He put it now on the bedside table. He undressed and hung up his suit. In the bathroom his nakedness, in a strange mirror, among strange angles and surfaces, suddenly perplexed and alarmed him. Would that hearse have arrived yet? Should he have been there for it, waiting in the twilight? He wouldn't have liked to drive a big hearse through the high, narrow lanes around

Marleston, let alone with darkness coming on. He saw its headlights rippling along the rooty banks.

What was in that coffin? He ran the tap. And those other two coffins—with their flags still wrapping them—where were they now? Pickering, Fuller. He'd scarcely given them a thought.

He lay in the bath, his knees raised so it could contain his length. The water had gushed and was hot. How had Tom died? The bath was better, safer than the swaying bed. He felt like a man on the run. He felt a great desire not to know who he was.

It was barely seven when he went out. There was no waddling woman, though there was chatter from along the hallway and the noise of a TV. So he hung on to his key. He'd picked up the medal again and put it in the zip-up pocket of his parka jacket. He didn't dare not have it about his person. It was like carrying a key. He had only one plan. To find a pub—definitely not the Globe itself—a pub that did food. To drink as much as it took, then to get back and crash into bed with as little as possible still stirring in his brain.

He was lucky with the pub. It was called the Fox and Hounds and was barely three minutes from his hotel. It had, at this early-evening hour, just the right number of customers, so that he wouldn't stand out nor, on the other hand, be swamped. Furthermore, one of the other customers, he almost casually observed now, was Tom. Still in his battle kit, but leaning against the bar like some regular, one hand plunged into one of many pockets as if he might have been jingling loose change, or perhaps a hand grenade. He'd looked round as his brother came in, as if to say, 'Jack! What'll you have?' Then, as before, he was gone.

Jack ordered a pint and saw that there were plastic menus on the tables. He didn't care: any food. He took a table by the wall. The wall had fake black beams running down it and in between were framed pictures of hunting scenes that were standard issue for pubs in country towns. He drank the first pint fairly quickly, then, when he went to the bar for a second, ordered the steak and chips. Fox and hounds, steak and chips. From the feel of the beer inside him, he reckoned another pint after this, or a large scotch, should be sufficient. He generally knew his limits. As many of the Lookouters who went to the Ship at Sands End could vouch, Jack wasn't a big drinker—two pints sipped slowly. His big body seemed to contain them easily, but not to need any more. But now he was drinking to a purpose.

Someone had left a convenient copy of the *Daily Express* on one of the other tables, to give him something to do. He looked at it, rather than read it. Fortunately, it was yesterday's news. He didn't want to look at any local paper. He didn't want to look at the television when he got back to his room. There was no television—it was something he'd consciously checked—in this bar. He wanted to be disconnected. Yet the voices around him were like voices he'd once known and he had the feeling again that he might suddenly be recognised. Equally, he had the thought that he was sitting—quite unnoticeably, in fact—in an ordinary pub in Okehampton when only seven or eight hours ago he'd been mingling with lords and ladies and generals and God knows who. He'd been where drums had been beaten, bugles blown and swords had flashed.

Guess where I've been today?

Was it the beer starting to work? In the wrong direction? While he waited for his food and looked at the *Daily Express*—though as if the newsprint might have been mere gauze—it seemed suddenly to Jack that he was perfectly capable of becoming one of those strange men in pubs who can rear up suddenly and accost others with their uninvited stories, their riddles, or their sheer, frothing rage. That sort of thing could happen, after all, at the Lookout (it could happen in the Ship, but then it was not his business). The furies that a fortnight's holiday could sometimes, oddly, release. The pressure-cooker of a caravan under three days of rain. It seemed strange to Jack that he could actually exert a calming influence in such situations—or maybe just look like a man no one would want to take on. A gangster even, apparently. He'd entered that hardly intimidating hotel like a mouse.

He was better at stopping fights, perhaps, than picking them, better at quelling anger than venting it. Yet now he felt he could almost go up to the bar and thump it and be one of those desperate, belligerent men. He might get out the medal, unlock it from his clenched and brandished fist. 'See this? See this, everyone? See what I've got here?'

A girl appeared from nowhere, bearing his steak and some cutlery wrapped in a paper napkin. Black skirt and white blouse. Her brief attentiveness (though she would never know it) entirely defused him. She gave him, as she put down his plate, a quick, direct smile. He couldn't see why he deserved it or why it should have come just as his thoughts had begun to boil. Did he look as if he needed soothing? That was two warm female smiles he'd had in the last two hours. Did he look as if he needed mothering?

He ate his steak and chips, drained his second pint. Before ordering a third drink he went for a leak. It was one of those places out the back along a short exterior alleyway exposed to the elements. The strip of air was like a knife. The band of sky above showed a glittering star or two. Frost tomorrow, he thought, like a farmer crossing a yard. Frost—a white dusting on the hills, on the distant heights of Dartmoor. Ten-thirty at Marleston church. It was really happening. Babbages had said, 'Leave it with us.' Undertakers would say that. Leave it with us.

It was pisshouse air, but it was the undeniable air of Devon. It was like the air of a cowshed. He splashed steamily against stained stainless steel. When he returned to the bar, Tom was sitting there in his place—saving it for him, so it seemed. He got up and vanished as soon as his brother entered. Jack went to the bar and ordered a large scotch. No pudding. His belly felt full and he thought the odds of getting a second smile from that girl were against him. He wanted not to spoil the first. The beer was working. He took his scotch slowly—still remarkably engrossed by the *Daily Express*—then left. It was barely half-past eight, but what else could he do? At Jebb, in the winter, they were sometimes all in bed at nine.

The streets were empty and quiet, as if under curfew. He walked pointlessly, in the cold, around a corner or two, along a street or two, then back. But it was all right now, he judged. He wasn't thinking about anything much. The girl's smile. Boots, Martin's newsagents, NatWest Bank. He walked with no sense of being shadowed or accompanied, but he felt that he himself, now, had become like some gliding ghost. He found his way to the Globe again and stepped in with a strong need not to be noticed. But the reception desk was empty. He made it to the stairs. There was a murmuring along the hallway in the hotel bar, the sound of a football-match commentary. He unlocked his room, switched on the lights and the clicking heater, though the radiator seemed to be functioning now. He was sure, as he entered, that Tom must have been lying on the bed, his soldier's boots crossed over each other, his helmet beside him. But the dent in the bedspread was his own.

It was not yet nine. He could phone Ellie. He could flick on his mobile phone at last and see if she'd left any message. He could call her. But what should he say? I'm in Okehampton, Ellie. So's Tom.

I'm in Okehampton, Ellie. Why aren't you?

He pulled back the bed covers so that the warmth of the heater might directly reach the sheets. It would have to be a frosty night. He saw the dip of Barton Field. But he didn't want to think of anything. He undressed. He put the medal on the bedside table. Then after getting into bed—it was perhaps only a beery whim—he took it from the table and placed it under his pillow. Within minutes, curled beneath the covers, all the lights switched off and the heater, for good measure, left on low, he'd crashed, just as planned and wished, into unknowingness.

But at some point later—he couldn't tell how long he'd slept—he woke up in the darkness as if some quite distinct and alarming event or perhaps some terrible but instantly forgotten dream had roused him, his pulse racing, his head throbbing, his teeth grinding like mill-stones.

And clutching a medal.

26

JACK HAD EVERY REASON to remember that last Remembrance Day.

November, 1994. Just him and Dad. Almost a year since Tom had gone—his name no longer being mentioned, and Jack himself no longer suffering (though he had for months) any proxy punishment for his brother's absence. A kind of muddled realignment, as if his father might have said now of Tom, in the way he might have spoken of any reconsidered investment, any shelved bit of farm planning: Well, we did the right thing there, Jack boy, didn't we, not to press ahead with *that*. As if Tom's departure had only revived the fortunes and workability of Jebb Farm. Which it very clearly hadn't.

But that anniversary had been coming up—the anniversary of Tom's departure which was also, anyway, his birthday. And before that there was Remembrance Sunday, with its tradition of dogged observance in the Luxton family. And how would they deal with that now—now that Tom had gone off to be a soldier?

Jack had left it to his father, and wouldn't have been surprised if Michael had said (though it would have been the first such omission, so far as Jack knew, in the annals of the household): 'In case you're wondering, we'll give it a miss this year.' And even spat.

But his father had said: 'I hope you've got your suit ready for tomorrow.' And then had said: 'I got these when I was up at Leke Cross.' And had handed over one of two paper poppies with their green plastic stalks.

None of this, on the other hand, had been done with much animation, and Jack's assessment had been that his father couldn't lose face in front of the village. As Luxtons, they simply couldn't neglect their annual duty. Michael's later, unspoken but manifest decision not to enter the Crown for the customary drink—where, of course, he might get drawn into some discussion about his younger son's whereabouts—seemed to go along with this. He would turn up for the ceremony, but he drew the line at anything else.

Jack didn't have then in his vocabulary (he doesn't really now) the word 'hypocrisy'. It would have sounded then to him like a word a vet might use—something else cows might go down with. As for getting his suit ready, he didn't know what that could mean other than taking it off the hanger where it had hung all year long.

But there was a seriousness, even a strange conscientiousness, about Michael's behaviour on that Remembrance Day. He seemed to present himself in the farmhouse that morning more painstakingly, more brushed and scrubbed about his face and hands, than he'd ever done before. He fixed the poppy in his lapel not cursorily, but with a degree of care, as if it might have been a real flower and he was going to a wedding. He'd duly produced the medal and in plain view, like a conjuror beginning some solemn trick, slipped it into his breast pocket so that Jack would note it. On the other hand, after he'd examined Jack's turnout—rather rigorously, and that too was untypical—he'd given a weird smirking expression, as if to say, 'Well, this is a bloody joke, isn't it?'

Outside, the air was clear and still and sharp, the sky a blazing blue. At ten o'clock the frost had barely melted from the fields and the hills lay powdered with white. The woods still had their yellows and browns. On the oak tree in Barton Field you could have counted every motionless, bronze-gold, soon-to-drop leaf.

It was a day as etched and distinct as Jack's memories of it would be, a day of which you might have said, at its brilliant start, that it was a fine day for something, whatever that thing might be. Even a Remembrance Day ceremony would do. And when this fine day changed— when Michael, after the ceremony, made his evident decision not to hang around, not to enter the Crown and buy his older son a drink and so let his younger son's name come up in conversation, it wasn't the simple, if unprecedented, skulking-off it seemed.

It had been for him, Jack, to say? His father was leaving it to him? But he hadn't said it. Not at first, when the little group round the memorial dispersed, nor after they'd stood by Vera's grave, nor all the way back, in that sparkling sunshine. They'd halted at the top of the track. Still he might have spoken. But he'd got out to unfasten the gate, then closed it behind his father as he'd driven through, then known it was definitely too late.

He'd pulled back the bolt. He remembers it all now. Two ridiculous men in briefly donned suits, in a worse-for-wear Land Rover, its exhaust pipe juddering and still steaming in the cold air; his father's uncustomarily combed head not turning as he re-entered Luxton territory, then stopped, with a loud yank on the hand brake, and waited for his son.

He'd swung shut the gate. The throbbing Land Rover was like some stray beast he'd herded back in. The decision had been all his. Maybe. But he'd also thought, his hands on the cold wooden rail and then on the even colder, rasping spring-bolt: You bastard, for leaving it to me, you bastard for not doing the decent thing yourself.

And thought it ever since, gone over it repeatedly in his head. It was somewhere, even, in the terrible dream out of which he surfaced, years later, in a hotel room in Okehampton. The simple opening and closing of a gate. He'd swung it back, perhaps, with extra force. And if he'd grasped that decision as he'd grasped and swung that gate—for God's sake, if he'd just bought his father a bloody pint—how different the consequences might have been.

That same night—this is what Jack told those he had to tell, and he had to tell it several times and never without great difficulty—Michael left his bedroom and the Luxton farmhouse at some early hour of the morning, possibly around three o'clock. It was another cold, still, frosty night, the sort of night on which no one leaves a house or even the warmth of their bed without a very good reason.

There's a version of it all that Jack tells only himself, an over-and-over revisited version that allows more room for detail and for speculation, but it's essentially the same version that he gave others and that for many years he's, thankfully, had no reason to repeat. Though one of the reasons why he sits now at the window of Lookout Cottage with a loaded gun on the bed behind him is the suddenly renewed and imminent possibility (which he hopes absolutely to avoid) of having to repeat it.

Michael had not been drinking, though drinking is not an uncommon accompaniment to events of this kind, which were themselves, around that time, becoming not so uncommon on small and hard-pressed dairy farms in the region. Not only were the Luxtons not great drinkers, but Michael had not even had a pint or two that lunch-time, which was one of the rare occasions when it might have been expected of him.

Nor has Jack, at his window now, been drinking. He is entirely sober. It's not a good thing to be drunk when handling a gun, in any circumstance.

Michael left the farmhouse on a freezing November night, long before dawn, and Jack would speculate to himself (though others would speculate too) why his father did everything that he did, not just in the cold but in the dark. It was not like when Tom slipped out that night, needing to do so by stealth. Though perhaps it was. Tom had needed only to find the track and climb up it. Dad's path was less marked. But Dad knew every inch of the farm and every bit of that field—Barton Field—back-wards. He knew it better than Tom. He knew it blindfold.

As Jack knew it too, and still knows it. He is perfectly able, still, without having been there for over ten years, and in the darkness, as it were, of his head, to retrace his father's movements that night as if they were his own. And right now he has a peculiar and unavoidable interest in doing so.

In any case, it was a clear night. There was starlight and there was a good chunk of moon, almost a full one, Jack had noted, which, by the time he noted it, had come up over the far hills. The question was never how, but why. Why in the *cold*—on such a night, and in those coldest hours before dawn? Though perhaps the answer to that was simple. It was dark and cold *anyway*. Michael Luxton was dark and cold inside. It was November. Winter, with the farm in ruins, stretched before them. Jack can see now the logic. Had it been springtime, with the first touch of warmth in the air, it's conceivable that Michael wouldn't have done what he did. But perhaps the truth is that if you're ready, such considerations are irrelevant. You don't consult, or much mind, the weather.

It's November now, although far from frosty. A strong, wet, gusting south-westerly.

Perhaps the crucial thing was that it was the night after Remembrance Sunday.

Jack, usually a sound sleeper, would puzzle over what it was that woke him. The shot, of course. But then if the shot had woken him, he later thought, he wouldn't have *heard* it, he would have wondered, still, what it was that woke him. In Jack's recounting of things—understandably confused—there was always a particular confusion about this point. He *had* heard the shot, yet the shot had woken him—as if in fact he was already awake to hear it, had known somehow beforehand that some dreadful thing was about to happen.

He was sure he hadn't heard his father leave—though his father must have made some noise and would have put on a light, downstairs at least, when he got the gun from the cabinet. There was a distinctive squeak to that cabinet door.

Then again, with the windows shut, the shot wouldn't have been so loud, not loud enough, necessarily, to wake a heavy sleeper. It would have carried in the frosty air, it's true, and been accentuated by the silence of the night, and it would have come from just a little nearer than the shot that had signalled Luke's death. But Jack had heard that from outside, in the yard, and he'd been expecting it.

Jack has always asserted that he heard the shot. It either woke him or, by some mysterious triggering inside him, he was awake to hear it. But he heard it. And he knew at once both where it had come from and what it meant. It might as well have been, as Jack has sometimes put it, in language unusually expressive for him, the loudest shot in the world.

And he has certainly thought what it might have been like if he *hadn't* heard it, if he'd slept through it. And has certainly blamed himself, of course, again and again (a point he also asserted to others that morning), that he was not awake even earlier. If he hadn't woken at all, he would have made the discovery only gradually. His dad might have been like a block of ice. Though could that have made it any worse?

But Jack has never wondered—at least when sharing his recollection of events—why his father chose the exact spot and position that he did. Among all the possible spots. Or why he, Jack, once awake, knew exactly where to go. He could explain this very easily by saying—though you'd have to be a Luxton to understand, you'd have to have spent your life on that farm—that if he'd ever been pushed to such a thing himself (and here, in some of Jack's earliest statements, his listeners, who'd included policemen and coroner's officers, had felt compelled to avert their eyes while they acknowledged a certain force of feeling) he'd probably have chosen exactly the same spot.

That oak, Jack might have added, was reckoned to be over five hundred years old. It had been there before the farmhouse.

Michael had put on the same clothes that he might have put on, a little later that morning, to do the tasks that had to be done about the farm: a check shirt, a thick grey jumper, corduroy trousers, long thick socks to go in Wellington boots—all of this in addition to the long-john underwear which in winter he normally slept in anyway. The suit he'd briefly worn only hours before (this was later noted) was back in the depths of the wardrobe. Then he'd put on his cap and scarf and his donkey jacket with the torn quilt lining, and the olive-green wool mittens that stopped short at the knuckles. So you might have said that he'd certainly felt the cold, given that he'd dressed so thoroughly for it. But all this was the force of habit. These clothes were like his winter hide, which he merely slipped off overnight. And, of course, he *did* have a task to complete. He even needed to make sure his fingers wouldn't go numb and useless on him.

He took the gun from the cabinet and took two number-six cartridges and either loaded them straight away, with the kitchen light on to help him, or loaded them at the last minute, in the dark and the cold. At either point it would have been an action of some finality.

The question would arise, which Jack, since he was asleep himself, could never answer, as to how much, if at all, Michael had slept that night: how, in short, he'd arrived at his course of action and its particular timing. He could hardly have set his alarm clock. Jack discovered no note, though he didn't tell the investigating policemen that he didn't find this surprising, and when asked by them if he'd noticed anything strange in his father's behaviour on the preceding day, he'd said only that they'd gone together to attend the short eleven-o'clock remembrance service beside the memorial in Marleston, as they did every year, because of the Luxtons who were on it. One of the two policemen, the local constable, Bob Ireton, would have been able to corroborate this directly, as he'd attended the ceremony himself, in his uniform, in a sort of semi-official capacity. It wasn't, therefore, a typical Sunday morning—they didn't put on suits every Sunday morning—but there was nothing strange about it, as PC Ireton would have wholly understood. It would have been strange if they hadn't gone. The only things that were strange about it, Jack had affirmed, were that Tom wasn't there (though the whole village knew why this was) and that they hadn't gone for the usual drink in the Crown afterwards.

And Jack had left it at that.

There were two other peculiarities about that (already highly peculiar) night that he might have remarked on, setting aside the peculiarity of where the act occurred—which Jack, in his fashion, suggested wasn't peculiar at all. One was that when he'd got up that night, suddenly galvanised into wakefulness and action, having somehow heard the shot and having somehow known what it meant, he'd naturally looked, even before hastily dressing and before (torch in hand) he left the farmhouse, into his father's bedroom—into what had always been known as the Big Bedroom. And had noticed that the bedclothes, recently pulled back, had an extra blanket—a tartan one—spread over them. There was nothing special about an extra blanket on a cold night, so in that respect it was unworthy of mention. Only Jack knew that he'd never seen that blanket spread over his father's bed before. Only Jack knew its history.

And Jack never mentioned either—was it relevant?—that there was a dog buried a little further down that field.

The second peculiarity—which Jack did point out, though the police might soon have discovered it for themselves—was that when Michael had dressed that night, he'd slipped a medal into the breast pocket of his frayed-at-the-collar check shirt. It was the same medal, of course, that Jack knew had been earlier that day in the pocket of his suit.

Why, later, the medal was in the pocket of his shirt was anyone's guess, but it would have meant—though Jack didn't go into this in his statement—that he must have been conscious of it during the intervening hours, and perhaps never returned it to its silk-lined box. He might have put it, for example, on his bedside table when he went to bed and before he slept, if he did sleep, that night. Perhaps—though this was a thought that would not crystallise in Jack's mind till many years later—he might even have clutched it in his hand.

These were considerations that Jack felt the police and, later, the coroner need not be interested in. Any more than they need be interested in the fact that Vera had died (and hers wasn't a quick death) in that same big bed with a tartan blanket now lying on it. Or that he himself had been born and, in all probability, conceived in it.

But the fact was that Michael had died wearing, so to speak, the DCM.

When the police had asked Jack how he'd discovered this so soon—after all, his father had been wearing two layers of thick clothing over his shirt, and anyway Jack was having to confront much else—Jack had said that he'd slipped his hand inside his father's jacket to feel if his heart was still beating. The policemen had looked at Jack. They might have said, if they'd had no regard for his feelings, something like: 'He'd just shot his brains out.' Jack had nonetheless insisted, with a certain dazed defiance, that he'd wanted to feel his father's heart, he'd wanted to put his hand over it. That had been his reaction. He didn't say that he'd wanted to feel not so much a beating heart—which would have been highly unlikely—but just if there was any last living warmth left on that cold night, beneath the old grey jumper, in his father's body.

But he said that he'd felt something hard there. Those were his actual words: he'd felt 'something hard there'.

When Jack said these things the two policemen—Ireton and a Detective Sergeant Hunt—had looked away. Jack was clearly in a state of great distress and shock. God knows what state he would have been in when he actually came upon the body. Bob Ireton knew Jack Luxton to be a pretty impervious, slow-tempered sort. He was looking now, for Jack, not a little wild-eyed. Bob had been at the same primary and secondary schools as Jack. He'd known, from its beginning, about Jack and Ellie Merrick—but then so did the whole village. Save for Ellie and his recently absconded brother (and Tom, as Bob would later observe, was not to reappear for the funeral), Jack was pretty much alone now in the world.

Bob Ireton was basically anxious—he couldn't speak for his plainclothes superior—to get this whole dreadful mess cleared up as quickly as possible and spare its solitary survivor any further needless torture. Poor man. Poor men. Both. Bob's view of the matter—again, he couldn't speak for his colleague—was as straightforward as it was considerate. Michael Luxton had killed himself with a shotgun. His son had discovered the fact and duly reported it to the authorities. In a little while from now, though there'd be a delay for an inquest, poor Jack would have to stand again in that suit he rarely wore, but had worn, as it happened, only the day before the death, beside his father's grave.

This was not the first time, in fact, that Constable Ireton had been required to attend the scene after the suicide of a farmer. Following the cattle disease, there had been this gradual, much smaller yet even more dismaying epidemic. One or two hanged themselves from a beam in a barn (sometimes watched by munching cattle), others chose a shotgun. A shotgun was marginally more upsetting. Bob frankly didn't attach much weight to the odd circumstantial details that sometimes went with a suicide, the strange things that might precede it, the strange things that might (it was not a good word) trigger it. It was a pretty extreme bit of behaviour anyway. Who could say what *you* (but that was not a good line of thinking and anyway not professional) might do?

But, sadly, he was not unused to the thing itself, no longer even surprised by it. The underlying causes were fairly obvious—look around. He was both glad and a little guilty to be a policeman, drawing his steady policeman's pay, while farmers all around him were going under. He should really have been like some odd man out within the community—though a policeman, a sort of outlaw—a stay-at-home version of Tom Luxton joining the army. Yet now his services were peculiarly called upon. He'd known that the Luxton farm, especially after Tom had withdrawn his labour, was near the limit. None of it was surprising, and the best thing was to clear it up as tidily as possible.

Had he been told when he became a policeman that he'd one day be officiating over all the wretched consequences of a so-called mad-cow disease, he'd have said that such an idea was itself mad. He hadn't supposed—though he hadn't sought a quiet life and there was such a thing as rural crime—that he'd become one day a sort of superintendent of misery. He'd never be (nor would DS Hunt, he reckoned) any other sort of superintendent.

And all this was years before the foot-and-mouth (by which time he was, at least, a sergeant). More dead cattle

—great crackling heaps of them. And a few more deaths among the 'farming fraternity'. Was it Jack Luxton who'd once passed on to him that phrase?

Poor men. Poor beasts. Both.

Michael crossed the yard and, skirting the Small Barn where the pick-up and the Land Rover and the spreader were housed, entered Barton Field by the top gate. Barton Field, only six acres and a roughly shaped strip of land, buckling and widening as it descended, was the nearest field to the farmhouse, its upper, narrow end meeting the shelf in the hillside where the farm buildings stood. Its challenging contours made it the least manageable field at Jebb, but it was the 'home' field of the farm and formed its immediate prospect. At the top, at its steepest, it bulged prominently, turning, further down, into a gentler scoop, so that its flat lower end was hidden from even the upper windows of the farmhouse. But this only enhanced the view. From the house you looked, over the fall of the land, to the woods in the valley and to the hills beyond, but principally took in—perfectly placed between fore-ground and background—the broad top third or so of the big single oak that stood near the middle of the field where its slope levelled off. The oak's massive trunk could not be seen, nor the immense, spreading roots which had risen above the surrounding soil. But between these roots, where the grass had given up, were small hollows of that reddish earth that Jack would notice on the last stages of a strange, westbound journey. The roots themselves were thick and ridged enough to form little ledges or seats, for a sheep or a man.

The oak was, of course, a great stealer of the surrounding pasture—its only value to provide shade for the livestock—but it was a magnificent tree. It had been there at least as long as Luxtons had owned the land. To have removed it would have been unthinkable (as well as a forbidding practical task). It simply went with the farm. No one taking in that view for the first time could have failed to see that the tree was the immovable, natural companion of the farmhouse, or, to put it another way, that so long as the tree stood, so must the farmhouse. And no mere idle visitor—especially if they came from a city and saw that tree on a summer's day—could have avoided the simpler thought that it was a perfect spot for a picnic.

None of these thoughts had particularly occurred to Michael or to Jack (or, when he was there, to Tom). They were so used to the tree straddling their view that they could, for most of the time, not really notice it. Nonetheless, it was straight to this tree that Michael walked on an icy November night, carrying a gun. Or as straight as the steep slope allowed.

Exact evidence of his path was left by the tracks in the frost that Jack, only a little later, picked up by the light of his torch. At one spot it was clear that his father had slipped and slid for a yard or more on his arse. It was very strange for Jack to think of this minor mishap at such a moment—of his father perhaps swearing under his breath at it and suffering its jolting indignity. As it was strange to think that this slip might not have been a simple slip at all, given that his father was carrying at the time a possibly already loaded and closed gun. There might have been a much nastier accident.

Had the frost not begun to melt—unlike the previous

morning—even before daybreak, it would have left a very clear record of the activity in Barton Field that night: Michael's tracks, with that slip, going in one direction, and Jack's going, separately, in both directions (and, despite the great agitation he was in, without a single slip). But all of them converging on the oak tree.

In his statements Jack had voluntarily made the point that when he'd spotted his father's tracks he'd both followed and avoided them, even carefully skirting round the broad mark where the slip had occurred. He had instinctively not walked through them, not out of forensic considerations, but because, as he failed really to convey clearly but as his listeners may have grasped, they were the last footsteps his father had taken.

Of course, this meant that the descending pair of tracks might have given the appearance that the two men had walked down together. There was certainly only one set of ascending tracks. But all this was neither here nor there, since by dawn and even by the time Jack made his phone call—he'd delayed the call because of the state he was in, but also because he knew not much could practicably be done while it was still dark—a change in the weather occurred. A breeze got up, bringing in cloud cover, and the air warmed appreciably.

By the time the two policemen arrived and descended the field with Jack—who was clearly dreading what he would have to see in daylight—the sharp night had turned into a grey, gusty morning. The top branches of the oak tree made a continual whirring above them, and dislodged leaves spun down. The frost had gone. There was even a touch of drizzle. So the policemen perhaps wondered why

Jack had needed to speak about the tracks he'd seen by torchlight that were no longer there—unless, of course, it was simply because he couldn't help reliving, and reliving again, every detail. Both officers were not unused to this. It was strange how the silent ones could suddenly become the gushers, while the regular gabblers could lose their voices.

But what both officers had mostly thought was: What must it have been like, to shine a torch on *that*?

The frost was there, anyway, when Jack first walked down, and would have sufficiently reflected the moonlight to make the torch barely necessary. The dark mass of the oak tree, against the ghostly silver of the field and the woods beyond, would have been visible of itself, Jack knew, to his father, who'd carried no torch. Perhaps his father had calculated even this, had waited for the moon to rise and light him. He would have been able to take a final look around. He would have been able, when it came to things closer to hand, to make out the roots under the tree and the gun he was holding: its dull metal glint and his own fingers on it.

Michael sat down at the foot of the oak. There was a sort of bowl in one of the thickest roots, close up to the trunk, which was ideal for this. He took his donkey jacket off first, despite the cold, the better perhaps to manipulate the gun, but also to spread under him before he sat. This precaution was as strange as it was natural: he'd wanted to spare his arse, already damp maybe, from any chilly hardness. It was like that extra blanket on the bed, though Jack didn't say this. Nor did Jack express to anyone his private view that his father would have removed his jacket so as to be better able to feel, through his remaining layers, the wrinkled bark and supporting, towering, centuries-old solidity of the tree against his back.

Michael had removed his cap as well, as if out of respect for something. He would have pressed the back of his head, too, against the trunk and its slight inward slope. This might have been mechanically necessary, but Jack had no doubt either, though he didn't say it (wasn't it plain—why had Michael gone to this spot at all?), that this was out of the same dominant motive. His father had simply wanted to press his head, his skull and his back hard against that oak tree and feel it pushing back. Spine against spine.

Jack knew—he knew it from climbing up the track in winter to get the school bus—that when you shine a torch at night it lights your way but makes the surrounding darkness several times darker. When he arrived beneath the tree he partly wished he hadn't brought a torch. It made the scene look like something horribly staged just to be lit up and it made everything else, despite the moonlight, pitch-black. Though Jack was technically prepared for what he would find, this had not made the discovery any less shocking, and how to describe what he'd felt at this moment was beyond him. Though he'd walked downhill—perhaps it was more of a scramble—he was panting for breath and his heart was banging inside him. Perhaps it was because of this that he'd reached out to feel for his father's heart, as if while one heart was beating so violently another could surely not be lifeless. To touch his father's breast certainly made more sense, in any case, than to touch any part of what was left of his head.

Thus he'd felt the small, hard object in his father's

shirt pocket and known exactly what it was. He didn't dare remove it. Why should he have removed it? He was overcome by conflicting instincts, to touch and not to touch. In its recoil, the gun had jumped from between his father's lips and from his fingers so that its double barrel lay now aimed at his waist. Even before stooping to feel his father's chest, Jack had automatically removed the gun, as if Michael was still in danger.

This was all wrong perhaps, he should have touched nothing, but it was what he did. He hadn't known if his father had loaded—or used—both barrels or if there was still a cartridge in place. He didn't know if he should have broken open the gun to check. Or indeed if he should have carried the gun back with him to the safety (though that was a strange idea) of the farmhouse. Normal procedure had been suspended. You didn't ordinarily leave a gun, especially one that might still be loaded, in the middle of a field, even if it was the small hours of the night. You didn't normally leave your father in a similar position. In any case, he moved the gun from where it had fallen and placed it to one side in a cleft between the roots. Then, after feeling his father's inert and medalled chest, he just stood—he couldn't have said for how long—over the body.

He couldn't have described his feelings at this time, but anger must have been part of them—a very large part of them—since, though this had no place at all in his subsequent relation of events, what he began to say, aloud and more than once in the middle of a dark field to his dead father, was: 'You bastard. You bastard.' Even as he shone a torch on his father's shattered features: 'You bastard.' He would never remember how many times he said it, he wasn't counting, but he couldn't stop saying it. 'You bastard. You bastard.'

It was the wrong word, perhaps, since it's not a word you use of your father or of any father, it's a word that works in the other direction, but he kept saying it, and the more he said it, the more it seemed not just an angry word but a useful, even encouraging word in the circumstances—the sort of word you might use to someone who wasn't dead but just in a precarious situation, to help them pull through it. 'You bastard.' It kept coming to his mouth like a chant or some regular convulsion, like the only word he might ever say again.

He was saying it when, after standing for however long it was, he actually sat down beside his father, his own back against the tree—it was easily broad enough—and wondered if he shouldn't stay there with him, freezing as it was, at least until dawn, or if he should take the donkey jacket from under him and wrap it round him, or—since that would have its problems—if he shouldn't take off his own jacket and wrap it round him. 'You bastard. You bastard.' He was saying it when he wondered whether to pick up the gun or leave it where it was. He was saying it, at intervals, when after deciding to leave the gun—it seemed to belong there—he made the climb back up the steepening field to the farmhouse, his breath coming like the strokes of a saw through his chest: 'You bastard.' He was saying it as the farmhouse and the lights he'd left on rose monstrously over the hump of the field above him, and as he passed by the Small Barn into the yard. By now it had become like some hoarsely uttered password. 'You bastard.'

He continued to say it during the period between

regaining the farmhouse and making the call he knew he would have to make, when he had no clear sense of the passage of time and when he continually wavered between the thought of making the call, which would make things final and definite, and the thought that he should go back down to the oak tree, because what had happened perhaps might not really have happened at all. Or because he should just be there with his father. Up here, in the farmhouse, he'd already deserted him. 'You bastard.'

He said it as he wondered whether he should wash off the muck that had got on his hands or whether he should leave it there for all of time to erase or ingrain. 'You bastard.' And he'd got so rhythmically used to saying it, that when he finally made the call and was able to get out that other word, 'Police', it's not inconceivable that he might have said, 'You bastard,' too, into the phone.

He didn't mention his repeated utterance of this phrase to Bob Ireton and his senior companion (or to anyone else), nor did he mention that during the preceding day and evening, following the Remembrance Day gathering, he had also uttered the phrase, if not aloud, but inside himself or perhaps under his breath. But the fact that he'd vented it, one way or the other, so much beforehand somehow enabled Jack to regain a degree of composure—it was his strange way, even, of haranguing himself—and to give the detailed and relatively focussed account of events that he gave. All of which, together with the actual evidence lying there in Barton Field, added up to the overwhelming conclusion, to be endorsed by the inquest, that Michael Luxton had taken his own life.

Neither policeman felt it was his place to comment on the strangenesses, so far as they knew them, of Jack's behaviour—who wouldn't behave strangely?—or on his technically inappropriate actions. He shouldn't have touched the body or even have moved the gun. But this was his own father lying there. Jack was hardly some meddling third party. The poor man had done what he did and could—when, quite possibly, he might have slept through the whole incident. And he was plainly mortified by the fact that, had he been awake just a little earlier, he might have prevented all of it from happening.

One didn't have to search far for a motive. Michael Luxton was like others. The peculiar circumstances of Remembrance Day seemed tragically to have precipitated something. Michael had either gone to bed with the not quite complete intention of acting, or he'd woken in the dead of night to form that soon-executed intention.

Detective Sergeant Hunt gave permission for the body to be moved by the ambulance men. It was a laborious and upsetting job transporting it up the steep field. The gun and Michael's donkey jacket and cap were taken separately as evidence, to be returned later. Likewise everything in Michael's pockets, including the medal.

Thus it would have been possible for the two policemen, out of curiosity as much as anything, to inspect the medal and see what was written on its reverse. It had been one of Michael's infrequent, sombre-faced, hard to gauge jokes that the medal had been a good one to give a farmer's boy, since what it said on the back was 'For Distinguished Conduct in the Field'.

DS Hunt had thought it right, for safety reasons, to examine the gun straight away. It was unlikely that there was a cartridge still in there (why should Michael have done things by halves?) and it was confirmed that both barrels had been recently (and it must have been simultaneously) discharged and that the gun was now unloaded. Sergeant Hunt also asked Bob, after the ambulance had departed, if—while he himself remained with Jack at the farmhouse—he couldn't find a bucket or two of water and (it would be a grim chore, he knew) carry them down to the oak and give things a slooshing down. It would be a decency. This was technically interfering with evidence too, but DS Hunt felt he had seen and noted carefully all the evidence necessary, and it would be a sort of kindness. PC Ireton felt likewise.

It was unfortunate in one sense, but fortunate in another, that Jack couldn't help overhearing this, and so offered to drive them all down in the pick-up with a jerry can of water, buckets and even a stiff-bristled yard brush. He appeared in need of things to do, no matter how gruesome. Bob had said that no, that wouldn't be necessary, but it might help if he could borrow the pick-up and be told where the jerry can was.

Jack was also manifestly and increasingly worried about his livestock and about several regular morning tasks not attended to. He seemed, in fact, to have a gathering sense that the farm was about to disintegrate around him—which had only been Michael's apparently no longer tolerable situation. But all this was duly taken care of. Both Constable Ireton and DS Hunt had the forethought to appreciate that a farm, even in extraordinary circumstances, cannot simply shut down. So there had been some necessary, discreet communications and a prevailing upon a horrified but quickly rallying community spirit. It wouldn't have been long anyway before word spread around.

It certainly wasn't long before a battered Land Rover containing Jimmy and Ellie Merrick, dressed as for a hard-working day on their own farm, pulled up in the Jebb yard. This was the first time Jack had seen such a thing. But then he'd seen other things today he'd never seen before. Jimmy and Ellie had come the short way—by the route with which Jack was very familiar—across the fields, through the boundary gate and over Ridge Field, which adjoined Barton Field. The direct route would then have been along the top of Ridge Field, to enter the Jebb yard close to the Big Barn, but Jimmy hadn't hesitated to drive along the bottom of Ridge Field and then, despite slipping wheels, slowly up by the low hedge alongside Barton Field, so getting a good view down across the dip to the oak tree. The body was still there, though about to be moved, and mostly and perhaps mercifully hidden behind the tree trunk. Jimmy and Ellie could only really make out two very still Wellington boots.

When the Land Rover arrived in the yard it was impossible, particularly for the two policemen, to read precisely the expression on old Merrick's face. It had a gnome-like quality that could have meant anything—triumph or shock or perhaps a recent quick but significant intake of alcohol. In any case, he'd stuck his head out of the window and explained to DS Hunt (they knew Bob Ireton) that they were neighbours, they were the Merricks, who were long and good old neighbours of the Luxtons, and they were here to help.

Ellie, in contrast, had been silent and had looked, for a while, rather white. But she soon began to make herself useful. In fact she made her busy presence felt around

Jebb Farm that day as if she herself might have owned it. It even looked at one point as though she might have been preparing to stay the night, which would have been another first. Jimmy might actually have conceded it. But just when it had begun to seem a distinct possibility, Mrs Warburton, with cardboard boxes of provisions she thought appropriate, drove over from Leke Hill Cross. She was older now, but she had her memories of Jebb Farmhouse and of when she'd been of vital assistance before. And, like some woman picking over a battlefield, she herself voiced the question that, above that still-insistent chorus of 'You bastard', was also tolling through Jack's head.

'My God, what would your poor mother have thought?'

27

JACK PULLED BACK the curtains—warily, as if expecting horrors—on the town of Okehampton. Sleep hadn't entirely deserted him, but he'd passed a dreadful, see-sawing night, uncertain of what was truth or dream. Surely, he'd fleetingly convinced himself, it was only a dream that he was lying here, in a hotel room in Okehampton, on this journey that was all some evil product of his mind. Yet he could remember (the two nights had seemed to merge together) islands of similar, wishful delirium during the terrible night he'd passed after his father's death. Surely it could not be so. Surely it was still only the night before and his father was still asleep, across the landing in the Big Bedroom (whether under a tartan blanket or not), and he, Jack, had never heard the shot that had sent him along that nightmare alleyway of events that had never occurred.

The clear blue sky over the rooftops mocked him with its sharp reality. It would have to be a day like *that* day, that Remembrance Day. Some of the roofs were grey with frost, others, where the sun had already struck, were a mottling of sparkling white and glossy black. Okehampton, like any country town at daybreak, was a huddle of re-emerging familiarities, and this was the sort of crisp, bright morning that could only make its inhabitants more confident of their world. But Jack felt like a spy behind enemy lines.

So it was true then, it was all true. Today he had to do some things (having done some things yesterday). He had to attend a funeral—in less than three hours. Then he had to drive a hundred miles to an off-shore island where (though the idea now seemed strange to him) he had his home. That was all he had to do.

Today he had to be in a place he hadn't been in for over ten years—had believed he might never need to be in again. The last funeral he'd attended there had been his father's, when Tom, because of his inflexible military duties (or so it was generally understood), had been absent. Now, and for the same reason, Tom would most certainly be present. What was left of him would be present. But once again it would be Jack who would be the only living member of the Luxton family visible, the eyes of the whole village on him, now as then—on him and boring into him, into what might be inside his head.

Though 'head', back then, had not been such a good word to call to mind. And that wasn't, quite, the last funeral he'd attended in Marleston. Since not long afterwards—how could he forget?—he'd stood by the grave of Jimmy Merrick, offering his arm (and shoulder to weep on should it be necessary) to Ellie.

And where was Ellie Merrick, in her supportive role, today?

When Jack had stood by his father's grave, he'd already had the thought (partly anticipated for him by Sally

Warburton) that at least his mother had never had to know how her husband had died. Though he'd also had the thought that, now the two of them were in a manner of speaking reunited again, she might get the whole story—underground, as it were—direct from the man himself.

And now it was true, with the same possible proviso, that neither Michael nor Vera would have to know how their younger son died. Vera had never even had to know that Tom had left the farm. Nor that Jack—even Jack—had left it too.

When Jack needed to arrange Michael's funeral he'd had to discuss with Malcolm Brookes, the rector (who would be officiating today), the delicate question—or the notion that had somehow got into Jack's head—of whether, given the nature of his father's death, his funeral would actually be allowed. In Church ground. Brookes had expressed his opinion of Jack's quaint idea in language surprisingly graphic for a clergyman ('This isn't the damn Middle Ages,' Brookes had said), but had then added with a sort of patient smile, 'Do you think, for any reason, I'm going to keep those two apart?'

So Brookes believed it, then? In the meeting—the re-meeting—of souls. But then, after all, Brookes would.

Death, Jack thought, looking out at brilliant, exposing sunshine in Okehampton, was in many ways a great place of shelter. It was life and all its knowledge that was insupportable.

He thinks the same, looking from his rain-blurred window, now.

*

It was a little past seven-thirty. A faint smell of frying bacon reached him even as he stood surveying the street. Breakfast was being cooked downstairs. And, even in his present state of mind, the smell caused a benign reaction in his stomach. Jack had sometimes been heard to observe—down among the caravans on those dewy August mornings when pans would be generally sizzling—that the smell of frying bacon was the best smell in the world. None of his listeners had ever disagreed. Instead of 'best', he might have said (consulting his memory) 'most comforting' or 'most consoling'. Sally Warburton, whose boxfuls of emergency items, that awful morning, had included a fair amount of prime bacon, had been surprised, if also relieved, to see Jack wolf down several rashers. Though it was almost noon by then and the poor man had been up, apparently, since long before dawn.

If they'd all been pig farmers, Sally had thought, if this had just been pig country, none of this would have happened.

But the smell now entering Jack's nostrils heartened him also by simply suggesting that he might not, after all, be the only guest in the hotel. He would not be alone, perhaps, and so under unrelieved scrutiny by the proprietor or her deputies when he appeared for breakfast. Though not being alone, being under the eyes of other guests, might have its problems too. Before the funeral, this would be the only point at which he'd have to run the risk of other people's curiosity. Or suspicion.

On the pavement opposite, two early-rising inhabitants of Okehampton had stopped to exchange energetic greetings, as if they might not have met for years. Their reddened, beaming faces seemed to Jack to go with the thought of bacon.

Within half an hour, shaved and wearing a clean white shirt and the dark trousers of his suit, he'd made his way, as advised the night before, to the 'back bar'. He could as easily have followed his nose.

It was a sunken, low-ceilinged place, which at other times might have been poorly lit, but was now pierced by bands of blinding light from the low sun shining through a gap in the buildings across the street. The shafts caught the polished surface of the bar, where the pump handles had been draped with tea-towels, and the glinting cutlery on several laid-up tables. There was obviously a kitchen close by, since the shafts were full, along with dancing motes, of bluish swirls.

Two of the tables, half in and half out of sunshine, were occupied by solitary men intently chomping food and studying newspapers. Jack was relieved to find that they required nothing more from him than a nod and a muttered, 'Morning,' and that, like him, they wore smart, open-necked shirts. They might have been three of a kind. He was in a hotel which in November catered, if it catered for anyone, for travelling reps with limited expense accounts. It seemed suddenly to Jack an innocent and honourable league to belong to, and he began to invent for himself—in case he should come to be questioned—an alias as a salesman. What might it be? Agricultural machinery? No, caravans, of course. All those sites that in winter might be considering replacements. He was travelling—in caravans.

He was also relieved to see that the proprietor seemed to be in sole charge of the kitchen and the serving of breakfast. Hers was at least a familiar face and, so long as she was busy, he felt, an unthreatening one.

He ordered the Devonshire Breakfast. It was no different in its basic components from a breakfast you might have had in any county, but it was, when it came, very good. The bacon in particular was very good. It was so good that for a few minutes, despite what lay before—and behind—him and despite the miserable night he'd passed, Jack's whole being relaxed into that of a man solely given over to the consuming of breakfast. It really was extremely good. He felt amazingly restored.

But no sooner had he finished eating than he'd looked up and seen, in the small porthole window of the swing door leading to the kitchen, not the face of the proprietor, but the face of Tom, peering in and peering directly at him. Since it was only his face, Jack couldn't tell if he was in his combat gear again (or if, for example, he was wearing an apron), but he was looking in as a mindful chef might briefly look in to see if the customers—and one particular customer—were happy.

It was Tom who'd made this breakfast, Tom who'd cooked his bacon.

Tom's face had disappeared. Then Jack, who'd scrupulously avoided the morning papers lying on the bar and had picked up instead an unhelpful brochure—'Things to Do in North Devon'—had glanced towards the front page obscuring one of his fellow breakfasters and seen the caption 'Heroes Return' (it wasn't the top story, but it was there in the corner) and had also seen the photo. He couldn't tell which of the coffins it was. Nonetheless, he was sure.

So everything that had happened yesterday was really

and undeniably true. It was publicly the case. Though for that man sitting there at his breakfast, concealed by his newspaper, and perhaps for thousands of others doing the same, it was not even drawing his eye.

Less than an hour later Jack drove northwards from Okehampton towards Marleston, the long shadow of the Cherokee leaping out ahead of him. His last act before leaving his hotel room had been to slip the medal into the breast pocket of his suit (his fresh white shirt had no pocket). He was quite sure by the time he settled his bill that the woman really knew who he was, but wasn't saying. Or, at least, that when she looked later at her paper (hadn't she looked already?) it would simply jump out at her: Luxton, I thought it rang a bell.

The traffic was light and the road shone. He'd delayed his departure so that he could pace this short final leg comfortably, without having to stop or cruise around to kill time. He filled up with petrol just outside town.

During these few miles Tom didn't appear at his side again. Jack took this to mean that Tom was now entirely sure that he, Jack, would complete the journey, would keep his appointment. Nonetheless, during this last stage Jack felt constrained to say aloud a number of times, softly but purposefully, 'I'm coming, Tom. I'm nearly there.' He would hardly have needed to do this if he'd felt that Tom might in any sense have been his passenger.

Ten-fifteen, he'd reckoned. Ten-fifteen for ten-thirty. He couldn't, of course, be late, but, just as with yesterday's ceremony, he didn't want to be so early as to be trapped by people. He didn't know how many there would be.

A sprinkle, or—given that it was clearly national news—a multitude? He should be just sufficiently early as was decent and as would allow him to make his presence known and to get his practical bearings. Perhaps, he vaguely anticipated, he could then ask to spend a few moments somewhere safely alone.

He was aware that being who he uniquely was might grant him excuses for behaviour that might otherwise seem clumsy, inadequate, even rude. He was relying on playing this card. He'd played it, strongly, yesterday. His principal plan—he didn't disguise it from himself—was to get away with as little as possible: time, involvement, talk. Pain. He would do the essential thing, he wasn't shirking that, but he wasn't up for any extras.

The arrangements he'd made—all by phone—had been minimal. He'd spoken to Babbages. He'd spoken to Brookes. And he'd spoken, of course, to Major Richards. No flag, please, the battalion could keep it. A non-military funeral, thank you. He'd been surprised at his own firmness. He'd not made a point of notifying people, let alone inviting them. He'd left that as a matter between Brookes and his parishioners. He knew that he was supposed to organise and host some gathering afterwards. But where could that be? There was only one appropriate place: Jebb Farmhouse. Impossible. The Crown? No. In any case, he knew he couldn't go through with it. Be the living centrepiece. Make a bloody speech (having not made one yesterday). Whatever poor form it might be, he couldn't do it. He would be present, that was the main thing.

A simple word had come, theoretically, to his aid: 'private'. Today's thing was private, if yesterday's hadn't been. Arguably, the whole thing was immeasurably private, and Major Richards had even framed for him that statement—for public release—that 'Corporal Luxton's family' (though there was only one) 'hoped that their need for privacy and peace in this time of great sorrow would be respected'.

But Jack could equally see that private was a thin, even treacherous word. A war memorial, for example, was not a private thing. It was a public monument, the names on it were for all to read. And how did a common soldier, serving his country in its public causes, ever get to be called a private? Fuller, Pickering. (Where were they now—and those clusters that went with them?) In any case, life in a village was never private, Jack knew that. Everyone eyed everyone else. This was one respect in which, today, he could envy the inconspicuous existence of those who lived in cities.

Yesterday's event should have trained him up, perhaps, for exposure. This little affair in a country churchyard ought to be a doddle in comparison. But Jack knew— seeing now the line of frost-speckled hills that he hadn't seen for over ten years—that it wasn't so.

Brookes and Babbages had been good to deal with. He'd been both pleased and troubled that it was still Brookes, since the rector's voice, even on the phone, took him straight back to the burial of his father (and of Jimmy). Brookes had said, 'I don't know what to say, Jack. The last time we spoke was when . . . And now this.' It was reassuring somehow to know that a man of the Church didn't know what to say. But Jack didn't like that linkage across twelve years—first that, now this—as if the two things were actually connected and the later one would unearth the other. Perhaps Brookes, who'd been so solid that first time, might be stretched past his limits now. A suicide—now *this*?

Brookes had asked Jack, among other things, if at the service he might want to say a few words of his own. Jack had said no, he couldn't face it, which was only honest, and Brookes hadn't pressed the point and had said, 'Fair enough.' Then Brookes had asked Jack if he wanted him, in his own address, to say anything in particular—possibly something about those two Luxton brothers on the memorial outside? Jack had thought for a while and said no, he didn't want that, and Brookes had also seemed to think for a while and had said again, 'Fair enough.' By then Jack was getting the comforting impression that Brookes understood that what he wanted was really only what he'd wanted that first time, twelve years ago, when they'd spoken face to face. As little and as simple as possible.

Brookes, indeed, was well aware by now (he'd been rector for over twenty-five years) that it was what most people really craved at such events, even when there were no extraordinary circumstances to acknowledge, as little and as simple as possible being really the essence of the thing, the bare bones, so to speak. So: a simple service, just the one address, and he would have to find some way—but he'd somehow done it before—of referring to the exceptional (and violent) manner of the death. He'd have to give it some thought and come up with something. The coffin would lie in the church overnight and, after the service, be carried out to the churchyard—Jack as principal bearer (this was the bit, Brookes noted, that seemed to matter most to the man)—for a simple burial. Hardly more, as Brookes knew very well, than eighty paces.

These thoughts had gathered in his mind even as he'd spoken to Jack on the phone. 'So,' he'd said, sensing that Jack didn't want to prolong the conversation, 'he'll be next to his mum and dad again.' And had heard a silence down the line. He'd added, 'It'll have been a long journey.' Then, hearing only more silence, he'd asked (he'd known he'd have to ask it and this was the only chance) whether there would be a flag, a Union Jack, over the coffin? And if not, would he like them—the parish— to organise one? Or anything else along those lines? Never having presided over an event of this kind before, Brookes was not at all sure how things worked. But Jack had finally spoken again to say no, he didn't want a flag. There wouldn't be a flag. And Brookes, after a pause, had said, 'Fair enough.'

Brookes would be there, Jack thought, looking older. Who else? Sally and Ken Warburton? How might Sally shake her head this time? Bob Ireton? Still the local bobby? The whole damn village would be there—remembered or half-forgotten faces leaping out at him like flash bulbs—but, given that the thing was on the front pages, Jack thought, so might the whole bloody world.

As well as speaking to Brookes, to Babbages, to Major Richards and to some other necessarily connected parties, Jack had in recent days been obliged to speak—or had avoided speaking—to quite a few people who wanted to speak to him. Most of whom had wanted to know, above all, how he felt, what his feelings were at this particular time, and had given the impression that they thought he might be only too grateful to be asked to share them. Jack had used the supposedly exempting word 'private' with these people, but it hadn't often worked, and he'd opted instead for a basic policy of evasion which, on the other hand, had felt shaming and—evasive. At yesterday's event he'd successfully given the reporters (he'd noticed their presence, like a different kind of cluster) the slip. He'd given everyone the slip. But now, as he approached his ultimate destination, he had the feeling he'd had before of being liable to arrest.

Ireton, yes, Ireton would be there. With a set of handcuffs. After the burial, and all its due allowances, he might say, 'Now, Jack, come with me.'

As he drew nearer, he was in fact already and very intently planning his escape. Right now, with his mobile still firmly switched off, no one knew exactly where he was, or if he'd even appear. Let alone how he felt. Ten-fifteen. And away—by when? If he was not under the immunity of privacy, then he was surely under the protection, the alibi of grief.

While he couldn't have feared more the clutching actualities of the occasion before him, Jack was hoping that he might pass through them like some shadow—both there and not there. Who could come near his situation? His compounded situation. First that, now this. He would be untouchable. He would be, in effect—and what could be more appropriate and more purely expressive of his situation?—like the corpse he would nonetheless have to bear on his shoulder. This was how he felt.

And perhaps because he wished it enough or perhaps

because, in the event, he was so simply and helplessly dazed and stunned by the whole process, this was how it was.

He turned onto a narrow minor road (there was still the same ivy-shrouded tree stump on the corner), and the matter felt out of his hands. It seemed impossible that the familiar sights now thickening round him could still be here, or else impossible that he'd been away. He surrendered to their ambush. That strange word 'repatriation' came again into his head. He said again, softly but firmly, 'I'm coming, Tom. I'm nearly there.'

And very soon he was. After some more turnings the narrow lanes became the deep single-track trenches he remembered. In summer grass would sprout in the middle. He'd chosen a route that avoided approaching Marleston from the east—past the entrance to Jebb—but, coming to a brow, he spotted through a gateway the church tower, across the valley that included both Westcott and Jebb. Then, having not encountered any other delays since turning off the main road, he immediately came up behind not one, but two, three, four—perhaps more—cars all heading in the same direction, and grasped at once where they must be going, as well as something of the actual numbers at this strictly private event.

He became now part of a general, creeping congestion, as if he were no more than some frustrated minor attender at the occasion ahead. This turned all his other misgivings into a wild exasperation that was outwardly just the self-important rage of someone stuck in traffic. In all his journey so far, even in Portsmouth, there'd been no significant jams. Now here he was, less than a mile from Marleston and crawling. But what could he do? Press his horn? Flash his lights? This was Devon, where both sides of a vehicle almost touched the hedges. Let me through. Let me pass. I'm a brother.

Such was his panic that he wouldn't clearly recall later precisely how he arrived—how he parked or how he got himself from his car to the church. But he would remember having to say more than once, to clear a path, 'I'm Jack Luxton, I'm Tom Luxton's brother.' Though wasn't it blazingly obvious? Who else did people think he was?

He would remember noticing that the Crown and the war memorial were still there, still uncannily in place, though he didn't want to look straight at them, and the same applied to all the milling people—you couldn't quite call it a crowd, but it certainly wasn't a handful. Something like a lock in his neck kept his gaze fixed on the gate to the churchyard and, beyond it, the church porch, so that even if he'd wanted to seek out and acknowledge familiar faces, he couldn't have done so. He was in a tunnel. Pressing on into the churchyard, he registered, at the edge of his vision, the gravestones of his mother and father and, close to them, a specially prepared area with some vivid green carpeting spread over the turf, but he didn't want to look directly at these things in case they might somehow render him unable to walk.

Then suddenly moving towards him—to meet him but also, it seemed, to rescue him—there was Brookes, in a white surplice that reminded him of those army padres, and with him, like some little unit under his command, a group of men who included Derek and Dave, the hearse drivers (how strangely good it was to see them),

267

and Ireton. Yes, Ireton, in a smart-looking uniform with three stripes on it, Ireton who'd once sluiced down his father's gore from the bark of an oak tree.

They all looked at him with the relieved and now activated looks of men who'd been waiting, perhaps with mounting anxiety, for nothing other than his arrival, and Jack realised, even as he also seemed to be floating absently and powerlessly, that he was the one who was here to make this thing click and function and cohere. He might have snapped his fingers and given orders if he'd been so disposed.

Derek and Dave greeted him like old friends. Their faces seemed to say, 'You didn't think we'd miss it, did you?' Then Ireton said, deferentially but quickly, like a man not wanting to waste valuable time, 'I'll be your other shoulder, Jack, if that's okay with you.' Your other shoulder? Then Jack understood. And, though he'd not given any previous thought to who might occupy this position, felt now he could have put his arms round both of Ireton's dark-blue shoulders and wondered why he'd ever supposed that Bob—Sergeant Ireton—might be here to clap him in handcuffs.

Six men, Ireton rapidly explained: the two of them in front and, behind, four men from Babbages, including Derek and Dave who would take the rear positions. 'Unless—' Ireton had hesitated and his head had done a strange swivel towards the crowd (perhaps it really could be called a crowd) standing at a discreet distance though seeming to have the church surrounded. 'Unless there's anyone else? Unless you'd like some other arrangement?'

It seemed that everyone was ready to defer to him. He was like a king. At the foot of the church wall, he'd glimpsed, along the whole grey, weathered flank, stacks of resting flowers. Bunches, wreaths, two and three deep.

No, Jack said to Ireton, it was fine. The other two men from Babbages had introduced themselves and he'd shaken their hands and said, 'Thank you,' and shaken everyone's hand and said, 'Thank you,' and this had seemed suddenly the most important and exclusively detaining thing, the names and the gripping, knuckly hands of these men.

But Brookes now intervened, pulling up a sleeve of his white robe to look at his watch. 'It's just gone twenty past, Jack. Everything's ready, but we haven't let anyone in yet.' He coughed. 'If you'd like a moment first, just to be alone, the church is all yours. Let us know when you're ready. Take your time.'

And then there he was, alone but not alone, in the stony hush of the church, with the coffin and the single circle of heavy-smelling white flowers that he'd ordered through Babbages now resting on it. It was the first time it had been like this, just the two of them, and it would never be like it again. He felt for a moment that he was in some box himself. He seemed to need to break through the wall of air that surrounded the coffin before he could put his hands on it (again), then his cheek to it, then his forehead, then his lips. These were actions that he hadn't planned or foreseen, but was simply commanded by his body to do. He said, 'I'm here, Tom. I'm here with you.' Then he said, as if he'd not made something clear, 'We're both here.'

The coffin was plain oak. Was it English oak? He felt its smoothness, examined the grain in the wood, breathed the scent of the flowers. It was suddenly like some inextricable riddle Brookes had set him, to be alone like this with the coffin, a dilemma beyond solving. 'Take your time.' How could any time be long enough? Yet it had to be limited—outside were all those people. On the other hand, Jack couldn't find the words, the thoughts or whatever it was, beyond his physical presence, that might have properly filled this unrepeatable interval.

It was extraordinary that while Tom had appeared to him clearly several times in the last twenty-four hours, he was now nowhere to be seen. Was he hiding somewhere else, behind a pillar, in this church? No, Tom was with him, here in this box. All there was of Tom was here. He felt, though he couldn't see Tom, couldn't hear him, couldn't see the signalling flickers in his face, that they were like two people waiting for something together, for the next thing to happen, and neither of them was sure who should make the first move, though it was foolish perhaps to delay. You decide. No, you. A sort of game. So he finally lowered his lips again to the coffin—he had never kissed any piece of wood like this, he had never kissed Tom like this when he was alive, except when he was very small and wouldn't ever have known about it. Then Jack said, 'Well, shall we get on with it?'

For a while, after that, it was like nothing so much as a wedding. He had to sit right at the front near the aisle, near the coffin, like a waiting groom. Eyes were on his back, he didn't know how many eyes, but he felt it was all right that he didn't turn, it was all right, it was even the correct thing, to keep his eyes to the front. Were the eyes behind him thinking he was like a bridegroom too? Were some of them thinking: Where's Ellie?

It seemed now impossible that the coffin before him was the same coffin that he'd watched yesterday being carried off a plane and that had been flown all the way from Iraq. That it had come all that way and by such a remarkable chain of events and arrangements, to stand now quietly here. There seemed no connection. There was no sign of the connection (he hadn't noticed—in his not-looking—any Union Jacks) and no one so far had made any mention of it, so that it seemed there might be some silent communal effort around him to make it not exist. As if Tom had died, at a tragically early age, just a little distance away. A tractor accident, perhaps.

But then Brookes had got up and said, among other things, that they all knew why they were here and they also all knew why Tom was here, though he hadn't been here, some people would know, for a very long time. He'd been in other parts of the world. But he didn't want to talk about how Tom Luxton had died and what he'd died for, because this wasn't that sort of occasion and other people had spoken of those things and might still speak of them. But what he wanted to remember, as he was sure others here would want to remember—as some of them really *could* remember—was 'the boy who was born in Marleston'.

That was what Brookes had said: 'the boy who was born in Marleston'. Though he might have chosen to say (and Jack knew why he didn't) the boy who was born at Jebb Farm. It wouldn't have been true, of course. It wasn't even true that Tom had been born in Marleston. Didn't Brookes know? He'd been born in a maternity unit in Barnstaple. And nearly killed his mother in the process. It was Jack who'd been born in Marleston, Jack who'd been born at Jebb. Jack who was really the boy—

But he'd known what Brookes had meant. He had the medal in his jacket pocket. He didn't know any more clearly now, if he'd known at all, why he'd brought it all this way. It wasn't Tom's medal. It went with one of the names on the memorial outside—or you might say with two of them. But his hand went, as Brookes spoke, to the small, round solidity against his chest.

Then Brookes had stopped talking and there was a hymn and a prayer or two, and then this whole part of it was over and it was time for the thing that was the most important thing for Jack, that was really why he was here. He had to go forward now with the five men whose hands he'd shaken and be their leader, even while they, in a sense, would all carry him. Just as they would all carry Tom. He would have to walk with Ireton on the other side and Tom between, facing the congregation now, facing the whole lot of them, but it would be all right if he didn't smile, it would be all right if he didn't look anyone in the eye. This wasn't a bloody wedding. It would be all right if he didn't show anything in his face, which came quite naturally to him anyway. He would have to be both like and not like one of those six soldiers yesterday. He should have shaken their hands too. He would have to walk, a finite number of paces though he would never count them, with his cheek against the coffin, his shoulder against the coffin, these parts of him closer to Tom than they would ever be again, feeling, sharing Tom's weight.

And so it was. They emerged through the porch into the painful brightness of the November morning. Behind them the congregation began to file out and follow, but it was as though, Jack thought, the church might have turned into a great grey empty-bellied plane. For the first time now, since he was looking straight towards it, Jack couldn't avoid seeing the same exact line of hills, across the valley—Dartmoor in the far distance—that could be seen from Jebb Farm.

It wasn't difficult, as a physical task, it wasn't so difficult. Ireton was a big man too. He felt the whole thing might be on a backward tilt, and that would be tough on the two at the back. But then the downward slope in the churchyard corrected that. And it wasn't heavy. Though Tom had been a big man, like his brother. Was it because of the distribution of the load among six? Or because—? What was inside? He knew how his mother had died, he knew how his father had died. His brother's death was a mystery. He suddenly wanted, needed to feel the weight of his brother. It seemed that, with his cheek and one palm pressed against the wood, he was urging Tom to let him feel his weight.

It was a matter of perhaps twenty steps now, a steadily diminishing number of steps. Jack could see the opening of the grave before him, see, close by, but didn't want to look and so see the names, the gravestones of his parents, and, yes, he felt sure at last that he could feel, inside, through the wood, through his cheek, through his hand, on these last steps, the shifting, swaying, appreciative weight of his brother. He would be all right now, he felt sure, so long as this weight was on his shoulder. He wanted it to be there for ever. And with each last pace he said now, inside, 'I rocked you, Tom, I rocked you.'

28

MICHAEL LUXTON died instantly. The double cartridge-load of shot that passed through the roof of his mouth, then through the back of his head, smashing and impelling outwards everything in between, might as well have been, at that absence of range, a single solid bullet. It continued to pass, along with fragments of bark, skull and brain, some significant distance into the oak tree against which he'd been leaning. It could be said that the tree felt nothing. The tree never flinched and no more registered Michael's death than Michael did himself. For an oak tree that big and thick and old, to have a parcel of compacted shot and other matter embedded not even deep in its flesh was of no importance. Trees endure worse mutilation.

But the hole, some three feet or more up the trunk, remained, its aperture reduced but defined as the bark grew a ring-like scar around it. It was there when Jack, with five others, lowered his brother's coffin into its grave. It's there now. The surrounding stain on the bark remained too, despite that sluicing down on the day itself by PC Ireton. Unlike the stains on the ground, which soon disappeared, it weathered gradually and came to look like some indeterminate daub of the kind sometimes seen near the base of trees, or like some fungal blemish associated with that odd puncture in the trunk. What was it there for? Had someone once tried to hammer something, for some strange agricultural purpose, into the wood?

Of course, Jack knew how it had got there, and a few other involved parties would have been able to explain, very exactly, its cause. But to any outsider or newcomer to Jebb Farm—and there would be newcomers—the hole would have been a puzzle, if not a very detaining one.

One person who certainly knew how the hole was made was Ellie. She and Jack stood one warm July day under the tree—it was the summer after Michael's death—and Jack watched Ellie put her finger into the hole. He didn't stop her. He'd done it himself, though not at first. It had taken a long time, in fact, before he'd felt able to and even then he'd felt that he shouldn't. But it was a hole that, all other considerations apart, begged to have a finger put in it, even two. An ignorant outsider, who might not have been especially bothered by the mystery of the hole, would have found it hard to resist putting a finger in it. By the time Jack returned to Marleston to bury his brother, quite a few fingers, young and old, had been idly poked into that hole.

But Ellie's putting her finger in it—without, as it were, even asking Jack's permission—marked a decisive moment in the history of Jebb Farm. Her own father had died even more recently. It was an act of impudent penetration that had to do with the absence of more than one parental constraint. It was as though Ellie were saying, 'Look, I can do this now. *We* can do this now. Look, I haven't been struck down. The tree hasn't fallen on us. We can do anything we like now.'

And so they could. They were standing there, for a start, just the two of them, by their own choosing in Barton Field. Despite the geography of their long relationship, this was something they had never done before. With a poke of her finger Ellie was endorsing the obvious and tangible truth that Jack, even after eight months, couldn't quite bring himself to accept or believe: that the tree was his, all his, everything around them, for what it was worth, was all his. Or, as Ellie might have put it, 'Ours'.

The tree didn't mind a bit.

And the fact was that this simple yet outrageous act of Ellie's—she allowed her finger to probe and twist a bit—rather excited Jack. It aroused him. Ellie was wearing a dress, a flower-print dress, something he hadn't so often seen, and he could tell that before she'd driven over ('Something to tell you, Jacko,' she'd said on the phone) she'd taken some trouble to look her best.

In any case, Jack would have said that she was simply blooming. Nearly twenty-eight, but blooming. Something he would be able to confirm to himself a little later in the Big Bedroom—another first—when that dress would be draped over the back of a chair. Ellie was another summer older and her dad had recently died, but she was a better-looking woman than she'd been a year ago. She didn't look like a farmer's daughter (and she wasn't, in the sense that she no longer had a father). She looked like some wide-eyed visitor to his lordly estate. That even seemed to be her knowing, teasing game. 'Show me around, give me a tour. It's a beautiful day. Take me for a walk down Barton Field.' She even said (and it was an oddly appealing idea), 'Pretend you don't know me. Pretend I've never been here before.'

A beautiful day. So it was. An afternoon in full summer, not a freezing November night. It had once seemed to Jack that he would never get the coldness of that night out of his bones, but now he felt warm to his marrow. Ellie drew her finger from the hole and beckoned. Blooming in herself—and with something, so it seemed, she still had up her (sleeveless) sleeve. A blotch of sunshine reached her through the canopy of the oak and rippled over her bare shoulder.

'Come on'—she might almost have licked her lips— 'put your finger in it too.'

He didn't say that he'd already done so, guiltily, by himself. It anyway seemed that if he didn't make a move, she would grab his finger and thrust it in for him. So he put his finger in the hole. Then Ellie squeezed a finger— it was a tightish fit—alongside it.

'There.'

It was like a pledge. And more. Years ago, when they were children, they might have carved their initials, though they never had, next to each other on a tree. But that seemed a bygone and dainty idea now.

Jack had rushingly and hotly thought: they might do it right here, right this minute, up against the tree itself. To prove that they really could do anything now. The bark that had pressed against his father's spine pressing against Ellie's. Could they do that? Could they do such a thing? Or they might do it over there, in the July-dry grass, near poor Luke's resting-place. There was no one to see, only some cropping cows and the big blue sky.

But Ellie had said, 'I think we should go back up to the house, don't you? You could give me a tour of that too. I think we could do with a cup of tea, don't you?'

And later she'd said, a mug of tea cradled against her bare, bright breasts, that they should throw in Barton Field with the house, that's what they should do. With the house and the yard, all for private development. A shared right of way on the track, maybe. No, forget that. The consortium could make their own entrance, they could use the Westcott Farm track. But Barton Field, with that view, with that oak tree—that would clinch it, that would do it.

'Mark my words, Jacko. Fifty thousand on the price.' She'd taken a sip of tea and smiled encouragingly. 'As long as we don't say anything about that hole.'

Though when the Robinsons, who already owned a house in Richmond, Surrey, acquired Jebb Farm (or, rather, 'Jebb Farmhouse') and when he and Ellie upped sticks, having between them sold to the dairy consortium the remaining Jebb land and all of the adjacent Westcott Farm, Jack sometimes nursed the uncharacteristically devilish fantasy of phoning up one day, even dropping by, to let the Robinsons know that there was something he'd meant to tell them, about that hole—perhaps they hadn't even noticed it—in the oak tree.

But he could hardly have driven over from the Isle of Wight. And by the time he did make the journey, a decade later, for his brother's funeral, the Robinsons had put their own indelible marks on Jebb Farm. After paying, at least by Jack's reckoning, a small fortune for it and spending another small fortune on, as they sometimes put it, 'making it habitable', they'd effectively transformed the farmhouse and its immediate surroundings. So that Jack might have been as shocked by what he saw as the Robinsons might have been by any belated piece of information he had to bring them.

In any case, the Robinsons wouldn't have been in residence. It was mid-November. Their last visit had been not long ago during their children's half-term holiday. And since they mixed with the locals no more than politeness demanded it was only to be expected that on an occasion like this they'd choose to stay away.

Many of those from Marleston who attended Tom Luxton's funeral might have brought Jack up to date on the changes at Jebb, assuming he hadn't learnt about them in some other way. Bob Ireton and several others might have told him—if they'd ever had the chance. If Jack hadn't been in such an obvious and desperate haste, once the thing was over, once Tom was in the ground, to make his exit fast and not to talk to anyone. It was a rough and dramatic thing, Jack's departure, as rough and dramatic as his arrival, screeching to a halt like that. (Who is that madman, some had thought, until they'd realised it was him.) But then he'd always been a big rough creature, even bigger than his dad (big and rough, though generally, in fact, as mild as a lamb), and that dark suit he was wearing didn't make him look less rough. It made him look like a . . . 'bodyguard' was a word that came to mind.

A mad dash of an exit, and in one sense you couldn't

blame the poor, distraught man. It wasn't an ordinary sort of death (nor had it been with his dad). You couldn't make rules for such a thing or say that the way he'd left was wrong and unpardonable, but if he'd hung around they might at least have told him that Jebb Farmhouse was empty right now. So that if, for any reason—and if he was ready for a surprise or two—he'd wanted to go and take a look around, then it probably wouldn't have been a problem.

Of course, it was equally possible that he might not have wanted to set eyes on the place ever again.

But anyway he'd simply driven off in that big blue beast of a thing—that was actually like something the Robinsons might have driven—without saying his good-byes (or, in most cases, his hellos), even looking like a man afraid of being chased. Though he'd driven off, it's true (some noted it wasn't the way he'd driven in), along the road that would take him past the entrance to Jebb Farm. As was.

Ellie had said, that mug of tea nudging her tits, that he could do it now—they could do it now. When she spoke, the 'he' kept slipping into 'they', as if the words were almost the same thing, or as if what he alone might have hung back from ever doing was a different matter once the 'he' changed to 'they'.

And now, of course, he'd seen the letter that Ellie had been waiting all that time to show him. Though it was so sudden for Jack that for a brief while he'd wondered if the letter was real, if it wasn't some trick, if Ellie might have written it herself. The letter wasn't just their way out, it was 'cream on the cake' (Ellie's phrase). Uncle Tony—from beyond the grave—was offering them not just a rescue plan, but a whole new future 'on a plate' (Ellie's phrase again). They'd be mad not to grab it.

So there was a plate with a cake on it with cream on top. And here they were taking tea at Jebb.

If they sold up—in the way Ellie was proposing—they'd wipe out the debts and have money to spare. They might even have, courtesy of Uncle Tony, a little money to burn. Or . . . they could stay put and each be the proud and penniless owners of massive liabilities.

There was a third and not so far-fetched option (not nearly so far-fetched, in Jack's mind, as the Isle of Wight), which Ellie didn't mention and Jack didn't mention either. If he was going to mention it, he should have mentioned it a whole lot earlier, but the time for mentioning it was past.

And of those two options starkly presented to him by Ellie, was there any choice? Couldn't he see, she'd said, sensing his at least token resistance, his getting guilty in advance, that there was such a thing as good luck too in the world, such a thing as the wind for once blowing their way? And, Jesus, Jack, hadn't they served their time and been patient long enough?

Through the window before them, the crown of the oak tree had stirred in the sunshine and seemed to offer consent. People would pay, Ellie had said, for a view like that. They'd pay. The dairy consortium couldn't give a damn. They'd think of the cost of having that tree taken out.

It seemed to Jack that Ellie had certainly picked her moment—a day when all that he was now the master of had never looked so fine—to tell him it was time to quit. She might have picked, instead, some bleak day in February. And she'd never looked so fine, like a new woman even, herself.

But Jack knew that this new (but not unrecognisable) Ellie hadn't just sprung up, in her daisy-dotted dress, overnight, or even with the warm summer weather. She'd started to appear, to bloom even the previous year, after Michael had caused that hole in the tree and when they'd found out soon afterwards the contents of his will. Yes, for what it was worth, he was sole lord and master now.

And she'd bloomed a bit more, he thought, when later that winter and into the spring, Jimmy—tough-as-thistles Jimmy Merrick—had become ill. Slow but one-way ill, a bit like Luke. His liver and his lungs. Both things, apparently. The worse Jimmy got, in fact, the better, in some ways, Ellie looked. Then in May Jimmy had been hospitalised and—whether it was the shock of being away from the farm where he'd spent all his life or whether, seeing how things were going after the cattle disease, he'd simply been ready to give in—he'd succumbed pretty soon.

And Ellie hadn't stopped blooming, as was now very clear. But then she'd have had cause to bloom, despite having a sick dad to nurse, if she'd had that letter up her sleeve all the while. It was dated mid-January. For six months she hadn't breathed a word. That was all, in one sense, entirely understandable. What point in sharing that letter with anyone, so long as Jimmy, ailing as he was, was master of Westcott Farm and she was in his thrall?

Jack didn't say anything to Ellie—though he came

very close—about the length of time she'd kept the letter to herself. He understood, anyway, that he was now in Ellie's thrall. (But hadn't he always been?) He felt the letter taking away from him any last argument, any last crumb of Luxton pride or delusion. Mastery? He was in Ellie's hands now. 'They' not 'he'. He knew that keeping the farm, for all its summer glory, was only a picture. Ellie had stuck her finger through it. Now she was pointing to their future.

He'd dipped his face to his mug of tea, but looked at that view.

'Cheer up, Jacko,' Ellie had said. 'Lighten up. What's there to lose?'

He might have said that everything he was looking at was what there was to lose.

Ellie stroked his arm. 'People leave,' she said. 'People go their own way and take their chances.' Then she added, 'My mother did.' As if she might have said: 'And didn't she come good?'

Then she said, in her way, the thing he should have said, in his way, first. The thing he should have got in first, and differently.

'And so did Tom.'

He didn't say anything to this. He was trying to work out the answer. The word 'Tom' was like a small thud inside the room. But Ellie got in first again. She looked at him softly.

'If he cared, Jack, if he wanted his stake, he'd have been in touch by now, wouldn't he? If he can't be bothered to tell you where he is—'

'He's a soldier, Ell.'

'So? He went his own way. Now we should go ours. I don't think you even have to tell him that you're going to sell.'

There was a silence while the house, filled with summer breezes, seemed to whisper to itself at what it had just heard.

'Forget him, Jack. He's probably forgotten you.'

Tom wasn't dead then, Jack thinks now, even if neither he nor Ellie knew where he was (Tom's Service Record would one day tell Jack that he was in Vitez, Bosnia), but it was as though at that moment, Jack thinks now, he might have been.

Then Ellie had switched the subject brightly back.

'Anyway, have you any idea how much a house—just a house, no land—in some parts of London can cost these days?'

Jack had no idea, and he didn't like the sudden, alarming implication that he and Ellie should buy a house in London. Hadn't they just been talking about the Isle of Wight?

'No. Why should I?'

Ellie had floated a figure across him that he'd thought was crazy. Then she'd said, 'And have you any idea how much some people in London who can afford that kind of money will pay, on top, for their own away-from-it-all place in the country? Just to have that view'— she'd nodded towards the foot of the bed—'from their window?'

Jack didn't know how much, though in one sense it seemed to him that the view from the window, which was simply the view that went with the house, didn't and couldn't have any price on it at all. How could a view that didn't really belong to anyone even be for sale? And when Ellie mentioned another figure, again he'd thought it was crazy.

Later on, when he did find out what people—specifically the Robinsons—really were prepared to pay for that view and all that came with it, he'd think it was strange that he'd lived for twenty-eight years in a place that might be so prized as an 'away-from-it-all place', but now he, or rather 'they', wanted to get away from it.

And sitting now by the window at Lookout Cottage, looking out at what, in less obscuring weather, might be thought of as another priceless view, Jack is of the firm opinion that the place known as 'away from it all' simply doesn't exist. He happens to have some idea roughly how much Lookout Cottage might currently fetch. But how little he cares about that.

'Throw in Barton Field,' Ellie had said, 'throw in that oak, and they'll think it's their own little bit of England.'

And wouldn't it be, Jack had thought.

Before she'd produced the letter—even when they were still down in Barton Field—he'd actually believed that Ellie had come round that day in her summer dress to put forward the option that he himself hadn't got round to broaching. It wasn't for him, he'd foolishly thought, but for Ellie to propose it, since she was the one who'd have to take all the steps while he wouldn't have to budge. Yet there would have been nothing outrageous or surprising about it and it was only what, sooner or later, one of them surely had to suggest. Namely that she (they) should sell Westcott Farm and Ellie should move in with him. That might clear the two lots of debt and then they might make a go of it. Then they might become Mr and Mrs Luxton and share the Big Bedroom for the rest of their lives, as was only right and proper. Luxtons at Jebb.

His mum would surely have been glad. Even Tom would hardly have been taken by surprise. And there would always be a place for him, for Tom, if he wanted it. Jack would have wished—when the subject arose—to make that small stipulation.

When Ellie had said they should go back up to the farmhouse and when, no sooner were they there, than they were up the stairs and in that bed, he'd thought she'd only been about to announce (getting in first as usual) this proposal he'd also been nursing, but that she'd wanted to do it in style and with a bit of pre-emptive territory-claiming. But she'd clearly had other ideas. Caravans.

'I've thought it through, Jack, trust me.'

He'd looked at that sunny view outside the window, which he'd never really thought of as purchasable, and felt, even then, that he was being asked to contemplate it for the last time. He wondered what his father had thought when he'd come up here, that November day, to change out of his suit, to take the medal from the pocket—only to put it later in another pocket. His last look in full daylight (had he known it?) at that view. The oak with its leaves ablaze in the cold sunshine. What had gone through his head?

For a moment, in that warm, July bedroom, Jack had shivered.

'Don't sell it all as a farm. Sell the land. And sell the house—just as a house. A country house.'

A country house? But it was a farm and he'd never thought of the farmhouse as a separable entity, as anything other than the living quarters of a working farm.

'What about the parlour? The yard, the barns?'

'Nothing that a decent builder and an architect and landscaper couldn't sort out.'

Architect? Landscaper? Jack supposed that Ellie must have recently been reading magazines again, something he knew she liked to do. *House and Garden, Country Homes.* He saw again the piles of worn magazines in the day room at the hospital in Barnstaple where he'd gone with Ellie— it was barely a month ago—to visit Jimmy for what was to be the last time.

The old bugger was sitting up in bed, making a show of it, holding a mug of hospital tea. He'd looked at Jack, eyes still bright as pins, and Jack had known he was looking right through him to his father. Then he'd raised the mug of tea to his lips and grimaced.

'It's not like Ellie's, boy,' he said. And winked.

Holding a mug of Ellie's tea now, and sitting up in bed, Jack got the odd impression that, had Ellie been another woman, a rich man's wife, she might even have been interested in buying Jebb Farmhouse and carrying out the renovations herself. She might have found the prospect exciting and absorbing.

'But keep Barton Field,' she said, 'to go with the house. It never was much of a farming field anyway, was it? A big back garden, a big back lawn. Throw it in with the house and you could make a bomb.'

She put down her own mug of tea, ran the smooth of her nails down his arm and sidled up.

'Just as long as we don't breathe a word about that hole.'

29

JACK DROVE OUT OF Marleston village. Who was the runaway now? There they all were, housed together again, under the same roof of churchyard turf, and, once the thing was done, he couldn't wait to turn his back on them. He'd borne Tom's coffin and he couldn't bear any more. It was hardly proper, hardly decent. But who was going to stop him? No one had stopped him yesterday, and it was all suddenly again like yesterday. (Only the voice of his own mother, impossibly calling to him— 'Jack, don't go'—could have stopped him.)

But he wasn't quite the total fugitive. He'd taken the eastbound road, in the direction of Polstowe, and had known he couldn't drive straight past. It was a sort of test. At a familiar gap in the hedge on the right-hand side of the road, about a mile from the village, he pulled across and stopped.

Or it was familiar only in essence. The double line of hedges, meeting the roadside hedge and marking the ascending path of the track, was still as it had been, but the old five-bar gate was gone, along with the old, hedge-shrouded gate posts. So too was the concrete churn platform, and the wooden mail box on the latch side of the gate with the carved, weathered sign above. Instead, there was a large white thick-railed gate with a built-in mail box and the words 'JEBB FARMHOUSE' in bold black letters in the middle of the top rail.

Well, you couldn't miss it.

Even more noticeable was that where there'd once been just the grassy, often muddy, roadside recess, with nettles and brambles sprouting round the churn platform—all deliberately left untrimmed (so no fool would go and park there, Michael used to say)—there was now a clean tarmac surface. On each side of the gate there was even a neat quarter-circle of low brick kerb. And, beyond the gate, it was obvious that the whole track, disappearing down the hillside, had been surfaced too. Jack could only guess what that must have cost.

But this was hardly his principal thought. He got out and stood by the gate. He left the engine running and the door open and wasn't sure if this was because he intended opening the gate and driving through or because he might, in a matter of seconds, wish to drive off again in a hurry. The gate had no padlock. It wasn't that sort of gate. Its boxed-in latch mechanism suggested some sophisticated, perhaps remotely controlled locking system, and set into the right-hand gate post—as thick and pillar-like as gate posts come—was a complicated metal panel that was either an entry-phone unit or key-code device, or both.

So, the damn thing could be unlocked, he thought, even opened and closed perhaps, from the house. The Robinsons, he remembered, had wanted to know quite a lot about 'security'. There hadn't been much he could tell them.

He stood by the gate, slightly afraid to touch it. Though the air all around was brilliant and still, a faint, extra-cold breeze seemed to siphon its way up the shaded trackway between the hedges. There was the sound of rooks below. They would be in Brinkley Wood.

The Robinsons, he supposed, weren't around. This was their summer place. It was November. Or their weekend place, and it was a Friday morning. In any case, he imagined they wouldn't be here, not now. Definitely not now. They would have read their newspapers, put two and two together and—if they'd had any notion at all of driving down this weekend—would have chosen to avoid any awkward association with the property they'd bought. A funeral in the village. Not their affair.

They wouldn't be here. They'd be safe in their other house, their main house, in Richmond (it had sounded to Jack like a place where rich people lived and had stuck in his mind).

So there was nothing, in theory, to stop him from opening the gate and driving down. Except the wired-up booby trap of the gate itself. Except, even if he got past that, a possible minefield of burglar alarms further down the track. But who would blame him, on this of all days, who would accuse him of unlawful intentions? Trespassing, intruding? On his own birthright?

And if the gate was beyond opening, there was still the option—though he'd have to leave the car by the road like some glaring advert of his presence—of climbing over and walking down. Gates were there to be climbed over. And even if the Robinsons were, by some unlikely chance, actually in occupation—so what? They'd get a surprise. Would they call the police? (The police would be Ireton.) I'm Jack Luxton. Remember me? I sold you this place. I was passing, and I thought I'd—. I've just buried my brother.

So there was nothing to stop him. He stood by the gate, putting his hands on it, gingerly at first. His hands just straddled the black name on the top rail. He felt again the wood of the coffin under his palms.

Tom would have climbed over the gate, Jack was sure of it, quickly dropping his backpack over first, like a thief. But on that dazzling morning, so like this one, he, the big obedient brother, had opened the gate for his father, then, before going to re-join him, had swung it shut, a great fiery rush, despite the coldness of the air, billowing inside him.

He stood in his funeral outfit, his white shirt and black tie matching the white paint and black lettering, the medal still in his top pocket. His mother had once told a story about the medal, which had ended at this very spot. Though it wasn't a true story, it had never happened. It wasn't even possible for it to happen. It was his mother's invention.

His grip tightened on the rail. The Cherokee chugged expectantly beside him. It seemed to be begging a decision—climb over, for God's sake! Drive away! But he could do neither, as if he might stay here, stuck for ever. At the same time, he had the growing conviction that some hurriedly organised posse of funeral attenders might be heading, even now, down the road from Marleston to round him up.

He gave the gate a sudden heaving shake, as if he

might have ripped it from its hinges, then turned and got back in the car, slamming the door behind him as though slamming a gate upon himself. His hands gripped the steering wheel as fiercely as they'd gripped the rail, and perhaps half a minute passed as he remained staring at the alien black-and-white structure that had so effortlessly defeated him.

He saw in his head the old bare-wood gate. His eyes were blurred, in any case. Thus he failed to notice that he'd left behind two distinct, even identifying indications of his presence.

No traffic had passed in either direction while he'd been stopped and no traffic, pursuing or otherwise, was visible as he set off again, so no one was to know about this almost immediate interruption to his headlong flight (though a whole crowd had witnessed that). But at least until the next rain—which in a day's time would come sweeping in on the back of south-westerly gales—anyone (including the owners of Jebb Farmhouse, had they been in occupation) might have seen two hand-prints on the top rail, one either side of the black-lettered name. They'd been made by large hands that had obviously grasped the rail with some force, and they were hands that had recently plainly been in contact, for whatever reason, with reddish-brown earth.

He flung the car back onto the road. There were already traces of the same red earth on the steering wheel and when, a little later, as he drove, he violently yanked off his black tie, he left a similar smudge on the white collar of his shirt.

So, he'd at least confirmed one thing. The last time he'd touched and passed through that gate—not *that* gate but the old one—had truly been after he'd taken his last-ever look at Jebb Farm. At least Ellie had been with him then. She'd already taken her last look at Westcott, and without much difficulty, it seemed. And as they'd left Jebb together (various items that had escaped the auctioneer's hammer—including a shotgun and a medal in a silk-lined box—in the back) she was in the driving seat, because he'd expressly wanted to be the one to get out and open and close the Jebb gate for the last time and take a last look down the track.

Ellie had been with him then. They were driving to the Isle of Wight. It had been all Ellie's doing. He'd stood beside her while her father was buried. More to the point, he'd helped carry the coffin.

Now, with a great, unearthly howl that no one heard, he drove madly on.

30

ELLIE SITS IN the lay-by near Holn, not driving anywhere.

When Jack had returned in the dark last night she
couldn't help having the thought: a wounded soldier.
That was how the sight of him, in the beam of light from
the cottage door, had framed itself for her, as he'd slowly
emerged from the car in which she sits stranded now.
He'd looked shattered, exhausted. But what had she
expected, after such a journey? A wounded soldier. Even
so, there he was.

Or was he? For two days she'd lived with the possibility
that he might not return at all, but one possibility she clearly
hadn't anticipated was that he might return, but that he
wouldn't be Jack, or not the Jack she knew. And in the
eyes of the strange figure who'd blundered towards her she'd
seen, she thought, his anticipation of yet another possibility: that he might return to find her gone. But how
could that be? Hadn't he read or listened to any of those
messages?

And since she *was* there, why hadn't he looked pleased
to see her, or at least relieved?

Even so. There he was, and so was she, standing in that doorway where she hadn't stood, it's true, to watch him go. If she hadn't been watching then, she was watching now—had been watching and waiting, in fact, for a good half-hour. Knowing only what he'd said before he left, that he'd booked himself on the four-thirty Friday ferry, she'd been waiting in an agony since five-thirty (which would have been pushing it, it's true). She'd even gone up to the bedroom window so as to spot his lights as soon as they came up the hill.

And Jack, Ellie thinks now, must have seen, as he passed this lay-by, the distant lights of the cottage. A pretty sure sign that someone was there and waiting for him. But had he been looking and did he care?

And what difference did it make, now, if he were never to know how anxiously she'd watched and waited? How she'd seen at last his lights—at such an hour they could only be his—take the turn for Beacon Hill, then travel, like the passage of some luminous, scurrying animal, up the first, hidden stretch of road before appearing, with a full blaze, at the bend by the old chapel. How she'd said aloud, 'Jack. Jack,' and how she'd sprung up, to run downstairs, to be at the door, to put right, to reverse all the events of two mornings before.

A casserole was on in the kitchen. A bottle was on the table. All the lights were on. He would surely have understood that she was there. Now he was too. And as she'd stood in the doorway she'd said again, 'Jack, my Jack.' Had he even heard?

It had even seemed, as he walked towards her, that he was sorry not to find her gone.

Though what had she expected? And what, since she

hadn't gone with him, did she deserve? But he was here. Or, say, half here. The other half she might still have to wait for. She'd fed him and put him to bed, realising that she couldn't demand much more of him, in his condition, than his presence. 'Ask me later, Ell. Ask me tomorrow.' Realising also that she couldn't expect much talk from him now, when two mornings ago he hadn't had a single word from her.

She'd put him to bed. And he'd slept, in fact, for over twelve hours, not surfacing till after nine (which wasn't like him at all). But if she'd hoped that a good sleep would really bring him back to her and if she'd hoped that a good breakfast—an all-day breakfast if necessary—would get them talking as they should talk, she was wrong.

He didn't seem to want any breakfast. He still looked like some invalid. It had all suddenly reminded her of when her dad had begun to get ill, years ago, and she'd flitted coaxingly and motheringly around him, thinking foolishly that a good breakfast might put some life back in him. And maybe for Jack there'd been some weird equivalent of the same memory, and that was how it had begun.

'You wanted him out the way, didn't you?'

She'd thought at first he'd meant Tom, and then thought: well, so be it, now she had some facing up, owning up to do. Even so, she hadn't thought that 'out the way' meant any more than that.

Then he'd come up with the really crazy stuff.

'I've always wondered, Ell, how come your dad died so soon after mine? Did they have an agreement?'

This wasn't about Tom's death at all. Or was it?

Still he hadn't yet said anything appalling. She might

even have laughed at him. He'd made a sort of joke. And yes, though she'd never said anything to Jack, she *had* thought at the time that there was a sort of agreement. A connection. The real cause was the state of his liver and the state, on top of that, so it proved, of his lungs. He had lung cancer, the two things were racing each other. Nonetheless, there'd been a trigger. A bad word in the circumstances. Jimmy had started to go downhill soon after Michael's death. Hardly a cause, but a kind of kinship. It was as if, she'd thought at the time, her father had lost a brother. Or he'd won some contest of survival and had nothing left to prove.

'It was just how it was,' she said. 'You know that. It was just how it happened. He had a bad lung and a bad liver.'

'And it was handy.'

'Meaning?'

'You know what I mean.'

His next words were the same—worse—as if he'd got up, leant across the table and hit her.

'You helped him along, didn't you, Ell? You put something in his tea. Or in that flask of his. Wormer, teat dip, I don't know. Some kind of cow medicine. You put something in his breakfast.'

Strangely, her first thought before she exploded was to continue to picture her father sitting in the kitchen at Westcott, in the chair he always sat in—to think of all those breakfasts she'd cooked for him. Then her second thought was to wonder, almost calmly, whether Jack—or this man in front of her—actually thought she'd put something in *his* breakfast and that was why he didn't want any.

Then she'd exploded. She might have just laughed. Could you laugh at such a thing? Was Jack—or this man—really saying this? Had he simply come home to her with a great dose of madness? So she said it.

'Are you mad, Jack? Are you *mad*?'

It was the wrong thing to say, perhaps, to a man who might be really mad. Even to a man who'd come back from all that he must have been through (and she was still to hear about). But she'd said it. And then she'd said, with a great roar of outrage, like some matron barking down a hallway, 'How *dare* you say such a thing to me? How *dare* you?'

And the madness must have been catching, quickly catching, because only a little while later, after he'd said things to her by way of mad explanation, she'd said back to him, by way of retaliation, things that were equally mad, equally ludicrous and certainly like nothing she'd ever thought might escape her lips.

But, in any case, and almost in the same hot breath, she'd grabbed her handbag, her keys were in it, and opened the door and walked out to the car from which he'd stumbled only the night before. And had got in and screamed off. The rain was only just starting to spit, from a darkening sky, but by the time she got to the main road it was coming down in great slapping squalls, like a warning. But she could hardly turn round now, just because of the weather. And, almost because of it, she drove madly on.

31

ELLIE SITS BY Holn Cliffs. And Jack sits, looking towards her but not knowing it, and seeing again for a moment that white gate at Jebb, though not his now washed-away hand-prints.

Everything is mad now, everything is off its hinges. He'd gone to bury Tom, but now all the things that had once been dead and buried had come back again, and there was only one way forward, he was sure of that. Even Tom himself hadn't been really buried. He was with him now, in this cottage, he was sure of that too, even if he hadn't seen him. It was Tom's trick, Tom's choice, to appear or not, he knew that by now. Tom might be standing even now at his shoulder. A sniper.

If Ellie had come with him, if she'd only come with him, then perhaps between the two of them they might have buried Tom properly. As they'd been trying to bury him, not properly, for years. Then none of this might be happening. But Tom wasn't the only one, it seemed to him now, that they'd tried to bury not properly. And he'd gone and said so.

Everything is off its hinges. But his mind is quite clear

and steady and decided. As if some last forbidding gate has now been simply opened for him. All he has to do is walk through, and shut it.

Breakfast was spread over the table. It still is. The smell of bacon reaches him even now.

'In his tea, Ell. In his breakfast. In his fucking bacon and eggs.'

He knew that he was off his rocker, right off it. But it was the only way he could get to do—calmly and coolly—what he had to do. The trouble was that Ellie had been here. If she hadn't been, he could have done it already, last night. He could have got the gun. But Ellie was here. But, still, that was all right. It was better, even. He'd seen that it was only proper that Ellie was here. It removed one important complication. He'd slept on it—beside her, though hardly aware of her, so deeply and committedly had he slept. He hadn't had a single dream. Then he'd thought it out further, lying in bed, while he'd heard her in the kitchen below. There had to be an explosion. An explosion before the explosion—what a policeman might call a 'domestic situation'.

He hadn't reckoned on Ellie's doing, and doing so quickly, what often happens in such situations: storming off. And with a threat, a further complication, on her lips.

'I'm not saying he didn't die of what he did. I'm just saying you speeded the process up.'

'You're off your rocker, Jack.'

But he knew that. He had to be. Ellie was looking at him as she'd never looked at him before, but he supposed it must be the same the other way round.

'It's not true, then?'

'How *dare* you?'

'It's not true?'

'Jack. Jack—come back to me. Of course it's not true. Of course it's *not fucking true*. It's about as true as me saying you killed *your* dad.'

He hadn't expected that. He wasn't sure if it further complicated or only clarified the situation. If it was even the nub of the matter.

'He shot himself, Ell.'

'Exactly. As true—as fucking mad—as me saying you got the gun and did it yourself.'

He stared at Ellie. She thought that might settle it. Tit for tat. She thought that might end this whole situation. All this would be a joke.

And how could he be mad, if he was so clear-headed?

'Well, if it comes to it, how do you know I didn't? How do you know I didn't?'

It was a subject they stayed clear of, his father's death. As if to enter it might mean reliving it. But hadn't he been doing just that recently? Wasn't he doing it even now?

'Of course you didn't.' Ellie gave a strange, dry, quivery laugh.

'How do you know?'

'Jack—is this all to do with Tom?'

'How do you know?'

'I know. I know *you*.'

But she was looking at him as though she was no longer certain on that last point. And whatever Ellie knew, she didn't know and couldn't know what had only ever been in his head.

Even Jack himself couldn't be sure of how it really was.

That it wasn't the shot that woke him. He'd been awake, perhaps for some time, before the shot. Had he even heard his father creeping—as once he'd heard Tom creeping—from the house? In his terrible dream in Oke-hampton he'd even heard the little squeak, from below, of the gun cabinet. Was it a dream? Or the dream of a dream that he'd had *that* night, before, in fact, the shot had woken him? Or was it simply how it had been?

In his dream, in any case, he hadn't heard the shot. There wasn't yet any shot. He'd heard his father's move-ments downstairs. He'd heard the kitchen door open, even the blunt scuff of Wellington boots on the frozen mud in the yard. And before he'd dressed and gone downstairs himself, before he'd hurried down Barton Field, a torch in his hand and his heart in his throat, he'd stood on the landing and seen the left-open door of the Big Bedroom, and gone in.

He wasn't sleep-walking, surely. He hadn't switched on any lights, but he'd seen, even so, that extra blanket on the bed. Yes, there was a moon by then and, despite the cold, the curtains hadn't been closed—or else they'd been only recently pulled back. So he was able to see, with just the aid of the moon, the tartan pattern of the blanket.

But more than that. He'd gone into the room—or in his dream he had. And he'd stood by the window, where his father, perhaps, would have stood only moments before, and seen what his father would have seen: the moon, over the oak and the frost-gripped valley. But more than that. He'd been just in time to see—or he'd seen in his dream—from above and behind, his father's tall black form, his whole body first, then just his shoulders and head, disappearing as he descended the upper section of Barton Field. The moon was almost full and its light was coming brightly off the frost. So it was even possible to see his father's inky, night-time shadow slipping out of sight, rippling down the slope after him, and to see the footprints, like black burn holes in white cloth, that he left behind.

Even to see what he was carrying.

And Jack hadn't moved. He'd stood there at the window—as he'd stand, years later, at a white-painted gate—thinking: Shall I? Shan't I? Thinking: Will he? Won't he? Can I? Can't I?

He couldn't have said (it was like other passages of time that night) how long he'd stood there, as if hypnotised, as if in his mind—but wasn't he dreaming anyway?—he might still have been back in bed and asleep, not knowing that any of this was really happening. Till the sound of the shot—but had he even seen, from the window, the quick poke of light?—had woken him, out of all dreams, into truth.

But Ellie couldn't have known any of this.

'How do you know I didn't, Ell? How do you know I didn't march him down that field and make it look as though he'd done it himself?'

It was no surprise, though he hadn't reckoned on it, that at that point she'd simply got up, grabbed her handbag and fished in it quickly to make sure she had her car keys. Did she look frightened? Of him—for him? No, she looked furious. She looked a little mad herself. If he'd already got hold of the gun he might have stopped her, he might have brought this thing to an end, there and then, as intended. But she was standing between him and the door, and how could he have got the gun and loaded it without her getting away first?

He should have got the gun to begin with. He should have crept down the stairs, as his dad had crept down the stairs, and somehow got the gun from the cabinet and loaded it (both barrels) before she'd even called up that she was putting breakfast on. He should have just appeared in the doorway, in his dressing gown, with the gun. But he knew he couldn't have done it like that, without any explosion first.

So it was good, in fact—he thought now—that it had all blown up and she'd gone.

She'd clutched her car keys. For a moment they'd stared at each other, not like two people who'd known each other all their lives, but like two nameless enemies who'd come face to face in a clearing. Jack understood that to prevent Ellie leaving he'd have to use physical force, his big weight, against her. But he'd never done that, in all the time he'd known her, and couldn't do it now. Even though, if he'd had the gun—

'Where are you going, Ell?'

Outside, the clouds were thickening, but the rain hadn't begun.

'Where am I going? Where am I going? Ha! I'm going to Newport police station. I'm going to tell them what you've just told me. I'm going to tell them what you are.'

And she looked like she meant it. She really did. She looked like she was going to fetch the police.

She walked out. Slammed the door. The wall seemed to shake. He heard the Cherokee snarl off. Rain started to pepper the window. He'd thought: this had caught him out, this had upset plans. Then he thought: no it hadn't. After a little while, after hearing only the wind and the rain, after switching off the grill section of the cooker, where several rashers of bacon still waited, warm, well-crisped and untouched, he went to the gun cabinet. He got the gun, he got the box of cartridges. When had he last fired this gun? There'd been every reason to get rid of it. There'd been every reason not to. The last thing his father had touched.

He went up to the bedroom and put the loaded gun on the bed. Put some cartridges from the box in his pocket. This was actually better, this was good. He was prepared now, he was calm. The weather had gone wild, but he was calm. And, whether she'd do or not what she'd said she'd do, Ellie, he was sure of it, would soon have to come circling back. There was even a sort of justice to it. As if her journey was just a smaller, tighter version of his.

32

THE ROBINSONS had bought Jebb Farmhouse over ten years before Jack stood by the white gate bearing that name, and it was the Robinsons, Clare and Toby, who'd made the extensive and costly renovations, few of which Jack was to see, since he didn't go beyond the gate, but which entailed having the drive (it had ceased to be the 'track' and become the 'drive') properly surfaced—which Jack did see—and the gate itself.

There had been the purchase, and there had been the renovations. Their investment had turned into an investment of time as well as money. After a lengthy planning and permissions stage, the building work—including a new extension (which they called the guest wing), a total overhaul of the original house, the demolition of the outbuildings, the construction of a double garage and the laying out of the gardens, turning-area and drive—took, all told, well over two years. So that their actual period of occupancy and enjoyment had really been only seven years, and then mostly in the summers.

Nonetheless, they spoke now of their 'Jebb years', their 'Jebb life'. Toby said, in his credit-claiming way, that it had 'paid off'. Clare, who'd always been the more effusive, felt she was justified in having imagined it from the start not just as their possession, but as a permanent legacy to be passed on through future generations of the Robinson family—their place, their 'country place'.

But Clare would always remember (and always keep to herself) the day—though it was little more than a moment—when this whole vision had seemed to totter and shake, all its radiance had faded. And this had occurred, oddly, during one blissfully sunny weekend when everything in the picture was complete and just as she would have wished. It was only ever, she told herself, some weird sensation *inside* her. It was nothing, surely, to do with the *place*. But it was lingering enough in its effect for Clare to ask herself: Is there something wrong with me? Am I cracking up? And since her answer to those questions was a robust no, it must then be to do with the place. This place into which they'd put so much.

For a while Clare actually contemplated having to tell her husband that she was very sorry, but she no longer felt—comfortable—at Jebb. But that, of course, would suggest that there really was something wrong with her, since no one else was having any problem. And how would Toby take it? Rich as he was, he'd spent more money than she cared to calculate on what might now become, thanks to her, a failed enterprise. And he'd doubtless choose to say that he'd really only done it all for her—because she'd got so gooey-eyed about it in the first place.

But he might also be—she knew her husband—rather witheringly pragmatic. It was his way with anything that went wrong. The facts were that he'd blown one year's bonus to make the purchase, another year's on the renovations. If they had to give up on the place (if she *really* felt like this) then it wouldn't have broken the bank. (He was a banker.) And, the way prices had moved, they might still make a bit on the sale.

'No permanent damage', he might even say—though perhaps implying that *she* might be the one who was permanently damaged. What was the matter with her? And such magnanimity, she knew, might only be a convenient tactic. He could afford to be agreeable. In the early stages of the building work, Clare had come to realise that he was using their expensive project as a sort of shield for his ongoing affair with Martha, his PA (though in the time it took to finish the renovations she acquired some loftier status). It deflected attention from it—it quite often meant that Clare would be down there, with the children, when he wasn't. But it was also a sort of pay-off. How could she complain, when he lavished so much on his family?

Clare even wondered if her moment—her 'shiver', as she would think of it—hadn't really been to do with her suppressed recognition that the Martha thing wasn't just a temporary toying (it had gone on and on like the building work), and that though they'd bought this solid and beautiful portion of countryside, her marriage was really a rather flimsy, unlovely affair. She pretended and even believed, most of the time, that this wasn't so. For the sake of the children, of course, but also because she'd been given the bribe of this handsomely refurbished farmhouse in its splendid setting.

*

Fortunately, her 'moment' was isolated enough for none of these awful showdowns—with either her husband or herself—to occur. When Jack stood by the gate, the Robinsons still possessed Jebb Farmhouse, though they were not in residence at the time. Toby and Clare remained married (though the Martha thing still went on). The three children—and there had only been two when the purchase was made—had now enjoyed several happy summers at Jebb. So had their parents.

Clare, masking her feelings, had been pragmatic in her way too. Before making any foolish announcements, she'd waited for a recurrence of her 'shiver'. None had come, which perhaps indicated it was all a nonsense in the first place. Time had passed and, in the absence of any further symptoms, she'd almost been able, until very recently, to forget her temporary, perhaps imaginary disease.

And what she'd experienced recently wasn't really like that first shiver at all. It was, in the first instance, only a letter, an unopened letter, that had nothing to do with her. They'd been at Jebb during the children's half-term break. It had coincided with Guy Fawkes' Night and Toby had made quite a thing of the fireworks. Then a letter had arrived, which only she had noticed and which she'd quickly redirected. They received very little mail at Jebb and, by now, virtually nothing relating to the former occupant, but the letter had borne the name Luxton and also the words 'Ministry of Defence'.

She'd wondered what the connection could possibly be with a now long-defunct farm, but she'd felt conscientiously impelled to see that it was forwarded at once. She'd crossed out the address, written in the one they still had for the Isle of Wight (assuming it still applied) and, on the pretext of some other errand, driven straight up to Marleston to re-post it. Perhaps it was more a case of wanting it, for some curious reason, out of the way as soon as possible and it was almost a relief when she dropped it in the village box. No one else knew about it.

Then only days later, back in Richmond, she'd glanced at a newspaper and spotted a name and a face, and this time felt a true shiver. The name was Luxton again, and the face was even faintly familiar, though it plainly wasn't the face of a farmer. For a while the cold sensation had concentrated in her hand.

She wished at once that she'd never seen the item in the paper. So often, you looked at a newspaper without noticing half of what was there, and what you don't see can't trouble you. But she'd seen it. And now she wondered what she should do about it. Though there was nothing, really, that could be done about it.

But she felt distinctly disturbed. She felt that at least she should mention it to Toby. Had he noticed it—and drawn the same conclusion? But she knew that if she did mention it, he would say he hadn't noticed, or hadn't remembered the name, whether he actually had or not. And she knew that if she spelt it out for him (let alone mentioned the redirected letter) he would simply shrug. So what? He might even look at her as if she were behaving pretty strangely.

The Robinsons, as Jack recalled, had been very concerned about 'security' (it was one of their words), and solid evidence of their concern was that heavy white gate with its built-in electronic features. 'Control of Entry', Jack had momentarily thought. But the Robinsons had reflected that while a gate that couldn't be opened might deter intruders in a vehicle, it was no barrier to intruders on foot. In such an event—and assuming the intruders would trip the alarms in the house and grounds—it was important, when the Robinsons were not in residence, that the police *could* get through the gate and so catch the thieves red-handed.

So it was that Sergeant Ireton, as well as the Robinsons, possessed the means to open the Jebb gate, and thus he might technically have found himself—had Jack decided, that morning, on some impromptu intruding himself—in the position of arresting the man who, minutes before, he'd, so to speak, shared a coffin with. Though it was also possible that if Jack had actually asked whether there was any way he might take a quick look at Jebb, Bob might have said, 'Of course. I can open the gate for you. I even know how to cut out the alarms.'

Security, in the broad sense—security of incomes, of livelihoods and even of lives—had become a real enough concern in a region afflicted first by BSE, then, years later, by foot-and-mouth. But security as the Robinsons meant it and as it might affect a local policeman was something different. Bob Ireton might have said it was something the Robinsons brought with them from London, but he might also have said that it was something that, like those cow diseases, was now just spreading through the air. The feeling that nowhere was really immune, even quiet green places in the depths of the country. Marleston and Polstowe were not exactly incident-free, but it was only recently that Bob had begun to feel that his safe little job as a country policeman—safe in the sense that it was far more secure than the jobs of dozens of farmers—was actually bound up, as if he might be involved in some latent war, with a larger, unlocal malaise of insecurity. And he'd felt this particularly, like a palpable burden and responsibility, when he'd offered his shoulder to help carry Jack Luxton's poor dead brother.

When the Robinsons had asked Jack about security—as if it formed part of the sale—Jack had been inclined to say (after some puzzlement about the word itself) that they never bothered, here, with burglar alarms or even with locking vehicle doors. But Ellie had already warned him not to make the Robinsons feel silly about anything they asked. He might equally have said that it always helped to know—should it come to it—that there was a gun in the house. But this might not have been wise either. So he simply said that they never had any trouble, not in this part of the world. And he'd given Toby Robinson one of his most neutral looks.

The Robinsons weren't interested in the kind of security—or insecurity—that had mattered to Jack, that was causing him to be selling his farm. They saw this as only offering them their opportunity. They—or Mr Robinson—saw cow disease and distress sales as possibly working to their advantage. Toby had told his wife that north Devon was off the beaten track. It was still genuine, undiscovered countryside. Everyone went to south Devon and Cornwall where prices were already beefed up, and—talking of beef—this BSE business could only mean there might be some real bargains around. Toby Robinson, investment banker though he was, had in certain situations, Clare knew, the instincts of a huckster, loving nothing better than to beat down a price. It was perhaps why he'd got to where he was. And also why the word 'countryside' seemed strange on his lips.

Toby had thought Jack was an extraordinary character to have to deal with (he wouldn't have meant this as a compliment), but he was very careful not to appear to look down on him. He didn't want to give the impression that a sum of money that to Jack, so he guessed (and guessed right), might be eye-popping, was to him, Toby, still almost within the bounds of pocket money. At the same time he had a sort of visceral respect for the man. Farmers went to market, didn't they? (Or did they any more?) They couldn't be *so* different from people who worked in the City.

What the Robinsons meant by security was the kind of security that might prevent the possession and enjoyment of their new property from ever being impaired or violated. Nonetheless, what Clare Robinson might have said of the effect upon her of seeing that newspaper item—though her physical well-being had in no way been harmed and though their possession of Jebb Farmhouse remained happily intact—was that it made her feel insecure.

Had Bob Ireton and Jack found themselves together, soon after the funeral, on what was now the Robinsons' property—and whether or not Jack would have been theoretically guilty of trespassing—they might have had a conversation about security. They might have sat in Ireton's police car, on the new, immaculately bricked turning-area, amid all the new landscaping and terracing, but looking at the essentially unchanged view before them (less impeded now after the removal of the Small Barn), down Barton Field. Bob might have brought Jack up to date about all the changes at Jebb—visible as they were around them—but they might have moved inevitably, even despite themselves, onto this larger subject.

Bob might have said, alluding to the Robinsons and their kind and the fears manifested by their elaborate alarm systems, that such people had a problem. They didn't know how fortunate they were, they couldn't just be glad of what they had, and they didn't know the real meaning of loss, did they? Here, Bob might have looked at Jack carefully. Both men, sitting side by side, might have been feeling still a detectable, angular pressure on one shoulder. But on the other hand, Bob might have said, the world—the world at large—certainly wasn't getting any safer, was it? So, he might have added, with an attempt at weary humour, he'd picked the right job, hadn't he? But would have stopped short of saying anything to the effect that some people might have concluded that Tom (though Bob knew it could hardly actually have been his motive) had picked the right job too. Keeping the world safe. Security. That was the argument that always got used, wasn't it? Though it could be used, couldn't it, to justify just about anything?

Bob, though a practical policeman, had become a not unreflective man and, while keeping these thoughts to himself, might have looked soberly across the frost-whitened valley before them.

Jack might have said, 'And a sergeant now, Bob.' Remembering all the stripes and gold braid and sashes he'd seen the day before. And Bob might have kept to himself how he'd had his uniform specially dry-cleaned and pressed for the morning's occasion, how he'd inspected himself in the mirror. Jack might have felt, all the time, the medal burning in his pocket.

Bob, looking at Jack also contemplating that frosty view and seeing his Adam's apple rise and fall, might have begun to wish this topic of security hadn't emerged, prompted as it was not just by the burglar alarms at Jebb, but by his local policeman's need to give some context to the death of a once local man in a far-away country. But Jack might at last have begun to take up the theme by saying that in his current line of work security was actually quite a factor. It wasn't just that now and then he had to step in to deal with little episodes that could make him feel a bit like a policeman (he might have looked shyly at Bob), but there was the whole question of guarding the caravans during the off-season months. Like now. Though he probably wouldn't have mentioned that he had a contract with a security firm (he didn't just rely on the local police) and this was especially necessary when they —he and Ellie—took their holidays (though not this winter) in the Caribbean.

Jack might have said that it was a funny thing, but the caravanners, on their holidays, often wanted to talk about the general state of the world, how it wasn't getting any safer. Just like him and Bob now. And Jack might have put forward the idea that there was no such place really as 'away from it all', was there? Then he might have made a stumbling effort at a joke. He might have explained that he lived these days in a place called Lookout Cottage that had once been a pair of coastguards' cottages. It had once been where two now-forgotten souls had had the task, in theory, of guarding the whole country against invasion. But now everyone had to keep a lookout, didn't they?

Both men might have gazed out over the valley and Bob might have picked his moment to say, 'But you're doing okay, aren't you, Jack? Things are okay?' Or to say, 'And how's Ellie? I couldn't help noticing she wasn't here.' But thought twice about that question and perhaps about asking any others, because he wasn't honestly sure what might make Jack, sitting here amid all the transformations that had occurred at Jebb, suddenly burst into tears.

A silence might have passed between them, broken only by the cackling of rooks, in which they might both have stared at the crown of the oak tree. How could they say between them whatever it was that needed to be said about the death of Tom Luxton?

Jack might have looked at Bob and thought: Is he going to arrest me anyway, after all, for something much bigger and worse than being found on private property? But Ireton might have looked at his watch and said, in a shepherdly way, as if he'd simply chanced upon someone who'd got lost, 'Well, Jack, I can leave you here to carry on trespassing by yourself, or I can drive you back up to the road and see you on your way.'

Looking back, Clare Robinson could admit that her first, shadowy misgiving—even before that 'shiver'—had been the foot-and-mouth. She'd been able to tolerate the long dragging-on of the building work. After all, they'd let themselves in for it. If they'd been over-ambitious, it was their own fault. On the other hand, if it all bore fruit the way they visualised, it would have been worth the waiting. Fruit was meanwhile borne anyway—and rather unexpectedly—in the form of their third child, a girl to go with the two boys, and Clare vaguely believed that this had happened precisely because their 'country place' awaited them. Since, apart from all its other virtues, it would be a haven, a perfect paradise for the children. Another child could only justify it all the more, and sanction the scope of their intentions for it. And little Rachel simply took up their time and made the continual postponement of when they might actually 'move in' seem only practical. They'd move in when she was old enough to know about it.

They started to joke about the whole thing as their 'millennial plan'—would they or wouldn't they move in before the next century?—but they became excited all over again and forgot about all the time and money consumed, when at last it neared completion and they saw what actually splendid things had been achieved. The builders finally left and they 'moved in' in the autumn of 1999, though they didn't make their first proper use of the place till the following summer.

Her husband had said that the foot-and-mouth outbreak, in the spring of the next year, wasn't their problem and it would blow over. In any case they didn't have to *be* there, that was the beauty (though Clare thought this was a rather sad argument) of its being their second place. Nor were they. It was a sacrifice, of course, and all rather galling. They watched the TV pictures of vast piles of cattle being burnt from the safety of their living room in Richmond. It seemed best. It *was* nothing to do with them. They'd look insensitive, perhaps, if they went down there. And by the summer, anyway, it would surely have all been dealt with.

But, even at a distance, Clare hadn't liked this thing happening so plainly and upsettingly close to their new property. She felt it as if she *were* down there. She didn't like the idea of the smoke from that huge pyre being carried on the wind towards Jebb Farmhouse. Her husband's remark about its blowing over had been unfortunate. She felt it like a contamination. And, though it wasn't logical and Toby would have scoffed, she felt it as something they should feel responsible, even vaguely guilty for, in a way they couldn't have felt about the BSE which had struck, as it were, before their time.

Mrs Robinson was glad when it did, so far as it might actually impinge on them, 'blow over'. She'd perhaps been over-reacting. And when, in fact, something far worse— far worse for the world at large—occurred later that year, she didn't feel nearly as troubled as she might have done had their 'country place' not now been fully up and running. She felt that the whole exercise was now vindicated. She felt glad and relieved. When those planes hit the towers that September, everyone said that the world had changed, it would never be the same again. But she'd felt it less distressingly, if she were honest, than the foot-and-mouth and those previous clouds of TV smoke. Since now they had this retreat, this place of green safety. It had been a good decision.

One of the big issues for her and Toby had once been choosing between flying off for holidays in exotic places (something they very much liked to do) and putting all their eggs, so to speak, into this basket in Devon. It might have its limitations, not least the English weather. But then again, with the children at the age they were—even before the new baby—going abroad had begun to have its limitations too.

Now the whole prospect of foreign travel, of having to deal with airports and people in states of crowded transit, seemed to Clare (her husband still travelled on business) touched by something sinister in the global atmosphere. So their purchase of Jebb Farmhouse seemed right in every respect. It seemed provident, even vaguely patriotic. How simple and comforting, just to have to drive down the M4.

By the summer of 2003 their presence at Jebb was a familiar reality. They would invite friends to join them—with their children—and the friends would be suitably impressed and envious. To cap it all, the weather that summer smiled for them. That the Martha thing seemed still not to have blown over made little effective difference. She made a pact with herself to push it aside, if not quite to ignore it. Everything else was too marvellous, too precious. It wasn't worth risking all that they now abundantly had by making an issue out of it. And surely, one day, Toby might take the same view—about his carrying on with Martha. He might put an end to it. Especially if, she rather perversely argued to herself, she was—lenient.

It was the only blot, and when they were all at Jebb it could sometimes seem to evaporate completely. The place had a healing effect. And yet, that dazzling Sunday in early July, as if some silent, invisible explosion had occurred, it had all seemed suddenly, deeply *wrong*.

That weekend the Townsends and their two children were staying. One thing they liked to do with guests on

Sundays, if the weather allowed, was to hold a grand picnic under the big oak tree. It was really a case of a late and lazy breakfast on the terrace gradually spilling over into a late and extended lunch in the field beneath. It was absurd, in one sense, to have a picnic so close to the house, yet it seemed exactly what that field and that tree were intended for. So, while the children ran on ahead and used the field (just as once imagined) as their exclusive playground, all the components of a picnic would be carried down in stages. Everyone would enjoy the feeling of a small-scale, rather preposterous expedition. The several trips down the steep slope and up again worked up a thirst and added to the general fun. It wouldn't have been in the right spirit to pile everything into the Range Rover and drive down—though the Range Rover was usually employed to cart everything back.

That day, the picnic was almost at the point of complete assembly. She and Tessa Townsend were occupying the rugs while the men did the last lugging and puffing. The children were happily amusing themselves. The oak tree was too massive and challenging for any climbing, but Toby had rigged up a rope swing, with a proper wooden seat, from one of the lowest branches. This was now in operation and the rugs had been placed some distance from the base of the tree, but still within reach of its ample shade.

It was hardly a talking-point with visitors like the Townsends, but every member of the Robinson family had by now noticed that strange little hole, with the faint discoloration around it, low down in the trunk, and had wondered how it got there. Clare, sitting on the rug with Tessa, noticed it today as the children swung past it. It surely couldn't have been formed naturally. A fixing point for tethering some mad bull had once been Toby's theory, a scary idea that had appealed to the children—and he'd done a brief imitation of a mad bull for their benefit.

He and Hugh Townsend were now bringing the last shipment of picnic supplies down the hill. The children—or their Charlie and the Townsends' pair—were busy with the swing. The oak tree itself was softly rustling every so often in a gentle breeze and there was a cooing of pigeons from the wood.

Then everyone's attention had turned to Toby, who, with a loud oath, had suddenly tripped and slithered several yards on his backside down the glossy grass of the field above, dropping and scattering the contents of the box he was carrying—which had included two bottles of pink champagne, now rapidly rolling away from him.

He hadn't hurt himself, though for a micro-second Clare had thought: Has he broken a leg, an arm, an ankle? Was this whole, marvellously materialising Sunday not to be, after all? But, in fact, he'd merely provided entertainment and laughter for all, something he acknowledged, when he regained his feet, by taking a theatrical bow. It was one of those moments of potential disaster rapidly transformed into comedy which are like some extra blessing. Clare had noticed, as her husband fell and slid and his short-sleeved shirt flew up, the plump wobbliness of his paunch above the waist of his shorts and, as his straw hat flew off, the shiny, receding patch in his hair, catching the sunlight. For some reason these things—the flashes of pink, vulnerable skin—reassured her. Yes, she knew that she loved him. She could not, would not lose him. He was even for her, at that moment, like some big fourth child.

And now, while all the actual children seemed to be in stitches, he was making a show, like some hired clown, of gathering up everything he'd spilt and pointing out that the champagne would now have really acquired some fizz. What a sweet fool he was. How had he become a banker? This was all, she realised, her heart strangely brimming, the perfect moment, the perfect scene. But it was only minutes later that she'd looked up at the broad, sun-filled canopy of the oak as if to see in it some approval of her joy (this wonderful oak tree—they owned an oak tree!) and felt that something was very wrong.

What was going on? A picnic was about to begin, that was all. A happy picnic heralded by rounds of laughter and, now, by the loud pop of a champagne cork. Everything was in place, but, as so often, once the thing was ready and though there'd been expressions of impatience, the children were being slow to come and get it. But that hardly mattered. What was happening? Charlie had pointed out to Laura Townsend the hole in the tree, the 'mad-bull' hole—and Laura had decided to put her finger in it. That was all. It was something Clare had never done herself—she'd felt, for some reason, there might be something in the hole she wouldn't like to touch. Though what was so awful, right now, about that little, natural, childish act of sticking a finger in a hole?

Yet she'd looked up at the oak tree and at once began to fear it. There was something now about it that, even on a warm July day, made her feel cold. Its leaves, stirring in the breeze, seemed to shiver with her. Its shade, which should have been only delightful on a summer's day, seemed, momentarily, simply dark.

She hid all this, tried to dismiss it as the picnic proceeded, and, as it turned out, never said a word about it to her husband. Though the truth was that it really took most of that summer for this 'moment' to go away. She was on guard against its repetition. She eyed the tree as if she and it were outfacing each other. She could no longer be sure that there wasn't something sinister rather than glorious about the way it dominated the view, its crown rearing up above the brow of the field, like the head of some giant with brooding designs on the house. She thought of it lurking at night. Then all this simply receded, to the point where she wondered if she hadn't really just imagined it all.

When Jack (with Ellie's advice) sold Jebb farmhouse and Barton Field to the Robinsons, nothing was said about the hole in the tree. Jack had even thought of filling it, disguising it, but had known that this was taking things too far. The hole had to stay. To anyone else it was just an insignificant hole in a tree. Nothing had been said, of course, about how Michael had died, though Jack had let it be known, in a sombre way, that his father was 'no longer around', and the Robinsons had expressed their sympathies and taken this to be connected with why Jack had to sell. It inclined Clare at least to a certain pity towards Jack (what a big, slow creature he seemed) and even Toby felt he shouldn't make too much of a contest over the price, though he also felt this might have been Jack's motive in mentioning the subject.

If the Robinsons subsequently began to suspect at all that the older Mr Luxton had committed suicide, it was not because of some understanding of how a cow disease might also reduce the human population (though they'd cut down, themselves, on eating beef) and certainly not because any of their new, seldom encountered neighbours had told them that Michael had shot himself under that tree. Their neighbours knew better than that. How would it have helped? It certainly wouldn't have helped poor Jack negotiate his sale. Even the solicitors had kept quiet. It wasn't exactly their direct business and it wouldn't have advanced a transaction which had its complications, but which both sides clearly wanted to complete as soon as possible.

If the Robinsons nonetheless had their inklings, they certainly didn't want to pursue them. They were happy not to know. Those two years and more while the building work went on acted like a curtain, and once they were in real occupation they kept themselves apart. They were not permanent residents anyway. They were effectively surrounded by a dairy consortium, and so rather conveniently ringed off from any real local inhabitants. They'd bought a centuries-old farmhouse, but they'd altered much of its ancient fabric and they were notably uninquisitive about even its recent history.

When Jack sold Jebb to the Robinsons he got the strong impression that for Toby Robinson at least, Jebb Farm was just an item, like anything else he might have chosen to buy, and perhaps even sell again later. This had at first astonished Jack: that someone might want to buy what the Luxtons had possessed for generations in the same way that they might buy a picture to hang on their wall. It had even, for a while, disinclined him to proceed, but Ellie had told him not to be a bloody idiot. Jack suspected that if Toby Robinson had found out that Michael had blown his brains out under that tree, he might simply have used it, without being fundamentally perturbed, as a pretext for getting something off the price. But at the same time he felt that Clare Robinson's 'investment', in the broadest sense, in Jebb was of a different nature. To her, in some way, it really mattered— she was the one who really wanted it. So when the sale looked like going through, he hoped she would never find out about that hole. He hoped no one, at the last minute, would go and tell her.

Had Toby Robinson inadvertently learnt that Michael Luxton had committed suicide—and how—he might have simply thought: So what? So what? It would have made his mad-bull notion a bit unfortunate, but was that tree— were they?—any the worse? But Clare might have suffered some more decisive occurrence of that transitory shiver which she would keep to herself. And the upset she felt through simply glancing at a newspaper might have been more unsettling too.

'Thomas Luxton.' Should they go there, she'd thought, should they *be* there? If the poor man had grown up in 'their' farmhouse should they put in an appearance? She had two boys of her own, Charlie and Paul, though she hardly saw them as soldier material. But they'd just been down for half-term, and was it really any business or obligation of theirs? She resolved not to let it cast a pall.

She wouldn't mention it to Toby, if he didn't mention it himself, and she knew he wouldn't.

It would be like never mentioning Martha's name, which had become a sort of rule. Clare knew that if she mentioned it, though she had every reason and right to, it might be a fatal thing to do. It might cause a catastrophe. So much time had passed, in fact, without Martha's being mentioned, that Clare couldn't actually be sure if Martha still featured. And this was a comforting uncertainty, as if consistently not mentioning her name was gradually making Martha not exist. Though Clare would never have said that she wished Martha dead.

So their happy possession of Jebb Farmhouse continued. Their 'Jebb years', their summer stays. Even their picnics with visiting guests under that wonderful oak tree. It was five centuries old, they'd once been told (by Jack Luxton), which rather put her temporary little disturbances into perspective. Clare would never have lasting cause to regret the acquisition of their country place. Or to feel she'd been overdoing it, that summer evening years ago, when, after they'd first seen Jebb, she'd intertwined fingers with her husband's over the dinner table in an expensive hotel on the fringes of Dartmoor and said—not unmindful of everything they already possessed—that it might even be like their 'very own little piece of England'.

33

JACK DROVE MADLY ON.

On that cold, clear Remembrance Day, when Tom wasn't there, Jack had swung the gate shut behind his father in the Land Rover, not knowing then (had his father known?) that Michael would never set foot outside Luxton territory again. He would walk that night down to the oak tree.

As he'd shouldered Tom's coffin, Jack had felt the overwhelming urge to be not just Tom's brother but the second, secret, cradling father he'd sometimes felt himself to be. And as he'd stood and dropped his handful of earth onto the drumming coffin lid—before he was unable to stand there any longer—he'd even wanted to be Tom's real father, *their* father, who could never, except through the living breath of his older son, have the chance to say, to let the words pour repentingly from his lips: 'My son Tom. O my poor son Tom.'

But Michael was lying now just yards from his younger son, and who knows how the dead may settle their scores? All at once Jack had remembered what Tom had said, about that other death down in Barton Field—

about what Michael had said: 'I hope some day someone will have the decency . . .'

He'd fled the churchyard, the only living Luxton left, then had needed to stop by that monstrous, mocking gate. Now, as he drove on, turning his back on Luxton territory, he knew why Lookout Cottage was the only place to go. It wasn't that he thought any more that it was where he belonged. It was the gun, his father's gun.

He had his dad's example. He even had Tom's example—a gun-carrying soldier, a sniper. How many had Tom killed? But Tom, who in his days as a soldier must have had to see many things, had never had to see what he, Jack, had once had to see in the darkness under that tree.

It was the gun, waiting for him now.

As he sped away from Marleston, Jack couldn't have felt less like a man who, instead of stopping to confront a gate, might have paused to call his wife and say he was coming home. His mobile phone (with its several messages) remained switched off. Yet on this homeward journey—if that was what it was—he followed a route he'd taken once before with Ellie and, had he been in a different state of mind, he might have felt he was travelling back, in more than one sense, to her.

Ten years ago, after closing the old Jebb gate for the last time, he'd got in, beside Ellie, in the passenger seat and so technically in the position of navigator. But Ellie already knew the way. Ellie had already gone—so Jack had learned one July afternoon—to spy out their future on the Isle of Wight, seizing the chance to do so secretly when Jimmy had been admitted to hospital. And that was one reason, Jack had told himself, why she'd kept that letter from Uncle Tony to herself for so long. She couldn't share it till she'd checked its validity—on the spot—and she couldn't do that while her dad was around.

So Ellie had driven them both, with the memory of her first trip to guide her, but Jack hadn't been just the passive, ignorant passenger. In the early stages of their journey he'd suddenly realised there was a coincidence of memories and of routes. The road signs had chimed with him: Honiton, Axminster, Lyme Regis . . . Ellie had passed along this road before, but then so had he.

'Ellie, I've got an idea.'

So they'd found themselves together at Brigwell Bay. And standing on the beach there with Ellie, having taken one of the great initiatives of his life (to think they might have sailed past the turning only for the idea to have hit him miles further on), Jack had made one of the great declarations of his life. It took the form of one of his rare jokes, but it was too gallant—and too successful—to be just a joke.

'There you are, Ell. Here you are. "Wish you were here." Now you are.'

Then he'd blurted out, 'And always will be.'

And just for his saying this Ellie had hugged him, almost squeezed the breath out of him, and said, 'My hero,' while he'd smelt the strange, forgotten smell of the sea.

Honiton, Axminster, Lyme Regis. He took the same route now, but at the turning—he knew when it was coming—

he didn't even slow. It was like another shut gate. What lay down that road? He and Ellie clasped in the embrace of their life? That wasn't the point. What lay down that road was a six-year-old boy on a caravan holiday, legs spattered with wet sand, who'd become a soldier in Iraq. He'd sometimes felt like Tom's father then.

He didn't even slow down, but he let out another great, unheard howl.

He reached Portsmouth well before four. Realising that he might be even earlier, he'd stopped at a service station, outside Southampton, on the M27. These anonymous places, in which to piss, eat and kill time, seemed to draw him like a second habitat—a habitat that was no habitat at all. But he wanted nothing more. He'd booked himself, to allow for all kinds of eventualities that might follow the funeral, onto the four-thirty ferry. There'd been no even-tualities, except for his swift exit, his encounter with a gate and the eating up of road.

Once he joined the queue of waiting vehicles, the long, cross-country loop of his journey was complete. There remained only the short sea-trip which, when he'd done it that first time with Ellie, had seemed momentous, like an ocean voyage. It was momentous now. He would never return to the mainland, he was sure of it, this crossing would be his last. The thing was so fixed now in his mind that he no longer paused to consider, as he'd sometimes done on his long journey, whether he was mad.

Nor did he pause to consider—since it had simply never occurred to him, and it had never been part of Vera's story—that it might have been from here once, from the Solent, that those two Luxton brothers, on the memorial near which he'd stood just hours ago, had been shipped out, never to return. So what Jack was very soon to do, but hadn't even thought of yet, had no premeditated link with them. It was just another of the sudden initiatives of his life.

The ferry's ramp and yawning hold reminded him of the plane. The deafening car deck was like some state of alert. After grabbing his parka and leaving his car, he made for the open decks above, not wanting to show his face. He stood by the rail. It was getting dark. The wind that had got up during the day gusted round him. A deep Atlantic front was moving in.

Would Ellie be there? Did he want her to be? Would it be like a final sign to him if she were not, so that he could simply take out the gun? Even now he shunned his mobile phone, when to use it would have been the most natural and normal thing to do. As he'd maintained silence for so long, it might even have been a stupendous thing to do. His voice might have sounded like that of a man given up for lost. Ellie, I'm on the ferry, I'm on my way.

How had Tom died?

With a clank of its raised ramp and a churning of water, the ferry slipped its moorings. The lights of Portsmouth were on, reflected in the surface of the harbour, but night hadn't quite fallen and the sky still glowed in the west. Beyond the shelter of the harbour mouth, the fitful wind combined with the movement of the boat into a steady, bitter blast. A few hardy souls—to appreciate the sunset or to indulge the brief sensation of being on the high seas—lingered for a while by the rails. And some of them would have noticed one of their number, a large, strongly built, even rather intimidating man, feel for something in the region of his breast pocket, then, clutching it tightly for a moment in his fist, hurl it into the sea.

Though it was small, it must have been metallic and relatively heavy, since, catching a quick, coppery gleam from the sunset, it sliced cleanly through the wind into the waves.

34

ELLIE SITS IN the lay-by at Holn Cliffs, not admiring the view. Even the seagulls have vanished as if swallowed by the greyness.

There is no end to this. She might sit here for ever, or she might drive on, circling the Isle of Wight for ever. Islanded, either way. Unless she were really to cut loose. Cross the water, take the ferry (in weather like this?). Like Jack did two days ago. Though where would she go?

Or . . . The thought comes to her only like some idle, abstract, teasing proposition: she could cross the soggy verge to her left, burst through that shuddering hedge, and simply drive on. Cut loose that way. She's a farmer's daughter and she knows how to hurl a four-wheel-drive vehicle across a muddy field. But such a thing, she knows, simply wouldn't be her.

She looks, all the same, towards the edge of the cliffs, considering the possibility like some malicious insinuation that has just been whispered in her ear. And then the other thought comes to her that isn't idle or abstract at all, more like a kick to her heart. She's a farmer's daughter and once upon a time—even when she was sixteen and knew how to handle a Land Rover—she knew how to handle a gun.

The gun. That bloody gun, which he could never bring himself to get rid of. Which she could never persuade him to part with. Why had he kept it? Were they plagued with rabbits down at the site? The gun which he'd kept in that cabinet all this time, as if it might be his dad in there. And the gun which—quite absurdly, but only to answer outrage with outrage—she'd gone and suggested he might have aimed at his dad himself.

Ellie's heart bangs. She has entirely overlooked that she has left Jack alone, in these—extreme—circumstances, with a gun. If she has the means, theoretically, less than fifty yards away, then so does he. And he has a precedent too.

A great blast of terror hits her as, in fact, the blinding buffets of weather temporarily relent. In front of her, Holn Head looms darkly but distinctly, its whole outline visible, like a ship keeping to its steady course. The clouds still engulf Beacon Hill, but that doesn't prevent Ellie thinking she sees now in the distance, at that crucial spot in her vision, a tiny, quick flash of light.

My God. The engine of the Cherokee starts as if it's not her doing but the direct consequence of the pounding in her chest. By a strange seeming-telepathy, the silver hatchback up ahead moves off too, as if it's taken its hint from her, or doesn't wish to be left alone. Or, to a neutral observer, as if they've both been simply prompted by the brief mercy of the weather. Are we going to sit here all day?

Ellie follows the hatchback down the descending road into Holn—wishing it would go faster. When she has to slow at the turn for Beacon Hill (though it's more of a skidding, rocking attempt to both slow and accelerate), she experiences a moment's odd desolation as the silver car carries on, up the rise ahead, in the direction of Sands End. She feels sure now it wasn't just waiting out the storm, but confronting, too, some Saturday-morning catastrophe, the story of which she'll never know.

She tears along the straight section of steeply banked road before the hill proper, even as the rain begins its onslaught again. But she's near enough now for the cottage to be plainly visible, if only for a few seconds before the bends of the road and the high banks obscure it, and she can see that its lights are on. Hardly surprising in this weather—they would have been on when she left. But she can see that they include the bedroom light, which she interprets first as a good sign, then as a bad sign, a terrible sign, then as a sign that need not signify anything at all. Then remembers how she'd watched for Jack from that same window last night and how she'd seen his lights. He'd come back!

All of this flashes through her mind, even as, frantically, she flashes her lights, as if a watching Jack—if he's watching—will instantly understand their coded message: 'Jack, it's me. I'm coming. I love you. Don't, Jack, DON'T!'

But of course her lights are hidden by the roadside banks, and he's not perhaps looking anyway. He's not perhaps looking at anything any more.

Her heart hammers and, as she mounts the hill proper, still sheathed by the high banks which only give way at the bend by the old chapel, it seems she has no choice but also to go down that hill Jack once went down, alone on foot. To enter that dark but silvery, frosty tunnel that he must have gone down again and again in his mind. And, in truth, in her mind, she's often gone down it with him, holding his hand and hoping that what was there at the bottom of the hill might not, this time, be there. Even wishing she might have gone down it with him that first time when it wasn't in the mind but entirely, terribly real, so at least he might not have been alone, at least she could have been with him.

But how could that ever have been? And she wasn't even with him yesterday, or the day before. And now she may have to go down that dark tunnel all by herself—Jack can't be with her—and see what he saw at the end of it.

35

THE CARAVANS loom through the greyness. Jack feels an ache for them. What will become of them? More to the point, what will become of all their would-be occupants in the season to come? Only November, but the bookings sheets are already filling up with the names of regulars: the same again next year, please. What will they think? What will they do when they find out, via the reports that will surely cause some noticeable blip on the national news? If they missed the other thing or failed to make the connection, then they surely won't miss *this*.

'Tragedy in the Isle of Wight'. Or (who knows?) 'The Siege of Lookout Cottage'.

Jack doesn't want to disappoint any of them—the Lookouters in their scattered winter quarters all over the country. It seems for their sakes alone he might almost decide not to do what he intends. But nor, mysteriously, does he want to disappoint the caravans themselves, which he has come to see, now more than ever, as patient, dormant, hibernating creatures needing their summer influx of life. Who will look after them now?

'The Lookout Caravan Park is closed till further

notice.' Pending future ownership. But who, with such a blot upon it, will want to take it over? A taint, a curse, and a lot more glaring than a hole in a tree.

The rain batters the window. Always, of course, the gamble of the weather. No, he couldn't guarantee it. Even farmers had never found a way of doing that. A risk you took, no money back. And it cut both ways: a wet July, a sudden spate of cancellations. And what could you say to those who braved it? There's always Carisbrooke Castle. Have you been to Carisbrooke Castle? Did you know (Jack certainly hadn't known till it became part of his rainy-day patter) that Charles I had once ruled England, or thought he did, from Carisbrooke Castle?

Always an eye on the weather. Even in August it could sweep in, just like now. No, not called the Lookout for nothing. But on a good Easter, say, in good spring weather, when they started to show up in numbers, knowing they'd hit it right, it was like turning out the heifers for the first time. They felt it, you felt it. Even the caravans felt it.

He looks at them from the window, as if he's abandoned them and they know it. Only the rapid events of the last two hours, only the shifting and sharpening of his basic plan, mean that he's here now and not down among them, with the gun, even in this weather. That his brains, and all that they've ever comprehended, aren't already strewing one of them.

He might have done it on his return, had Ellie not been at home. And he might even have done it now, in her absence. He might have damn well walked down the hill, even in this rain, the gun under his parka, and taken the keys and chosen any one of the thirty-two. Pick a number. And *that* surely would have marred for ever the prospects of the Lookout Park. No chance, then, of happy holidays to come.

But he needed Ellie. He needs her now. He fully understands it. That final, still solvable complication. He needs her to be here. If he has gone mad, then he's also rational. He needs her to return and, if she returns, to return alone. He's prepared to deal with all comers, seriously prepared: a whole box of cartridges, this upstairs position.

But he thinks—he could almost place a bet—that Ellie will return, and alone, and that it won't be long now. Delayed only by this evil weather, sent this way and that by the weather, like some desperate yacht (he's sometimes watched such a thing from this very window) trying to make it round Holn Head.

It was all a hysterical bluff, perhaps. But he isn't bluffing. And he needs her.

Jack hasn't changed the will he made soon after their arrival in the Isle of Wight. There'd be no reason—or opportunity—for doing so now, but he momentarily thinks of how he sat one day with Ellie in the offices of Gibbs and Parker (the same firm who'd acted for Uncle Tony) and of how the solicitor, Gibbs, had delicately pointed out that they should include in both their wills a standard provision for their dying at the same time or nearly so.

They'd done two things. They'd got married (his

declaration at Brigwell Bay was almost a proposal) and, being man and wife and business partners, they'd made wills. It was a flurry of wills—Michael's, Uncle Tony's, Jimmy's—that had brought them to this new life, so they were not unfamiliar with such things, and for Jack this sensible if slightly grim undertaking had even been comforting.

Simple, reciprocal wills in favour of each other, with the provision in his case that, should he die having survived Ellie and without children, everything would go to Tom.

That provision had strangely consoled him, even though it rested on the dreadful precondition of both Ellie's and his own death, and had sown in his mind the exonerating notion that Tom might one day come to own Lookout Cottage and run the Lookout Caravan Park—not a bad prospect for an ex-soldier. As Tom was eight years his junior it was not improbable that Tom might survive him. On the other hand, as Tom was a serving soldier . . . But when Jack's mind turned in that (improbable) direction it flicked away.

It was a notion he never mentioned to Ellie and which he didn't indulge so much himself, since it had its morbid aspects. But it was really a hope, a dream, a variant of a simple, secret wish: that one day Tom might just appear. One day he might just stick his head round the cottage door.

And it was all one now: the notion and the wish and the contents of his will—even that gruesome addition Gibbs had advised, which, in theory, would have speeded Tom's inheritance.

He'd sometimes embroidered the wish with fanciful

details—Tom might have become an officer, with a peaked cap, or he might have quit soldiering and signed up as a gamekeeper—but the fantasies had always stopped as soon as he thought: But what might Ellie feel if Tom were suddenly, actually to show up? And they'd vanished completely whenever he reflected: And what might be Ellie's secret wish?

People can help in all kinds of ways, Jack thinks, by dying—death is a great solution. That doesn't mean you should anticipate or wish it. But he's past the point of separating wishes and reality, and, perched at this window with a gun on the bed behind him, he's all anticipation.

But people also didn't help by dying. Because someone had to pick up the pieces. It was a bastard thing to inflict on anyone that they should pick up the pieces, a bastard thing. Jack knew this. He and Ireton had picked up the pieces, so to speak, yesterday, though neither of them had resented Tom for it. Tom hadn't meant it or been a bastard about it. It wasn't Tom's fault. They'd put the pieces on their shoulders and Jack had wondered if Ireton had thought (but surely he would have done) about other pieces they'd once had to pick up.

And it could be said now that Jack Luxton had picked up everyone's pieces. He knew about picking up pieces, and for that reason he wasn't going to inflict the same thing on Ellie. He'd make sure he'd never inflict such a thing on her.

He looks at the empty caravans. And what will Ireton think, he briefly considers, when he finds out? As he surely will. What will he think? Jesus God, he'll think, I was with him only yesterday, I was right beside him. And what will Ireton think (though Jack doesn't really believe it's likely now) if a squad car of armed police is involved?

Could Ellie really have done it—said it? On a Saturday morning, on this filthy-wet morning, in a police station? And even have added: 'I don't like to say this—but there's a gun in the house. He's got a gun.'?

Jack doesn't really think it's likely, but he's prepared. A whole box of cartridges, some in his pocket. And he thinks it's likely, in any case, that Ellie will have remembered the gun.

The rain stops beating against the window. It's only a fleeting break in the storm, a parting of dark clouds to reveal paler ones behind, but Holn Head suddenly emerges in its entirety and the caravans seem to gleam for a moment almost as if the sun is shining on them.

Do caravans *know* things, have feelings, premonitions? It's a stupid thought, like wondering if the dead can know things (and Jack is trying very hard now not to think of his mother). Do caravans know when a death is going to happen?

At Jebb it was something there was always plenty of opportunity to think about—to observe and assess—if you wanted to. Did *cattle* know things? Did they know when trouble, death even (as it quite often could be) was on its way? Did they know the difference between madness and normality? A cow was only one notch up, perhaps, in thinking power, from a caravan. At Jebb, Jack had occasionally thought that he wasn't that many notches up from a cow. All the same, he knew things. Did they know things? Luke had known things, Jack had never doubted that. Luke had surely known, when Dad had bundled him out to the pick-up. He'd known.

For an instant Jack sees himself driving again the old rust-pocked pick-up, with Luke in the back, over to Westcott, over to Ellie, not knowing, any more than a cow might know, that thinking of doing just what he was doing then might one day be one of his last thoughts.

And Luke not knowing then, either, that the last ever journey he'd make would be in that pick-up.

But as Jack has these thoughts about the pick-up he sees the rain-drenched Cherokee emerge from behind the old chapel building and, travelling fast, start to mount the steep last section of the hill beneath him.

The rain has already resumed and Jack can't see Ellie herself, still some hundred yards away, through its blur and through the wet windscreen in front of her. But there certainly aren't any police cars. No sirens. No lights, save Ellie's own. Jack decides accordingly, if for no other reason than last-minute tidiness, to slip the box of cartridges into his sock drawer.

Then he turns from the window to pick up the gun and, as Ellie drives the final yards, walks with it to the bedroom door, to the top of the stairs, then down them. No police, just Ellie. The air still reeks of bacon. He'll need to be very quick and decisive, but he feels quite calm. He'll need to appear with the gun only when she's shut the door behind her. If she calls out 'Jack?' or 'Jacko?' he'll need to ignore it. Or perhaps, as he emerges through the doorway from the foot of the stairs, he'll say, 'Here I am, Ell. I'm here.'

It's as though something he can't prevent is simply

happening to him. Though everything is quick, there also seems ample time to do it in. He has the spare cartridges in his pocket, but he hopes it will be as unfumbled and clean as possible. His own death he is ready for. He could have done it already. He might even have done it yesterday, if he'd busted through that gate—and if he'd had a gun with him—but that would have been inconsiderate to all concerned, including the bloody Robinsons.

And he'd needed this gun.

He can bear the thought, very easily now, of the world without him, of the world carrying on without Jack Luxton, but he can't bear the thought of Ellie having to carry on in it without him, of a world with Ellie but not him in it, and of Ellie having to pick up his pieces. He knows he can't inflict it on her, it would be a crime.

Which leaves only one option. And final complication. Also, if he deals with Ellie first, he knows he won't hesitate to deal with himself, he'll do it all the quicker. Not that in his case it will be so mechanically simple to do, but he'll make sure it's done. He knows that it can be done.

Now that it's happening it doesn't feel mad at all, it even feels—only right. As if his death has arrived in the form of Ellie and there's no getting away from it and no other way he would wish it. And she'll understand perfectly, he knows that too, even as he lifts the gun. From the look in his face, in his wall of a face, she'll know what he's doing. He's sparing her. He's sparing her from finding what he once had to find and look at. He's simply sparing her. This was always a double thing, just him for Ellie and Ellie for him, and there are two barrels to this shotgun.

He hears, through the sound of the rain, the approaching car and decides—a sudden, impetuous change of plan—to come forward, raising the gun, from his position of concealment at the foot of the stairs. Only to see Tom standing with his back pressed against the inside of the front door through which Ellie must enter, in a barring posture that's vaguely familiar.

He's in his full soldier's kit, head to toe, he's in the clothes he died in, and in his face and his eyes, too, he looks like a soldier.

And this time he speaks, though it's hardly necessary.

He says, 'Shoot me first, Jack, shoot me first. Don't be a fucking fool. Over my dead fucking body.'

36

ELLIE TURNS BY the old chapel and makes the final climb to the cottage. Never in all her life has she felt so monstrously late for anything, and so absolute is her hurry that she takes this itself to mean that the worst must be true. Why else should she be hurrying? It's a false logic, but persuasive. On the other hand, if the worst is true, hurrying can make no difference.

No amount of hurry, however, can reverse the recent sequence of events. She simply shouldn't have left. She shouldn't be travelling in this direction at all. Two mornings ago it was her crime to stay, today it was her crime to leave. And she has never in any serious way walked out on Jack before. She has never even thought of it, though now it might already be her irrevocable situation: life without Jack.

Her final charge up Beacon Hill is, anyway, quite unlike the slow but deliberate approach of Major Richards last week, which could be said to be the cause of why she is careering up the same road now. Haste, in his case, would have been quite inappropriate, though so too would have been lateness, or any hint of evasion.

For a moment Ellie, who only seconds ago has thought that she is like Jack, heading down that dreadful slope of Barton Field, wishes she might be Major Richards, still making his solemn way to Lookout Cottage. That the sequence and allocation of events might be reassembled. Then all this might be undone and have a second chance to unfold. Or rather Ellie thinks, even as she races in her unmajorly way up the hill, that she would rather be Major Richards, bringing the confirmation of Tom's death, she would rather be Major Richards with his unenviable duties as the messenger of death than be the woman she is, in the plight she is in, right now.

But it's as she briefly shares her being with Major Richards that Ellie gets the distinct sensation that she has been preceded, even now, by a military visitation. As if during her absence, her manic driving this way and that and her sitting helplessly near the edge of a cliff, Major Richards has in fact contrived, even in this weather, to pay another, surprise call. To let them know it was all a mistake. That it wasn't Tom, after all. A mistake of identities. Bodies, you understand. It was some other poor luckless soldier, whose family, of course, have now been informed.

'Carry on.' (Major Richards's cap drips with rain water.) 'Carry on. As you were.'

And for the first time Ellie realises that she wishes Tom not dead. Truly.

So had she wished him dead? Was that the logic? Had she? Wish you were not here? She wishes him not dead now and for a moment even wishes she might *be* him. Not Major Richards, but Tom. She wishes she might be Tom, in his soldier's kit, speeding now up Beacon Hill to prove that Major Richards's last, swift, miraculous visit, in the middle of a storm, wasn't itself a deplorable error.

Never, in any case, since the news of Tom's death, has Ellie felt such a tangible sense of his living presence—a big burly corporal—and to her surprise and in all her haste and terror for another man, and even as she comes to a lurching halt outside the cottage, her eyes and throat thicken and she splutters out as if she might even have been the poor dead man's wife, lover, mother, sister: 'O Tom! O poor, poor Tom!'

And no sooner has she done so than the feeling of Tom's presence (that military presence was his) is gone.

She cuts the engine. The cottage, despite its lit windows, looks deserted. The rain lashes down. The very worst thing now would be to hear a shot from inside. The very best would be to see the door open. The door stays shut.

After her headlong drive, there's no logical reason for her not to move as fast as she can to open that front door herself. But she stays stuck where she is—how long do you give such a moment?—afraid of what she will find, or longing to remain for a further instant, then a further instant, within the time before she will find it. Or simply willing that other, miraculous thing to occur: that the door will open.

Then it does open.

It is opened slowly and sheepishly, as if, she will think later, by a man emerging half-believingly from some awful place, or a man who, having sought desperate refuge, has just been told that it's safe now, it's perfectly

349

safe, to come out. She opens her door too, and perhaps they both look, in looking at each other, as if they've seen a ghost. Jack stands in the doorway, and he grasps with both hands and points before him something long and slender which, had the light been even poorer or had she been looking from a different angle, might have made her blood run cold.

But she sees what it is. There's an identical article in the back of this car.

He struggles to open it, fumbling with the catch. Then he does open it, and disappears for a moment behind its expanding circle. Ellie sees before her, through the pelting rain, a burst of black and yellow segments, with the word LOOKOUT, repeated several times at its rim. Then she sees Jack, stepping forward, holding the umbrella uncertainly up and out towards her, in the manner of an inexpert doorman.

'Stay there,' he says hoarsely.

But Ellie doesn't stay there. She takes almost immediately the few, wet paces that will enable her to meet Jack halfway, thinking as she takes them: The things we'll never know.

And among the things she'll never know is how Jack had stood, for an interval he'd never be able to measure, with a gun aimed, as had never been his intention, at his protesting but unflinching brother. How so shocked was he by this situation (and so fixed had been his intention) that he couldn't alter his posture or grasp the fact that the spectacle he was himself presenting must be no less extraordinary than the one before him. Then this second shock had hit him, as if he'd seen not Tom, but himself in a mirror.

But Tom was standing there, and Jack was pointing a gun at him.

Ellie will never know, either, how with Jack's shock had come a small, impossible explosion of joy. Tom was here, in this cottage. How Jack's muscles had frozen, then melted. How he'd lowered the gun, for which, he knew, the cost would be the disappearance of his brother, though it was not nearly so great a cost as the cost of not lowering it, and in lowering it he knew too (and knew that Tom knew it) that it would never be fired again.

How he'd stood, staring now only at a closed door, and how he'd shaken and gasped for air, as if he might have returned from the dead himself, and how he'd felt that though Tom had vanished he was still with him, and how he might even have groaned out loud, 'For God's sake help me, Tom.'

How suddenly the power to move had returned to him. How in a giddy, panting frenzy of reversing actions and in the very limited time available (though only moments before he'd felt that time was calmly slowing and stretching), he'd returned each glaring object to where it belonged. The gun, that is, to the gun cabinet, as if it had never been taken out, along with the loose cartridges in his pocket, though not before removing the two from the gun itself, his fingers burning against what might have been, in these same rushing seconds before him, the means of ending everything.

Panic had spurred him. Sweat had pricked his skin. His breath had hissed. In his haste to hide the evidence and in his all-consuming terror that Ellie might forestall him, he'd considered slipping the gun—the loaded gun —temporarily into the umbrella stand. But she'd surely notice it and how would he explain? In his haste too, he'd failed to deal with the box of cartridges lurking upstairs among his socks.

But thank God it was safely concealed up there. He'd deal with it, hours later and in less of a frenzy, while Ellie was taking a bath, and while the thought would come to him that he would simply get rid of all this weaponry, he'd get rid at last of the gun and that when he did so, Tom would finally be laid to rest. But was it Tom, still with him, who gave him this thought? Was he here? Had he gone?

Rain would still rattle at the window and he'd tremble to be alone again (but was he alone?) in the bedroom where he'd been alone before. He'd smooth the almost-forgotten dent in the bed. Could Ellie possibly have guessed?

He'd sell the gun. Or—better, quicker—there was plenty of sea all around, which had already, regrettably but permanently, swallowed a medal. He'd have to explain that too, sooner or later: the absence of the medal. He'd say that he'd taken it with him—which was true—and had thrown it in Tom's grave. It was a lie, but it was a white lie. He'd see again, as he smoothed the duvet, that white, closed gate. Then the thought would seize him that he could really have done it—dropped the medal in the grave, it might have been the thing to do, the right place for that medal. All his useless, too-late thoughts, arriving after the event, but this one still had a use, and some thoughts were best never enacted. His hand would shake as he retrieved the box of cartridges. He'd hear the splashing of Ellie in the bath.

But all this—while he had still to open the door that

his brother had guarded—was yet to come. His scramble to return the gun to the cabinet meant there was a significant delay. It was just as well Ellie had delayed too, willing the door not to stay shut, and his foolish idea about the umbrella stand had prompted a more practical course of action.

Jack walks towards Ellie, holding a seaside umbrella. Ellie walks towards Jack. Then the umbrella covers them both, the wind trying to wrest it from Jack's battling grip, the rain beating a tattoo against it.

NOTE

This is a work of fiction that does not aim to give a documentary account of the repatriation process of dead British servicemen and any specific similarities to any such actual repatriation are unintended and coincidental.